Deadly waters

In a scrabble of white foam, the frantic man clutched the buoy, apparently trying to climb on top of it. Ben began to pull him in.

Sass, sitting on the roof of the deckhouse, let out a sharp cry. "Ben! Shark!"

The high, crescent-shaped dorsal fin and blurry gray form of a huge hammerhead shark cut through the water straight toward the swimmer. The little man commenced screaming hysterically, renewing his efforts to get on top of the buoy. The frantic churning only excited the great predator; it executed an attack turn with a tremendous thrash of its tail. Ben pulled with all his strength, yanking the shrieking swimmer closer to the boat.

Then, like a nightmare, one side of the hammerhead came out of the water, the eye rolling back white and dead, as the shark turned on its side and opened its jaws, rows of razorlike white teeth inches from snapping shut on the victim's leg. . . .

D0459631

Also by John McKinna

Crash Dive

TIGER REEF

John McKinna

AN ONYX BOOK

ONYX
Published by New American Library, a division of
Penguin Putnam Inc., 375 Hudson Street,
New York, New York 10014, U.S.A.
Penguin Books Ltd, 27 Wrights Lane,
London W8 5TZ, England
Penguin Books Australia Ltd, Ringwood,
Victoria, Australia
Penguin Books Canada Ltd, 10 Alcorn Avenue,
Toronto, Ontario, Canada M4V 3B2
Penguin Books (N.Z.) Ltd, 182–190 Wairau Road,
Auckland 10, New Zealand

Penguin Books Ltd, Registered Offices:
Harmondsworth, Middlesex, England

First published by Onyx, an imprint of New American Library,
a division of Penguin Putnam Inc.

First Printing, May 2000
10 9 8 7 6 5 4 3 2 1

REGISTERED TRADEMARK—MARCA REGISTRADA

Printed in the United States of America

PUBLISHER'S NOTE
This is a work of fiction. Names, characters, places, and incidents either are
the product of the author's imagination or are used fictitiously, and any resemblance to actual persons, living or dead, business establishments, events or
locales is entirely coincidental.

Dedicated to the wild places
and the things that inhabit them,
and
To my wife, Teresa,
who searches them out with me.
I love you.

ACKNOWLEDGMENTS

Many thanks, as usual, to Jimmy Vines,
literary agent *par excellence*,
for his career guidance and encouragement;
and Joe Pittman, my editor,
who knows exactly what to leave in
and what to take out.

Prologue

The tigress moved through the steaming Sumatran jungle as silently as a ghost. Her early-morning patrol had taken her into higher country, up around the flank of a lushly forested mountain and well above the gullies and wet meadows that were her usual haunts. It was not hunger that compelled her to leave familiar territory. She had been aware of the big male shadowing her for more than a week.

Normally, she would have shunned him, instinctively respecting his territoriality and solitary nature. If she had had cubs, she would have avoided him at all costs, knowing that the great males of her species were savage, lone killers, capable of disposing of a litter of their own kind without hesitation. Tiger and tigress maintained separate lives most of the time, occasionally stalking the same silent jungle paths and, upon encountering each other, passing by with plenty of room to spare.

But not all the time.

The tigress was in heat. The age-old need to mate had turned her normal wariness of the male into interest. He possessed something she needed, and she would get it. But female instinct directed her to handle her powerful suitor carefully, with subtlety. She would wander through his territory, in no particular hurry, and attract, entice . . . bewitch.

She was beautiful. And highly unusual. She was a white variant: a tigress with peridot-green eyes and a white coat with blue-black stripes. Not an albino, but a natural, healthy variation within the species' gene pool, she was even more regal in appearance than her normally colored relatives.

The big male, eyes glazed and nostrils filled with her rich scent, thought so.

The tigress, well aware of him slinking through the undergrowth a dozen or so yards behind her, paused at a small opening in the trees. Far off, across the rich green expanse of treetops below, lay the indigo-blue reaches of the vast Pacific Ocean. She blinked her eyes and sniffed the wind; the aroma of salt drifted in and out on the breeze. It was a good spot.

Settling down on her belly, her forelegs resting sphinxlike on the ground before her, she casually turned her head and watched as the male tiger emerged from the cover of the trees. By Sumatran standards, he was huge: over five hundred pounds of muscle and sinew, draped in a glorious coat of fiery orange and black. Though the tigress was not small, he was almost twice her weight.

As he neared her, she rose, tail twitching, and lowered her head. Peering up at him, she began to slink closer, pausing once to stretch languorously, then sidled around him. The language they shared was one of grunts, purrs, body movement, and eye contact.

The tiger raised his great head high and looked sideways at her.

Carefully, the tigress slunk provocatively around in

front of him, keeping her head low, and brushed his nose with her tail.

The tiger bared his fangs in a lethal grimace, and from his throat there came a long, low, rumbling growl.

With exquisite care the tigress placed herself on the ground in front of him and rolled over on her back, writhing a little. She reached up with one paw and brushed his whiskers . . .

She rolled back onto her belly and lifted her tail aside, crouching. The big male, his eyes and brain fogged with testosterone, was on her in an instant, crushing her down with his weight. For a few brief moments his powerful haunches thrust rhythmically, his canines bit into the loose hide of her neck, and the jungle reverberated with a deep, moaning growl . . .

And then it was done. No sooner had the tigress felt the hot gush deep inside her loins than she abruptly lost interest in the procedure at hand—as did the male. When he was slow to move off her, she hurried him along with a vicious open-clawed slap to the muzzle and a savage snarl. Too nonplussed to react, he sat back on his haunches and dumbly licked his stinging chops.

Without a look back, the white tigress sauntered off into the trees, carrying deep within her the prize she had sought. Now, once again, she walked the shadows alone.

The tigress was back in the low country, padding her way silently through the dense coastal jungle near the town of Bengkulu. She had come to know that the occasional goat could be taken from the rice paddies on the outskirts of the town, and although she did not like the sounds of machinery and the voices of the *Two-Legs* that always seemed to be near the fields, the possibility of snatching a sweet young kid was irresistibly tempting. She would patrol the edges of the paddies, just out of sight in the undergrowth, and once in a while, luck would be on her side. A goat—perhaps two—would be foraging in the rice close to the jungle's edge. One ferocious headlong dash into the open, a savage, vertebrae-crushing bite, and seconds later she would be back into the trees with her easy feast.

The sound of a cracking twig froze the tigress in her tracks. It was followed by the murmur of voices. With four powerful bounds she was thirty feet to the side of the narrow path she had been following and crouching under a tangle of broad-leafed vines, invisible. Only a few feet to her right a deadly poisonous krait, its rest disturbed, slithered away from her in haste. She paid the snake no mind.

Down the trail in single file came the *Two-Legs*. They were short and wiry, lean of face and sharp-eyed. As was their custom, their heads were swathed in bright cloth, and all carried strangely shaped black sticks. The tigress's green eyes narrowed, and her chops curled back in a sneer of fear and hatred. She had encountered such *Two-Legs* before, and had felt the terrible thunderclap-sting that came from their mysterious black sticks.

She stayed hidden beneath the vines until the *Two-Legs* were long gone, listening for the sound of their voices. When no sound came, and when the smell of sweat, tobacco, and curry was no longer in the air, she rose from her hiding place and continued on down the path in her original direction. A soft shower of warm rain began to fall, pattering on the broad leaves and raising a thin, living mist of agitated insects. The tigress paused to lick the drops of rain from her whiskers.

The bleat of a goat, very near, filled her ears. Instantly, all her keen senses focused toward the sound, her ears swiveling forward, her eyes probing the jungle ahead. Very slowly, crouching low, she crept forward several paces and peered over a small rise.

Tied to a stake in the center of a small clearing was a young black goat. Its bleating became more frantic as it caught the tigress's scent and bucked at the end of the rope that restrained it.

Something told the white tigress that this goat could not escape. Unhurriedly, she trotted forward to take her prize.

Like virtually all wild animals, the one direction in which the tigress almost never looked was *up*.

As one, four Indonesians leaped from their perches twenty feet up in the trees, dropping onto ropes that were attached to four corners of the heavy net on which the tigress was walking.

The ground erupted around her, showering her with dead leaves and detritus, and then she was balled up in the net fifteen feet in the air, disoriented, spitting and clawing in a futile, fearful rage.

Beneath her, the *Two-Legs* jumped and cavorted like monkeys, their voices jubilant, strange, and terrifying in victory.

Chapter One

Ben Gannon cranked another full turn on the *Teresa Ann*'s mainsheet winch, tightening his boat's big mainsail, and glanced up toward the bow. Sasha Wojeck was silhouetted against the spectacular purple-and-gold sunset, her long blond hair flying out behind her, her legs locked expertly around the stainless-steel railing of the bow pulpit to secure her in place. She was scanning the ocean ahead with a pair of binoculars. Far off the port bow, outlined in misty tones of gray-black, the coastal highlands of western Java emerged from the rolling, shimmering waters of the Java Sea.

The big double-ended cruising ketch bucked gracefully over the dark evening swells as she made her way steadily to windward, leaving behind a hissing white wake of salt foam. Ben tapped the compass, nudged the wheel a couple of degrees to port with his knee, and reset the autopilot to steer the slightly corrected course. He eyeballed the compass for a few seconds, making sure the *Teresa Ann* settled onto the right bearing, then watched as Sass made her way back toward the cockpit.

He smiled to himself at the sight of her; lithe and tanned at thirty-six, barefoot, dressed in cutoff denim shorts and a yellow foul-weather jacket, agile and sure on her sleek athlete's legs as she picked her way across the roof of the boat's deckhouse. The wind whipped her sun-bleached hair across her face as she jumped down into the cockpit, and she made a comical puffing sound as she blew the strands away from her mouth.

"Whoops." She sat down hard as she lost her balance momentarily.

Ben laughed. "C'mere, babe. Lemme get that." He braced a knee on the cockpit bench and moved in close to her, brushing the hair away from her eyes with one work-scarred hand. She turned her face up to him, smiling.

"Thanks, Captain," Sass said softly, and he grinned before rechecking the compass.

Sass looked at her companion of nearly ten years. Six feet plus, a hundred ninety pounds of lean muscle kept in tone by hard physical work, he carried his thirty-nine years gracefully. His face was open and a little weather-beaten, with steady gray-green eyes that crinkled into crow's-feet at the corners, the result of a lifetime of squinting into the sun. His mouth seemed fixed in a lopsided half smile, as though he was perpetually amused by the world around him.

She watched the vein pop a little on his sun-browned biceps as he reached over to the shelf on the steering pedestal and retrieved a small notebook. When he leafed through its pages, the movement of tendons made the commercial diver's tattoo on his right forearm ripple. She smiled and tapped his calf with one outstretched toe, making him look up.

"You look good, Gannon," she said. "Make a girl get a warm itch just sitting and looking at ya."

He grinned and patted her leg. "As long as I make *this* one itch, that's good enough for me."

Sass sat up and began to pull her tousled hair back

behind her head, wrapping it with a black fabric elastic. "How long has it been since we left New Orleans, again?" she asked. "Seems like another century."

Ben glanced at the date on his watch. "Six months, three weeks, and four days," he announced. "And we left the Pacific coast of Panama seventy-one days ago. With only a few short stops between here and there, that's a full three months at sea together in this old girl." He slapped the *Teresa Ann*'s stout teak cockpit coaming.

"Amazing, huh?" Sass replied coolly. "A man and a woman together on a forty-four-foot boat for that long, almost continuously, and we can still *sort of* stand the sight of each other."

"Amazing," Ben concurred, rolling his eyes. "Particularly when you figure in the PMS factor . . ."

Sass reached up and scratched the stubble on his cheek. "Ah, hahaha. Funny boy." She leaned back against the side of the cockpit and rolled her head in an arc, stretching her neck. "You know, I love you to death, but I'm not going to mind having you go do that pipeline diving work when we get to that port city in Sumatra. What's it called?—um, Bandar Lampung. How long is the job contract again? Six weeks?"

"Six full weeks offshore," Ben confirmed. "I take over for Jake Logan in three days. And it was damned nice of him to offer me the job contract, too. We could use a little cash infusion into the bank account right about now, and this old oil-field diver needs to get back to work on a rig or pipeline again. Before he forgets *how* to work." He smiled at her and gently took her chin between his thumb and finger. "And I know what you mean. I love you, too, but we could both use a little break from each other."

He sat back. "Besides, you do need to hop a flight to the Florida Panhandle and check up on your marina in person. Not because Jimmy and Anna can't run the thing right, but because you need to go there and see how the place is doing firsthand, before you drive yourself nuts thinking about it."

Sass pouted. "You got that right. The phone calls from time to time don't cut it. I need to be there. Just to be sure."

He stood up and scanned the horizon. The dying sun lay nested like a golden egg amid the gleaming cloud billows to the west. Cupping his hands around his eyes, he squinted hard into the ebbing light.

"Sumatra's only about twenty-five miles from Java," he said, "but I can't see it. Not quite yet." He dropped his hands. "Huh. Still a little too far, and too much direct glare out on the Sunda Strait."

"Ben," Sass said sharply. "Who are those guys?"

Ben turned to look at her, then followed her gaze astern. Cutting through the dark swells four hundred yards behind the *Teresa Ann*, and approaching fast, was a high-bowed motorized junk of the type common to Indonesian waters. Ben frowned, then took the binoculars from Sass and focused in on the overtaking vessel.

"Fishing junk," he said. "About sixty feet long. Got some horsepower in her, too, by the look of it." The muscles in his jaw tightened. "No running lights. I don't like that."

He stared through the binoculars for a few more seconds, then abruptly turned and handed them back to Sass. "Watch 'em," he said, and disappeared down the main companionway.

Thirty seconds later he reemerged carrying two Colt

AR-15 semiautomatic rifles. The sport version of the famous M-16 combat rifle, the AR-15 retained all of its fully automatic military cousin's menacing appearance. Ben handed one to Sass, along with a black wool watch cap.

"Put that on," he said. "Cover up all that blond hair. And sit in the cockpit where they can see you, but don't show your legs. I don't want them to know you're a woman, if possible. And prop that rifle up at a good angle, so they can see it, too." He softened his concerned expression by force of will. "Stay cool. It'll be fine."

Sass nodded back at him, her eyes full of alarm but her mouth set and determined. She tugged the watch cap down over her ears and turned up the collar of her foul-weather jacket, then slid into the aft corner of the cockpit and tilted the AR-15 up at a ready angle.

Ben pulled on his own watch cap and stepped up to sit on the aftermost section of the deckhouse roof, in plain view. Cradling his rifle in the crook of one arm, he stared astern at the approaching junk, his face hard and watchful.

The clanking roar of a large, badly tuned diesel engine grew louder as the junk surged across the *Teresa Ann*'s clean white wake and began to pull up even with the sailing yacht's stern fifty feet to starboard. The vessel was a low-freeboard fisherman, painted black, with the traditional good luck spirit-eyes drawn in white and red on her bows. Oily black smoke belched from her stern exhaust, and her wood-planked sides ran with rust stains from her corroding fittings. She was stout, but poorly maintained.

Lining the rail facing the *Teresa Ann* were a dozen men who appeared by their build and dress to be Indonesian, and whose faces and heads were either covered by bandannas and headbands, or completely concealed by balaclava-style hoods. All were armed to the teeth, most with what looked like Chinese AK-47 combat rifles.

"Ben . . ." Sass said, her voice a little shaky.

"Sit still," Ben told her quickly. "Don't smile. Don't wave. Don't do anything." He shifted the AR-15 upward and put the butt end of the stock on his thigh, continuing to stare coolly at the junk, which had now slowed and was pacing the *Teresa Ann* at about seven knots.

"They know we've seen them," he said softly. "They know we're armed, and they know we're ready." He paused. "Right now they're trying to decide if we're worth the trouble."

Sass shifted her rifle a bit. "Supposing they decide that we are?" she muttered.

Ben cleared his throat before answering. "Well," he said, "let's hope they don't." He glanced down at her and smiled fleetingly. "If the shooting starts, hit the floor of the cockpit. I'll be right behind you."

"Then what?"

Ben turned his gaze back to the junk, saying nothing. Sass kept looking up at him for another few seconds, then flexed her fingers around the cool metal of the AR-15 and stared across the narrow stretch of dark, rolling water at the row of cloth-swaddled faces examining the *Teresa Ann*.

Abruptly, the junk's engine gunned and a cloud of sickly black smoke spewed from the stern exhaust. Her bows rose as her propeller dug into the water, and then she was lunging rapidly ahead of the *Teresa Ann*, veering off to the northwest as she did so. Spray flew out from her sides as she bulled her way through troughs and swells. In less than three minutes she was a barely visible dark speck off the yacht's starboard bow.

Ben jumped down into the cockpit and laid his rifle on the leeward bench. He looked over at Sass and pulled off his watch cap.

"Whew," he said.

He searched the fast-encroaching darkness in the direction the junk had gone for a moment, then stepped over and sat down beside her. Her hand, still wrapped around the muzzle of the AR-15, was shaking slightly. Gently, he took the weapon from her and put an arm around her shoulders.

"Okay?" he asked.

She looked into his eyes and nodded. "Yup. You bet." Then she rested her head on his collarbone and gave a long, shivering sigh. "Glad you were here, Captain."

He let out a hollow chuckle. "Hell, I'm glad I wasn't here *alone.*"

The wind gusted hard, heeling the *Teresa Ann* over on her leeward rail. Ben leaned opposite the roll, then reached down to collect the two rifles from the cockpit bench. "Let me secure these below," he said. "I'll put them under the companionway ladder—just in case we need them again." He stepped through the open hatch. "But I hope not. Single-shot sport rifles against fully automatic weapons. Not very even."

When he returned a moment later, pulling on an old gray sweatshirt to help ward off the humid cool of the evening, Sass was gazing out into the gathering darkness in the direction taken by the departing junk.

"Maybe we should try to radio the authorities," she said.

Ben tapped the compass and checked the boat's course again. "And tell them what? That a fishing junk full of men we can't identify pulled up alongside us for two or three minutes and then left?" He sighed.

"You've got a point there," Sass agreed, nodding. "But it sure feels like we ought to do something, doesn't it?"

Ben's lopsided smile was ironic. "Yes, it does. It's a cinch those guys aren't out here to hand-line bonito."

Sass got to her feet impatiently. "I'm going to see if I can spot that junk," she declared. "I doubt if I'll be able to sleep at all tonight after what just happened. I might as well keep an eye out for those creeps. You put those new night-vision binocs in the chart-table drawer?"

"Yeah," Ben replied. "Right-hand corner."

She dropped through the companionway hatch, rummaged around below, and came back up carrying a set of high-powered green-scope glasses, the commercial application of the sophisticated optics developed by the U.S. military for night fighting. Like a cat's eye, the special lenses in the binoculars collected the ambient light that was present at night—but invisible to the human eye—and concentrated it into a startlingly clear, green-lit image of the object under scrutiny. The resolution of the new units was amazing; it was possible to identify a person's face in pitch-darkness at over two hundred yards.

"If they're still around here," Sass said, "I'll find them."

"You do that," replied Ben. "It isn't every day you run into real-life modern pirates. Which is what those guys were, no question." He reached inside the hatch and came up with a thick, leather-bound book about the size of a small atlas. "I'm entering this little encounter into the logbook. Position, time, and description. Who knows? Maybe we can report it when we get to Bandar Lampung . . . if anybody there gives a damn."

"There are at least half a dozen freighters out there tonight," Sass mused. "Look at all the running lights." She pointed toward the western horizon. Far ahead, dots of white, green, and red light were moving slowly across the Java Sea's black horizontal plane.

Ben nodded. "They're either coming in or going out of the Sunda Strait," he said. "Busy shipping lane. You've got Djakarta right beside us to the south here in Java, Bandar Lampung and Palembang on Sumatra just ahead, and beyond that—Singapore, the Malacca Strait to the Indian Ocean, Bangkok, and then all of mainland China, the Philippines, and Taiwan farther to the north. This area is one of the great crossroads of maritime traffic in the world."

"And the single worst place for modern piracy in the world," added Sass, looking ahead through the night glasses. "If I recall what you told me correctly."

"You got it," Ben said. He began to write in the log. "It varies, but the most dangerous area of them all is the Malacca Strait. So many ships have to crowd through that narrow channel between Sumatra and Malaysia, and thread their way through all those little islands, that it's a virtual bottleneck. The ships have to slow down, and when they do, these fast-moving small boats loaded with armed men approach out of nowhere—like they did to us just now—and the next thing a captain knows, he's got bandits scrambling all over his vessel. These Southeast Asian pirates are murderous, too. They've killed dozens of people during ship hijackings over the past fifteen years."

"Thanks for talking me into coming here," Sass remarked, grinning.

Ben gave her a withering look. "I told you all this before," he pointed out, his voice full of mock annoyance. "Back in Panama. I seem to recall that you still wanted to see the South Pacific. What I don't recall is twisting your arm and forcing you."

Sass lowered the glasses and smiled at him. "You didn't, Ben," she said. "I wouldn't have missed it for the world. Go ahead, babe, I interrupted you."

"Well,"—he shrugged—"the thing is: there are over seventeen thousand islands in the Indonesian archipelago. Only six thousand are inhabited. That leaves an awful lot of widespread, isolated real estate in the middle of this great big ocean for pirates, hijackers, and smugglers to hide out in. That's the problem; the bad guys have hidden bases all over the place, and there's no way the Indonesian authorities—or anyone else, for that matter—can locate even a fraction of them. Too big an area. These guys just hit and run, usually at night and in fast boats, and then disappear into the islands. Poof. Gone."

Ben's eyes turned forward, narrowing. The running lights of a small freighter, some distance ahead, were moving from port to starboard across the *Teresa Ann*'s course line. He reached down and flicked the power button of the small radar scope mounted on the steering pedestal from STANDBY to ON. In a few seconds the scope began to display a series of glowing green contacts behind its rotating sweep arm.

Ben identified the nearest contact as the freighter

in question and flicked the switch that brought up the scope's distance/scale rings. "About three-quarters of a mile ahead of us," he announced. "Bearing about oh-three-five degrees. He's gonna cut across our course line almost at right angles." He glanced up at Sass. "No problem. We'll miss each other by half a mile, unless he decides to veer into us for some reason."

"Well, he's not likely to do that," Sass said. She put the night glasses up to her eyes and located the freighter in the lenses. "Not very big. It has one large shipping container on the central deck amidships. Aaand . . ."

Suddenly, she lowered the glasses.

"Ben," she said. "Our pirate junk is right underneath the stern of that freighter."

Chapter Two

Ben stepped out from behind the steering pedestal, and Sass handed him the night-vision binoculars. He braced himself against the rear bulkhead of the cabin and quickly adjusted the glasses' focus.

In the unit's circular viewing field, lit with eerie green light, a startlingly clear image of the freighter's high stern—the junk racing along just underneath it—presented itself. As Ben watched, grappling hooks and lines were heaved up from the knot of men crowding the junk's bow and over the larger vessel's stern railing. Lithe as cats, two of the pirates, their weapons slung over their backs, began shinnying rapidly up the ropes that now connected the two boats.

"Dammit!" Ben said, keeping the glasses to his eyes. "That freighter's being boarded, and I doubt if the crew even realizes it!" He searched the ship's stern, his jaw working. "Name, name . . . There it is! The *Loro Kidul.*"

Sass handed him the VHF mike before he could ask for it. He thumbed the talk button and began to speak in a fast, clear monotone:

"*Loro Kidul, Loro Kidul, Loro Kidul.* This is sailing vessel bearing two-four-five degrees approximately one half mile off your starboard stern quarter. You are being boarded at your stern by personnel from

suspected pirate vessel. Repeat: you are being boarded
at your stern by personnel from suspected pirate vessel. Take immediate action to defend yourself! Please
acknowledge. Over."

Ben released the talk button and waited. Second
after second, the only sound coming through the
speaker was the harsh, raw crackle of static . . .

In the wheelhouse of the *Loro Kidul*, the helmsman,
a twitchy-faced little Indonesian named Lom Lok,
reached up and turned off the overhead VHF radio
upon hearing the sound of English. He snickered and
made a coarse comment in Bahasa Indonesia, the predominant Indonesian language, to the crewman who
was lounging and smoking by the open port-side door
of the wheelhouse. The man cackled with glee, then
coughed, hacked up a large wad of phlegm, and spat
it over the rail.

A moment later a door in the rear bulkhead opened,
and the Caucasian captain, one Jakob De Voort,
stepped into view. He spoke harshly in Bahasa to Lom
Lok, glared momentarily at the smoking crewman,
then stepped back into his cabin and banged the door
shut. The little helmsman's pinched, Asiatic face
twisted into a snarl, and he muttered something under
his breath.

Without warning, a spray of machine-gun bullets
shattered the glass of the entire port side of the wheelhouse, sending razor-sharp fragments and paint dust
flying. The smoking crewman screamed once, his body
shaking like a rag doll's under the impact of twenty
slugs, and crumpled into a heap on the outside catwalk. The deafening chatter of automatic weapons
filled the night air.

Lom Lok, his instinct for self-preservation long since honed to a fine edge, didn't miss a beat. Without a second thought, he abandoned his station at the *Loro Kidul*'s wheel and bolted for the starboard door, leaping for the rail. He was nothing but a sudden blur to the hooded pirate just reaching the top of the external catwalk stairs from the lower deck. His body turned over slowly in midair as he dropped the forty-five feet from the wheelhouse to the black water below, where he landed full on his back with a sickening smack.

The pirate loosed off a quick burst at him from his AK-47, then spun and leaped into the wheelhouse, followed by three accomplices. The mangled steering station was empty but for another of his cohorts, hooded and holding a smoking AK, peering in from the opposite door. Simultaneously, their eyes both settled on the entrance to the captain's cabin.

They stepped inside, followed by six others, and leveled their weapons at the wooden door's handle. A clipped word, and the two pirates opened up. The handle and lock mechanism disintegrated, along with half the door itself. It swung open, and for a moment there was virtual silence as the night wind swirled a light haze of cordite fumes about the men's heads.

And then, in the blink of an eye, the hulking, black-clad form of Jakob De Voort materialized in the doorway. In each of his hamlike hands he gripped a Mac-Ten machine pistol; he was firing them both before the pirates could tighten their trigger fingers. The deadly little weapons did not chug or rattle like the slower-recoiling AK-47s. The sound they made, with their incredibly high rate of fire, was more akin to that of a chain saw biting into wood: *Brrrrrrrrrrrrrrrrrp! Brrrrrrrrrrrrrrrrp!*

All eight of the pirates were cut down, none getting off a shot. De Voort continued to fire until he had emptied both Mac-Tens into the pile of writhing bodies, then quickly released the spent clips and banged new ones home. His bearded, heavy-browed face was expressionless as he stepped over the dead Indonesians and paused at the starboard door.

"Jesus Christ, you hear that?" Ben exclaimed as the faint popping sound of automatic weapons fire came across the black swells. "Machine guns."

"Isn't there anyone else we can call" Sass lamented. She put her arms around Ben's shoulders. He slipped his free hand around her waist and squeezed.

"I'll try again," he said. "These waters are patrolled by Indonesian gunboats, but they're so few and far between . . ." He let the words trail off. "If I could only raise an American or British warship, but dammit, we haven't seen any."

He looked through the night glasses again, then handed them to Sass. "She's getting too far away to see anything now. She's doing something like twenty knots." He reached through the companionway hatch for the VHF mike again. "All we can do is try to inform the authorities over the distress frequency and hope someone's listening. Maybe in Djakarta, or ahead in Bandar Lampung—but nobody's getting here in time to do anything useful . . ." He shook his head in helpless frustration and brought the mike up to his mouth.

Sass centered the shrinking *Loro Kidul* in the binoculars' green viewing field once more as Ben began reciting an ongoing distress call. The freighter had not slowed at all, and the junk was no longer beneath her stern. Sass assumed that the attacking boat had pulled up along the far side of the bigger vessel and was no longer in sight. The *popopopop* of intermittent gunfire still reached her ears, barely, but she could not make out any human movement on the *Loro Kidul*'s decks.

Shivering, though it was not at all cold, she kept the night glasses trained on the ship's rolling stern as it faded, like a phantom, into the darkness.

De Voort stepped out of the wheelhouse side door and began to inch his way aft along the external bulkhead, leading the way with his brace of machine pistols. As he reached the stairwell that led down to the main deck level, a turban-wrapped head, its face obscured by a bandanna, rose through the opening. De Voort obliterated it with a dual blast from his Mac-Tens. The decapitated body tumbled backward and slid down limply to the next landing.

Moving with surprising speed for such a large, heavyset man, De Voort dashed around the aft catwalk to the opposite side of the ship, just in time to encounter four more turbaned pirates charging up through the other stairwell. This time both parties opened fire simultaneously. De Voort dropped two of his adversaries before an AK burst caught him on his left side, stitching him vertically from knee to collarbone. He let out a bellow of pain and rage as the slugs spun him halfway around and knocked the machine pistol from his hand. Even as he was driven back against the stern catwalk railing, he continued to fire with his remaining Mac-Ten.

Another short burst of AK slugs hammered into his

right upper chest and shoulder. Still bellowing like a
dying bull, he lost his balance, tumbled backward over
the railing, and disappeared from view.

The two remaining pirates, one of them clutching a
stomach wound, rushed to the railing and looked
down. Some twenty feet below, De Voort lay sprawled
on the steel plate of the narrow poop deck, motionless. The two Indonesians grunted in satisfaction,
then turned and walked back to the wheelhouse door.
The one with the stomach wound let out a high-
pitched, yammering call and waved off the junk, which
was still pacing the *Loro Kidul* amidships on her port
side. The single helmsman aboard her waved back,
then spun the wheel and gunned his pitching boat off
into the darkness in a fast, hard turn.

The pirates pulled down their bandannas, revealing
typically thin, high-cheekboned, slit-eyed Indonesian
faces. The one with the stomach wound leaned back
against the chart table, grimacing with pain, his fingers
clasped over his gut leaking blood. The other pirate
impassively stepped over the bodies of his late associ-
ates, yanked a first-aid box off the bulkhead, and
tossed it to him. Then he searched the wheelhouse's
instrument array for a few seconds, located the engine-
room intercom, pushed a button on its speaker box,
and began to talk rapidly into it in Bahasa.

A curt reply came back in the same fast, chattering
language. The pirate drew his lips back in a yellow,
gap-toothed grin, then moved over to check the compass course and turn the ship's wheel. Behind him, the
wounded man was wadding a pile of absorbent cotton
over the ugly, puckered bullet hole in the right side
of his abdomen and taping it into place, all the while

letting out an ongoing stream of gasps and grunts. The pirate at the helm paid him no heed whatsoever.

Below, on the poop deck, the *Loro Kidul*'s engineer emerged from a small hatch about ten feet from De Voort's sprawled form. He was fat, particularly for an Indonesian, with a distended belly that protruded from beneath his grease-stained white T-shirt. He looked at his former captain, at the bullet-torn clothing and the puddle of blood collecting on the deck plates, then hissed an obscenity and spat on him. Stepping over the big man's body, he mounted the stairs leading up to the wheelhouse.

Once inside, the engineer accepted the offered cigarette from the pirate at the *Loro Kidul*'s helm and beamed in satisfaction. It had been child's play to fake a compression problem in one of the ship's two diesels, slowing her enough to allow the pirates to intercept and board her just after dark, as prearranged. Who would ever know? The entire crew was dead, including the hated Dutchman, De Voort.

His new employer would be most pleased with his performance. The chubby engineer drew deeply on his cigarette and fantasized about the reward he would receive. Perhaps even a generous share of the wealth to be derived from the *Loro Kidul*'s unusual and extremely illegal cargo would be his. The thought sent a shiver of greedy elation through him.

The helmsman growled a comment back over his shoulder about the damaged autopilot. Exhaling smoke, the engineer stepped forward and examined the bullet-shattered unit. After punching a few buttons and opening the rear panel to probe around inside, he looked up at the pirate and shrugged. There was no hope of fixing it. They would have to steer manually.

The helmsman scowled and made it clear that he'd be damned to the netherworld by every god he knew if he was going to steer this creaking pile of steel for the rest of the night. He drove the point home by dropping one hand to the haft of the wicked-looked *kris*—the serpentine-bladed dagger of Indonesia—that he wore in his belt.

The engineer, who was by nature more of a lurker than a fighter, gulped hard and rapidly assured the pirate that he had every intention of taking his turn at the wheel. Trying to suppress the nervous tic that had suddenly developed at the corner of his right eye, he backed up against the chart table and looked down apprehensively at the array of bodies strewn around the wheelhouse floor.

The pirate with the stomach wound, who was sitting on the deck next to the starboard door with his back against the bulkhead, let out a long, rattling groan. The engineer glanced over at him with little interest, taking in the ashen, drawn face and the hands clasped over the hemorrhaging belly. With a dismissive snort, he turned away to peer out through the broken forward windscreen of the wheelhouse, sucking on the last of his cigarette. When the mortally injured man let out a sharp gasp, the engineer was almost too annoyed to bother looking over at him again. But he did anyway.

The gut-shot pirate lay crumpled over on his side, the ivory handle of a seaman's knife protruding from his throat. And lying up against the doorjamb, soaked in his own blood, his face horrific and his eyes maniacal, was the dreaded captain, Jakob De Voort. As the shaking Mac-Ten came up level, the engineer had just time to begin a babbling scream of terror . . .

De Voort's life ebbed away as he depressed the trigger, spraying the two men standing by the ship's wheel with a lethal hail of bullets. Through darkening eyes he saw them dance and claw the air as they were cut down; heard their screams and the angry blast of his machine pistol as though the sounds were coming down a long tunnel. The Mac-Ten sagged to the deck as its firing pin fell on an empty chamber, and the last thing Jakob De Voort felt as he rolled over and died was the pure, vicious satisfaction of *winning*.

The *Loro Kidul* sailed on into the equatorial darkness of the Java Sea, manned by a crew of dead men, her aimless helm allowing her to wander farther and farther to the north, out of recognized shipping channels and into the island-dotted, reef-infested waters southwest of Borneo.

Chapter Three

Ben hung the VHF mike back on its clip in disgust. "My emergency call isn't bringing back anything but static." He glanced out to the south, toward the island of Java, invisible in the darkness. Faraway glimmers of heat lightning were illuminating the horizon every few seconds. "The transmission's probably getting lost in all that electrical activity over the Sunda Strait. Night squalls cluttering up the airwaves."

Sass was sitting behind the *Teresa Ann*'s wheel, peering intently into the scope of the radar unit, her high cheekbones lit with green light. She adjusted the control knobs, fine-tuning the picture.

"I've still got the *Loro Kidul* on radar," she said. "Her course track shows her curving away slightly to the north. Out of the shipping lanes, it looks like." She looked up at Ben. "She's still moving at something like eighteen knots. We're going to lose her off the scope in just a few minutes. Out of range."

Ben regarded her for a few seconds, then sighed and shrugged. "Well, we're not following her up into the shoal waters south of Kalimantan." Sass furrowed her brow. "That's the new name for the Indonesian part of Borneo," he elaborated. "Anyway, we've done what we can. I don't know what's happened aboard that freighter, but we can't do anything useful by trying to follow her.

"We'll make a full report to the port authority when we reach Sumatra tomorrow," he said. "Right now I'm going to take a Sat-Nav reading and get us back on course for Bandar Lampung."

"I'll make note of the *Loro Kidul*'s course readings until I can't see her anymore," Sass declared, looking back into the radar scope. She felt around for the notebook on the steering pedestal shelf. "Maybe it'll help the authorities locate her later on."

"Good idea," Ben said with a nod. "Who knows where that ship will be tomorrow? Or her crew. Poor bastards. I hope they're not all dead."

He ducked below momentarily, then stepped back out into the cockpit holding a small electronic unit about the size of a cellular phone. It was a Magellan Satellite-Navigation device, a remarkable instrument that could pinpoint its own location anywhere on earth, within fifty yards, by collecting position signals from orbiting satellites. Ben smiled a little as he punched the unit's buttons. For centuries men had sailed the seas using the stars and complex mathematics as their only guideposts, the art of celestial navigation so crucial to bygone empires that it had often been considered a military secret. And now a child of ten who was familiar with computer games could find out exactly where he was in seconds, anywhere on the planet, simply by manipulating a few buttons.

Ben and Sass were both experts with the sextant, the primary sighting instrument used in traditional celestial navigation. But the little Sat-Nav was fast, easy to use, and accurate. They kept their skills honed by taking sextant sightings every day and working through the daunting mathematics of converting sun or star shots to actual chart positions, but for fast "where the hell am I?" information, nothing beat the little Magellan.

The unit beeped twice, and a lat/long position displayed on the LED screen. Ben hit a few buttons to lock it into memory as a way point, then read off the magnetic course they'd have to steer to make landfall at Bandar Lampung.

"Let me check it manually against the chart," he said, and stepped down into the companionway, disappearing below.

Sass blinked hard as the green blip on the radar scope that was the *Loro Kidul* faded off the edge of the last range ring. Sitting back, she jotted down the last course heading and position of the freighter and then rubbed her eyes. Her nerves were jagged from the events of the preceding two hours.

She was looking up into the star-pocked night sky when she heard it: a high-pitched, barely audible wail. Abruptly she dropped her head and sat up straight. The keening cry of a night-flying bird? The eerie song of a whale? She'd heard both sounds before, many times. The ocean at night was often full of strange noises.

There it was again. A ragged, despairing scream that faded rapidly to a choking gasp. Sass jumped up, lifted the cockpit bench seat, and pulled a large halogen searchlight from the storage compartment, tucking its long coil of cord under one arm. As she let the seat drop back down with a bang, Ben appeared at the top of the companionway stairs.

"Okay, I've got the new course checked and plotted," he said. "We—what are you doing?"

"Ben," Sass said breathlessly, "there's somebody out there. I heard a scream. She stepped up on the cockpit coaming. "I'm going forward to see if I can spot them."

"Wait." Ben grabbed her sleeve. "You're not going up to the bow at night without your harness on and being clipped in. That's our rule, remember?"

He reached inside the companionway and took a heavy-webbing harness off the clothing peg mounted on the inner bulkhead. "Here," he said, holding it open. "Slip this on."

"Right, right." Sass pulled the harness up over her shoulders and buckled it securely. Then she took the carabiner attached to the harness's short leash and snapped it around the horizontal jack line that ran from the cockpit to the bow pulpit. "Okay, I'm going."

She stepped over the coaming, and as she did both of them heard the scream again, much closer than before.

"What the hell . . ." Ben muttered, staring out into the darkness. He stepped back behind the *Teresa Ann*'s wheel and disabled the autopilot, steering manually.

Sass picked her way rapidly over the roof of the deckhouse, the carabiner sliding along the jack line behind her, and paused as she reached the foredeck. Uncoiling about twenty feet of searchlight cord, she bent down, uncapped a waterproof electrical receptacle mounted in the forward part of the deckhouse, and inserted the cord's plug. At that moment Ben pushed the starter button for the *Teresa Ann*'s small diesel generator. As power surged through the boat's AC system, Sass flicked on the searchlight.

The brilliant halogen lamp sent a concentrated column of light stabbing out ahead of the yacht like a long, probing white arm. Moving forward to the bow pulpit, Sass locked her legs around the stainless-steel railing and scanned the dark sea ahead. She gimbaled her upper body on her hips as the bow rose and fell over the crests and troughs, as sure of her balance as a human gyroscope.

Back at the wheel, Ben took the night glasses from their holder on the steering pedestal. Powering up the unit, he brought them to his eyes and began searching the shadowy seas for any signs of human life. Even with the night-vision optics, picking out a small, unlit boat or raft on a dark ocean was a very long shot. A person in the water—one chance in a million.

He chewed his lip as he moved the glasses over the swells. Whoever had let loose with that desperate cry was going to be left far behind in just a few more minutes . . .

"Haaaaiiiiiiiiiiiii!"

Ben jumped at the nearness of the shriek, the hair prickling on the back of his neck. Dropping the glasses from his eyes, he thought he caught a faint, unnatural motion on the crest of a swell some forty or fifty feet directly abeam of the *Teresa Ann*'s starboard side.

"Over here!" he shouted, but Sass was already swinging the searchlight beam toward the correct spot. A frantically waving arm flashed through the beam of white light on the crest of another gently foaming swell.

Ben spun the wheel hard to starboard, laying the yacht over on her port rail as she came around up into the seas. On the bow pulpit, Sass flexed her legs around the railing and hung on with her free hand, leaning hard against the sudden heeling.

"Keep the light on him!" Ben yelled, knowing she was trying to do that anyway. He punched the starter button of the boat's auxiliary engine, and the primary diesel roared into life. Sails loose now and flogging the air, the *Teresa Ann* began to plunge up-sea, motoring into the oncoming swells.

Scrambling back over the roof of the deckhouse, Sass kept the searchlight centered on the person in the water, never taking her eyes off him. Ben too looked away from his target as little as possible. As the yacht moved upwind of the swimmer, Ben brought her around and allowed Sass to fall off toward him.

Steering with his knee, he unhooked the throwing buoy and line from its bracket on one of the stern stanchions and got ready. As the *Teresa Ann*'s bow came even with the swimmer, he slipped the throttle into neutral, braced his leg against the cockpit bench, and hurled the buoy in the victim's direction, aiming for a point well beyond the bobbing head.

It was a perfect toss. The buoy hit the water eight feet behind the victim, and the line dropped cleanly across his shoulder. In a frantic scrabble of white foam, the swimmer clutched the line and then the buoy, apparently trying to climb on top of it.

Sass, sitting on the aft roof of the deckhouse and keeping the light on the swimmer as he drifted aft along the starboard side, let out a sharp cry. "Ben! Shark!"

The high, crescent-shaped dorsal fin and blurry gray form of a huge hammerhead cut through the illuminated water scant feet from the swimmer, propelled by rapid, jerky sweeps of its powerful tail. The little man clinging to the buoy commenced screaming hysterically, renewing his efforts to climb out of the water

onto it. The frantic churning only excited the great
predator; it executed an attack turn with a tremendous
thrash of its caudal fin. Ben pulled on the line with
all his strength, yanking the shrieking swimmer closer
to the boat.

One side of the hammer came out of the water, the
eye rolling back white and dead, as the shark turned
onto its side and opened its jaws. Its rows of razorlike
white teeth were seconds from snapping shut on the
victim's kicking leg.

Ben sprawled under the safety lines between the
stanchions, half overboard, and slapped both hands
onto the back of the swimmer's soaking shirt as the
Teresa Ann rolled to starboard. Seizing the wet cloth
in his fists, he heaved upward with all his might as the
yacht rolled back.

The fortuitous roll saved the swimmer a leg. He was
yanked clear of the water like a gaffed fish, his feet
grazing the top of the shark's hammer head as it
snapped at prey that was suddenly no longer there.
Sass watched transfixed as the great animal disappeared beneath the *Teresa Ann*'s stern.

"Arrrgh!" Ben's groan of effort snapped her out of
immobility. Dropping the searchlight, she unclipped
the carabiner from the jack line, leaped down from
the deckhouse roof, and threw herself across his buttocks and thighs, saving him and his feebly kicking
load from going headfirst into the Java Sea on the
yacht's next roll to starboard.

As the *Teresa Ann* came back to port, Ben used the
extra leverage Sass's weight gave him to heave the
swimmer back up against the cap rail. The little man
wasn't helping; he was still babbling and shrieking and
clawing at the air.

"Jesus H. Christ," Ben growled, panting hard. He squirmed his way farther back under the safety lines and onto the deck, his arms shaking with the strain of holding the swimmer. "Can you get a hand on him?"

"Haaiiieee! Haaii—haiii!"

"I think so," Sass panted. She flung out an arm and grasped the collar of the little man's shirt. "I—"

"Haaaaii! Haaa! Haiii!" One flailing forearm smacked Ben across the mouth.

"Son of a *bitch!*" he cursed, losing his temper. "Pull this little bastard in!" He gave a furious yank and wrenched the swimmer inboard across the cap rail, throwing him toward the cockpit. The little man thumped off the bench seat and smacked down onto the floor of the cockpit like a boated tuna. The shrieking abruptly stopped.

Sass turned to Ben, breathing heavily. "I think you've killed him," she said.

Ben was lying on his back on the deck, his chest rising and falling like a bellows. "I hope so," he wheezed.

"My God, Ben," Sass breathed, putting a hand on his arm and then pointing astern. "Look."

Ben rolled up on one elbow in time to see the yellow throwing buoy, which was being towed along on its shortened line, thrash madly back and forth across the surface of the water in an explosion of spray and foam as the giant hammerhead attacked it. The immense caudal fin swept up into the air, smacked down once . . . and then the remaining third of the buoy resumed its quiet, bobbing journey along in the *Teresa Ann*'s wake.

Sass and Ben looked at each other. "New buoy," they said simultaneously.

They laughed, relief flooding through them both like warm wine. Leaning on each other, they hoisted themselves up to a sitting position on the edge of the cockpit coaming.

"What a day," Ben said. "Nothing for weeks, and then pirates, castaways, and sharks all in one evening." He shook his head, then clapped his hands onto his knees and leaned forward, looking down into the cockpit at the feebly stirring form on the floor.

"What in the world have we got here?" he wondered aloud.

Chapter Four

The little Indonesian was mumbling to himself in a run-on whimper, still flat on his back, his eyes wide and staring up at the night sky. Not more than five-four in height, he appeared to have been constructed of thin sticks that had then been wrapped in tightly drawn yellow parchment. His thin black hair was plastered on top of his head and around his skull-like features. He couldn't have weighed more than a hundred twenty pounds soaking wet. Which he was.

Ben slid down off the cockpit coaming and onto the bench seat. Bending forward, he tapped the little man on the knee. "Hello," he said. "Are you all right?"

The swimmer jerked a little at the touch and lifted his head, his eyes darting around. He appeared very disoriented. Sass stepped down toward the companionway.

"I'll get a blanket," she said. "He acts like he's going into hypothermia or shock."

"Uh-huh," Ben said, nodding. "No telling how long he was in the water."

Suddenly the little man reached out and clasped Ben's ankle with both of his bony hands. *"Terima kasih!"* he cried, his voice ragged and exhausted. *"Terima kasih, bung!"*

Ben put a hand on the man's shaking arm. "Take it easy, friend. You're okay now."

"Terima kasih . . . terima kasih . . ."

Sass stepped back into the cockpit, carrying a heavy wool blanket. "You worked that job in the oil fields off Palembang in Sumatra a few years back, Ben," she whispered. "You know what he's saying?"

"I'm not sure," Ben replied, "but I think he's thanking me. I wasn't here long enough to pick up much, but I think *'terima kasih'* is 'thank you' in Bahasa—the most common Indonesian language. But there are hundreds of dialects." He grimaced down at the hands still clutching his ankle. " 'Bung' I remember. It's a respectful equivalent of 'brother.' I guess the guy's grateful."

"I would be, too," Sass commented. "This poor man was about two seconds from becoming shark food." She bent and spread the blanket over the swimmer's shaking legs and hips.

"How the hell did he get way out here?" Ben wondered aloud as the bony hands finally turned loose his ankle. "He must have fallen overb—" His voice trailed off.

Sass stared into his eyes. "You think? The freighter?"

Ben shook his head slowly. "Huh. I don't know. But what other ship have we been close to? He couldn't have been in the water since daylight; he'd have drowned or been torn up by sharks."

He looked down at the swimmer again and pointed his finger. "You? *Loro Kidul*? You?"

The little man nodded instantly. *"Ya, ya. Loro Kidul."* He slapped a palm on his bony chest. *"Loro*

Kidul." He was suddenly seized by a fit of coughing, salt water erupting from between his thin lips.

"Got residual water in his lungs," Ben said. "Good for him to cough it up."

When the spasms finally ceased, the man looked up at Ben again with bloodshot eyes. "*Minta, bung. Bisa bicara* Bahasa Indonesia?"

Ben shook his head, smiling. "No. *Tidak.*" He glanced over at Sass. "I think he just asked me if I speak Indonesian. I told him no. *'Tidak'* means no. One of the few words I remember."

The little man's skull face split into a somewhat hideous grin. "I speakee good *Ingles,*" he cackled. "Engleesh." He smacked his chest again. "I Lom Lok."

Ben and Sass smiled at each other in surprise. "I'm Ben," Ben said, tapping his own chest. He pointed at Sass. "She's Sasha. Sasha."

Lom Lok clapped his bony hands together, showing an array of jumbled yellow teeth. "Ben," he said, pronouncing it easily. "Ben." He looked over at Sass. "Say-sha. Sayyy-sha." His eyes lingered hungrily on the long tanned legs. She picked up on it instantly and, uncomfortable, moved her knees together. Her jaw tightened.

Sass glanced over at Ben. He'd missed it completely. Typical male, she thought, suppressing a twinge of irritation.

She looked over the little Indonesian again, taking in his shifty eyes and obsequious manner. Something about him set off all her alarm bells, and she decided then and there that she didn't like him.

Ben, the lunkhead, was regarding him with the same open, frank smile that he presented to everyone. Sass had to remind herself that quite often even *she* couldn't tell what he was thinking from his expression. Rarely was anything written on his face but quiet amusement.

Lom Lok started shivering violently, and Ben leaned forward to put a hand on his shoulder and pull the blanket up around him. "Come on, friend. Let's get you below and into some dry clothing."

He helped the little man to his feet and ushered him down the companionway steps into the *Teresa Ann*'s main salon. The rich teak interior was dimly lit with yellowish twelve-volt lights, giving it a warm, snug appearance. Ben guided Lom Lok through the salon to the forward cabin berth, and pulled an old khaki welding shirt and a pair of Sass's worn jeans out of a drawer. He tossed them onto the bunk.

"Here," he said, smiling and pointing at the clothes. "You put these on. Okay?"

Lom Lok grinned. "*Ya. Terima kasih.* Thank you."

"Okay. Then come out to the main salon when you're dressed, all right? You understand me?"

"*Ya.*" Lom Lok's head bobbed energetically, the yellow-toothed grin splitting his face from ear to ear. "Understand."

Ben stepped out of the forward berth and closed the door. Sass was sitting on the top step of the companionway ladder when he reentered the main salon, sipping a mug of something hot.

"I boiled some water for hot chocolate," she said, indicating the galley stove, "and set the autopilot on course again. The auxiliary engine's still idling. You want to shut it down? Sails are set properly and pulling."

"Yeah," Ben replied, moving over to the gimballed

stove and tearing open a packet of hot chocolate. "And we need to haul in that ate-up buoy, too. Jesus!" he said, shaking his head.

Sass chuckled into her mug. "I did that already," she told him. "There's not much left of it. Can hammerheads digest closed-cell polyvinyl foam? If not, that fish is gonna have one hellacious bellyache. He bit off a big helping."

"I hope he chokes on it," Ben groused. He dropped the stirring spoon into the small metal sink and took a sip of chocolate. "Damn critter has some nerve, eating chunks of our boat gear."

Sass sighed. "Ben. What do you think about our guest?"

Ben sipped again. "Hard to say. He's getting changed. I'm gonna let him lie back on the settee here, and then ask him a few more questions. He says he's off the *Loro Kidul,* so he must have a good idea of what happened aboard her. I'm sure he's going to want to talk to the authorities about her as soon as possible, just like they're going to want to get all the information they can from him . . . and us."

Sass lowered her voice. "I don't like him."

There was a slight pause. "Is this your female intuition?"

"You might call it that. I'm serious, Ben."

"And I'm taking you seriously," Ben reassured her. "Gut feelings are often right." He drank the last of the hot chocolate and set the mug in the sink. "Let's talk to him a bit and see what we can find out." The door to the forward berth opened. "Here he is."

The little Indonesian shuffled into the main salon, his eyes darting around furtively. Ben's shirt looked like a tent on him, and Sass's pants were far too long in the leg. He'd rolled the cuffs up to just beneath his knees, revealing calves that weren't much bigger around than Ben's wrist.

"Here," Ben offered. "Lie down." He beckoned to Lom Lok and indicated the settee. The little man hesitated, then shrugged and settled down onto the dark green cushions. He kept his bare feet flat on the floor, which twisted his body awkwardly as he lay back. Sass approached, holding a fresh mug of hot chocolate she had just mixed up in the galley.

"Um . . . . what's he doing?" she muttered quietly to Ben.

"Being polite," Ben answered, arranging a pillow beneath Lom Lok's head. "In Southeast Asia, it's considered rude to show someone the bottom of your feet, since they're the lowest and most impure part of the body. They're really sensitive about it. The oil company gave us a short orientation at Palembang— so we wouldn't get into trouble when we got into town. Lots of different customs to get used to."

He spread a dry blanket around Lom Lok's legs and feet, and gently lifted them up to the settee, smiling and nodding that it was all right. The Indonesian grinned again and took the mug Sass offered him.

His eyes had a habit of darting, ferretlike, around the room when he wasn't being addressed directly, Ben noticed. The mannerism certainly didn't inspire confidence. He leaned back against the teak partial bulkhead at the aftermost end of the settee and folded his arms, smiling at the Indonesian.

"You feeling better?" he asked.

Lom Lok grinned broadly again over the rim of the mug. "*Ya, ya, bung!* Yes. Okay now. Thanking Ben and Say-sha for saving me."

Ben nodded slightly and kept smiling. "Glad to help. Now look, friend; we're going to be reporting this incident with the *Loro Kidul* to the authorities as soon as we get into Bandar Lampung tomorrow. I'd report it now, but I can't radio through the lightning static out in the Strait. You understand that?"

"*Ya.* Radio no good."

"Right, more or less," Ben said. "Anyway, it would help me put together a more complete report if you could tell us what exactly happened after the pirates got aboard the *Loro Kidul.* Okay?"

Lom Lok's eyes began to rove furiously as he sipped slowly at his chocolate. He didn't make any attempt to answer. Ben appraised this reaction for a moment, then leaned forward.

"Perhaps you didn't quite understand me," he said gently. "I asked you what happened tonight after the pirates got aboard your ship."

Lom Lok lowered the mug and looked directly at Ben, his eyes slits. Then he shrugged. "Pirate? No pirate on *Loro Kidul.*" An artificial smile appeared on his face. "You make joke, *ya*?"

Ben stopped smiling. "No, I'm not joking. The *pirates.* The men in the junk with the automatic weapons who climbed aboard your ship and started shooting. We saw them attack your vessel. We called you on the VHF trying to warn you."

Lom Lok stirred under the blanket. "No pirate on *Loro Kidul,*" he repeated. "Not know what you mean." He grinned again, his eyes shifting restlessly.

"Are you telling me," Ben pressed, "that *nobody* attacked your ship this evening?"

"No attackings," the little man replied.

"But we *heard* the gunfire. We *saw* the pirates

board over the stern through our night glasses. What
the hell are you telling me, here?"

Lom Lok shrugged.

"Okay, look," Ben said, exasperated, "how did you
end up in the water?"

"Water?"

"Yes. *How did you fall over the side*?" Ben felt his
patience shredding.

"Ahhhh!" Lom Lok grinned once more. "Drink
much tea. On watch, to keep awake. Have to must go
whizzy. Whizzy, whizzy." He made a slightly obscene
gesture over his groin area. "Pee-pee. Slip near rail
and fall into sea. Ship sail away, bye-bye."

"Oh, for God's sake," Sass exclaimed from the galley, "he's trying to tell us he slipped and fell off the
boat while he was taking a leak?" She shook her head
in disgust.

"How long were you in the water, friend?" Ben
asked. "Did you fall in before or after dark?"

"Oh, in nighttime," Lom Lok said quickly, nodding
his head. "Very dark. I swim in black water maybe
forty-five minutes. Maybe more."

Ben gazed at him steadily, frowning. "Are you sure?
That's all you want to say?"

"*Ya,*" the little man replied. "No pirate. I fall into
water. Ship sail away."

With a sigh, Ben turned away and walked over to
where Sass was standing in the galley, scowling over
at Lom Lok.

"He's completely full of shit, Ben," she whispered
harshly, her blue eyes snapping.

"I know," he answered, his back to the Indonesian.
"He freely admits that he's off the *Loro Kidul*. The
way our courses were intersecting, he had to have

gone into the water at some point *after* the pirates got aboard her and started shooting, because we altered course slightly to the north to try and follow her to see what was going on. If he'd fallen in *before* they got aboard, we'd have missed him completely, since he would have been way to the south of our course line. He's lying through his teeth. But, for the life of me, I can't see the reason why."

Sass looked over Ben's shoulder at Lom Lok. "Maybe he's one of the pirates," she whispered. "Maybe one of the crew got the better of him and knocked him over the side."

"Possible," Ben agreed. "We aren't taking any chances with him between here and Bandar Lampung, that's for sure. Brew me up some coffee, will you? I'm not sleeping tonight. I'm keeping an eye on our guest."

"Huh!" Sass said caustically. "You think I am? After tonight, and with *him* in here, I'd rather sleep in Dracula's Tomb with the Undead."

Ben chuckled and kissed her on the ear. "That's my good-natured gal," he said. "Never at a loss for words."

She smiled at him, pressing her lips together in suppressed irritation, as he turned back toward Lom Lok. He stepped across the salon and took the empty mug from the Indonesian's bony fingers.

"Look, friend," he said, "I don't know why you don't want to talk about the attack on the *Loro Kidul,* but like it or not, I'm reporting it when we get to Bandar Lampung tomorrow, and *you* are part of the report. I don't know if you're scared, or hiding something, or *what,* but you can take it up with the port authorities yourself. Right now, all you've gotta do is lie there and get some sleep. Understand?"

Lom Lok stared at him, his jaw slack and mouth slightly open. "Me," he said. "I go to Bengkulu. No Bandar Lampung. *Bengkulu!*" It was as though it were the first time the fact that they were headed for Bandar Lampung had penetrated his mind, Ben observed.

He laughed. "We're not going to Bengkulu, Lom Lok. We're going to Bandar Lampung. Where you go after we get there is your business."

Lom Lok's face suddenly twisted into a hateful mask. *"Tidak!"* he snarled. "You take me Bengkulu! take me Bengkulu! *Bengkulu!*"

Ben's pleasant expression hardened. "You'd better calm down, friend. On my boat, *I* decide where we go."

The little Indonesian struggled up onto his elbows, straining, his face contorted. "Bengkulu!" he shouted again. *"Bengkulu! You take me there!"* Ben started to put a hand onto his chest to restrain him, but his eyes suddenly rolled up in their sockets and he passed out, sagging back onto the settee cushions.

"This just gets weirder all the time," Sass whispered, standing behind Ben. He checked Lom Lok's breathing for a few moments, then straightened up.

"He's out," he said. "Exhaustion. We'll let him sleep. He's less trouble when he's unconscious, apparently."

"What was that last rant and rave about?" Sass inquired. "Where's 'Bengkulu'?"

"Up on the southwestern coast of Sumatra, if I remember correctly," Ben replied, moving over to the chart table. "Yeah," he said, tapping a finger on the chart. "Right here. Through the Sunda Strait and up the coast about two hundred seventy-five miles."

"What's there?" Sass wondered.

Ben shook his head. "I remember reading about it in one of the guidebooks," he said. "It's kind of a backcountry, seaside town; not big at all. Let's see what I can remember: it has beaches, small docks, a few historic buildings . . . not much. Oh, and something else."

"What's that?" Sass asked. "Streets paved with gold brick?"

"No," Ben said. "Tigers. Wild tigers."

Chapter Five

The *Loro Kidul* sailed on through the night, a charnel
ship manned by dead men, in a wide, wandering arc
that took her first to the northwest, and then directly
north. She was not a soft-helmed vessel; her rudder
tended to stay where it was set whether or not there
was a hand on her wheel. Thus, she did not lapse off
her course into a series of tight, spiraling turns until
her engines either seized or ran out of fuel, as so many
abandoned ships do. Rather, by dawn, traveling at
twenty knots, she had put nearly two hundred fifty
miles between herself and the attack location.

As she cut directly north across the Karimata Strait,
the wide arm of the Java Sea that separates southern
Borneo from the island of Belitung, a British Petro-
leum supertanker was forced into an emergency
course alteration to avoid colliding with her. The extremely annoyed captain, barely into his morning cup
of tea, sent some scathing remarks highly unworthy
of an English maritime officer over the airwaves, but
neglected to identify the *Loro Kidul* by name or jot
the incident down in his log. The freighter and her
crew of dead men passed through the shipping lanes
without encountering any other vessels.

The seas northeast of Belitung and southwest of
Borneo are dotted with unnamed small islands, and

booby-trapped by hidden reefs and shoals that often rise without warning out of waters three or four hundred feet deep. The *Loro Kidul* entered this deadly maze at nearly full throttle, a bone of white foam in her teeth.

Her luck held for nearly two hours. She bypassed twenty islands and atolls over the course of forty miles, lightly grazing the edge of one reef, but not holing herself. At a couple of the islands, native fishermen hand-lining from outrigger canoes in the early morning light gazed in astonishment as the black-hulled freighter charged past reefs with only feet to spare.

But at last, the volcanic cone, jungled hills, and blue-green, breaker-ringed lagoon of a small island presented itself dead on the *Loro Kidul*'s bow. The distance was closed with frightening speed.

In the final eighth of a mile between the freighter and the island, the water shoaled from three hundred fifty feet to less than ten over the ring of coral that protected the lagoon. The *Loro Kidul* drew sixteen feet.

The doomed ship drove onto the reef at twenty-one knots, striking with a grinding clash that turned coral into rubble and shook her from stem to stern. She staggered and shuddered like a bull skewered by the matador's sword as her own momentum gutted her on the fangs of the reef. The sheet steel of her bottom peeled and split like tinfoil as she careened off into deep water again, her diesels still roaring even as water surged into the engine room through her lacerated hull. Dying, she powered along for another minute before her engines flooded out and stalled. Settling fast, and without any thrust from her propellers, her headlong rush finally ceased. She drifted to a stop and, almost as if tired, began to lie over on her port side as she sank.

Displaced air screamed out of vents and stacks as she slipped beneath the surface, sending geysers of spray into the air. She went down rapidly, her bow sinking just ahead of her stern, listing to port at about forty-five degrees. As her mast disappeared in the center of a vortex of swirling bubbles and foam, debris began to pop up to the surface. life rings, buckets, lengths of rope, oil cans, garbage bags—the final talismans of a dead ship.

She struck the bottom at three hundred twenty-five feet in an upright position, then canted over onto her port side, stabilizing at about sixty degrees of list. Streams of bubbles continued to escape from her as water seeped in and displaced air from every compartment, nook, and cranny. For the next hour, the ocean reverberated with screams of twisting steel as the ship settled, agonizingly, into her final resting place.

And in a small jungle clearing high up on the volcanic shoulders of the island, the lone human witness to the death of the *Loro Kidul* kept his failing eyes trained on the spot where she'd gone down, his mind a whirl of fear and confusion.

Chapter Six

Dawn had broken over the Sunda Strait with nary a cloud to be seen, the squalls of the previous night having dissipated completely. The wind had died to a light, feathery breeze, barely enough to etch ripples on the shimmering surface of the sea.

Now, at ten in the morning, the equatorial sun was laying a blanket of heat over the glassy expanse that separated the islands of Java and Sumatra. The *Teresa Ann,* her sails furled, was motoring along at eight knots, her sharp bow slicing through water so clear and blue it looked like liquid sapphire. Ben and Sass sat at the rear of the cockpit, Ben steering, looking up toward the immense headlands of southern Sumatra, only seven miles away.

The great island rose from the Pacific like a mythological giant, its mangrove deltas and jungle-covered mountains wreathed in drifting mist and dancing waves of heat. Freighters, ferries, and fishing boats of every description dotted the waters ahead, the marine traffic generally moving in and out of the main ship channel to Bandar Lampung.

Sass wiped away a bead of sweat that was running down her temple and looked southward, to port. It was unbelievably hot; the kerchief she wore as a headband was already soaked in perspiration. She blinked more sweat out of her eyes and focused in on a pillar of dark smoke far off on the horizon, in the middle of the Sunda Strait.

"What's that?" she asked, pointing. "It looks like something on fire."

Ben squinted southward into the glare. "That oughta be Krakatau," he declared. "Or what's left of Krakatau. I think they call it 'Krakatau Anak' now."

Sass looked over at him. "Is that the volcanic island that blew up in the late 1800s? The one that sent the tidal waves all over the Pacific and killed thousands of people?"

"The same. I was reading up on the best way to enter the harbor at Bandar Lampung, and the chart notes mentioned it. If I remember correctly, the initial explosion and the tsunamis—or tidal waves—it generated killed thirty-six thousand people on the island itself, and on Java and Sumatra. The sound was heard in Australia three thousand miles away, and a cloud of volcanic ash was thrown twenty miles into the air. It encircled the Earth for three years."

Sass grinned. "Wow, Professor. You may be in the wrong line of work."

"I'm just regurgitating what I read this morning," Ben said, chuckling. "No original thoughts here. Sorry."

"Humph!" Sass rolled her eyes. "You think professors don't regurgitate? It's what they do *best*."

"You're probably right about that."

There was a scrabbling sound, and Lom Lok's haggard face appeared in the companionway, his ferret eyes blinking and darting in the bright sun. Getting his bearings, he stepped out into the cockpit and grinned at Ben, yellow teeth flashing. With a yawn he moved aft and sat down on the starboard bench.

"Bengkulu?" he inquired, pointing southwest and nodding hopefully.

Ben shook his head, his smile thin and hard like the rim of a cup. "No. Bandar Lampung." He jabbed his finger dead ahead, for emphasis.

Lom Lok's drawn face exercised itself, but he said nothing. For a few minutes he appeared to be having a silent conversation—or argument—with himself, his lips working and his head shaking. Sass curled her legs up in the corner of the cockpit, watching him with distaste.

Ben was tired. All night long he'd stayed awake to keep an eye on the *Teresa Ann*'s odd guest. Lom Lok had done little except snore lightly from time to time. Now Ben had had enough. He wanted the little Indonesian off the boat—safe, on land, but off the damn boat.

"We're heading for a small shipyard run by a Dutch family named Zwolle. When we get there, we're going to check in with the port authority. At that time, I'm handing over my log entry information, radar data, and my own written statement concerning the events we witnessed last night aboard the *Loro Kidul*. That includes a full recounting of the rescue of a seaman claiming to have fallen off the freighter during the night—*we* figure, at the time of the pirate attack."

Ben fixed his even gray-green eyes on Lom Lok's. "I assume you're going to want to accompany me to the port authority. Aren't you?"

Lom Lok looked like a man holding duds in a million-dollar poker game. "Sure, sure." He nodded, his eyes darting at light-speed. "Go make report. But no pirate."

"Jesus," Ben muttered, shaking his head. He

bumped the *Teresa Ann*'s throttle up a little more and tapped a finger on the rpm gauge, looking thoroughly disgusted. Sass reached out and put a hand on his shoulder, rubbing his tight trap muscles.

"You see 'im go which way?" said Lom Lok suddenly. Ben's head came up and he looked at him.

"What?"

"You see *Loro Kidul* go which way?" the Indonesian repeated. "You know where ship go to?"

Ben shrugged. "We've got radar-tracking records, position records. I couldn't tell you where she is right now . . . but I know where she was headed last night. Assuming she didn't change course—which she probably did—you might be able to guess where she'd be this morning. Of course, it would be just that: a *guess*."

"Where records?" Lom Lok asked, his eyes bright.

"In the ship's log, the radar log, and in my supplementary notes," Ben replied. "Why?"

"I need," Lom Lok stated. "Need for ship's owner."

"Now, why would the owner need those," Ben growled, "when *you* say nothing at all happened to the *Loro Kidul* last night?"

Lom Lok spluttered to himself in his native tongue, ending with "I need records!"

Ben was silent for a moment, then shook his head. "No, everything will be in my report to the authorities. If you want to make a statement yourself, feel free to join me. If not, you can tell the owner he can identify himself to the appropriate enforcement office and get all the details he needs from them.

"My vessel's logs stay with my vessel." His gaze bored into the Indonesian. "If you want access to information, you need to decide to play ball with me *and* the port authority. You understand, Lom Lok?"

"Ya." The little man fell silent, his jaw working under the taut yellow-brown skin, and stared at the floor of the cockpit.

Ben eyeballed him another moment or two, then wiped the back of his hand across his dripping brow and turned to Sass. "Take over for a few minutes, will you, hon? I'm gonna rinse down. I've got a frigging headache. Too much heat, I guess." He scowled at Lom Lok's lowered head and got to his feet.

Grabbing a plastic bucket with a short rope attached to the handle, he stepped up onto the cockpit coaming and made his way forward along the port rail. A school of small flying fish erupted from the jewel-blue water next to the boat in a sudden flurry and sailed off around the bow, several of them smacking into the hull. One cleared the rail and landed on the foredeck ahead of Ben, thrumming its tail in a frantic effort to find a way back to the sea.

Ben paused, holding on to the *Teresa Ann*'s shrouds, and squinted down into the glare-bright water. In a second or two he spotted the predators that had spooked the flying fish into flight: two bullheaded, electric-blue-and-green dolphin fish—mahi-mahi—rocketing ahead of the boat in pursuit of the school, twin four-foot living torpedoes.

Ben continued onto the foredeck, bent down and scooped up the thrashing flying fish, and tossed it back over the rail. Then he stripped off his faded denim shirt and put it on the deckhouse roof along with his sharp-visored swordfisherman's hat. Taking up the bucket, he knotted the tail end of its retrieval rope around one of the port stanchions and threw it forward into the water. As it came back even with him, before it could drift aft far enough to tighten the rope, he jerked it back up to the rail and inverted it over his head.

Sass gazed at him from the cockpit as the silvery water sheeted over his brown shoulders and down his back. He was preserving himself well, she decided with a private smile. He kept himself fit, but was utterly without the desperate vanity and denial of aging that led so many men and women to starve themselves sick and spend a mint on a health club. Ben liked his beer, and carried the hint of a roll on his hips, but Sass knew that it was barely enough for her to pinch between her thumb and forefinger.

As he dashed another bucketful over his head, her eyes fixed on the ugly, Y-shaped scar beneath one shoulder blade. Ten years before, on a salvage job in the Gulf of Mexico, Ben had inadvertently cut into a hidden gas pocket in a sunken barge with a thermal torch. The blowback explosion had thrown him into a pile of jagged steel on the sea floor, ripping open his back. The memory of seeing him lying unconscious in a New Orleans hospital still gave her shivers.

Even now, after more than a dozen years together, she sometimes wished that he had not chosen the life of a freelance commercial diver; moving from contract to contract, oil field to oil field; welding, rigging, and salvaging under a variety of conditions, all of them as dangerous as they were lucrative. He was often gone for weeks—if not months—from their home aboard the *Teresa Ann* in Wojeck's Marina on the Florida Panhandle—the family business that Sass had inherited from her father.

But he came back. He always came back. And always with his lopsided, rueful smile. She watched him pour one last bucket of water over himself, then shake his head vigorously and untie the retrieval line from the stanchion. He started back toward the cockpit, but paused at the port shrouds to have a look at the unusual vessel that was about to pass them, headed in the opposite direction.

Coming out of the Bandar Lampung ship channel—bound for Java, evidently—was a double-ended fishing schooner of around fifty feet in length. Extended bow and stern pieces, upturned like the toe of an Arabian slipper, exaggerated her lines. Her wooden hull was painted black, but decorated with white, yellow, and red lines; some straight, some laid on in an exotic, curlicued motif. Large good-luck eyes adorned her bows.

Her relatively flat deck and small stern house were painted a brilliant blue-green. The lateen-rigged, triangular sail was furled, laid back amidships across the roof of the deckhouse. Her mast looked more like a neon Las Vegas motel sign than a means of supporting a sail. It was barely twenty feet high, and consisted of a flat, gaily painted wooden representation of an Islamic warrior with a ferocious facial expression supporting a large, stylized octopus on his shoulders. Atop this—as if the lower assembly was not sufficiently impressive—was a scale model of a square, tiered mosque. A gold-painted crescent moon was mounted on a slender spindle on its roof.

Brilliantly colored flags and pennants fluttered from the vessel's rigging, many displaying the motif of the good-luck eye. Her decks were crowded with men and women wearing traditional Indonesian dress, all clapping and singing along to a screeching contemporary sound track being blasted from unseen speakers. As she passed the *Teresa Ann*'s stern and the racket of gongs, drums, and caterwauling voices receded, Ben stepped down into the cockpit.

"Must be some kind of celebration," he said, stowing the bucket in the lazaret. "I wonder what it is?"

"Fish festival," Lom Lok said tonelessly. "In Merak." He waved a hand disinterestedly toward Java.

Ben just looked at him. "How about that," he said. He turned to Sass. "Ever see a boat like that before in all your life? It looked like a float in the Mardi Gras parade."

Sass smiled. "It was beautiful. And never mind the boat—did you check out that *mast*? I've seen billboards that weren't that good. How can they actually sail with all that artwork in the way?"

"Sail just fills out behind it all," Ben replied. "It's a lateen rig; you only need a short, stubby mast for one of those. And that figure is Islamic—see the little mosque with the crescent moon up top? Islam is the predominant religion in Indonesia"—he grinned at Sass—"and sailors are a religious lot . . . remember?"

" 'There are no atheists in a storm at sea,' " Sass said, reciting the old quote.

"Amen to that."

Ben squinted into the glare, looking ahead. The jungled headlands at the mouth of Lampung Bay were drawing closer, and the ship traffic was increasing. Pocket freighters, ferries, fishing schooners, junks, and outrigger canoes were all beginning to cluster in the ship channel leading to Bandar Lampung, at the head of the bay.

"Time to start paying attention," Ben muttered, and stepped behind the *Teresa Ann*'s wheel once more.

*   *.   *

Lampung Bay is a wedge-shaped divot carved out of Sumatra's southern tip. Forty miles wide at its mouth, with mountainous highlands to the west and lower plains to the east, it extends inland, narrowing, almost the same distance and terminates at the city of Bandar Lampung, the fourth largest city in Sumatra.

Idling the *Teresa Ann*'s engine in neutral, Ben let her drift slowly behind a large red can-buoy, just out of the channel, as he surveyed the crowded waterfront four hundred yards away. A rust-pocked tramp freighter, overloaded, listing, and with the waterline well above her Plimsoll line, vibrated past on her way southward down Lampung Bay, her props churning the milkshake-brown water of the harbor into creamy froth.

Sass put a hand on Ben's shoulder. "Six hundred thousand people in Bandar Lampung," she said, "according to the cruising guide."

"And they're all right here on the waterfront," Ben commented, squinting into the early-afternoon haze.

The level of activity on the docks, seawalls, and streets of harborside Bandar Lampung was incredible. There appeared to be literally not a single inch of available dock space in either direction as far as the eye could see. Pocket freighters, tramp steamers, fishing schooners, rusty barges, cargo junks, galvanized-tin houseboats, and a variety of other knock-together vessels that defied description were tied up four and five deep along the entire length of the waterfront.

Over these boats, atop the seawalls, and along the street that paralleled the water, swarmed a tremendous crush of humanity; colorful, noisy, and constantly in motion. Fishermen hauled nets across decks next to engineers repairing anchor winches beside fishwives in brilliant sarongs cradling infants on their hips while cooking food over charcoal braziers on the deckhouses of live-aboard junks. Stevedores and longshoremen lugged crates, sacks, and boxes of goods and supplies on and off vessels, dodging pedestrians and *becaks*— the three-wheeled bicycle-rickshaws of Indonesia—on the main street. Ancient trucks, belching smoke, nosed their way through the ebbing and flowing mob, their horns blaring in impatient protest far more often than they were silent. The general din of human activity rose into the steaming air, hummed across the water, and enveloped the *Teresa Ann,* rocking gently beside the channel buoy, in a muted jangle of white noise.

"The Zwolle Shipyard, such as it may be, is supposedly down there to the left," Ben said, pointing. "The chart and guide say to veer north once we hit the number sixteen green can in the west channel."

"Right," Sass mused, poring over the paperback cruising guide. "It says we have to look for a U-shaped concrete seawall surrounded by wood-piling piers, and a big galvanized-steel building with 'Zwolle' painted in red over the main sliding doors."

"Great," Ben said, stepping back behind the wheel and slipping the engine into gear. He gazed back and forth at the congestion along the docks and smiled. "Man, I'd hate to have to come into this harbor after dark and try to sort out all the lights." He turned to Sass. "Just out of curiosity, does the guide say anything about navigating in here at night?"

She nodded. "Yes."

"What's it say?"

Sass shut the book and grinned. "It says, 'Cruising yachts are advised not to attempt to enter Bandar Lampung at night.' "

Ben laughed. "That'd be us."

He spun the wheel and gunned the *Teresa Ann* back out into the channel. As the big double-ender drew abreast of and then cleared the next buoy, Ben turned her to the west and began to motor along parallel to the waterfront. Sass sat up on the aft end of the deck-house and began scrutinizing the passing shoreline with a pair of binoculars.

Ben sighed and settled back on the steering bench. It would be the old routine of hunting cautiously through an unfamiliar foreign harbor for a particular marina, mooring, or in this case, small shipyard.

His eyes settled on Lom Lok. The little man was seated on the starboard rail, looking toward shore, his arms crossed atop the lifeline and his bare feet dangling above the water.

What the hell, thought Ben. Maybe he knows.

"Lom Lok!" he called. The little man's head jerked up and around. "You know where the Zwolle Shipyard is?"

Lom Lok's face twisted into something halfway between a snarl and a grin. His eyes were slits. "*Ya,*" he said, his voice a croak. "This way we go. *Satu jam . . .* one hour."

"You can point it out to us?"

"*Saya mau pergi ke Bengkulu!*" the Indonesian shouted, his face contorting even more. "I want go to Bengkulu!"

"You can forget it," Ben answered firmly. "We're not going there."

Lom Lok lapsed back into a sulk, sinking down onto the lifeline and staring at the muddy water bypassing his feet.

Ben shook his head and bumped the throttle higher,

pushing the *Teresa Ann* along the channel at a slightly increased speed.

Fifty minutes later they were motoring westward beside a somewhat sparser—albeit still dock-infested—waterfront when Sass stood up suddenly and waved at Ben.

"I see it!" she called, putting the binoculars to her eyes. "There's a big steel warehouse-type building with 'Zwolle' painted on it in red."

"Okay," he replied. "And this green can up here"—he indicated an approaching barker buoy with a nod of his head—"must be number sixteen. You can't tell about most of them; all their numbers are worn off."

He glanced over at Lom Lok as the *Teresa Ann* drew abreast of the buoy, suppressing a twinge of irritation. Thanks for speaking up, you little jerkoff.

The Indonesian's head barely stirred as Ben turned the wheel and brought his boat around in a ninety-degree swing to starboard, setting her bow on the warehouse.

As they approached the shipyard, Ben could make out the concrete bulkheads of a central haul-out slip, spanned by the massive blue-painted steel framework of a large Travelift—a mobile device designed to lower a set of heavy slings beneath a floating yacht, winch it out of the water, and then "travel"—or motor—with it to a nearby on-land location for storage or repair.

There was room for the *Teresa Ann* to dock at the end of one of the creosote-stained wood-piling piers bracketing the central slip. Ben gunned the engine and put his boat into a wide turn, lining up the approach.

"Starboard side to, Sass," he called. "No current, no wind; should be easy."

She was already kicking bumpers over the side, checking that they were tied securely as she made her way to the foredeck. Coiling the bow line in her hands, she put a foot on the pulpit railing and got ready to climb up onto the dock. In the cockpit, Ben checked that his stern line was ready to heave, then reduced the *Teresa Ann*'s forward speed to a mere crawl as she neared the pilings.

Lom Lok was sitting amidships on the deckhouse roof, apparently in a trance. Ben briefly considered asking him to handle the stern line, but dismissed the thought. They'd do it themselves.

Just as the *Teresa Ann*'s bow was about to graze the first piling, Ben threw the wheel hard to starboard and gunned the diesel in reverse. The backward prop wash churned out to port past the flattened rudder, the stern kicked in toward the dock, and the bow-pulpit railing missed the oncoming piling by six inches. The *Teresa Ann* came to a stop, and Sass jumped off onto the pier, trailing the bow line. Throwing two turns over the piling, she half-hitched it and immediately trotted back opposite the cockpit to catch the stern line Ben tossed her. Making it fast to a rusty cleat mounted on the pier's toe rail, she stood up, breathing hard, and smiled at him. The *Teresa Ann*'s bumpers hadn't even touched the pilings yet. Perfect docking.

Ben was about to say something complimentary when Lom Lok suddenly went into motion. Leaping up as if jolted by electricity, he took a step, cleared the lifeline with the agility of a gibbon, and dashed off down the pier, his bare feet slapping on the sun-bleached boards. Halfway to solid ground he collided with an Indonesian mechanic carrying a bucket of greasy engine parts, knocking both of them to the deck. The engine parts went every which way, the mechanic yelled in rage, but Lom Lok wasn't stopping for anything. Rolling to his feet as quickly as he'd fallen, he dashed across the main yard, ducked between two chocked-up fishing junks, and made it through the main gate of the Zwolle property's high chain-link fence.

"Hey!" Ben shouted, well after the fact. He looked up at Sass, bewildered and disgusted. "How do you like that?"

"Some gratitude," Sass commented, her hands on her hips. She head-tossed a strand of blond hair out of her eyes. "Glad he changed back out of my jeans."

"And my welding shirt," Ben added. "Hell of an odd way to say thanks to two people who just pulled you out of the Java Sea in the middle of the night."

"I told you he was an asshole," Sass said pointedly. "I hope we never see him again. He made my skin crawl."

Ben shrugged. "Probably we won't." He punched the kill switch on the *Teresa Ann*'s main engine and listened to the diesel die smoothly.

"Okay," he said. "Let's snug up these lines and go see if we can find the main man around here."

Humbert Zwolle mopped his dripping neck and jowls with one of a dozen soiled handkerchiefs lying balled up on the top of his huge, cluttered desk and sucked in another tremendous lungful of smoke from a black-paper cigarette. With his free hand he continued to write furiously on an assortment of yard contracts, the rapid movements sending jiggling tremors up his pudgy arm and into his fat-padded torso. At well over three hundred fifty pounds, he appeared to be permanently wedged into the ancient oak armchair in which he sat.

Ben and Sass were seated opposite him in the shipyard owner's office, trying not to gag on the incredibly acrid combination of body odor and spicy smoke that permeated the small, airless room.

Her eyes tearing, Sass broke the silence: "Just out of interest"—she coughed—"pardon me . . . Could you tell me what kind of cigarettes you're smoking? They're . . . unusual."

Zwolle looked up, stopped writing, and stretched his wide, rubbery lips into a smile. "Ahhh, you like it, *ja?*" The Dutch accent was strong, although his English was fluent. "These are *kretek* cigarettes, a product for which Indonesia is world-famous." He drew heavily on the remaining butt, plucked it from his mouth, and held it up for observation. "The unique flavor comes from the artful blending of tobacco and cloves," he elaborated, smoke leaking from his lips, his corpulent face beet-red with cardiopulmonary strain. "They are my life-blood. Would you care to try one?"

"Noooo," Sass said quickly, putting up a hand. "No, thank you. I was just curious."

Zwolle shrugged and smiled, and went back to his frenetic scribbling. As he did so, he extracted a fresh cigarette from a carved sandalwood box on his desk without looking, lit it with the stub of the one he'd just been smoking, and got the end glowing brightly with another immense, rattling inhalation.

Ben felt a burning sensation beneath his breastbone just watching and listening to Zwolle. The man was a walking heart attack. Astonishing the amount of abuse the human body could take, month after month, year after year.

"There we are," Zwolle announced, putting down his pen. "Contract for haul-out, a bottom scrub and antifouling paint job, and six weeks of dry storage in the best corner of the yard, chocked up and tied down to the ground in case of storm winds." He tore off the triplicate carbon copies and handed a set to Ben. "How would you care to pay, please?"

"Credit card," Ben replied, extracting his wallet from his shirt pocket. "Will Visa be all right?"

"Absolutely," Zwolle said agreeably. "We've found that taking major credit cards is one of the best ways to accommodate foreign yachtsmen who stop in. They rarely have bank accounts in Sumatra, ha-ha. Of course," he added, grinning like a car salesman, "we still take cash. Preferably American."

"Of course," Ben said.

"So," the Dutchman continued, taking Ben's card and swiping it through an electronic validation unit, "you will be vacationing in Sumatra for some time, *ja?* Six weeks of storage is unusually long for a stopover."

"Well, it's not really a vacation," Sass explained. "My guy here will be working on a pipeline job in the offshore oil field just northeast of Lampung Bay. The contract runs six weeks."

"Ahhh, I see." Zwolle beamed, exuding smoke. "In the new Pertamina oil field just north of Bakauheni. Excellent." He directed a courtly smile at Sass. "And how will the lovely lady be occupying herself while you are away working on this project for our illustrious government-owned oil company?"

"The lovely lady," Sass said, "will be flying home

to the United States as soon as the *Teresa Ann* has her bottom scraped and painted and is secure on shore. She has a boatyard of her own to run. A marina, actually."

"Indeed?" Zwolle remarked, his eyebrows raising. "How fascinating. Technically, that would make us competitors, wouldn't it?"

"I suppose," Sass answered. The unbreathable atmosphere was getting to her. Between the clove smoke, the cramped quarters, the steaming temperature, and the Dutchman's redolent body odor, she felt positively claustrophobic.

"You know," Zwolle went on, "my family has been in the maritime-services business in Indonesia since 1831, initially in the pepper-exporting trade, and subsequently in shipbuilding and repair. There was that nasty business of the Japanese occupation between 1942 and 1945, when the Zwolles were forced to take an extended holiday in southern Australia, but . . ."

He went on. Sass turned to Ben, a pleading look in her eyes. He grinned and got to his feet.

"Well, Mr. Zwolle," he announced, extending a hand, "I'd like to thank you for accommodating us on such short notice; we really appreciate it. But, you know, we have to get into the center of town before dark. Perhaps you could tell me where I might locate the office of the port authority, and recommend a good hotel?"

Zwolle recovered from the interruption of his narrative flawlessly. "Certainly, Mr. Gannon, certainly I can. The port authority you will find just sixteen streets down, in an unmistakably horrendous pea-green building opposite the monument to President Suharto. One of many such monuments throughout

Indonesia, I might add. I'm afraid our former glorious leader had nearly the same fondness for being immortalized in vulgar socialist statuary as his predecessor, Sukarno, and perhaps even Stalin. You see, in the history of Indonesia—"

"Fascinating, Mr. Zwolle. And a good hotel, not too far from here?"

"Yes, yes. Well, there is the Sheraton Inn Lampung on Jalan W. Monginsidi, not far at all. And then there is the Hotel Arinas, on Jalan Raden Intan, up in the old town of Tanjungkarang. You will have a more Western experience at the Sheraton, of course, but you will save money and still enjoy luxury accommodations at the Arinas. Now, in *my* opinion, the Arinas is where you want to go. The European Bakery, which operates in that hotel, serves the most exquisite Viennese desserts imagina—"

"Wonderful, Mr. Zwolle," interrupted Ben once again. "And we will be able to reenter the boatyard after hours just by identifying ourselves to the night watchmen, if we need to get back aboard the *Teresa Ann* for some reason?"

"Absolutely." Zwolle nodded. "Sutan and Yos are on duty from sunset until eight in the morning, and are aware of your presence here. They will open the gate for you."

"Thank you. And now, if you'll excuse us, we need to head into town. Appreciate all the information." Ben took Sass's arm and ushered her toward the door. She was only too happy to accept the prodding.

"My pleasure, Mr. Gannon." Exerting a vein-popping effort, Zwolle actually half rose to his feet, smoke billowing from his lungs, his fleshy, cotton-clad hips expanding alarmingly as they escaped the arms of the chair. "Now, I recommend that you take a *becak* into town, and don't pay a rupiah more than four hundred for the trip. You must dicker with these infernal rickshaw drivers until—"

"Thank yooooouuuu," Sass called, pulling Ben outside as she reached behind her and shut the door.

Chapter Seven

Having escaped the interminably sociable Humbert Zwolle, Ben and Sass relaxed in the double seat of the two-passenger *becak* and watched the kaleidoscopic scenery of urban Bandar Lampung creep, cruise, and occasionally fly by—depending upon the whim of the tirelessly pedaling driver behind them.

Basically a reversed tricycle with two wheels in the front supporting a rattan seat, and rigged with a small overhead awning, the *becak* could weave in and out of the tangle of pedestrians, cars, trucks, buggies, bicycles, animals, and other *becaks* with impressive agility. The Indonesian who maneuvered the vehicle was typically slender and small of stature, but the power in his thighs was startling. More than once Ben and Sass felt themselves pressed back in their seats by a sudden forward surge as the driver propelled the *becak* into an opening in the street's melee.

After weaving down the roadway nearly a quarter mile, they entered what was apparently one of the city's market sections. Stalls and booths loaded with fresh produce lined either side of the street, the proprietors hawking their fruits and vegetables, meats and fish, to the passing throngs. Many vendors were engaged in rapid-fire negotiations over the price of *mangosteen* or *rambutan* or some other exotic fruit with equally hard-bargaining, sarong-clad women—the raging debates each appearing to be a case of an irresistible force meeting an immovable object.

Ben and Sass both winced, laughing, as they bypassed by scant inches a five-foot-tall woman in a gorgeous green, blue, and gold batiked sarong who was directing a chattering harangue at an equally animated jackfruit seller. The sheer volume of sound coming from the little woman could have blistered paint off a steel hull.

Noticing something up ahead, Ben looked back over his shoulder and beckoned to the driver with a smile. Whispering something in the man's ear, he gestured at an upcoming stall and passed him a thousand-rupiah banknote. The man's seamed face split in a cackle of delight as he stuffed the money into his belt and veered over to the right side of the street.

"Where's he going?" Sass asked as the driver stopped the *becak* and jumped off.

"Time for a snack." Ben smiled, slipping an arm around her shoulders.

"Pizza?"

Chuckling, Ben gave her a squeeze. "No—takeout, Indonesian style."

In a few minutes the driver returned, holding half of a large, oval fruit with a spiky green exterior and pockets of creamy white flesh inside. Grinning at Ben, he bowed slightly to Sass and held it out to her, his eyes twinkling.

"*Durian,* missee?" he inquired.

Without warning, Sass found her nostrils assailed by the most god-awful stench imaginable; something like a cross between Limburger cheese and the outflow of a backed-up septic tank. She recoiled violently, wrinkling her nose and clutching Ben's knee.

"Good *Lord!*" she gasped, her face paling, "what the *hell* is *that?*"

Ben and the driver convulsed with laughter, as did nine or ten people standing near the *becak*. All the other aromas of the street market—ginger, curry, pepper, charcoal smoke, exhaust fumes—were overwhelmed by the incredibly vile smell of the spiky green fruit.

Ben beckoned to the driver, who could barely stand for laughing, and took the fruit half from him. Sass was holding her nose and breathing through her mouth.

"This," Ben said, holding the offending item up between them, "is durian fruit. It's one of the most famous fruits in Southeast Asia, and is often described as smelling like hell, but tasting like heaven." He looked at Sass with a devilish smile. "Care to sample it?"

"What?" she replied incredulously. "*Eat* that? Are you out of your *mind*?"

In response, Ben dug a section of creamy white flesh out between his thumb and forefinger and popped it into his mouth. Sass stared at him in disbelief. He held the half out to the driver, who also extracted a piece and bit into it, his shoulders still shaking with laughter.

"I think you need your head examined," Sass declared. "This is some kind of little-boy joke, right? Ha ha. I'm amused." She tried to look put out, but couldn't keep the smile off her face. "Is it really edible?" she asked timidly.

"You'll never know until you try," Ben remarked, chewing. He held the durian out.

Taking a deep breath, Sass dug out a piece of the white flesh, hesitated, then put it gingerly into her mouth. A few chews later her expression softened and she looked at Ben in surprise.

"It's *good!*" she said in astonishment.

"Yup." Ben nodded. "It's a delicacy. Hard to describe, isn't it?"

"Uh-huh." Sass scraped out another section and licked her lips. "Tastes like . . . onion-flavored ice cream."

Ben turned to the driver, who was climbing back on his bicycle seat behind them. "*Terima kasih,*" he said.

"*Kembali,*" the man replied, still grinning broadly.

As the *becak* pulled away from the curb, Sass held up a piece of the white durian flesh and examined it. "How can something that tastes that good smell so bad?" she asked. "Taste and smell are linked."

Ben shrugged. "I don't know. You notice how, when you eat it, the smell seems to lessen? I think you just get desensitized to it after a short while." He laughed. "That only happens if you're eating it, though. If you're just standing nearby, the smell will run you out of town."

The driver was able to move a little faster as they left the market area and began to cruise along a slight downhill to the next section of town. The faint breeze thus created provided them with a few moments' relief from the simmering heat of the late-afternoon sun, and Ben settled back with a relaxed sigh. It would be at least a quarter hour or so before they reached the port authority offices.

In contrast to the effusive Humbert Zwolle, Captain Achmed Supratman of the Bandar Lampung Port Authority was the very picture of the bored, midlevel, backwater bureaucrat. Studiously uncommunicative, and emitting, like a gas, the sense that he was having his valuable time sorely wasted, he listened to Ben's account of the attack on the *Loro Kidul* with a bleary-eyed, hangdog expression. Sitting beside Ben, Sass couldn't help but wonder if Supratman was on some kind of drug.

"And so," Ben said in conclusion, "I hope that my information is helpful to the Indonesian authorities in tracking down the *Loro Kidul*, and hopefully locating any of her crew who might have survived." He dropped a typewritten copy of his oral report onto Supratman's desk, clearly fed up with the official's sulky indifference.

"Mmmm," Supratman intoned, fingering the papers. He rubbed his eyes wearily and looked out the greasy window to the right of his desk. With a sigh, he got up and put Ben's report into one sweat-stained armpit. "*Loro Kidul* was an Indonesian-flagged vessel?" he muttered.

"Yes," Ben said, Sass nodding beside him. "The home port of 'Djakarta' was painted beneath her name, and she was flying the Indonesian flag at her stern."

Supratman looked sadly out the window again, then disappeared silently through a door behind his desk. A moment or two later there was some grumbling and shuffling from the adjoining room.

Sass reached up and touched Ben's flexing jaw muscle. "You're gritting your teeth again," she said.

Ben's expression softened and he relaxed his jaw. "This is bullshit," he growled. "We're trying to help these people. This is the most unprofessional reception

I've ever had from a port official with regard to a crime at sea, and I mean *ever*. Even the damn *Nigerians* showed some interest when our construction barge got robbed on that job in West Africa a few years back."

"I know, I know," Sass murmured, patting his forearm. "We'll be out of here in a few minutes. With any luck."

After a while Supratman reentered the room, carrying a three-foot-long, torn-off computer printout. Reversing it, he laid it across the desk in front of Ben and sat down.

"No *Loro Kidul*," he said simply.

"What?" Ben leaned forward and looked at the printout.

Supratman tapped the wrinkled paper with one sharp, nicotine-yellowed finger. "This current list of all ships flagged Indonesia, over five-hundred-ton displacement. No *Loro Kidul* exist."

Ben's eyes ran down the alphabetical list of names, printed in both English and Indonesian. He looked back up at the sloppily uniformed man across the desk.

"Well then, I'd say your list is incorrect, Captain. We know what we saw."

Abruptly Supratman leaned forward and whisked the printout off the desk.

"List correct," he mumbled irritably, folding it into an uneven bundle.

Ben drew a breath. He would try one last time. If there were any working seamen on the *Loro Kidul* who were still alive, he owed it to them.

"What about Lom Lok?" he ventured. "The man

we rescued who claimed to be off the *Loro Kidul*?
We didn't imagine him."

Supratman sighed, fished in his pocket for a *kretek*
cigarette, and slipped it into his mouth. "Where Lom
Lok?" he asked.

"We told you," Sass broke in, exasperated. "He ran
away as soon as we hit the dock. We have no idea
why, other than he might have been with the pirates."

Supratman ignored her utterly, lighting his cigarette
with a paper match, and kept his eyes on Ben. "Where
Lom Lok?" he repeated.

Ben realized that the captain, a man of some authority, had almost certainly taken offense at having
a woman speak so forcefully to him. There was no
equality of the sexes in Indonesia. He leaned forward quickly.

"Lom Lok disappeared immediately after we arrived," he said quietly. "He's got to be around somewhere, and he knows more than he told us. His
description's in the report."

Supratman blew a cloud of clove smoke at the ceiling and rubbed his eye with the heel of his cigarette
hand. "No *Loro Kidul* listed," he stated. "No Lom
Lok, seaman from *Loro Kidul*. No distress call from
Loro Kidul. No report from other ship in area of *Loro
Kidul*." He permitted a ghost of a smile to cross his
face and shook his head.

"Dammit!" Ben said angrily, sitting back hard in
his chair and crossing his arms.

The captain looked out the soiled window again,
then got to his feet. He squinted at Ben through the
smoke trickling up from his cigarette.

"Last month, two hundred petty theft from boat in
Lampung harbor," he said. "All of Indonesia, many

thousand. Theft of all boat—fishing, houseboat, junk—more than four hundred. Theft at sea or hijack of freighter, ferry, or schooner: twenty-seven. *One month.*"

He shrugged. "*Loro Kidul,* if real, only one of many."

He crushed out the butt of his cigarette in the ashtray on the desktop and left the room.

Ben looked at the empty doorway behind the desk for a few seconds, then slowly unfolded his arms and got to his feet.

"Well," he said, "I guess we're done."

Chapter Eight

The *becak* driver was having a good day. As he pulled up in front of the entry gates of the Pertamina oilfield docks, Ben turned and handed him a five-thousand-rupiah note, at least twice the proper fare for the distance traveled. The man made a repetitive bowing motion with his head.

"*Terima kasih,*" he said, beaming.

Ben held up some fingers. "Seven o'clock, okay? You understand? Be around at seven, and you can run us up to the Hotel Arinas. Got it?"

The driver nodded. "*Jam tujuh,* boss. Seveen oh-clock." He tapped his cheap plastic watch.

Ben smiled, waved him off, and turned toward the gate, slipping his arm under Sass's.

"Just out of curiosity," she asked, "what are you actually spending when you drop five thousand rupiahs on someone?"

"About two dollars American," Ben replied. "For a custom-chauffeured scenic ride along the entire waterfront of Bandar Lampung, with two or three stops along the way—and that's *still* a dollar more than he's used to making. He shook his head, smiling. "Incredible."

"Think he'll be here when we get through meeting Burke? It'll be nearly dark by then."

Ben grinned. "Oh, yes. He'll be here. You can count on it."

Ben identified himself to the green-uniformed guard manning the watch booth at the main gate, and he and Sass were ushered through into a typical oil-field dockyard. Racks of drill-string and large pipe were stored here and there, interspersed with generators, compressors, fuel drums, stacks of galvanized grating and sheet steel, and coils of heavy cable. Several large cranes stood idle near the seawall, and along the docks at the far end of the yard a small tugboat, a rusty barge, and an oddly fat-looking, medium-sized freighter were tied up.

"I guess that'd be Burke's ship," Ben said as they strode down the dirt road toward the vessels. He pointed. "The freighter."

They picked their way across the short stretch of muddy ground separating the road from the quay and stepped up on the concrete of the seawall, pausing beside the big steel bollard to which the freighter's bow lines were secured. Ben put his hands on his hips and looked the ship over with a practiced eye.

"She's about three hundred fifty feet overall," he said, thinking out loud. "Midsized cargo freighter, with some conversions done on her for construction work." He gazed up at the high, flared, black-painted bow looming overhead. "She's got a lot of forward sheer for this kind of vessel; her bow's a real wave cleaver, like a North Sea oil-field boat. She looks like she was built in the U.S. or northern Europe, with lines like that."

He squinted sharply at the doubler-plates near the waterline on the ship's bow. "Jesus. Are those *rivets*?" Lines of small bumps, thickly coated with black paint, ran along the edges of the extra steel plates. "They *are*. Hot-hammered rivets. Boy, that dates her." Ben shook his head. "The last riveted ships were built just after World War Two. Soon after that virtually all shipyards converted to welding. This old gal's at least fifty or sixty years old.

"She looks strong and well maintained, though," he went on. "Look, you can see the modern stick welding where they've replaced some of her older plates." He pointed to a relatively smooth spot about ten feet back from the ship's stem.

"Neat," Sass commented, shading her eyes and looking up at the vessel's name, rendered high on the bow in square white letters.

"*Kraken*," she read aloud. "Port of registry: Honolulu."

"American-flagged vessel," Ben said. "A little piece of home working the Indonesian oil fields."

Sass looked down the length of the *Kraken* and frowned. "Why does she look so fat? What's that big bulge running along her side?" She indicated a long, half-tubular tank nearly twenty feet wide that was welded into the ship's hull above and below the waterline, extending from thirty feet aft of the bow almost all the way to the stern.

"That's a sponson," Ben replied. "There'll be one on her other side, too. It's just a long air tank that adds more width and stability to a ship that wasn't originally designed to be used as a construction platform. See that big pedestal crane mounted amidships? Without sponsons, lifting a really heavy load with that thing could actually roll the ship right over."

"That would be bad," Sass observed.

"Very bad."

They walked along the seawall, stepping over docking cleats and dodging bollards, and continued their appraisal of the *Kraken*. Amidships, Ben pointed out a support structure of steel girders on top of the quayside sponson.

"See how they've extended the deck out over the sponson?" he said. "Those beams brace it in place. Gives much more working room topside, and a clear drop to the water for doing over-the-side rigging and crane work."

"Pretty clever," Sass acknowledged. "Somebody took this old freighter and updated her for the kind of work that's available in these oil fields right now, didn't they?"

"Sure looks like it," Ben agreed. "Here we go. Here's the gangway."

He stepped up on the hanging stairs that were suspended over the side of the *Kraken* and reached back to offer Sass a hand. Together they climbed to the deck above. They were met at the rail by a crewman on watch; a weather-beaten Indonesian of about thirty with a thatch of flyaway black hair, wearing grimy navy-blue coveralls and work boots.

"Permission to come aboard," Ben said, smiling. "Captain Burke around?"

"Cap'n Boork?" the crewman responded. "*Ya, ya.* Boork here. You Gah-non?"

"That's right," Ben replied, nodding. "I'm Ben Gannon. The new diving supervisor."

The crewman grinned, showing missing teeth. "*Selamat datang.* Welcome. You come." He beckoned in the Indonesian manner, waving his fingers inward with the palm of his hand facing down, then turned and strode off down the deck toward the stern.

"That almost locked like waving good-bye," Sass whispered as they proceeded after him.

"Yeah," Ben said over his shoulder. "But it's their way. Beckoning someone like we do in the West. by crooking an upraised finger, is simply considered a rude gesture over here." He grinned. "Watch you don't forget and do it to someone by accident. In Indonesia, it's more or less like flipping a person the bird."

"Yikes," Sass exclaimed, widening her eyes and smiling. "I'll remember!"

The crewman waited for them at one of the open watertight doors in the starboard side of the stern superstructure, which housed the crew's quarters, galley, and up top, the bridge. He pointed into the passageway.

"Jalan terus," he said. "Straight on. Then climb stairs to bridge. Cap'n office and quarters behind bridge. Knock please." He leaned in conspiratorially. "Boork very strict cap'n. Never no funny bizness." He grinned and nodded, stuck one of the ubiquitous *kreteks* between his lips and strolled off, fiddling with an ancient Zippo lighter.

"Does *everybody* in Indonesia smoke those damn things?" hissed Sass as they entered the passageway.

"Pretty much," Ben said. "At least as far as I saw when I was in Palembang. Most Indonesian men smoke like furnaces." He sighed. "And the big American and European tobacco companies are only too glad to feed their appetites. Western brands are almost as popular as *kreteks* now."

They reached the end of the passageway and climbed several flights of stairs to the bridge. The steering station and command center of the *Kraken* was spacious and clean, with varnished teak, gleaming chrome, and polished brass and bronze everywhere. The bridge equipment was an unusual combination of the modern and the traditional. A brass-and-glass binnacle mounted in front of the ship's wheel looked at least a hundred years old, but the compass it housed was utterly modern, with coaxial cables connecting it to an array of electronic navigation instruments mounted in overhead racks. A solid bronze, early twentieth-century engine-room telegraph with a handle of genuine ivory stood next to a magnificently carved teak ship's wheel, while two feet away a computerized weatherfax machine continuously ran satellite weather information across a glowing liquid-crystal screen.

"Interesting ship," Ben said. "It's got someone's personal touch." His wandering gaze landed on a gilt-framed oil portrait affixed to the rich teak of the aft bulkhead. The man pictured was about sixty, wearing a blue merchant marine uniform and captain's hat. The face was classic New England Yankee; lean, austere, and unsmiling, with heavy black brows arching over piercing blue eyes and a gray-streaked, muttonchop beard framing a hard-set mouth. "I wonder if this is Burke."

"It is *a* Burke," came a clipped, commanding voice from the door that had opened, unnoticed, in the port side of the aft bulkhead. "My father, Captain Isaac Burke."

A broad-shouldered man at least six-four in height stepped through the doorway. Ben and Sass stared: minus thirty years and the muttonchops, it was as though the portrait on the bulkhead had come to life.

The same icy blue eyes under thick dark brows looked them up and down.

"I assume you are Ben Gannon," the big man said. "I'm Captain Joshua Burke." He extended a large, black-haired hand, which Ben shook. Burke was one of those men who liked to communicate their masculinity by mangling another person's hand in a handshake. Ben tightened his own grip to keep the burly captain from crushing his knuckles.

"Pleased to meet you, Captain," Ben responded, salvaging his hand. "This is my better half, Sasha Wojeck. As Jake Logan probably told you, we've been making a sailing passage across the Pacific from Panama over the past three months. We just got into Bandar Lampung early this afternoon."

"Mmm." Burke looked at Sass disapprovingly. "My pleasure, madam. Or should I say, Mrs. Gannon." His lip curled in something resembling distaste. "It is *Mrs.* Gannon, isn't it?"

Since he seemed bent on making an issue of it, Sass told him what he wanted to hear: "Yes. Wojeck is my maiden name." She slipped her arms around Ben, smiling like a good little wife. "Ben introduces me like that because he likes me to keep my identity. He's such a sweetie." She mooned up at him, batting her eyes.

Ben smiled down at her with a slightly pained expression on his face. She was laying it on a bit thick.

"Good," Burke announced. "Too many people fornicating and living in sin these days. The decay of Western society starts with a lack of respect for the institution of marriage. Pretty soon we'll all end up like these third-world heathens around here, breeding like monkeys and propagating all kinds of disgusting diseases."

Ben glanced at Sass as Burke whirled on one heel and reached overhead to grab an intercom microphone. She rolled her eyes.

"You'll take a little refreshment, of course," Burke stated. He thumbed the speaking key of the microphone. "Chang! *Chang!*"

A few seconds later a thin voice came back: "Yes, Cap'n?"

"Iced tea for three people on the bridge immediately, Chang. Hurry it up."

The voice was even fainter the second time. "Yes, Cap'n."

Burke jammed the microphone back into its overhead holder. "The ship's steward," he said. "An old Chinaman who started with my father back in the late forties as a young man fleeing the Maoists. After my father died about three years ago and I inherited title and command of this ship, I kept Chang on for sentimental reasons." He shook his head. "I'm afraid, however, that he's getting lax in his old age. This ship has been his only home for over fifty years, and he knows every inch of it, but his performance of his duties has been slipping. Very irritating." He tsk-tsked "Long-term crew or not, this will be his last six weeks at sea aboard the *Kraken*. I'm releasing him when we're through with the pipeline project."

"I see," Ben commented, unsure of what to say.

"I won't waste time, Mr. Gannon," Burke said, planting himself squarely in front of Ben and Sass again, his hands clasped behind his back. "You came highly recommended as a diving supervisor by Mr. Logan, whose judgment I came to trust during the course of our working together over the past year. I will leave you free to run the diving operations of this pipeline-laying project as you see fit, with a few simple provisions:

"One: ultimate authority aboard the *Kraken* belongs to me, and me alone. I will listen to the recommendations of my contractors, but my decisions are final and my orders at sea are to be obeyed without question by all personnel. I run the proverbial tight ship. Mr. Gannon, as did my father."

"I can appreciate that, Captain." Ben nodded. 'One ship; one master."

"Good. Two: I do not tolerate alcohol, drugs, or unattached women"—his gaze flickered briefly over Sass—"aboard my ship. Abstention from unhealthy habits and distractions keeps men's minds on their work. If you witness any violations of this rule you will report them to me immediately. Agreed?"

Ben nodded silently, his face a pleasant blank. Beside him, Sass fought to keep the blood from rising to her cheeks.

"And three: this ship is crewed by Malaysian, Indonesian, and Taiwanese nationals. In addition, there will be a pipe-laying and welding crew aboard to man the lay barge that will be tethered alongside *Kraken* at sea. You see those portable fiberglass buildings welded to the deck down there?" Burke pointed out the forward glass of the bridge at the main deck below.

"Yes, I see them," Ben said.

"The barge laborers will be quartered there. The crew occupies the first sublevel and main deck level of this ship's living quarters. Upper sections of this aft superstructure are reserved exclusively for me, my first mate, my chief engineer, and any Caucasian contractors—such as yourself—who may be onboard.

"Under no circumstances are any Southeast Asians

permitted to enter the upper three levels unless it becomes necessary in the performance of their duties. They live, eat, and work on the main deck and subdeck. We live up here. There is no casual fraternization between crew and ship's officers, for reasons pertaining to both the maintenance of authority *and* the differences in race and culture."

Burke smiled grimly. "Separate worlds, Mr. Gannon. They aren't like us. We have our ways and they have theirs, and the two do not mix well." He paused. "Does any of this disturb you?"

Ben's pleasant expression revealed no opinion whatsoever. "Your ship, Captain," he said.

"Excellent," Burke concluded. "Ah, the tea. Well, come on, Chang! Don't take all day about it!"

An aged Chinese of at least seventy shuffled slowly into the bridge, puffing from the climb of the interior stairs. He carried a large silver tray upon which rested three tumblers of ice and a glass pitcher of tea and lemons. His white steward's jacket was stained and threadbare, and wisps of gray hair protruded from beneath the small embroidered cap he wore. His eyes, deeply slanted and underscored with wrinkles and bags, appeared almost shut.

Burke seemed close to exploding with irritation as the old man set the tray down on the bridge console and began to pour the tea with unsteady hands. When he was finally done, he turned to the captain and gave a slight bow.

"Something else, Cap'n?" he asked softly.

"No, No! That's all, Chang!" Burke snapped the words out. "Run along."

The old man bowed again and shuffled out of the

bridge. Burke handed glasses to Ben and Sass, then raised his own.

"Cheers," he said. "To the next six weeks."

Ben and Sass tipped their tumblers in his direction and drank. The tea was excellent; lemony with a touch of ginger.

Burke drained his glass, then set it down briskly on the tray.

"All right, then, Mr. Gannon," he said. "I'll expect you and your personal gear to be aboard the *Kraken* the day after tomorrow at oh-eight hundred hours. You can complete your orientation and meet my mate and engineer on the way out to the oil field. Oh, and by the way, you can also meet your translator."

"Translator?" Ben's eyebrows lifted in surprise.

Burke looked vaguely amused. "Yes, 'translator.' Didn't Logan tell you?"

"No."

"You'll be working a crew of Indonesian divers. None of them speaks English." Burke let out a short, barking laugh. "So, unless you're fluent in Bahasa Indonesia, your every order will have to be translated.

"And now, if you'll excuse me, I have paperwork to file. You know your way ashore." The captain turned toward the entrance to his quarters. "I'll expect you the morning after next. A pleasant evening to you both."

He walked into his stateroom and shut the door.

Sass finished her tea, set the glass slowly on the tray, and looked up at Ben. She began to smile.

Ben put an index finger gently on her outthrust chin.

"Don't say it," he whispered, smiling back at her. "Just don't say it."

Chapter Nine

It had rained most of the night in and around Bengkulu. As the sun rose over the jungled hills to the east, its rays turned the town and surrounding fields into one immense steambath. The heat and humidity were relentless, claustrophobic. It was the kind of atmosphere that had, in the past, driven more than one European colonial mad.

Twelve miles north of town lay the sprawling oceanfront grounds of the Smuts Estate; a property owned for over a hundred fifty years by a Dutch family that had made its initial fortune operating pepper and rubber plantations. An early to mid-twentieth-century succession of alcoholic and/or idiot sons had done a remarkably efficient job of diminishing the family's net worth, and the Japanese occupation and successful post-World War II Indonesian struggle for independence from Dutch colonial control had more or less finished the task.

Since the early 1950s, the Smuts Estate had been owned on paper by a consortium of Indonesian businessmen—a front for the last few remaining members of the Smuts clan, who spent their time ensconced in villas in Monte Carlo, busily drinking and gambling away their family's last few remaining millions. For several decades the estate and its grounds had been for rent to anyone who could produce the necessary money, no questions asked.

The old stone great house and its surrounding buildings were dilapidated and nearly barren of furniture, and the courtyard and nearby gardens were overgrown and tangled with jungle vines, but for the past eighteen months, the estate had been occupied. It was isolated, had grounds that could easily be secured against intrusion, and came complete with a deepwater dock. That was enough for the current occupants, who were little concerned with niceties such as antique furniture and designer wallpaper.

In the cobblestone courtyard behind the great house, Malcolm Durant sat in a small, rusty patio chair, his long, booted legs stretched out in front of him, one hand cupping his morning coffee-and-bourbon. He was staring, unblinking, across the courtyard at the equally unblinking green eyes of the white tigress caged some twenty feet away. Already, though it was barely nine o'clock in the morning, sweat had soaked his khaki trousers and sleeveless hunting vest.

A drop of salty sweat trickled off the bridge of his large, broken nose and into his left eye, stinging it. With a curse, he blinked and rubbed it with the back of his hand, then got up and glared at the tigress. She continued to stare back at him, motionless.

Draining his coffee mug, Durant set it on the small patio table and walked over to a large-diameter fire hose that lay near the cage. As he picked it up, the tigress snarled and retreated to the rear of her little prison, pacing back and forth and baring her fangs. The big man dragged the hose over to the front of the cage, paused to chuckle at the tigress's alarm, then opened the valve on the bronze nozzle. A powerful stream of water shot out and hit the trapped animal full in the face.

The tigress went insane. Dashing from side to side, hurling herself against the bars that confined her, she screamed in fear and rage at Durant as he kept the hose trained on her, knocking her off balance and drenching her from muzzle to tail. Her claws raked across the cage as she made futile efforts to strike out at him, then cowered back under the stinging impact of the jet of water.

After tormenting the animal for a few minutes, Durant shut the nozzle off, chuckling to himself, and dropped the hose on the cobblestones. Shaking with fury, the tigress gnashed her hatred of him, then retired to a rear corner of the cage to lick herself dry.

Durant picked up a small towel from the table and mopped his dripping face, cursing the heat. Not that he really minded it—it was simply his habit to snarl at everything. At six-three and two hundred forty pounds, with tattooed, steroid-blown arms and the swarthy, battered face of a Neanderthal prizefighter, virtually everything at which he snarled got rapidly out of his way. Seven years as a U.S. Navy SEAL, along with an inbred cunning and utter lack of remorse, made Malcolm Durant a very dangerous man indeed.

Fleeing the United States after breaking his trust as a SEAL by attempting to sell several truckloads of classified weaponry out the back door of a military warehouse, Durant had spent most of the 1990s as a military instructor for hire to various terrorist organizations, during which time he had become one of the more wanted men on the planet. In particular, his involvement with a Middle Eastern terrorist cell responsible for the mining and subsequent destruction of one of the United States' premier high-tech oil rigs in the Gulf of Mexico, just the previous year, had made him a high-priority target for antiterrorism agencies around the world. The heat had gotten *too* hot; Durant had fled the Mediterranean region for the relative obscurity of Indonesia.

And now he had a new gig. One that allowed him to satisfy his killer instinct with little danger to himself. One with plenty of action, easy pickings, a big score just down the road, and little or no interference from any truly effective law-enforcement agencies. He ran a hand through his thinning tangle of greasy black hair and poured another slug of Jim Beam into his empty coffee mug. Life was good.

He lit a Marlboro and was about to sit down when the compact walkie-talkie on his hip buzzed. Unclipping it, he raised it to his ear.

"Durant," he rasped. "What is it?" The East Texas accent was strong.

As he listened, his expression shifted and hardened until his face bore a disturbing resemblance to that of a gargoyle.

"What?" he erupted. "Lom Lok? That little slimeball from the ship? What's he doin' here?" He glanced at the date on his watch. "He's supposed to be aboard the *Loro Kidul* right now, approachin' the Riau Archipelago!"

Irritably snatching a drag from his cigarette, Durant listened for a few seconds, then lashed out with one booted foot and kicked the small metal chair clear across the courtyard.

"Get that little bastard in here."

He slammed the walkie-talkie down on the table,

then jerked his head around as the tigress let loose a rumbling snarl. In one quick motion he grabbed the nearly empty Jim Beam bottle and hurled it at the cage. It smashed against the bars, showering the tigress with shards of broken glass and sending her cowering back into a rear corner.

"Shaddap!" Durant bellowed.

He paced up and down a few times, sucking furiously on his cigarette, until he had calmed himself enough to lean back against the table and sip some bourbon. In a few minutes two of his Indonesian trackers came into the courtyard, AK-47s slung over their shoulders and their sandals slapping the cobblestones, with Lom Lok hurriedly shuffling along between them. The little man came forward and bowed obsequiously to Durant, trying to keep his gap-toothed grin from deteriorating into a grimace of fear.

Durant's eyes were like two black coals set in his simian face. "What the *fuck* are you doin' here?" he rasped.

Lom Lok withered visibly under the big American's menacing glare. His grin faltering, he put his palms together in a gesture of deference. "Please, Mistah Durant. Something happen to ship. Something bad. I nearly killed, but get away."

There was utter silence as Durant's freezing gaze remained fixed on the smaller man. Lom Lok's eyes began to shift rapidly.

"Somethin' happened to the ship?" Durant hissed. *"To my shipment?"*

"Ya, ya, boss."

"What?"

Lom Lok eye-shifted around the courtyard, looking trapped and miserable. "Pirate raid, Mistah Durant," he explained earnestly. "Two day ago. They board ship at night, kill all, throw poor Lom Lok over side when he try to fight them. Bad, very bad. Much killings."

Durant uncoiled his massive arms, took one quick step forward, and grabbed Lom Lok by the throat, lifting him up on his toes.

"Don't lie to me, you little fucker," he said. "If there was a firefight, you'd have been the first sonofabitch to run for cover. You ain't never stuck your scrawny neck out once in your life." He lifted the little man clean off the ground until he gurgled. Lom Lok began to kick feebly, his eyes rolling up white in his head. "When I let you down, I want the whole story, quickly, without the fuckin' lies."

He tossed him backward, and the little Indonesian sprawled on the cobblestones at the feet of the two trackers, who made no move to assist him. Durant lit another Marlboro as Lom Lok gasped for air, rubbing his throat.

"Now," Durant said, turning, *"what happened to my ship?"*

His face creased with fear, Lom Lok blubbered in Bahasa for a few seconds, then switched back to his broken English. "Pirate come!" he sobbed desperately. "Take ship after we pass through Sunda Strait! Wear mask, have machine gun . . . kill all! I tell true!"

"What happened to De Voort?" Durant growled. "He's one mean motherfucker. No way he'd have let anyone take that ship."

"I not know!" Lom Lok went on. "I go into sea at night, hear much shootings! Thinking Captain De Voort dead, too. Too many pirate, too many machine gun."

Durant thought a moment. "So you went over the side, eh? What'd you do? Swim forty or fifty miles to land, then jog on up to Bengkulu?" His smile was deadly.

"No, Mistah Durant, no!" Lom Lok cried, shaking his hands and head. "I picked up by Americans in sailing boat. Save me from sharks. I come up on fast bus from Bandar Lampung to tell you all, Mistah Durant, sir."

"So you came up here to tell me that my ship, along with my shipment, has been hijacked by some other gang of freelancers, that it's fuckin' *gone,* but you got away? This is supposed to make me happy? You sniveling little prick." Durant reached behind him and whisked a four-inch killing knife out of its place of concealment in the small of his back. "I'm gonna cut your throat just to make myself *feel* better."

"Haaiii! No! No, Mistah Durant!" Lom Lok back-pedaled frantically, his mud-splattered sandals scuffling at the cobblestones. As Durant advanced, the knife gleaming in his hand, the little man flung out his arms. *"I know where ship went!"*

Durant paused. Casually, unhurriedly, he squatted down on his haunches and peered into Lom Lok's terrified face. "Well," he said with deadly softness, *"why don't you tell me about it?"*

"Two American on sailing boat!" babbled the little Indonesian. "Big man, nearly big as you, and pretty lady. They hear me, pull me out of water. They *see* pirate attack *Loro Kidul*! Record *everything—time, speed, position, bearing*!" He panted a couple of times, getting his breath. "They not friendly to Lom Lok. Not take me to Bengkulu; not give me records for Mistah Durant. Want me to talk to police. No, No!"

He shook his head vehemently. "I never talk to police. I run away, come to Mistah Durant in Bengkulu." Lom Lok glanced up, sheer desperation in his eyes. "You see, boss? No telephonings. I come to get you, maybe we find where *Loro Kidul* go from Americans on sailing boat."

Durant stared at him for a few seconds longer, then got to his feet and resheathed the killing knife. He snatched the walkie-talkie off the table, punched a button, and held it to his mouth.

"Get the Land Rover fired up and bring it to the front of the house," he ordered. "Move your asses."

He glanced over at Lom Lok, who was getting painfully to his feet. Grinning, he held out the coffee mug containing the remnants of his last shot of bourbon. "Here, you little weasel. Have a drink. Give you some guts." Durant watched, thinly veiled contempt on his face, as the little man sucked down the dregs. "We're goin' to Bandar Lampung and talk to your Americans. Go wait out by the Rover."

Lom Lok grinned and bowed, his hands clasped. "*Terima kasih,* Mistah Durant." He turned and nearly ran from the courtyard.

Durant snapped his fingers at one of the trackers still standing off to one side. "Get me a secure land line," he barked. The man whirled and trotted into the great house.

"Nobody steals my goods," Durant whispered to the white tigress across the courtyard. She stared at him, unmoving.

In a moment the tracker returned carrying an old rotary telephone, trailing a long cord behind him. He handed it to Durant, who took it and then waved the two trackers away. They left the courtyard silently as he dialed a number.

There was a rough click as the call connected. *"Ya?"* a voice said.

"It's Durant," the big man snarled at the speaker. "Gimme Jaeger. And tell him we got a major problem."

The white tigress lay in a rear corner of the cage and licked her damp paws. She didn't mind water; it was the terrible force with which it shot through the bars at her, the frighteningly unfamiliar feeling of something she didn't understand striking her body that sent her into a frenzy. And she could feel the malice of the *Two-Leg* that held the strange and fearsome water-spitting snake.

She watched through the bars of her cage as the creature paced back and forth, upright on its hind legs like *Choy-cho,* the giant cassowary bird. It was not as big as she, though it stood taller, and she knew she could kill it. But the *Two-Legs* had always terrified her. They were not benign; a scent of malevolent power emanated from them as it did from the *Buaya,* the great saltwater crocodiles, whom she also loathed and feared.

With an acceptance that was more instinct than conscious resignation, the white tigress laid her chin down on top of her paws and half closed her eyes, listening to the familiar sounds of birds calling from tree to tree and insects chirping and buzzing in the hot air. One eye she reserved for the *Two-Leg* that still walked back and forth, back and forth, talking in its strange language though no others of its kind were nearby.

If the chance came to escape the confines of this small cave with no entrance or exit, she would be well rested and ready.

Durant chewed the filter of his Marlboro and listened to the party on the other end of the phone line. The voice was male, but high-pitched and wheezy, as though its owner had bad lungs. The speaker rarely got through a sentence without pausing in the middle to suck in more air.

"I provide you with an untraceable ship, a generous outlay for fuel and other transportation expenses, and now you tell me that your captain, whom you assured me was reliable, has *lost* my ship, and our shipment along with it." There was yet another rattling wheeze.

"I am not pleased, Malcolm. Not pleased at all."

"Look, Anton," Durant said irritably, "I told you we were going to go talk to these two Americans down in Bandar Lampung and shake loose some info on where the fuckin' ship was headed. Okay? I'm also gonna grab me the logs and everything else they recorded on the night of the attack. At least we'll have some idea where the *Loro Kidul* may have ended up."

There was a patronizing sigh at the other end of the line. "Malcolm, Malcolm . . . You go to Bandar Lampung and assault two American citizens and they'll run straight for their embassy, creating all kinds of noise and attention in the process. What you need to do is kidnap them outright, along with their logs and documents. Then there will be no repercussions after we extract the information we require. You see?"

Durant shrugged. "Fine by me. Easy to get rid of two bodies in Sumatra. No end of swamps around here. But look: you gonna get your people out askin' questions in the islands? Somebody must have seen that freighter. You're supposed to be the man with the connections, ain't you? Maybe you can track it down while I'm tryin' to pump the two Americans at this end."

Another sigh. "Malcolm, as soon as you told me of the problem, I dispatched my senior lieutenants to initiate a search. I maintain a network of informants throughout the islands of the western Java Sea, particularly around the shipping lanes. But this is a large area, and time is of the essence since we are trying to locate a moving target. If you can get bearings and a last known position for the *Loro Kidul* from the two Americans who picked up your crewman, it will help to narrow the search."

"Right," Durant said. "I'd better get moving."

There was a bitter, wheezing chortle. "Yes," Anton Jaeger concurred, "you better had. I don't make investments in order to take a loss. And I don't let profits of this scale slip between my fingers due to the incompetence of others. De Voort was *your* captain, Malcolm. I'm going to be very put out if this ship and its cargo aren't recovered. Do you understand me, Malcolm?"

Durant let out a rasping laugh. This was familiar territory. "You ain't threatening me, are you, Anton?" he inquired.

There was an icy pause before Jaeger answered.

"I *never* make threats," he said softly, and hung up.

Chapter Ten

The morning of their third day in Bandar Lampung, Ben awoke in the upper-story suite of the Hotel Arinas to find Sass standing in front of the open window, gazing out at a red dawn breaking over Lampung Bay. She had wrapped a green batik sarong around her hips, but was naked from the waist up, her arms crossed beneath her breasts. The crimson glow coming through the window illuminated her tanned curves, cascading hair, long, elegant neck, and high cheekbones—as though, it seemed to Ben, she had turned into a living golden sculpture. He let his eyes roam over her. Time and time again, year after year, he would turn and glimpse her in an unguarded moment, and find her intoxicatingly beautiful.

Though he'd made no sound, she turned suddenly and looked at him. Slowly, she smiled.

"I could feel you looking at me," she said softly.

"Did it feel nice?" Ben asked.

"Yes."

She unfolded her arms and came back toward the bed, the green sarong contrasting richly with the golden-brown skin of her flat stomach. Kneeling on the sheet, she straddled his legs and crawled up to sit on his shins, her palms resting on his thighs. She gazed down at him, her eyes happy, crinkled at the corners.

"I love you," she said.

Ben reached out and grasped her upper arms in his big hands, pulling her gently toward him. She came willingly, the weight of her body on his chest, her eyes closing as his lips met hers in a slow, deliberate kiss. His shoulder muscles flexed under her palms, and once again she found herself reminded of how strong he was.

"I love you back," he said, smiling. He kissed the tip of her nose.

She squirmed on top of him, kicking down the sheet into a crumpled pile at the foot of the bed. Hooking her legs under his, she sat up on top of his hips.

"It's early," she whispered, pulling loose the knot of the sarong. Somewhere outside, a rooster began to crow as the dawn mists sifted through the narrow streets. She ran her hands through her sun-streaked hair, then laid back down on his chest.

"I miss you already, Ben." She nuzzled his neck. "Call and tell Burke you've changed your mind. You're not going away with him for six weeks. Okay?"

"Sure." He patted her head. "Sure thing."

"Liar. You're patronizing me."

"Yup."

"Oh, well," she sighed, shifting her hips to just the right spot. "Are you gonna use me for my body before you abandon me for a month and a half?"

Ben grinned. "Who's using who this morning?"

"Just answer the question, stupid."

"Okay: yes, I'm gonna."

Sass giggled and bit Ben's earlobe. "Oh, my goodness," she said. "Oh, *help*."

The *Kraken*'s engines were already warmed up and throbbing smoothly when Ben showed up at the ship's boarding stairs at ten to eight, lugging two large duffels and his dive-hat bag. Although it was relatively early, the temperature was close to ninety degrees, and he could feel sweat begin to trickle down his temple as he humped his gear up to the main deck. Pausing to catch his breath at the top of the stairs, he noticed a slender, well-groomed Indonesian in blue military fatigues standing by a rack of pipe, looking him over. The man was young, not more than thirty, and had a pleasant, open demeanor.

Panting, Ben nodded to him. He smiled immediately and approached. "Hiya. Can I give you a hand there?" Ben blinked. The man's accent was as American as apple pie.

"Sure. Thanks." He extended his hand. "I'm Ben Gannon, the dive supervisor."

"Kiat Padang." The young Indonesian clasped Ben's hand firmly. "Call me Ki. Everyone does." He pronounced his nickname *kee*. "Where do you want to stow your gear?"

"In the dive-control shack for now. Wherever that is." Ben laughed, and Ki's smooth face creased into a broad grin, his intelligent brown eyes crinkling at the corners. The young man was frank and easy in his manner, and Ben liked him immediately.

"It's over here," Ki said, and picked up Ben's largest duffel. "The smaller green building." He indicated a portable fiberglass shack that had been welded to the *Kraken*'s main deck near the starboard rail.

They began lugging Ben's gear down the deck. "I'm the Indonesian government representative on this job," Ki explained. "Basically, that means that I'm a sort of multipurpose type: part environmental watchdog, part Pertamina Oil official, and part translator."

Ben grinned. "Oh, so you're my translator. I was wondering how that was going to work out."

"Well, what d'you think now?" Ki asked good-naturedly, raising an eyebrow.

"Hell," Ben said with a laugh. "You don't just speak English. You speak American better than most Americans. I wish I spoke Bahasa Indonesia one-tenth as well, or any other language for that matter."

"Stick around for a while," Ki said, "and you just might surprise yourself."

They paused and stepped aside as a small gang of Indonesian deckhands trudged by, dragging a thirty-foot length of rusty, oversized anchor chain. It made a harsh scraping sound as it slid over the steel deck plates, leaving long streaks of orange corrosion. Ben shook his head. "Hope they're taking that to the junk pile."

"Are you kidding?" Ki replied as they resumed lugging Ben's gear toward the dive shack. "Burke'll have six men with wire toothbrushes on that piece of junk before we're out of the turning basin. A dozen cans of cheap cold-galvanizing spray, and that chain will be part of the *Kraken*'s ground tackle again." He caught Ben's look of surprised disapproval. "Yeah. It's scary."

"Well," Ben said, "he does seem like the type who might want to wring the last cent out of a dollar. New England Yankee stock. Course, I only just met the man the other day, so I don't want to judge him before I know him. He appeared to know his business."

"Oh, he does." Ki set the heavy gear bag down beside the door of the dive shack. "Being cheap doesn't necessarily make you incompetent. It just makes you, well, cheap."

Ben chuckled and set his bags down. "Well, whatever he is, I'm gonna have to make the best of it for the next six weeks. You?"

Ki nodded. "Six weeks. I got assigned for the whole shebang."

"You'll have to tell me about that later," Ben said. "I'm interested in what you do, working for the Indonesian government. Sounds fascinating."

"Sure. I'll bore you with the whole nine yards, if you like."

A small, blond-bearded Caucasian man wearing an officer's cap and carrying a clipboard was striding down the deck in their direction. Ben leaned back against the wall of the shack, watching him approach. He looked like the intense type.

"By the way," Ben asked Ki, "where'd you pick up all your Americanisms?"

"Pepperdine University." Ki grinned at Ben. "And four years of high school in Santa Barbara before that." He shrugged. "Hey, I'm a rich kid. Dad's in textiles, import and export from Bali and Java. I'm lucky. I got educated in the States. My family still has three homes in California."

Ben smiled at the easygoing, self-deprecating young man. "Luck of the draw counts in this life. No crime to be born with an advantage, as long as you do something good with it."

"My thinking exactly," Ki said. "Look out. Here's Bullock."

The stocky man with the clipboard arrested his forward momentum with a final stomp and touched his cap briefly to Ben in what was apparently an old, unconscious military reflex. "Mr. Gannon? First Mate Glenn Bullock. Captain Burke wants to look at the personnel manifest before we cast off. If you don't sign it, you're not here."

"Even if he's looking right at you," whispered Ki, too low for the mate to hear.

Bullock reversed the clipboard across his forearm with a brisk movement and extended a pen toward Ben. "Sign beside your name, please. Along with the date and time."

"Sure." Ben took the pen and signed. "If you wouldn't mind, please tell Captain Burke that I'll be up to check in with him on the bridge as soon as I do a quick once-over of the dive station. Okay?"

"I'll tell the captain, Mr. Gannon." Bullock spoke the way he moved. Everything was short and abrupt, with more energy than was needed. The man was like an overwound human spring.

Ki had a patient smile glued to his face. Bullock looked him up and down briefly, then spun on his heel and marched back the way he had come. The deck-hands tended to shy away from him as he approached, Ben noticed.

"Not too relaxed," he said.

"Not at all," Ki agreed. "And he doesn't like me one bit."

"Oh? Why?"

Ki took a second to refresh his smile. "I'm the wrong race."

Ben frowned. "I don't like the sound of that." He fished a toothpick from his shirt pocket and chewed on it momentarily. "You know, I picked up a little of that mindset from Burke, too, the other day."

Ki shook his head. "Nah. Burke's different. He doesn't actively despise people with skin color different from his. He just feels that we'd all be better off if we were white and saw everything his way. More of a control issue than racism. But Bullock—now he's damn near Klan material. He seems to hate everyone who doesn't look like they sprouted from the same family tree he did. I haven't been able to find out a reason why. That's just the way the guy is."

"Wonderful," Ben growled. He opened the door of the dive shack. "We're guests working in this country, and we've got some damned bigot running the deck. Perfect."

"Ah, it's not that bad." Ki followed Ben into the interior of the shack. "Bullock does his job. He knows he can't get too far out of line, regardless of his personal feelings."

"Glad to hear it." Ben began looking over the dive-control station, going through an equipment checklist in his head. The dive shack was little more than a large fiberglass closet with an air conditioner mounted on its roof. It contained a couple of swiveling office chairs, a countertop/desk running along one short wall, several wall-mounted dive radios, a VHF, a four-drawer filing cabinet containing dive records and pipe-laying specifications, and a gas manifold.

The gas manifold occupied one entire wall of the cramped shack. A complex arrangement of high-pressure steel tubing, pipe fittings, quarter-turn valves, check valves, needle valves, and pressure gauges, it was the means by which the dive supervisor controlled the amount and type of breathing medium—air or gas—delivered to the diver through his umbilical hoses. The manifold was supplied by sources of breathing media outside the shack: large cylinder racks of high-pressure heliox gas for deep diving, and volume tanks of air continuously refilled by diesel compressors for shallower work.

"Logan left it looking pretty good," Ben mused as he ran his hands over the valves. He looked over at Ki. "How'd you like working in here? You translated for Jake, didn't you? Sat right at his elbow relaying every word over the radio like you're going to do for me?"

Ki shrugged. "It was fine. I only went out to replace the previous translator two weeks before there was a scheduled break in the job, and Jake Logan left. They just wanted to give me a taste of what I was in for. Hey, I didn't mind it. Jake was a nice guy. I learned a lot from him about running dives and decompression chambers, and we spent the hottest part of the day in here in the air-conditioning." He grinned broadly. "Even us Indonesians like to beat the heat when we can."

"I bet," Ben said. He straightened up and put his hands on his hips, chewing on his toothpick. "Well, this looks okay. Later on I'll check the hoses and hookups out on deck, and we should be good to go. The divers are all aboard, I guess?"

"Yes." Ki nodded. "They're all sleeping in one of the deck buildings. They got back aboard late last night." He grinned again. "Too much *arak,* I think. You want to talk to them now?"

"Ouch." Ben winced. "Rice liquor's a mean drunk. Let's just leave 'em be for now." He opened the shack door. "You want to go up to the bridge? I need to check in with Burke."

"Sure."

They exited the dive shack and headed down the deck toward the stern, Ben carrying his personal gear

bag. The sun was high in the east now, and the deck
plates were already so hot that Ben could feel the
heat through the soles of his work boots. Overhead,
flocks of black and white seabirds wheeled across a
clear, azure-blue sky. As they walked, they suddenly
felt the powerful vibrations of the ship's main engines
revving high, followed by the sight of black smoke
billowing from the main stacks. Her props engaged,
the *Kraken* gave a metallic shudder, then began to
move away from the quay.

They watched the shoreline of the eastern end of
Bandar Lampung slip past for a few moments—the
hot coastal plain shimmering in the distance, the shadowy green mountains of southern Sumatra far beyond—then entered the stern superstructure and
climbed the long series of internal stairs to the bridge.

Burke was standing erect beside the *Kraken*'s wheel,
his hands clasped behind his back. He was wearing a
gray turtleneck sweater, a captain's hat with a spit-
polished black visor, and navy-blue dress pants. There
couldn't have been a more perfect model of a traditional New England sea captain, Ben thought, if Ahab
himself had carved it out of Moby Dick's jawbone.

He cleared his throat. "Excuse me, Captain. I'd just
like to check in with you and run over—"

Burke whirled on his heel. "No talking on the
bridge during inshore maneuvers!" He turned back to
the view of the Lampung Bay ship channel filling the
bridge's forward windows. "Correct course four degrees to starboard," he ordered. The helmsman, an
impassive Indonesian with a white bandanna wrapped
around his head, moved the big wheel slightly. "Fo'
degree, aye," he said.

There was a lengthy silence. Then Burke turned and

looked at Ben. "I'll speak to you in about an hour's time, Mr. Gannon, when the *Kraken* is in the middle of Lampung Bay." He looked back out the forward window. "In the meantime, Mr. Padang will be only too glad to show you to your quarters, which are two decks above his. Mr. Padang occupies a cabin between the upper officers' decks and the lower crew's decks. Caught between two worlds, you might say, but able to keep a toe in each. Much like his position in real life, actually."

Burke turned again and indicated the door, eyebrows raised. "Mr. Padang? If you please?"

Ki nodded his head slightly, a smile of infinite patience scribed across his face. "Of course, Captain. My pleasure."

He touched Ben's elbow. The two of them left the bridge and began to descend the stairs to the accommodation decks.

Sass stood back, one work-gloved hand on her hip, and wiped the grimy sweat off her brows with the back of her forearm. At two in the afternoon the heat was brutal—in excess of a hundred degrees. She could feel the sun wringing the moisture from her like water from a chamois cloth.

The *Teresa Ann* had been hauled and was sitting chocked up on her sturdy full keel in a secure corner of the Zwolle yard. Two Indonesians wearing old coveralls, their heads and faces swathed in damp rags, were removing the aging blue bottom paint from the big double-ender using electric grinders equipped with flexible sanding pads. Clouds of toxic blue antifouling paint dust flew as they worked under Sass's watchful eye. She wiped her arms with a rag in annoyance. Her sweat-slicked skin was powdered with the stuff. Great for the complexion, she thought.

One of the workers paused momentarily, and she stepped in to run a hand over the ground-out section of hull. "Here," she said, indicating a rough patch. "Little more, please."

The Indonesian looked at her wearily, tucked his bandanna up over his mouth and nose once more, and hit the missed area with the grinder. His demonstration of fatigue had absolutely no effect on Sass, who had spent a lifetime dealing with manual laborers in boatyards. The job had been paid for. The hull was going to be prepped properly for the new bottom paint if she had to look over their shoulders until midnight.

The grinders whirred for another hour before Sass was satisfied. *"Terima kasih,"* she said to the two men, who went hurrying off to the shade of the tool room, grumbling beneath their breath. She spent the next ten minutes going around to every through-hull fitting, checking for corrosion and leaks.

When she was finally done, she patted the hull of the old boat and stepped back. The *Teresa Ann* was as solid as a battleship. She had many thousands of ocean miles left in her. "You and me both, I hope, old girl," Sass whispered.

There was a crude shower made of galvanized pipe over in a tree-shaded corner of the yard, partly concealed by a paint-storage shed and well out of the general view. Sass looked down at herself in disgust. She was literally itching to be rid of the toxic paint dust covering her head to toe. Grabbing a large towel and a bottle of shampoo that she'd brought down with her earlier, she headed over to the shower.

She was wearing a bikini swimsuit underneath her sweat-soaked khakis and denim shirt. Prying eyes would just have to pry, she thought as she kicked off the sticky clothes and turned on the shower's single valve. The water that streamed out wasn't much cooler than the surrounding air, but at least it was wet. Pouring shampoo into her hand, she began to scrub off the thick film of blue dust and sweat, unaware that she was being watched.

Less than twenty feet away, hidden from view by a stack of oil drums, Malcolm Durant gazed appreciatively through the Zwolle yard's chain-link fence at the slim, tanned, nearly naked blonde soaping herself under the shower. He glanced briefly at Lom Lok, whose eyes were practically popping out of his head.

"That her?" he growled.

"*Ya, ya,* Mistah Durant. Say-sha, she called." He licked his lips.

Durant studied her again. "Now that's one inspirin' figure of a woman," he mused. "Ain't seen one that flavor for a while . . ."

He looked back at Lom Lok, then suddenly cuffed the leering little man across the mouth with the back of his hand. The Indonesian reeled, clutching at his split lip.

"Don't you be lookin' at no white woman like that," Durant snarled. He turned back to Sass, who was bent over squeezing shampoo out of her hair. "I believe I'll be stakin' a claim on this one myself."

Chapter Eleven

Sass woke up early the next morning and had a lei-
surely continental breakfast in the lobby café of the
Hotel Arinas, eating croissants and sipping dark Ja-
vanese coffee as rattan ceiling fans rotated overhead.
She took the time to admire the greenery and orchids
spilling out of wall-mounted clay urns throughout the
little patio restaurant, and lingered over a plate of
multicolored fruit slices with unpronounceable names.
All in all, it was a very civilized way to start the morning. Wouldn't be too hard to get used to, she thought.

She made a phone call at the front desk to confirm
her flight reservations for the following morning: a
shuttle from Bandar Lampung to Djakarta, switch
flights, then Honolulu, Los Angeles, New Orleans, and
finally Fort Walton, on the Florida panhandle. She
sighed as she ticked off the flight details in her notebook. It was going to be one of those never-ending
journeys.

There were still a couple more things to do at the
boat: pick up some personal items and check that it
was securely locked down. She rolled up the sleeves
of her khaki shirt, put on her mirrored sunglasses, and
walked out of the Hotel Arinas into the street. Already it was much too hot for jeans, but she'd decided
to follow Ben's advice about not wearing shorts and

attracting undue attention. She waved over a *becak* and sat down in the passenger seat. "Zwolle Shipyard, please." The driver nodded and the rickety vehicle lurched away from the curb.

A few blocks from the hotel, Sass became aware of an odd sound—a warm, mellow chiming that cut through the raw noise of the street, not by volume, but by virtue of its sheer tonal beauty. The harmonious sound grew and grew as the *becak* pressed on through the traffic, until a small, grassy park came into view on the right side of the street. The chiming music was coming from the base of a giant wandering fig tree that covered the entire park with an umbrellalike canopy of leaves.

Sass motioned to the driver to stop. Sitting on the great, gnarled roots at the trunk of the fig tree were five men dressed in orange robes and headbands. In front of each man was a small array of what appeared to be inverted bronze or brass bowls. Sass stepped out of the *becak* to get a better look.

Each man was striking his bowls with small mallets, keeping time to a subtle rhythm that seemed to change constantly even as it anchored the music. The tonal pattern the musicians produced was glorious: a collage of gonglike notes that was as harmonically rich as it was exotic. Sass found the little orchestra captivating.

She turned to the driver. "What is that?" she asked, pointing at the musicians.

"*Gamelan,* missee," he answered, grinning. "Pretty musics."

Sass nodded. "It's beautiful. Wait here a minute, okay?"

"*Ya.*"

She stepped forward through the small crowd of onlookers. It was noticeably cooler in the shade of the giant fig tree. The *gamelan* orchestra played on, filling the park with a flurry of ringing tones. The sound was similar to that produced by a xylophone or vibraphone, thought Sass—or maybe a half-dozen xylophones.

She listened for another minute, then turned and made her way back to the *becak*. As she was putting a foot up on the base of the rattan seat to board, she glanced up at the driver and stopped. A different man sat on the bicycle seat; a man marked with an almost disfiguring blue-black tattoo that crawled up out of the neck of his shirt and over the right side of his face. Same *becak*. Different driver.

She took her foot off the rattan seat. "Who are you?" she asked. "Where's the other driver?"

The stranger grinned, showing a mouthful of bad teeth. "He gone, missee. My cousin. He sick. He ask me to run *becak* for today."

"Huh." Sass appraised the man for a second. Ugly damn tattoo. "Well, if he left, he left. A ride's a ride. Guess I'll just pay you, eh? The Zwolle Shipyard, please."

The man simply kept grinning. Sass took that for a yes and got into the seat, trying to decide what his tattoo was meant to be. It was either a very fat dragon or a very thin elephant.

The *becak* pulled out into the street again, and the lovely sound of the *gamelan* orchestra faded into the distance. Sass was going over her boat checklist in her mind when she noticed that they didn't seem to be heading in the general direction of the Zwolle yard. She looked over her shoulder at the driver.

"I said I wanted to go to the Zwolle Shipyard," she stated.

"*Ya,* missee." The driver began to pedal furiously.

Sass glanced back ahead of them. The *becak* gained speed rapidly as it started down a mild slope, its wheels chattering over the rough roadway. Sass was nearly vibrated out of her seat, and clutched at the metal support rods of the sun canopy for a handhold.

"What the hell are you doing?" she shouted at the driver.

The tattoo-faced man did not answer, but bore down on the pedals even harder, his eyes staring intently ahead. Pedestrians, parked cars, and fruit stands went by in a blur as the *becak* careened down the hill. Sass hung on grimly. Too fast to jump. She'd break bones hitting that hard, cracked street surface.

"Stop this thing, you asshole!" she yelled, trying to reach back for his hair. He ducked away, and as the *becak* caromed off the side of a juice cart at the bottom of the hill, Tattoo-Face wrenched the handlebars to the left. The speeding vehicle turned on two wheels toward a large pair of heavy wooden doors set in the side of a ramshackle warehouse. Sass had barely enough time to squeeze her eyes shut and brace herself for the inevitable impact.

It never came. At the last second the wooden panels swung open and the *becak* shot through the doorway into the dark interior of the warehouse. The doors slammed shut again as Tattoo-Face stood back hard on the vehicle's pedals, desperately trying to brake. The *becak* skidded sideways, throwing up a cloud of dust, then flipped over and crashed into a stack of rattan baskets.

Tattoo-Face staggered to his feet, weaving badly,

and began to paw through the pile of rattan. He found Sass's upper arm and gripped it, attempting to yank her upright. To his great surprise, she came up out of the jumble of baskets willingly. To his even greater surprise, she promptly smashed her clenched fist into his mouth, dislodging his two front teeth. Reeling, he tried to get another hand on her, and she kicked him in the groin. His grip on her upper arm relaxed, and he sank with an agonized whimper back down into the baskets.

Sass clawed her way out of the crushed rattan and squinted into the dim light of the warehouse, trying to get her bearings. Four Indonesians were almost on top of her before she saw them. Dodging the nearest one, she sprinted farther into the interior of the building.

Door. She grabbed the handle and yanked on it. It was locked. She spun out of the grip of the first Indonesian to reach her and grabbed a rusty machete that was resting on top of a large spool of jute twine.

The four men spread out as if to encircle her, expecting her to back away, ineffectually waving the machete.

Sass did the opposite. Not giving them a chance to catch a breath, she charged at the nearest man with a yell, swinging the rusty blade in front of her. The man's eyes bugged out in alarm, and he fell backward over his own feet, throwing up his arms in a feeble attempt to ward off the slicing machete.

Sass didn't bother trying to chop at him. She simply ran right over his body, trampling him, and hightailed it for the big swinging doors with the other three Indonesians in hot pursuit.

Reaching the doors, she hauled on the latch with

all her strength. It wouldn't budge. Frantically, she tried again. It was locked. Exhausted now, she whirled and raised the machete into a striking position, waiting for her assailants to close.

They hung back, giving her plenty of room. In front of them had appeared a tall, broad-shouldered Caucasian wearing a sleeveless vest, camouflage pants, and military boots. His tattooed arms were almost deformed with muscle, and in one hand he held a large automatic pistol, a silencer extending from its business end.

Sass looked at him, raising the machete higher. His close-set dark eyes squinted in his coarse, apelike face, and his mouth twisted into a cruel parody of a smile. The muzzle of the silencer shifted slightly, and there was a sharp *chuff*!

Simultaneously, the bullet rang off the blade of the machete, spinning it out of Sass's hand. Wincing in pain, she balled her fingers into a fist and clutched them to her stomach. Backing against the doors like a wounded animal at bay, she glowered up at the big man, who was advancing on her with his pistol leveled at her chest.

"Stings, don't it?" rasped Malcolm Durant. He laughed—a nasty, gloating sound. "Now, you and me are gonna be friends, darlin'. We can do it the easy way or the hard way." His twisted smile returned. "It don't matter which one."

Sass head-tossed a few strands of blond hair out of her face and glared up at Durant, trying not to show any fear. She'd been handcuffed to a plain wooden chair, her arms behind her. The far rear corner of the warehouse was dusty and dim, barren except for a few fruit crates. A few thin shafts of light streamed into the dark interior from several tiny windows set high up above the overhead rafters, near the roofline.

"I hope you realize what kind of trouble you're in," Sass said hoarsely. "Assaulting and kidnapping a woman isn't looked upon kindly in *any* country that I'm aware of."

Durant smiled at her and lit a Marlboro. "You need to look at your situation, darlin'. It ain't me that appears to be in trouble at the moment."

Silently, Sass had to agree with him. He wasn't the type who was going to be out-bravadoed by her. She ran her eyes over him, taking in the steroid-blown arms and acromegalic face. He looked like one seriously mean son of a bitch.

"What exactly do you want?" she asked quietly.

Durant stepped in close and leaned down, putting his hands on his knees, his face inches from Sass's. "What I want," he said, smoke from the cigarette trickling up around his squinting eyes, "is your cooperation, 'Say-sha.' "

Sass recognized the mispronunciation of her name immediately. Lom Lok—that little bastard they'd hauled out of the Java Sea. He'd put this murderous ape onto her.

"My name's Sasha," she snarled. "And you can tell Lom Lok for me that if I had it to do all over again, I'd let that shark bite him in two."

Durant grinned in delight and blew a long cloud of smoke directly into Sass's face before straightening up and stepping back several paces. The four Indonesians hovering around Durant chortled briefly.

"Look, darlin'," the big man said. "Let's get down to cases. I want to know where you last saw the *Loro*

Kidul, what direction she was headed in, and who got aboard her. Also: I know you got logbooks on your boat with the *Loro Kidul*'s locations and bearings entered. I want those, too. Clear?"

Sass shrugged. "We only saw the *Loro Kidul* from a distance as she was being boarded by pirates. How the hell am I supposed to know who they were? One pirate looks pretty much like another to me. They were just a boatload of Indonesians with bandannas and guns.

"As for where the freighter was going: we ran into her at the northeastern end of the Sunda Strait, and she kept heading more or less directly north until she ran off our radar screen. Looked like she was heading up toward Borneo—Kalimantan—whatever."

Durant drew on his cigarette. "You got it all recorded in the logs?"

Sass shrugged again. "We made a few notes. Nothing more than what I've already told you."

"Got the keys to your boat?"

Sass paused, then nodded silently. Durant turned to Tattoo-Face, who was lounging against a wooden upright, and made a key-turning motion with his hand, tilting his head in Sass's direction. The gangly Indonesian trotted over to her and, with a lascivious grin, began to paw at her jeans and shirt pockets. He looked disappointed when he found her key ring almost immediately.

"Tell this sideshow reject he can take his fucking hands off me now," Sass informed Durant. The big man stepped in quickly, grabbed the keys, and cuffed Tattoo-Face on the jaw with his open palm.

"These boys ain't real refined, darlin'," he rasped.

"Now, one more thing: where's your old man? Ben, ain't it? Where's he at?"

Sass looked up at him. "I've told you everything you want to know. Why don't you just let me go? I won't say anything or press any charges. You can go chase your freighter all you want."

Durant leaned down again. "Right. You been real cooperative, like a good gal. And now I want to know where your old man's at."

Sass's mouth tightened into a thin line. "You can kiss my ass."

Durant's hand shot out and grabbed her hair, jerking her head back. "Oh, I plan on it, darlin'," he exclaimed. He slapped his other hand onto her right breast and squeezed until it hurt. "I'm long overdue for a taste of fine white meat like you. But first, I need to know where your fella's at."

"Fuck off," Sass spat.

Durant jerked her head once, let go, and spun on his heel. He strode over to the far side of the warehouse, almost disappearing into the darkness, and returned dragging something. Sass couldn't quite make out what it was . . .

The big man opened the valve on the fire hose, and a powerful stream of water hit Sass full in the sternum, knocking the wind out of her and the chair over backward. Durant kept the hose on her as she gasped for breath, the force of the water pushing her along the warehouse floor until she fetched up against the wall. She could feel herself blacking out, drowning in sheets of battering spray . . .

Durant shut the hose off. Barely conscious, lying on her side with the chair on top of her, Sass fought for air with great racking inhalations. When the coughing spasms had ceased, she turned her head weakly to see Durant's boots only a foot away, standing in a puddle of water. He squatted down, grabbed her hair again, and twisted her face upward.

"Now, darlin'," he said. "I got lots of water. We can do this half-drowning thing all afternoon, if you like. Or I can just do it like so." He suddenly shifted his hands, pinching shut Sass's nose with one and clamping the other over her mouth. He let her struggle futilely for air for a few seconds, then released her. Her head hit the floor as she sobbed for breath, her vision blurring and her chest aching.

Durant patted her shoulder. "That's okay, darlin'. You just let me know when you want to tell me where Ben is. We got nothin' but time."

Chapter Twelve

She told him, eventually. She wasn't quite sure *when* she'd given up the information as to Ben's whereabouts, or even exactly *what* she'd said. She just knew that somewhere around the fifth or sixth blackout by water and/or manual asphyxiation, she'd told Durant what he wanted to know. Now, as she lay drenched in a huge puddle of lukewarm water with hot tears of self-loathing stinging her eyes, she tried to convince herself that it would have served no purpose to end up choking to death. Ben wouldn't have wanted that.

Durant was stalking back and forth, smoking and talking into a cellular phone. As she composed herself, Sass noticed that the thin streams of sunlight from the warehouse's tiny upper windows were beaming in from the opposite side now. The sun had passed to the other side of the building. It was early or mid-afternoon.

"That's right, Anton. I sent one of my men down to the boat with her keys to get the logs, but she already done told me what she knows. You can count on that. Looks like the *Loro Kidul* was headed up toward Kalimantan, into those islands north of the Karimata Strait. Fuckin' maze of reefs up there, right?" Durant didn't seem to mind being overheard, by Sass or anyone else. He listened impatiently for a moment.

"Yeah," the big man went on, scowling, "I know you got all kinds of feelers up in those islands. We'll see whether all your informants are worth a flying fuck, won't we?" He gave a short, snorting laugh. "Pretty goddamn funny, Anton. You make your living running pirate raids against merchant ships when you're not running whores in those shithole clubs of yours, and some freelance assholes turn around and pirate *your* ship. Man, one of the reasons I threw in with you to move my goods was that you were supposed to have the pirate action from Sunda to Malacca *sewn up*. What a fuckin' joke."

Durant threw down his cigarette and stamped on it. "Find that goddamn ship, Anton. I'm startin' to think that I'm the one who oughta blame *you*. Two years' worth of goods, gone just like that. Where was my guarantee of safe passage from the high and mighty Anton fuckin' Jaeger? You—"

He stopped talking abruptly, and some of the purple color ebbed from his face. His knuckles, white from clenching the phone, relaxed slightly.

"Fine," he hissed. "Fine. When your flyboy gets back to you, you get back to me. I'll be available. Right. *Adios.*" He flipped the cell phone closed and jammed it into his vest pocket. The three remaining Indonesians shuffled their feet uneasily. Durant scowled at them.

"I ain't waitin' for Fat Anton too goddamn long," he said to no one in particular.

The sky was a brilliant, eye-burning blue over the far-flung archipelago of tiny islands and atolls north

of the Karimata Strait. Hundreds of feet below the
aircraft the calm sea was vivid with indigo deeps and
emerald shallows.

The small Cessna float plane banked sharply and
made another pass over the half dozen fishing canoes
that had congregated barely a quarter mile outside
the barrier reef of the unnamed, uninhabited island.
Surrounding the canoes was a thin, iridescent slick of
oil that stretched off downwind in a filmy path as far
as the eye could see. The Indonesian pilot removed
his tinted aviator frames and squinted down at the
little boats. A number of them appeared to be carrying
salvage items: life jackets, oil cans, buckets, and the
like.

The native fishermen stared up at the Cessna as it
buzzed overhead. Several of them waved. The pilot
banked around again, put the nose of the plane into
the wind, and came in for a water landing just fifty
yards from the canoes. The pontoons skipped over
a few low swells—*smack-smack-smack*—and then the
Cessna's weight settled into the water, curtains of
white spray whirling in the propeller's turbulence.

The engine roared as the pilot revved up to taxi in
close to the little knot of boats. Turning upwind of
them, he throttled back, then cut the engine alto-
gether. The Cessna went silent, drifting among the canoes at the edge of the oil slick. Opening the cabin
door, the pilot stepped down onto the port pontoon.
The water was crystal clear and dark blue. It was
deep here.

Hailing one of the older fishermen in his native
tongue, the pilot beckoned to him to come closer. The
old man did so, sculling his dugout canoe sideways
with a short, broad-bladed paddle. A young boy—

likely the old fisherman's grandson—sat quietly in the bow, examining the plane.

The pilot's eyes ran over the dugout's contents: several jerry cans, a number of lifeboat flotation cushions, a large coil of floating yellow polypropylene line, and two life jackets. He inquired as to where the items had come from.

He'd asked the right person. Stringy, leathery arms waving in the air, the old fisherman launched immediately into a detailed eyewitness account of a large black-hulled ship—obviously piloted by a crazy man—that had powered past his home island a dozen miles to the south only three days earlier. The ship had narrowly missed the shoals outside his fishing village only to run aground and crack her hull open on the barrier reef of the next island, then sink in the deep water outside the coral banks.

It had been a good wreck, he said, cackling, with rich pickings and no survivors to complain about his scavenging. Alas, though, most of the flotsam from the sunken ship had risen to the surface on the first day. Now all he could hope for was the odd jug or oil can to pop loose. Even if he had been young enough to free-dive, he lamented, the wreck was down too deep and besides, there were water demons there.

The pilot glanced down into the dark blue depths nervously at that last comment and put a foot up on the entry step of the plane's cabin. Thanking the old man, he climbed into the pilot's seat and checked his exact latitude and longitude using the aircraft's navigation instruments. After jotting the position down in a notebook, he adjusted his aviator glasses and fired up the engine.

The old fisherman sculled away hurriedly as the

Cessna turned into the wind once more and took off in a whirling cloud of salt spray Climbing fast, the plane banked sharply and headed off to the southeast, past the black volcanic cone of the densely jungled little island.

Sass was dreaming. In her dream, a great hammerhead shark had risen out of the Java Sea and plucked her from the cockpit of the *Teresa Ann*. Now it had her shoulder in its terrible jaws and was shaking her, back and forth, like a chunk of dead meat. *Een*, she tried to scream, but no sound came from her lips. She couldn't get any air . . .

"C'mon, c'mon, darlin'," Durant growled as he shook her upper arm. "Time to wake up."

Sass bolted awake, panting hard and blinking. Getting her bearings, she glared up at Durant and jerked her shoulder away from him. She had fallen asleep in her wet clothes, lying on her side in the middle of a large puddle with her hands still cuffed behind her. Everything ached.

"Let go of me, you ugly bastard," she said, her voice ragged.

Durant stood up and plucked the lit cigarette from between his lips. In his other hand he held his cell phone. Blowing a long stream of smoke, he gazed down at her. "Now, that ain't nice," he said. "How we gonna develop a healthy relationship when you got an attitude like that?"

Sass just turned her face away from him. There was nothing to say.

Taking another draw on his cigarette, the big man walked around to where he could look her in the eye again. When he spoke, there was a hint of admiration in his voice. "Tough little package, ain't you?" He coughed violently for a few seconds. "Well, I tell you what. We gonna get you cleaned up and take you for a little ride. See, my man Anton's people done found our ship."

"Great," Sass said hollowly. "Now you're going to take me back to my hotel, right?"

Durant shook his head. "Nooo. We need you to help us do something, gal. You're more important now than you were twelve hours ago. We—"

The cell phone rang, cutting him off. He flipped it open. "Yeah?"

He listened intently for nearly a minute, chewing on his cigarette. Then he plucked it abruptly from his lips and finger-snapped it onto the floor in a small shower of sparks. His face twisted into its ugly grin.

"You got it, Anton. The guy's a professional oil-field diver. He's runnin' a job out there off Bakauheni for Pertamina Oil aboard a big mother salvage vessel, layin' pipeline. He'll have all kinds of deep-diving equipment out there: air compressors, heliox gas, underwater cutting torches—hell, they gotta have at least one or two cranes on that boat, too. Everything we fuckin' need to get my—our goods back."

He paused momentarily, then scowled. "What d'you mean, 'if he cooperates'? Goddamn right he's gonna cooperate."

He turned and let his eyes run over Sass.

"I got me the winnin' wild card right here."

Chapter Thirteen

In the little cave high in the black lava cliffs on the far side of the island, the old man had been dreaming.

In the dream, he was writing a letter to his parents. He took care to make it look crisp and presentable, dipping the quill pen into the black inkwell with caution, avoiding blots and less-than-elegant penmanship. He chose his words carefully, after much thought, and when he was finished had covered the entire sheet of paper with his precise, almost calligraphic writing. Signing it, he set it aside to dry.

With a small pair of scissors, he trimmed the nails of his left hand, which he had been letting grow for two months, and collected the five crescent-shaped clippings. Then he reached up and cut a lock of jet-black hair from his left temple. Setting the scissors down, he pulled one golden silk thread from the scarf his mother had given him and tied it carefully around the lock of hair. The fingernail clippings he folded into a small piece of rice paper.

He picked up the letter and blew on the ink to complete its drying. Then he creased the sheet of paper into neat thirds and inserted it into an envelope. The lock of black hair and the fingernail clippings he slipped in beside the letter. Then he closed the envelope, dripped wax onto the seam from the small candle on the writing desk, and sealed it shut with the signet ring his father had given him.

Leaving the letter on the desk, he rose, straightened his uniform, and turned toward the door of his spartan quarters. It was getting late. The others would be waiting. He began to walk forward, toward the light, toward his comrades. But the farther he walked, the more the door receded, because the growing whine of an airplane engine was pulling him back and away . . . up out of the depths of his restless sleep . . .

The old man had jerked awake with an agonized cry, the walls of the cave reverberating with engine noise. In a panic, he'd run to the entrance just in time to see the Cessna float plane roar directly overhead not fifty feet up, bank around the vertical black rock of the volcanic cone, and descend toward the lagoon like a great white gull. It had landed on the deep water just outside the reef, near the scavenging canoes of the fishermen.

Quaking, he'd emerged from the cave entrance and begun to pick his way carefully down the steep rock toward a better vantage point in a clearing several hundred feet below . . .

It wasn't long before the Cessna took off again, disappearing into the blue haze to the northwest. The old man listened for a long time, turning his failing eyes skyward again and again, but no more planes came. The fishing canoes that had been loitering outside the reef hoisted their ragged sails and cruised off to the south, toward home. He was glad to see them go. They belonged on their own distant island, not his.

He stayed hidden from view in the bamboo cane at the edge of the little clearing until the shadows length-

ened and the sun dropped behind the island's black
volcanic cone. Then he gave a weary sigh, rose to his
feet, and made his way along the little upland trail
through the razor grass toward the high, black lava
cliffs that formed the island's western shore.

Chapter Fourteen

The *Kraken* had reached the work site in the offshore oil field well before dawn, the day after her departure from Bandar Lampung. Burke had wasted no time. The pipe-laying barge on which the welders would work had been anchored near the end of the submerged pipeline. He'd spun the *Kraken* expertly alongside the barge, rafted it to his ship's port side with tethering hawsers, and then run his four positioning anchors. The winch-controlled anchor cables formed a huge X with the *Kraken* in the center, holding her in place over the pipeline on the seabed.

By the time the sun's upper limb had just cleared the watery horizon to the east, the *Kraken*'s huge main crane had recovered the open end of the unfinished pipeline to the deck of the barge. Four hooded welders were hard at work attaching the next fifty-foot section, bent over sizzling pockets of sparking blue fire. Confident that he'd drilled the quick-minded Ki adequately in the basics of running the gas rack and radios, Ben had performed the initial hookup dive himself, guiding the crane line down through sixty feet of clear water and attaching it to the end of the pipeline with a wrapping sling.

It had felt good to get back underwater. Now, sitting in the dive-control shack with Ki, his wet hair tousled, he listened to the muted roaring sound of the water jet coming through the dive-radio speakers. One of the Indonesian divers had jumped to take the first two-hour shift on bottom, hand-jetting the coarse coral sand out from beneath the pipeline with a high-volume water nozzle as it was slowly welded and laid.

In the weeks to come, the ocean currents would fill the jetted trench back in until it was indistinguishable from the rest of the seabed. The hard underwater work was necessary; the Indonesian government had recently adopted the American policy of burying off-shore oil pipelines in order to prevent them from being snagged and ruptured by ships' anchors and fishing trawls.

"Ask him if he's got enough air," Ben said, listening to the diver panting as he worked.

Ki depressed the talk switch on the dive radio and leaned over to the speaker. *"Bisakah anda bernapas, okay?"*

"Ya. Baik," came the reply.

"Baik." Ki leaned back in his chair. "He says he's fine."

"Good. He's got an hour and forty minutes to go on his shift. He won't make it if he's gasping for breath down there." Ben rubbed his wet hair with a towel. "It's good to be back at work. I was feeling poor there, sailing all over the South Pacific and spending money like a tourist."

"Being a rich kid, I really don't know firsthand what it's like to be poor," Ki commented wryly. "But I've sure seen a lot of desperate poverty up close. I'm sort of a floater when it comes to working for the government. I fill in where I'm needed, you know? And since my specialty is environmental science, I spend a lot of time in rural and wilderness areas. Indonesia is vast, and there are people living in its more remote parts that don't make a hundred U.S. dollars a year."

"That right?" Ben replied. "Jesus. They must live off the land, I guess."

Ki nodded. "Pretty much. Fortunately, an incredible amount of food grows wild in our country, and the seas are full of fish. They get by. And you know what? A lot of them are very happy." He smiled. "Probably a lesson for the rest of us in there somewhere."

"That's a fact." Ben ran his eyes over the gas rack and tapped a sticky air gauge with one finger. "So what's your main concern as an environmental scientist in Indonesia?"

"Primarily the preservation of rare and endangered species," Ki said, "along with the ecosystems in which they're found. That can mean anything from sitting out here on the *Kraken* for six weeks making sure that a lot of industrial waste oil and chemicals from this project don't pollute the coastal waters, to crawling through caves collecting bat droppings for research, to counting tigers and hunting poachers up in the central and western highlands of Sumatra."

He smiled. "Confidentially, tigers are my thing. I've kind of made them my primary career concern. Not to brag, but just recently I was partly responsible for having the Sumatran tiger officially recognized in academic circles as a unique subspecies, distinct from the Indo-Chinese tiger of the mainland and the unfortunately now extinct Javan and Bali tigers."

He shook his head sadly. "You know, the last Bali tiger was shot in 1938. An irreplaceable subspecies, gone. The Javan tiger hung on until 1988, believe it or not, but even so we couldn't save it. There was no habitat left on the island of Java that would support a breeding population of wild tigers, so—poof! Another unique animal gone forever.

"We don't want the same thing to happen in Sumatra," Ki said. "That's why I'm so concerned about the status of the existing wild populations. It would be a profound tragedy if we lost all three tiger subspecies from the Indonesian archipelago in less than one century."

Ben glanced at his watch and checked the diver's elapsed time. "I'd say so. What's the biggest threat to the Sumatran tiger? You can control big-game hunting, can't you?"

"Sure." Ki clasped his hands behind his head. "We can declare a moratorium on legal trophy-hunting. What we can't control adequately is the poaching of tigers to supply the insatiable demand of the TCM market for genuine tiger body parts."

"TCM?"

"It stands for Traditional Chinese Medicine. Many of its remedy ingredients come from endangered animals like the rhino, the various Asian bears, and the big cats. All parts of the tiger—eyes, whiskers, bone, muscle, internal organs, sex organs—are used like prescription drugs in this ancient form of health care. And while it's difficult for Westerners to understand, the belief in the curative powers of a daily sip of tiger-bone wine or a tiny amount of ground-up tiger whisker dissolved in one's morning tea is deeply entrenched in the minds of millions of Asians.

"When they have a health problem, real or imaginary, they're as glad to pay a premium price for a few grams of dried tiger as any American is for penicillin, Prozac, or Viagra. They're convinced it will help them.

And there are literally countless TCM shops throughout Asia that are more than willing to provide them
with the traditional remedies. Even as we try to make
the trade in tiger parts illegal in all countries of the
world, the demand is serviced by the black market,
which encourages poaching and drives the price of a
dead animal higher and higher. And the rarer tigers
get, the more the few remaining ones are worth.

"You see?" Ki smiled sadly. "It's a vicious cycle.
Just recently, in fact, we've seen a sudden and drastic
decline in our southwestern tiger population. Some
kind of sophisticated poaching outfit at work, very
good at avoiding the armed wardens."

Ben shook his head. "Unbelievable. What's the dollar value of a dead tiger, anyway?"

"Ha!" Ki rolled his eyes. "Considerable. Let me
give you a couple of examples: we have video surveil-
lance of a Saudi royal family member offering an
undercover agent in excess of a hundred thousand dollars for a single wild Sumatran tiger pelt. He wanted
it for his wife, apparently. He wore lion, she was to
wear tiger. A rather expensive fashion statement, but
there are people on this planet who have far more
money than they need.

"And talk about Viagra. The Viagra of TCM is
tiger-penis soup. Yes, you heard me right. The dried
penises and testicles of tigers are ground up, simmered
in light broth, and served to believers as the ultimate
aphrodisiac. Drink this stuff and your—ahem—performance supposedly leaps from Hyundai to Lambor-
ghini in a matter of minutes. Cost: between three and
five hundred dollars U.S. *per bowl.* And yet there are
wealthy Taiwanese, Chinese, and others who will
gladly pay it.

"Lucrative?" Ki stretched his arms over his head. "You can get quite a few little bowls of watery soup from one dried tiger penis. So the TCM shop proprietors can afford to pay black marketeers a lot of money for a pound or two of genuine dead tiger.

"With the best connections, and getting premium prices for all the various parts of the animal, I'd say that, currently, a sophisticated black marketeer could clear well over a hundred thousand dollars for a tiger carcass.

"Cost of obtaining this valuable carcass: forty or fifty cents' worth of heavy-caliber bullets."

Ben whistled. "Not a bad profit margin."

"Not at all."

There was a knock on the door. Ben reached over and unlatched it. Standing outside, blinking in the merciless glare of the sun, was Chang, the old steward. He was holding a tray containing several glasses and a pitcher of his excellent lemon tea. He made no move to enter the dive shack, but bowed deferentially to Ben.

"Excuse me, Mistah Gannon. Cap'n Burke he say make sure you have plenty to drink in heat on deck. Sun make you sick, you forget to drink."

Ben smiled, holding the door open for the old man. "Thank you, Chang. Come on in. It's much cooler in here."

The old steward felt carefully for the jamb of the door, then stepped into the shack, moving noiselessly on his soft-soled black slippers. He bowed again and put the tray down on the radio shelf.

"Why don't you stay and have a glass with us?" Ben offered. "It's hot out there."

Chang smiled and pressed his hands together. "I go

back to galley," he said. "Have much work still. But kind of Mistah Gannon to ask. Many thanks."

"Okay, then," Ben said. "I won't press you. Careful . . ." He put a hand on Chang's shoulder as the old man nearly missed the step to the deck. Ki's shrewd eyes flickered over the steward, watching as he placed his hands carefully on the doorjamb and then the outer wall of the dive shack.

Ben watched Chang shuffle off down the deck, then closed the door, shutting out the heat once again. "This is pretty good stuff," he said, turning to Ki. "Iced tea from heaven. Want a glass?"

"Sure. Thanks." Ki was silent for a moment as Ben poured two tumblers. "You notice anything odd about old Chang?"

Ben handed him a glass. "As a matter of fact, I did."

Ki looked at him expectantly. Ben took a few swallows of tea before he continued.

"Just offhand," he said quietly, "I'd say he's going blind."

Chang moved through the galley, from food locker to freezer to cutting table, with the utter certainty that fifty years aboard the *Kraken* afforded him. He knew every inch of her: every ladder and walkway, every hatch, vent, duct, and bolt head. One didn't need clear eyes to move around a place that had been home for half a century.

He sighed as he worked, cutting bread and meat, squinting down at hands that were only blurry forms even in the glare of the galley's fluorescent lights. It was not just his eyes. He became tired easily these days. The stairs up to the bridge that he had run two at a time as a young man were now a dreaded obstacle. He knew that the young captain was becoming annoyed with him. Still, he persevered without complaint. One didn't shirk from one's duties. And he kept his failing eyesight hidden from Burke, who would certainly have terminated his employment had he known the full extent of his handicap. His duty was not yet done, his obligations not yet fulfilled.

He smiled as he thought of old Captain Isaac. Of course, he had never referred to him as such. He had been Captain Burke, as his son Joshua was now. But in the privacy of his thoughts, Chang had always identified the *Kraken*'s first captain by his given name. There had been a clear division of authority between captain and steward, but there had also been a bond— an unspoken mutual respect that had nothing to do with the outward trappings of rank, race, and position, and everything to do with the content of each other's character.

Chang's loyalty to the *Kraken*'s original master remained unwavering even now in the years following the old captain's death. When the wily American had given him shelter aboard his ship as a terrified young man fleeing a Maoist death squad on the docks of Shanghai in 1949, the twenty-three-year-old Chang had sworn himself to a life of service to his benefactor on the spot. Even now, fifty years later, he could still see the tall, black-coated figure of Isaac Burke standing alone at the top of the *Kraken*'s gangplank, a cocked British Webley revolver in one hand, facing down a dozen enraged, heavily armed Maoist soldiers who were howling for Chang's blood.

In that moment, the old man remembered, he had known with absolute certainty that no power on earth could have moved Captain Isaac Burke from the gang-plank of his own ship. Snarling like a pack of street dogs, hurling threats and insults, the death squad members had retreated, and Chang's service as the *Kraken*'s steward had begun.

He felt the second loaf of bread as he took it from its package. It was slightly firm, perhaps stale. He sniffed carefully. It seemed fine. It was the last of Captain Joshua's favorite dark German rye. Wanting to disappoint him even less now that he could sense the young captain's annoyance with him, Chang decided to go ahead and use it for the sandwiches.

He smiled again as he worked. Joshua Burke had become Captain Burke, master of the *Kraken,* like his father before him. But Chang remembered the awkward boy who had voyaged on his father's vessel in summers past, who had sat for hours in the galley plying the steward with questions as sea winds breezed through the open portholes, and who had sipped medicinal teas and called out his name when caught in the delirium of a tropical fever.

On the day Isaac Burke had lain on his deathbed in the master's cabin of the *Kraken,* he'd called his steward to his side. Chang could clearly remember the surprised irritation on Joshua Burke's face when his father had asked him to leave the room. When they were alone, the old captain had clasped his aging steward's hand in his.

"I'm dying, Chang," he said. "I can feel it. I'm losing."

"Yes, Cap'n."

"We've come a long way, you and I. More voyages than I can count." Burke's face contorted as a spasm of pain gripped him. Chang waited for it to pass, his hand firm on his captain's.

"Many voyage, Cap'n."

Burke cleared his throat. "My old friend, your record of service to this ship has been exemplary. Any obligation you've ever felt toward me because of that far-off day in Shanghai has long since been repaid, many times over. I want you to know that."

Chang nodded. "Yes, Cap'n. Thank you, Cap'n."

Burke tightened his grip. "But, Chang, even though you deserve it, I do not release you from your service. Not yet. Let me tell you why:

"A man is fortunate if, only once in his life, he comes to know another man he can trust without question. Someone whose word can be depended upon even from beyond the grave." Burke coughed. "You are such a man, Chang."

Another spasm seized the dying captain. He quelled it with the dwindling reserves of his great strength and will. "May I ask you one last favor, my friend?"

"Ask, Cap'n."

"My son will inherit this ship when I am gone. He is strong, even as I was, and capable. But he has his mother's disposition, her tendency to leap to judgment and strut authority. In time, experience will teach him the folly of such overbearing conduct.

"But, Chang, in a ship's captain, youthful lapses in judgment can be fatal. Joshua will be flushed with his own power and importance in the months—perhaps years—to come. I ask that you watch over him. Use all your influence and experience to keep him, the *Kraken,* and those aboard out of harm's way.

"It will not be easy. How do you control a headstrong person who has authority over you? But I must ask you to try. Will you do this for me, my old friend?"

Chang nodded without hesitation. "Yes, Cap'n."

Some of the strain left Burke's gray, thin face, and he clasped the old steward's hand in a final handshake.

"Thank you, Chang," he whispered. "Thank you."

Chang paused as he neared the top step, getting his breath. The climb from the galley to the bridge had made him dizzy, as it always did these days, but it would pass. The tray of sandwiches and iced tea felt very heavy in his hands, and he gripped it more tightly to keep it from sagging. Through the bridge entrance he could see the blurred shapes of men moving back and forth.

He steeled himself and mounted the last few stairs. From the entrance he recognized Joshua Burke's tall, dark-clad form as he issued orders to the mate, Bullock. Bullock touched his cap and departed through the starboard outer bridge door, and Burke was left alone, shuffling some papers.

Chang padded silently into the bridge. "Your lunch, Cap'n."

Burke jerked his head up from the papers, startled. "Ah. Chang. I didn't hear you come in. Very well. Set it down over there, by the chart table." He stalked forward as the old steward complied.

"Anything else, cap'n?"

Burke leaned back against the table. "Yes. Yes, there is. Since we're alone up here, this is the perfect time to address it." His tone softened imperceptibly. "Now, look, Chang: I know that you were with my father for a long time, and that you maintain considerable loyalty to him and to this ship. But you must acknowledge that there is a time for all men to retire. It's the way of things, Chang."

The old steward's face remained inscrutably serene after the oriental fashion, but inside his heart began to pound.

"You have been letting things go, Chang. Not keeping up to your old standards of cleanliness and attention to detail. Stained linens, dirt in corners, poorly polished brasswork—you've become slovenly. I won't tolerate it."

"I, Cap'n?" Chang could feel desperation rising in his chest.

"Yes, you, Chang."

"My work no good?" The old steward struggled to understand. He wished he could see Joshua Burke's eyes instead of the blur that was his face.

"No!" The captain's temper flared. "For example: that binnacle you polished yesterday—absolutely unacceptable. I mean, just look at it, man!"

In utter confusion Chang turned and padded over to the large brass compass housing in front of the ship's wheel. Numbly, he ran his hands over it, squinting hard, trying to force his dim eyes to focus. They wouldn't. He couldn't understand it. He had taken extra time polishing the binnacle so that it would shine as it had for the past fifty years.

"Oh, for God's sake, Chang! Don't pretend you don't see what I'm talking about! Around the port rims and the edge of the base—just look at the tarnish there! That brass looks as though it belongs on some scow, not the *Kraken*."

The old steward located a spot on the binnacle's base on which the sunlight shone directly. Keeping his back to Burke, he bent down until his eyes were only inches from the metal. Then he sighed. It was true. The brass bore several small areas that were discolored by black and green oxidation. He shook his head. It simply wouldn't do.

He turned slowly, head bowed and hands by his sides. There was nothing to say.

Burke exhaled impatiently and crossed his arms. "Do you see my point, Chang? And this is only one example." His voice moderated as his temper ebbed. "Now, as I said, a man can only go on so long, and then he must accept his age and retire. I'm sorry, but there it is. In view of your long service to my father and the *Kraken*, I'm going to let you stay on for the duration of our current contract. That is nearly six weeks. I know you have a small amount of money put away, and I will purchase a plane ticket to fly you anywhere you wish to go after we put into port.

"I know this is difficult for you, Chang, but I've made my decision. Try to understand." Burke reached down for a sandwich. "And make an effort to enjoy your last weeks aboard the *Kraken*. She's the ship she is largely because of your efforts over the years."

Chang stood in silence, his ears ringing. The tightness in his chest was overwhelming.

Burke brought the sandwich to his mouth, started to bite, then jerked it up in front of his eyes. With an oath, he threw it down onto the plate in disgust.

"Moldy bread!" he exploded. "A fully equipped galley and a new supply of fresh food, and I'm served a sandwich with green mold sprouting all over it! Dammit, Chang, here is yet another example of what I'm talking about!" He wiped his fingers forcefully with a paper napkin. "Steward, get this tainted food off the bridge right now and have something edible sent up! And for God's sake, make an effort to absorb what I've said to you this morning. Let me warn you: if this nonperformance of your duties doesn't improve immediately, I won't wait six weeks to release you from this ship. I'll have you off the crew manifest and transported in to Bandar Lampung in a matter of days!"

He scowled and waved a hand at the food tray. "Now get this garbage out of here."

Trembling, Chang moved forward to take the tray. Burke turned away from him, picked up his sheaf of papers, and stalked to the far side of the bridge. No more was said.

The old steward made his way down the stairs toward the galley, trying to calm himself and slow the pounding of his heart. He was gripped by fear such as he had known on only a few occasions in his long life.

He was not afraid of losing his employment or his home. Nor was he afraid of the young captain's wrath and scorn. He was not even afraid of being old, blind, alone, and unwanted.

The one thing that Chang feared to the depths of his soul was not being able to keep the last promise he had made to Isaac Burke.

Chapter Fifteen

The white tigress hadn't seen the sun for nearly two days. The small, lean-faced *Two-Legs* had surrounded her cage in the courtyard of the Smuts Estate, hooting at her, and thrown a dark canvas tarpaulin over her little prison. She'd roared in impotent protest as the cage had been dragged, jostled, and lifted. Eventually, she'd crouched down in a corner, trembling, to growl at sudden movements and noises on the other side of the canvas.

She'd been bounced over dirt roads in the back of a truck continuously, enduring foul-smelling diesel fumes, choking dust, no fresh air or water, and appalling heat. With her mouth drying out, she was losing her ability to pant and keep her body temperature low. Now she lay with her great head on her forepaws, weak from heat exhaustion and thirst.

She barely noticed when the motion of the truck suddenly ceased and its grinding diesel shut down. All was silent for a moment. Then the canvas tarpaulin was whipped back, revealing a night sky encrusted with stars, and fresh, tangy sea air wafted through the cage.

"You idiots," Durant snarled, looking at the prostrate form of the white tigress. "You drove her all the way from Bengkulu without giving her any water, right? You fuckin' *idiots*!" He lashed out at the head of the Indonesian standing closest to him, knocking his turban askew. The man ducked away hurriedly.

Durant spun on his heel and strode out onto the wooden dock behind the abandoned fish cannery. Off to his left, about a mile down the coast, the lights of Bakauheni winked in the darkness. The big man opened a rusty faucet mounted on a piling, filled a discarded oil pan with water, and carried it back to the cage.

"C'mon, c'mon . . . Open it, dickhead."

One of the trackers slipped the catch on the door of the cage's food slot and let it drop open with a metallic bang. The tigress jerked up her head at the sound. Durant slid the pan over to her on the cage's floor grating. She sniffed at it, then instantly rolled over and began to lap up the water as fast as she could.

"Get another pan ready," Durant ordered. "And keep giving her water until she doesn't want any more. *Apakah anda mengerti?* Got it?" There was a general nodding of turbaned heads.

Durant glared at his men for a moment, then walked out on the rickety wooden dock again. The calm, blood-warm waters of the Java Sea lapped at the rotting pilings beneath him, the slight disturbance setting off little glimmers of phosphorescence on the surface. A motorized wooden junk about forty feet in length was tied up near the end of the pier, yellow light emanating from the forecastle hatch.

Jumping down onto the foredeck, Durant squatted in front of the open hatch and dug a Marlboro out of his vest pocket. "How we doin' in here, sweetheart? You and your old buddy reminiscin' about good times?" He chuckled and lit his cigarette.

Sass was sitting on a burlap copra sack, her left hand manacled to a rusty eyebolt embedded in one of the junk's stout hull timbers. Beside her, pointing an AK-47 in her direction and leering happily, was Lom Lok. She pushed a strand of hair out of her haggard, dirt-streaked face and looked Durant up and down with cold distaste.

"What is this, some kind of mental torture? You've got me chained up in here—why do I have to look at this demented worm all night? Look at him looking at *me,* incidentally." She suddenly lashed out with her right foot, kicking Lom Lok hard in the shin. "Stop gawking, you pissant little creep!"

The Indonesian howled and grabbed his lower leg, dropping the AK-47 on the copra sacks. Acting on reflex, Sass seized its pistol grip with her free hand and, tucking the wooden stock under her arm, swung it up toward Durant. The hatch on which she trained the muzzle was empty but for a star-spackled night sky. A chuckling sound came from around the edge of the opening, followed by a puff of cigarette smoke.

"One tough little bitch," Durant said.

Lom Lok scrabbled sideways on the copra sacks a bit and Sass jerked the weapon down and lined it up on his chest. When she looked back up at the hatch again, Durant was peering at her with only one eye showing around the frame of the opening.

"Now what you gonna do?" he asked, still chuckling deep in his throat.

Sass swung the weapon up at him. "How about blow holes through the deck and you if you don't get down here and un-handcuff me?"

Durant laughed and coughed. "Sorry, darlin'. Won't work. Them little AK slugs won't make it through this deck. Cargo junk. Deck planks are doubled and five inches thick. Try it."

Sass gazed at Durant's eye for a moment, then dropped the AK back down onto Lom Lok. "Okay. How about this: if you don't toss the little monkey the key so he can unlock me, I'll turn him into an Indonesian sieve. Better?" She knew she was playing a dangerous game, but she was too dirty, tired, scared, and angry to care.

Durant did what she expected him to do. He rolled out of view and began to laugh in earnest. After about thirty seconds the harsh guffawing faded away, and another puff of cigarette smoke drifted across the open hatch.

"Why don't you tell me how many things are wrong with what you just said, darlin'?" Durant rasped.

Sass waited a moment, then sighed. "You don't give a damn whether I shoot him or not," she said in a monotone, gazing with hooded eyes at Lom Lok.

"That's one," growled Durant. Lom Lok looked up at the hatch in horror.

"Even if I shoot him, you'll just leave me locked up in here until I pass out."

"That's two."

"And if you got tired of waiting you could just toss a grenade in here and kill me with no risk to yourself. And Lom Lok, too, if he happened to be alive at the time."

"No great loss. That's three." Lom Lok gulped. The eye appeared around the hatch frame again. "You're a smart gal. So what you gonna do?"

Sass glared up at Durant's eye for a few more seconds, then abruptly threw the combat rifle at Lom Lok. It clattered off his bony knees, drawing fresh howls from him. Durant swung down through the hatch, his hulking form filling the forecastle, grabbed the AK, and began kicking Lom Lok in a fury. The little Indonesian screeched and tried to scramble for cover among the copra sacks.

"Goddamn useless piece *(thud)* of *(thunk)* shit! C'mere, you little *(thwack)* prick!" Copra dust flew as Durant attempted to stomp Lom Lok all over the forecastle's interior. Sass curled her legs out of the way and watched in amazement as the big man ran amok, his face purple with rage.

Finally, Lom Lok managed to claw and tumble his way out the open hatch, helped along by Durant's jungle boot. As the little Indonesian's howling faded and the copra dust began to settle, the hulking American sat down, panting, on one of the sacks. He leaned the AK up against the forecastle steps.

"You know," he muttered, lighting another cigarette, "it's embarrassin' to have to work with people like that. Can't even guard a handcuffed damn woman by himself without havin' her kick his ass and take his weapon." He spat on the deck. "Just pitiful."

Sass kept silent, watching him. Outside, on the main deck, there was a thumping sound and a chattering of Indonesian voices. Something heavy was being slid across the junk's coarse deck planking. Then Sass's ears caught another sound: a low, throaty rumble . . . almost like the growl of a large animal . . .

Durant got up and stuck his head out of the hatch. "Put her amidships, there. No, moron, not there— *there*!" He gestured angrily, then heaved himself out through the hatch onto the main deck. "Jeezus H. Christ."

There were some sharp exclamations in Bahasa,

more sliding and banging, and then silence. Sass watched the hatch, and in a couple of minutes Durant's grinning face came into view once again. He appeared amused about something.

"A thought done occurred to me," he said. "You say you ain't crazy about the roommate you had down there?" Sass didn't like the look of his widening grin. He swung down into the forecastle and grabbed her manacled arm. "Well, darlin'," he continued, "we got another one for you." He unlocked the handcuffs.

Sass started to kick, but he bent her arm up behind her back painfully and yanked her to her feet. He forced her up the forecastle steps and out onto the deck.

His breath was hot on her ear, the coarse black stubble of his beard scraping her neck. "We got us a first-class cabin for you right here," he whispered, grabbing her chin with his free hand and swiveling her head toward the center of the deck.

Sass's eyes widened. Secured to the deck by chain binders was a six-by-twelve-foot steel-barred cage. Inside the cage, pacing in a tight circle, was a huge white tiger. It bared its fangs as it walked, emitting a continuous low rumbling sound from deep in its throat and glowering with coallike eyes at the Indonesians standing nearby.

Sass barely had time to digest the scene in front of her before Durant shoved her toward the cage. "*Buka dia!* Open it!" he shouted.

The tiger let out a savage roar at the commotion. Sass gasped with alarm as she realized what Durant was going to do and tried to brace her legs on the deck, but the big man propelled her forward easily. She writhed desperately, trying to break free of his bear-trap grip, but he was too strong. One of the Indonesians slid back the bolt of the cage door with a metallic clank. The tiger roared again at the sound, its eyes locking on to Sass as she neared the cage, struggling.

The Indonesian swung open the cage door. In a panic, Sass reached back with her free arm to grab at Durant's head, face, hair—anything—but her nails only raked his cheek as he gave her one last tremendous shove, throwing her headlong into the cage. Cackling, the Indonesian slammed the door behind her and slid the bolt home.

Sass fell hard onto the steel floor grating on her knees and elbows, her mind whirling, and jerked her head up. The tiger roared into her face from six inches away, its breath hot and fetid. She shrieked involuntarily as a blur of white and black stripes, staring green eyes, and huge ivory fangs filled her field of vision. There was no time even to fall backward as the tiger brought its huge paw around, claws unsheathed, for a single killing swipe.

The deadly claws raked across the steel bars that divided the cage into two separate halves. Sass fell over on her back, kicking and thrashing to put distance between herself and the tiger, her eyes wide with primal fear. She fetched up against the door through which Durant had shoved her, gasping for breath, her heart nearly battering out of her chest.

On the other side of the dividing bars, the tiger snarled and licked its chops. Then it sat down on its haunches, cocked its huge white head, and stared at her with its immense, luminous green eyes.

The men surrounding the cage exploded into laughter, dancing and capering and back-slapping each other as they gestured at Sass and the tigress. Durant's hoarse, deep guffaw rolled through the high-pitched cackling. He sauntered over to the cage door where Sass lay shaking and twisted his fingers in the long blond hair at the back of her neck. She jumped at his touch, her nerves like live wires, but he held her head tightly against the steel bars.

"Really had you goin' there, didn't I, darlin'?" he rasped. "That's what you call a breedin' cage. Lets two critters get to know each other, but keeps 'em separated so's they don't fight. Hard to see them dividin' bars in the dark." He chuckled for a moment. "Now look: you get real comfortable with your new roommate. We gonna keep you in here and out of trouble while we take us a little run out to the oil field. And think about bein' a little more *friendly*"— he banged her head on the bars—"to ol' Malcolm in the near future. Or I might just get up a notion to put you in the other side of this here cage."

He turned her loose and began issuing orders to his men. Drained, still shaking, Sass felt her head spinning, felt herself slumping over onto the floor of the cage, and fainted.

The tigress lay up against the dividing bars, panting slowly, and examined the motionless *Two-Leg* with the long yellow hair that occupied the other half of the cage. It looked dead. She sniffed the air, turning her head this way and that. There was the faint scent of warm breath and estrogen.

Her ears flicked forward at the sound of a thin moan. The *Two-Leg* stirred, its limbs shifting slightly, then lay still again. It looked helpless, like a newborn fawn lying in the grass. The tigress yawned and licked her chops. It was certainly no threat, and would be easy to kill if it came too near.

She sniffed the air again. The estrogen scent told her that this *Two-Leg* was female. She did not know why—the tigress would live her entire life unburdened by the question "why"—but she felt no alarm at being in close proximity to this particular *Two-Leg*. It was feeble, perhaps injured, and had no young to protect. And, unlike the *Two-Legs* bustling around outside the cage—in particular the tall one that had tormented her with the water-spitting snake—it gave off no aura of malevolence.

For the moment, there was nothing to fear. The tigress set her chin down on her paws, her head leaning up against the dividing bars, and closed her eyes to doze.

Chapter Sixteen

Burke had decreed that pipe-laying operations would adhere to a schedule of sixteen-hour days, seven days a week, until completion of the project. Work, eat, and sleep—then do it all over again the next day was the never-ending cycle of life aboard the *Kraken*. It had been well after nine P.M. when Ben finished decompressing the last diver, recovered him to the deck, and shut down the dive station's air compressors for the night. The exhausted divers had staggered off to their bunks in the fiberglass deck buildings, too tired to even think about eating a late supper. And up from the lay barge had come four pairs of weary, grime-covered pipe welders, tough little Indonesians clad in sweat-soaked protective leathers, lighting up *kreteks* and engaging in the rough-edged ribbing that is universal among men whose working lives consist of long hours at hard labor.

Ben and Ki had stopped briefly in the galley to grab a plate each of the delicious Indonesian beef kebabs known as *sate,* with the accompanying fiery peanut sauce, and then trudged up to their respective cabins on the ship's upper levels. After finishing his daily paperwork—dive profiles, job log entries, and the next day's work rotations—Ben had collapsed onto his bunk and, his mouth numb from the afterburn of *sate* sauce, drifted off to sleep in minutes.

With work operations shut down for eight hours, the only sound aboard the *Kraken* was the muted hum of her main electrical generator, located deep in the bowels of the ship in the forward section of the engine room. To an old offshore hand like Ben, the steady, indistinct vibration was like a sedative; it meant that one of the vessel's key systems was operating normally.

Seamen like familiar sounds: the predictable throb of healthy machinery, the whooshing surge of open water moving past a hull. Conversely, the racing or lugging down of engines under strain, unnatural silences, and unidentifiable impacts—however faint— will immediately get their attention or even wake them out of a sound sleep.

The lack of any abnormal noise was the primary reason that Ben never knew something was amiss until just an hour before dawn the following morning, when he was awakened by the cold steel muzzle of an automatic rifle digging into his Adam's apple.

The Asiatic face at the other end of the AK-47 looked like a disembodied yellow skull in the dim light of the cabin. Ben blinked, trying to clear his sleep-fogged eyes, and twisted his neck away from the choking pressure of the gun barrel. The gunman jabbed the weapon hard into Ben's throat and flexed his fingers on the handgrip.

"Bangun!" he shouted. *"Bangun! Sekarang!"*

Ben stayed motionless on his bunk, his mind not processing the unfamiliar words. The gunman jabbed him with the rifle again, his lean, slit-eyed face contorting with anger. *"Bangun!"*

Then it came to him. *Bangun* was "get up."

"Okay, okay," Ben said, spreading his hands. "No problem. *Saya akan bangun.* I'll get up." Thank Christ Ki had been running over some Indonesian phrases with him.

He rolled to a sitting position, then cautiously leaned down and slipped on his boots. When he got to his feet he had at least a twelve-inch height advantage over the gunman, who was forced to aim his rifle up at a thirty-degree angle to keep it trained on Ben's head. But for the gravity of the situation, Ben would have laughed out loud. It was like having a ten-year-old child draw a bead on him with a pellet gun.

Short of stature though he was, there was nothing childlike about the gunman's expression. His lips drawn back in a threatening sneer, he jerked the AK toward the door, indicating that Ben was to go out ahead of him. Hands at his sides, Ben complied.

They stepped out into the passageway and headed toward the port stairwell. At the landing, Ben paused as a tremendous commotion sounded from the deck above. The gunman stepped in front of him and backed him up against the bulkhead, the muzzle of the AK in his chest. The scrambling and thudding of multiple feet echoed in the stairwell, along with a chorus of shouting voices.

In a moment Burke appeared, blindfolded with a dirty rag, kicking and struggling as half a dozen armed Indonesians rushed him down the stairs. The big captain threw his weight from side to side, pulling three of the smaller men off their feet at a time, but could not break free.

"Let go of me, you dirty maggots! By God, I'll have you all up on charges, you pirate bastards!" Burke's face was livid. He heaved the entire knot of men against the bulkhead as they reached the landing. "Goddamned nest of filthy heathens! *Get your thieving hands off me!*"

Yammering in Bahasa, one of the Indonesians drew a rusty .45-caliber automatic pistol from the sash around his waist and clubbed Burke over the head with it four times. Blood running down his temple, the dazed but still struggling captain was propelled down the stairs and out of view.

The little gunman with the AK stepped back, keeping Ben covered, and jerked the weapon in the same direction.

"Menggerakkan!" he commanded.

Move. That's clear enough, Ben thought.

He walked down the stairs, the AK's muzzle poking his back, and stepped out onto the main deck. The sky was still dark, but to the east the coming dawn was turning the far-off clouds a hazy purple. A small crowd of people was assembled beneath the towering boom of the *Kraken*'s huge walking crane, illuminated by the ship's powerful main deck spotlights. Here and there, turbaned or headbanded Indonesians carrying military rifles trotted across the deck, going from door to door, hatchway to hatchway, sweeping every corner of the vessel for more personnel.

As Ben neared the little knot of men, he could see that it consisted of the eight welders, six divers, and seven deckhands making up the bulk of the *Kraken*'s extended crew. Surrounding them were a number of shabbily dressed Indonesians, some with ammunition belts crisscrossed over their chests, holding combat rifles or submachine guns at the ready. Off to one side, blindfolded and gagged with their hands bound behind them, were Burke and the first mate, Bullock. The captain was still being actively restrained by several of the gunmen.

At the rear of one of the walking crane's immense caterpillar treads, Ben noticed, was Chang, the old steward. He was seated on an inverted five-gallon bucket, talking quietly to three of the armed Indonesians. As Ben watched, one of them smiled, reached out, and clapped the old man on the shoulder.

Strange, Ben thought as he was prodded forward by the muzzle of the AK. He felt oddly let down. He'd liked the old steward.

There was a cough at his shoulder, and he turned to see Ki being shoved along with a pistol at the back of his head. The young official had a nasty gash just over his right eyebrow, the blood leaking in two streams down his cheek. He glanced at Ben.

"This isn't good," he said softly, his face pale but composed.

"Sepi!" barked the gunman holding the pistol. Ki clamped his lips together and kept quiet.

Together they were herded across the deck, stumbling over chain, cable, and scrap steel, until they reached Burke and Bullock. *"Hentikan!"* Ben's rifleman shouted, stepping in front of them and waving his AK.

"He wants us to stop here," Ki translated under his breath. He weaved a little on his feet, and Ben grabbed him by the elbow.

"You all right?"

The gunmen moved back with their accomplices, covering the *Kraken*'s crew from a comfortable distance. Ki nodded. "Just a little dizzy. Bastard cracked me on the skull with his pistol when I tried to talk to him. I'll be okay."

Ben shook his head in bewilderment. "What the hell's going on?"

Ki opened his mouth to answer, but at that moment some high-pitched yelling broke out on the ship's starboard stern quarter. A shirtless Caucasian with a bald head and bushy red beard backpedaled into view from behind the aft superstructure, swinging a length of chain at four pursuing Indonesians. As the smaller men tried to grapple with him, he whipped the chain across the neck of his closest assailant. The momentum slammed the Indonesian headfirst into the starboard rail, dropping him to the deck as if poleaxed.

"Reinhardt," Ki whispered. "The engineer."

Roaring incoherently, the bald man lashed the chain back and forth, striking sparks off the deck plates. His three remaining pursuers dodged in and out, unsure of how to get him under control.

Then, as Ben and Ki watched, a tall Caucasian with heavily tattooed arms stepped out onto the main deck through one of the superstructure's watertight doors. Without hesitation, he strode over to the enraged engineer, raised a large automatic pistol, and shot him twice in the chest. The chain clattered to the deck as Reinhardt collapsed and lay still.

The killer shouted something to the three Indonesians, who promptly scattered and headed off across the deck in different directions. Then he stalked toward the crane, checking the breech of his pistol and looking like something off the cover of *Soldier of Fortune* magazine. The big man kicked aside an oil can as he neared the captives and shoved his handgun into a shoulder holster. He glared briefly at Ben and Ki as he went past, then stopped in front of Burke.

"Get them blindfolds off," he ordered. Two Indonesians standing nearby lowered their weapons and peeled off the rags binding the captain's and first mate's eyes. The two men blinked into the harsh glare of the deck spotlights.

Burke's face was crimson with rage. "Who the hell are you," he demanded, "and what the *goddamned* hell are you doing aboard my ship?"

Ben had to give Burke high marks for sheer balls, even if his choice of words seemed to indicate a serious underestimation of his current circumstances.

"I'm Durant," replied Durant, lighting a cigarette. "And guess what, admiral? This is *my* fuckin' ship now."

"Your ship?" Burke's voice rose in incredulous fury. "*Your* ship? You bilge-crawling son of a bitch! I won't bother quoting you the articles of International Maritime Law you're violating, in addition to the sovereign laws of Indonesia, whose coastal waters we're floating in! Piracy, hijacking, kidnapping, assault—"

"Murder," interrupted Durant, pointing casually over at Reinhardt's blood-smeared body. The captain snapped his eyes over to the starboard rail and examined his engineer's corpse for several long seconds. Then he took a deep breath and turned back to Durant.

"My friend," he hissed through clenched teeth, "rest assured that I am going to make it my mission in life to see that you get the death penalty."

"Omigod," Durant commented. He rubbed his eyes. "Now shut up for a minute, admiral. We got business to discuss, you and me."

"I'm discussing nothing with you. Get the hell off my ship."

Durant yanked his automatic from its shoulder holster and jammed the muzzle hard into the center of Bullock's forehead. There was an audible click as he thumbed back the hammer.

"Wrong answer," he said.

Bullock squeezed his eyes shut, grimacing. His jaw flexed as he ground his teeth together.

"Captain . . ." he choked. His hands shook slightly.

Burke stared at Durant with black, silent hatred. The seconds ticked by as Ben regarded the pair with mounting horror. Then the big man's apish face creased into its predatory grin, and he drew contentedly on his cigarette.

"Five, four, three, two—" he recited.

"All right!" Burke shouted.

Durant pulled the trigger.

There was a metallic snap as the hammer fell on an empty chamber. Bullock flinched violently—then his eyes rolled back in his head and he passed out, crumpling to the deck.

"Huh," Durant said. "Thought that chamber might've been empty." He jacked the automatic's slide once. "There. That's better." Lowering the hammer, he pushed the pistol back into its shoulder holster and smiled at Burke, sucking again on his cigarette.

Several more seconds passed before any of the captives could draw breath. Burke stared at Durant as though he were some kind of virulent disease in human form.

"You absolute bastard," he said quietly.

"Thanks for the compliment, admiral," Durant replied. "Now listen carefully: I pull this pistol again and someone's gonna die. When I ask questions, I want answers. Nod your head if you understand me."

Burke nodded.

"Good. How many men do you need to run this tub up north about two hundred fifty miles?"

"What do you mean, run up north?" the captain exploded.

"Answer the fuckin' question!"

Burke got himself under control. "I need a knowledgeable man in the engine room," he said, seething, "and at least two more men to trade watches at the helm."

"Okay," Durant declared. "So you need an engineer to run the ship. Forget the men at the wheel— my people can do the steering. You got enough fuel to run hard for one or two days?"

"Yes."

"Fuckin' great. Next: do you have the capability to get a diver and a crane line down over three hundred feet?"

Burke shrugged. "I don't know. You'll have to ask the dive supervisor."

"Where's he at?"

"Over there." The captain tilted his head in Ben and Ki's direction.

Durant stepped over in front of Ki and looked him up and down. "You sure ain't him, slant-eye." He turned his attention to Ben. "You look the part, sick. Ben Gannon, right?"

Durant's use of his name caught Ben off guard. "How'd you know that?"

The big man leered, puffed on his cigarette, and flicked the butt over the rail. "A real good mutual friend of ours told me." Seeing Ben draw a blank with that statement, he chuckled unpleasantly and went on: "So, diver man, can you get down to three hundred feet or so with the gear you got?"

"If I had a reason to, I could."

Durant laughed harshly. "Oh, I got a real good reason for ya, slick." He spat on the deck, then stuck another Marlboro in his mouth. "How about a crane line? Cuttin' gear? You can get those things down that deep, too?"

"I could."

"Perfect." Durant turned back to Burke. "Okay, admiral; we're goin' with Mike Nelson here, your engineer, and you. Anything else you need a warm body for, my guys'll do it. Your engineer ready to go?"

Burke scowled at him. "He would be," he snapped, "if you hadn't gunned him down a few minutes ago."

Durant looked surprised, then glanced over at Reinhardt's corpse. "That him?"

"Yes, you murdering bastard."

"Well, shit." He frowned and looked down at Bullock, who had come to and was lying on the deck weakly shaking his head. Durant nudged the sole of his shoe with the toe of his jungle boot. "What about him? He looks white enough to have half a brain. Can he keep them engines runnin'?"

Burke appraised his first mate. "Mr. Bullock can do it."

Durant grinned happily. "There, see? Another problem solved." Turning to several of the Indonesian gunmen standing nearby, he gestured suddenly at the divers, welders, and deckhands beneath the crane boom. "All right. Put 'em all down on the barge. *Cepat!* Move it!"

Shouting commands in Bahasa, the armed men

began crowding the little knot of captives with their rifles, herding them toward the port rail and the ladder leading down to the lay barge. Burke stepped forward, jerking free of the hands that tried to restrain him.

"What are you doing?" he shouted at Durant. The big man ignored him.

A gunman shoved Ki forward, prodding at him with his assault rifle. *"Menggerakkan!"*

Ben stepped between Ki and the weapon's muzzle and held up both hands. "Wait! I need this man. *Menunggu!"*

Durant turned, blew a cloud of smoke, and lifted an eyebrow. "Yeah? Why's that?"

"He's the only man on the ship who knows how to run the topside dive station," Ben blurted, thinking fast. "No one else has the training. Without him in the dive shack, I can't do anything down below."

"That so?" Durant thought a moment, drawing on his cigarette and looking Ki up and down again. Then he shrugged. "Fuck it," he said to the gunman. "Leave him."

The armed man nodded slightly and hustled off toward the captives being forced to descend the ladder to the barge. Ki stepped back beside Ben and let out a long, shaky breath. "Thanks," he whispered. "I owe you."

"Forget it." Ben chewed his lip. "I've got a bad feeling about this."

Burke watched helplessly as the *Kraken*'s extended crew was off-loaded onto the lay barge. "What are you going to do with those men?" he fumed at Durant. The big American smiled and silently drew on his cigarette. Burke's eyes searched the deck and finally came to rest on Chang. The old steward was standing beside several of the gunmen. Someone had given him a black bandanna to tie around his head.

Burke stared in disbelief. "What in the name of God are you doing, Chang?" he called. The steward looked over in his direction. "Chang? Answer me, dammit!"

The old man gazed at the dim form of the young captain who had ridiculed him, criticized him, and would soon exile him from his home of half a century. He turned his palms out slightly in a gesture of helplessness. There was nothing to be done; the decision had been made. He was committed.

"New boss on ship, Cap'n," he said sadly. "Have to must stay alive."

He shrugged, and the Indonesians standing nearby snickered, watching Burke's jaw drop. "You faithless, miserable old bilge rat," he said in a choked voice. "I should have gotten rid of you years ago."

Chang stood for a moment, his face expressionless, then turned away. Hovering near the armed Indonesians, he disappeared around the far side of the crane.

"Didn't take the old man long to make new friends and switch sides," Ben muttered. "Somehow, I never would have figured him for that." Ki just shook his head slowly.

"Fifty years," Burke said hollowly. "For fifty years he's been with this ship. And he turns away as if it meant nothing at all . . ."

"What do you expect from a fucking chink?" Bullock snarled, getting unsteadily to his feet. "The Asian races are subhuman. You get more loyalty from a dog." He locked eyes with Ki momentarily, then shifted his gaze as the young officer glared at him with cold disdain.

Durant strode over to the port rail and surveyed the men assembled below on the deck of the lay barge. They stood nervously among the acetylene tanks, welding cables, and pipe sections, their faces upturned and apprehensive. Several of the gunmen were climbing down the ladder as well, their rifles slung across their backs.

"Lock 'em in!" the big American shouted, pointing downward. The gunmen began herding the workers toward a small watertight door at the barge's stern. Ben and Ki shuffled closer to Burke to get a better view over the *Kraken*'s rail.

One by one, the workers were forced at gunpoint to pass through the doorway, which led down into the barge's interior. Ben nudged Ki.

"I haven't been belowdecks on that lay barge," he muttered, keeping his voice low. "You know what's inside it? A lot of 'em back home in the Gulf of Mexico are just dark, empty steel hulls. Don't even have any air vents."

"This barge has a single tool-storage room built into its interior," Burke said before Ki could reply, "like a long cage made of grating. That's where that hatchway leads. No ports, but it has small air vents cut into the underside of the main deck above. Lights, too, if the topside generator is running."

"Which it isn't," Ben observed. His expression hardened. "That's a small, dark hole those men are being forced into."

One of the turbaned gunmen slammed the watertight door closed after the last captive crewman and locked it by wedging a steel marlinspike through its hasp. He tugged on it, checking that it was secure, then turned and looked up expectantly at Durant.

The hulking ex-SEAL ran his cold eyes over the barge's deck once more, then plucked the spent cigarette from between his lips and flicked it over the rail. "Okay," he said. "Sink it."

Chapter Seventeen

For several seconds Ben, Ki, Bullock, and Burke stood frozen in stunned silence, Durant's murderous command echoing in their ears. Then as one, they surged forward against the wall of gunmen guarding them, Bullock lingering behind. Their shouts of protest were lost in the sudden roar of the main crane's diesel engine, now manned by one of Durant's turbaned henchmen. A cloud of dirty black smoke wafted over them as the gunmen forced them back, clubbing them with rifle stocks.

The crane boom swung toward the opposite rail of the *Kraken*, and a fast line with a ball weight and lifting hook began to descend from its top pulley. Durant stalked past the little knot of struggling men, deaf to the pleas and threats being hurled at him, and gestured impatiently for the crane operator to hurry it up. As the futility of his protests began to sink in, Ben noticed for the first time the gently swaying top of a wooden mast at the starboard rail. Some kind of vessel was sitting along the far side of the *Kraken*. Of course. Something had to have ferried Durant and his private army out to the offshore oil fields.

Durant stopped at the rail near the mast top and looked over the side. After barking a few orders, he turned, glared at the crane operator, and made a vigorous whirling motion with one hand, the index finger pointing down. The crane's engine gunned, and the fast line's ball-and-hook dropped rapidly past the rail, next to the mast.

Burke's face was purple and his lips flecked with spittle as he hurled himself against the crisscrossed rifle barrels that were forcing him back. "Durant!" he bellowed. "*Durant!* Rescind that order, damn you! You can't do it! You can't drown all those men! Get back over here, you bloody bastard!"

Out of earshot, the big American kept leaning over the starboard rail, looking down and giving languid hand signals to the crane operator.

Stumbling over each other's feet, Ben, Ki, Burke, Bullock, and the mob of angry gunmen attempting to restrain them surged sideways and up against the port rail. Pinned by sheer weight of numbers, and looking into the muzzles of over a dozen automatic weapons, the four of them gave up the fight, exhausted.

"Bloody . . . bastards . . ." Burke panted. His feverish gaze wandered over the rail and down to the barge. Then his eyes focused in shock. "God in heaven," he said.

Ben, Ki, and Bullock looked down. At the corners of the barge, pairs of Indonesian gunmen had disengaged the locking dogs on four large, red-painted flywheels and were turning them laboriously by hand. A soft rushing sound began to emanate from the deck air vents.

"They're opening the primary seacocks of the four underwater intake chests with the manual flywheels," Burke said in a hollow voice. "She's filling."

Someone began to hammer on the inside of the barge's locked hatch with a metallic tool. The watertight door didn't even shiver under the impact of the blows. A muted chorus of frantic shouts began to echo from the air vents. Then, as if to compound the horror, Chang came into view, still wearing the black pirate headband, and began to shuffle hurriedly from corner to corner, gesturing and nodding, encouraging the gunmen who struggled with the flywheels. As he picked his way along the deck of the doomed barge, he kicked shut the watertight covers of the air vents, dogging them securely with a few quick twists of his hand.

"That fucking animal," Bullock muttered. "He's taking the last breath of air away from those men inside. Maybe he figures they'll suffocate before they drown."

"Chang," whispered Burke. "I can't believe it."

Ben gazed at the stooped figure of the old steward as he groped about the deck of the barge, nodding to and cajoling the pirates on the flywheels, then dogging shut the remaining air vents. The old man secured the last one, cutting off the muted yelling from below, then backed up against the small storage shack containing the barge's life jackets, apparently exhausted from the energy he'd expended.

Ben was watching him reach inside the shack's open door when a rifle butt slammed into his right cheek-bone. He staggered back from the rail, dazed. Three gunmen wrenched him out of the little crowd and propelled him across the deck, one on each arm and another at his back, digging hard with an AK muzzle. They yanked him to a halt about ten feet from Durant, who had stepped back from the starboard rail and was watching the crane's fast line wind back onto its spool. The big man moved closer to Ben and stuck yet another cigarette between his lips. "Something here I think you oughta see, Gannon," he said, chuckling. His grin was ugly. "Hold him," he said to the gunmen.

Ben felt the Indonesians tighten their grips on his arms, He stood quietly, watching the crane cable rise above the rail.

"Ta-daaa," Durant intoned.

A large steel-barred cage was lifted into view. In it crouched a magnificent, extremely agitated white tiger—*tigress,* Ben corrected himself as the animal shifted position, rocking the cage on the end of the crane line. It revolved slowly as the crane boom swung inboard and began to lower it to the main deck.

"This'll be priceless," Durant muttered happily, fixing his gaze on Ben.

The cage thumped down on the deck plates and the lifting cable went slack. Ben blinked, uncomprehending. Sass stared out at him from between the steel bars, gripping them with her hands on either side of her face, like a prisoner at a jail cell window. Behind her, partly obscured from view, the white tigress paced back and forth, snarling.

"Ben!" Sass cried out, locking eyes with him.

Ben's lips moved, forming her name. Then his eyes snapped over to Durant, who was watching him with a twisted grin. Ben's teeth ground together. With a violent heave he yanked the Indonesian holding his left arm sideways, and lifted the one on his right arm three feet off the deck. Using his own momentum, he inverted the dangling little gunman in midair and, falling to his right, dropped him on his turbaned head on the steel deck plates. The Indonesian promptly let go of his arm.

"Whoa," Durant said, nodding appreciatively.

Rolling hard, Ben pulled the other frantically kicking gunman with him across the deck. He pinned his more slightly built opponent up against one of the walking crane's caterpillar treads with his weight, twisted suddenly, and drove the elbow of his free arm straight back into his assailant's face. Once. Twice.

"Ouch," Durant winced, exhaling smoke. "Check for swelling."

The Indonesian rolled away, moaning and clutching his smashed nose and mouth, but before Ben could get to his feet, four other gunmen tackled him. Two more followed, and under the combined weight of six men, Ben finally gave in, pinned to the deck and gasping for air.

Durant stepped over him, looking down, his bulky frame dark against the coppery dawn sky. "Never fails," he said, chuckling out tendrils of cigarette smoke. "Throw his woman into the mix, and an otherwise perfectly sane sumbitch goes all freaky on you." He paused, then toed Ben in the ribs hard. "You done now, diver man?"

Ben glared up at him, saying nothing. Durant grinned, then stepped back. "Get him up," he ordered.

Ben was pulled to his feet, disheveled, a livid bruise darkening under his right eye. He could feel his body shaking with adrenaline, his mind racing.

"Don't fight them anymore, Ben," Sass called. There was pleading in her tone. "I'm all right."

Durant came up close and pointed his lit cigarette at Ben's eye. "That's good advice, slick. I'd take it, if I was in your place." He grinned. "You wouldn't want anything to happen to her, now, would you? That cat looks kinda hungry."

As if on cue, the tigress let out a high-pitched snarl.

Ben watched Sass huddle up to the bars at her end of the cage, as far as possible from the great animal.

"No," he said quietly.

Durant nodded to the gunmen. "Let him go."

As hands dropped away from him, Ben stepped over to the cage and reached through the bars to hold Sass. She clutched at him in return, pressing her face against his chest. "I'll get you out of here," he breathed into her ear. "I promise."

"I know," she whispered back.

Durant snapped his fingers impatiently. "Hey, hey. Over here, slick. This ain't no fuckin' soap opera."

Ben turned to face him, and the big man continued. "You look like a smart boy, Gannon. At least, you got more brains than any of these yellow-skin niggers around here. I know you can figure out the deal."

"I dive for you, she doesn't get hurt," Ben muttered tonelessly.

Durant grinned, then drew on his cigarette. "I knew you was a smart boy." He waved his hand. "Get back over there with the others."

Ben walked slowly across the deck toward Ki, Burke, and Bullock, now standing quietly against the aft superstructure bulkhead at gunpoint. As he passed the cage, he reached out and squeezed Sass's outstretched hand, managing a wink. She smiled slightly.

"Who's that?" Ki murmured to Burke.

The big captain, blood running across his forehead in three thin streams, cleared his throat before answering. "Gannon's lady."

Ki didn't move for a moment, then slowly shook his head. "Shit." He made room as Ben moved in and stood at his shoulder. "I'm sorry as hell, Ben."

Ben set his jaw. "So am I."

Durant stalked across the deck, a train of raggedy gunmen following him. Two others were throwing chains over the tiger cage and binding it in place. He stopped at the port rail and looked down at the sinking lay barge, already low in the water next to the *Kraken* and drawing her tethering lines tight. Grabbing a machete from one of the Indonesians, he stepped over to the bollard closest to him, which anchored one of the barge's spring lines.

"Cut it loose!" he shouted, and began hacking at the four-inch woven rope. It parted on the fifth slash in a small explosion of nylon dust and fibers. At the bow and stern of the barge, gunmen chopped away at the remaining lines, severing them one by one, until the water gap between the *Kraken* and the sinking vessel widened, and nudged by a faint current, it moved slowly out onto the glassy surface of the windless sea.

"A steel coffin," Burke muttered. "My God, those men." His eyes fell on Chang, standing far down the deck, and a look of pure hatred blossomed on his face.

Durant watched the barge drift off for a few minutes, then whirled and strode over to the tiger cage. Removing the padlock that held the hasp closed at Sass's end of the little prison, he swung open the door, reached in, and pulled her out roughly by the arm. Walking quickly, he hustled her over to the four remaining crew members of the *Kraken* and shoved her at Ben. He caught her as she half fell, setting her upright again.

"Incentive, Gannon," Durant rasped. "Cooperate with me, and you and her will likely walk away from this thing. Try to *fuck* with me"—he punctuated the ugly word with a stab of his forefinger—"and you won't believe what you'll have to watch happen to her."

He turned to Burke, who was glowering at him with helpless rage.

"All right, admiral," Durant said. "Crank this tub up and let's go."

An hour and ten minutes later, having recovered her four positioning anchors, the *Kraken* pulled off the pipeline location, came around in a wide turn, and headed due north in the direction of the island of Borneo. Astern, the doomed barge lay wallowing in the glassy sea, her deck just barely awash.

The banging from inside her had long since stopped.

Chapter Eighteen

Ben and Sass lay together on the narrow sea cot in the captain's cabin just aft of the *Kraken*'s bridge. On the large master bed, two Indonesians were sitting cross-legged, AK-47s across their thighs, busily engaged in a silent, high-speed game of dice. Every once in a while, one or the other would look up and run his eyes over Ben and Sass—mostly Sass—then return to the game.

The *Kraken* had been cruising northward at top speed for over fifteen hours. Night had fallen again, and Durant, who never seemed to show any fatigue, had ordered Ben to take Sass into the cabin and get some sleep.

"Need you wide awake when we get where we're goin', diver man," he'd said. "And you, slant-eye"—he'd pointed at Ki—"you grab some floor and stay quiet." Silently, Ki had stretched out in a corner of the bridge, his head on a life jacket, and dozed off.

Burke had remained standing by the ship's wheel, his arms folded across his chest, scowling at the gunman who manned the helm. Like Durant, he showed no inclination to sleep.

Ben and Sass had fallen asleep in each other's arms, more from sheer exhaustion and relief at being together than any desire to rest. Ben had gotten six hours, Sass an hour more, before waking up to find out that it hadn't, in fact, all just been a bad dream.

"How the hell did this Durant get hold of you?" Ben whispered, his lips against her ear, eyeing the guards on the master bed.

Sass stirred, moving her knee between his legs and hugging his chest tightly. He felt her mouth press against the point where his jaw met his neck. "Lom Lok," she murmured. "The little insect works with Durant."

"Christ."

"Durant made me tell him where you were, Ben."

There was a hot trickle on his neck, and she tried to suppress a small, shuddering gasp. "I'm so sorry. I couldn't help myself. I—I don't even remember what I said . . ."

Ben put a hand in her hair. "Stop."

"But I—"

"No. Stop."

He put his lips to her ear again. "Don't you ever apologize to me for anything. Not ever."

Ben held her until she stopped shaking and her breathing once again became deep and regular with sleep. Then he closed his eyes, listening to the thrum of the ship's diesels, and stared at the inside of his eyelids, wide awake.

"Bangun! Bangun!"

The Indonesian guard repeated the command to get up, jabbing them with the barrel of his AK. Sass grunted as the steel muzzle dug into her ribs.

Bleary-eyed, Ben angrily batted the rifle away from her and rose on one elbow, glaring at the guard. *"Pergilah,* you little bastard. Back off."

"Jesus, Ben . . ."

"Hell, what's he gonna do? Shoot me? That'd make him real popular with his boss, wouldn't it?" Ben let himself sag back against the bulkhead, rubbing his eyes. He squeezed Sass's shoulders. "Guess we're wanted on the bridge, kiddo."

The two guards were hovering, unsure of what to do. They backed up a step, brandishing their AK-47s, as Ben swung his booted feet to the deck. He sat on the edge of the cot for a moment, scratching his head, then looked up at the Indonesians.

"Relax, pinheads," he said wearily, and got to his feet. He'd had enough of pint-sized gunmen barking semitranslatable commands at him and digging at his body with rifle barrels. Sass got up behind him, one hand holding his elbow.

Ben opened the cabin door and they walked out onto the bridge. Even through the tinted glass of the large forward windows, the brilliance of the daylight hurt their eyes. Burke was still standing beside the helm, now manned by a different Indonesian. Ki stood beside him, rocking back and forth on his heels. Durant was sitting up on the port side of the bridge console with his back against the bulkhead, his long legs stretched out, jungle boots resting on top of the expensive weatherfax unit. He was smoking and cleaning his pistol.

"Mornin', slick," he rasped. "Sleep good?"

Ben looked at him. "Okay."

Durant ran his eyes slowly up and down Sass. "How about the little woman? She too tired to give you a little poon-tang? Hope not. Man needs his relaxation. 'Sides, I need you to keep her limbered up for me."

Ben's jaw clenched and he balled a fist. His eyes

flickered over the disassembled pistol in Durant's lap. When he looked up again the big man was staring straight back at him. Ben hesitated for half a heartbeat, and in that brief moment Durant produced a small black automatic from inside his vest and leveled it. It was not disassembled.

Durant smiled around his cigarette. "Read your mind, slick." He moved the little pistol over slightly, lining it up on Sass. "Think twice."

Ben settled back off the balls of his feet and unclenched his fist.

"Good boy," Durant said. He plucked the cigarette from between his lips and fingersnapped it angrily at the two guards standing in the doorway to the captain's cabin. "*Awas!* Wake up, assholes!" He shook his head. "Just pitiful," he muttered.

Ben and Sass gazed out the forward bridge windows, squinting against the glare. The *Kraken*'s great upswept bow was swinging slowly through a postcard-like panorama of turquoise and emerald water that shoaled to the paler green of a lagoon, bordered by the white sand beaches of a small island. The backdrop to the scene was a steep volcanic cove, a black tower of rock that jutted up against the brilliant blue sky out of the island's densely jungled interior. Though the sea was flat calm, water surged and boiled around the jagged yellow coral of the outer reef that protected the lagoon.

"Ship killer," Burke growled. He reached over and tugged back the handle of the engine-room telegraph. Ching-*ching*! At the same time, he spoke into a microphone mounted just over his head. "Reverse one-quarter, Mr. Bullock," he ordered. "We'll bring her to a slow stop here."

"Aye." Bullock's disembodied voice crackled out of the intercom speaker.

The vibration of the main engines changed, ebbing to almost nothing as Bullock cut back the rpms. For a few seconds the *Kraken* ghosted forward under her own momentum as the gears were reversed. Then the bridge deck shuddered as the diesels revved back up and the propellers bit into the water in the opposite direction. Burke stepped in behind the wheel, shouldering the Indonesian helmsman aside as if he didn't exist, and grasped the teak spindles in his big hands, his eyes roving over the scenario in front of him.

A short channel of deep blue-green water cut through the reef ringing the lagoon, much too narrow for the *Kraken* to enter. As the ship came to a dead stop outside the channel's mouth, Durant swung his legs off the console and picked up a pair of binoculars. He moved over beside Burke.

"Hold her here," he instructed, and put the glasses to his eyes.

He scanned the palm-lined beaches of the lagoon for a few minutes, then grinned and focused in on something. "Beautiful, beautiful," he muttered. Reaching inside one of the large thigh pockets of his jungle fatigues, he extracted a small VHF radio. Continuing to look through the binoculars, he brought the unit to his mouth.

"Durant to Jaeger, Durant to Jaeger. You got me, Anton? Acknowledge." He lowered the VHF a little and released the talk button. "Come on, come on, ya fat fuck," he grumbled.

After a few seconds of static, a voice, high-pitched and wheezy, came over the air. "This is Jaeger. Are you ready to begin the recovery?"

Durant half turned toward Burke and Ben, looking disgusted. "How d'you like that? Not even a hi-how-are-ya from the asshole." He thumbed the radio's talk button. "Damn nice to hear from you, too, Anton. Yeah, we'll get set up as soon as you confirm the position coordinates." Durant dropped the binoculars onto the console and pulled a piece of crumpled paper from his pocket. "Read 'em off to me again."

He scowled down at the paper, eyes narrowing, as the oddly high-pitched voice recited a set of latitude and longitude numbers. "Okay. Got 'em. I'll talk at you later."

"Talk *at* me, as you put it, when you have recovered the cargo," the voice wheezed. There was a sharp click as the other speaker cut off transmission.

"Fat motherfucker," Durant cursed under his breath. He pocketed the VHF and faced Burke, who was standing at the wheel like a ramrod. "Okay, admiral, I need you to set this tub up exactly on this location." He slapped the piece of crumpled paper down on top of the brass binnacle. "We're gonna have us a quick salvage operation."

Burke glanced down at the paper, then stared back out the forward window. "That's barely a half mile from our present position. In deep water just northeast of the island."

"Right. Set up over it."

Burke said nothing. Ben glanced at his face. Fatigue and the strain of having his authority usurped, his ship hijacked, were bringing the man dangerously near the precipice of acting without thinking. Ben felt a sudden twinge of empathy for him, and reached out to touch Burke's sleeve.

"Best to do what he says, Captain," he said. "We have no alternatives."

Burke turned and looked at him, his face drawn. Then he nodded slowly and reached for the ivory handle of the engine-room telegraph. He pushed it forward, the chinging sound reverberating through the bridge, then tilted his head back and spoke into the overhead microphone.

"Engine room."

"Engine room, aye."

"Ahead one-third, Mr. Bullock. Prepare for a series of positioning maneuvers."

Two hours later, in the deep blue water some three-quarters of a mile to the northeast of the island's low, black lava sea cliffs, the *Kraken* floated motionless, held in place by her four anchors like a spider caught in a web of its own making. There were no swells, no waves, on the absolutely windless sea; the surface merely heaved, gently, imperceptibly, up and down, like the breathing of some immense animal. Directly overhead, the equatorial sun pounded down with the intensity of a blast furnace, imprisoning the ship in a cocoon of humid, boiling air.

Ben stood amidships at the port rail, gazing over the side at the myriad shafts of sunlight flickering down into the depths, sweat trickling down his temple. Behind him, in the dive shack, Ki was checking air and gas pressures at the main manifold.

A wad of phlegm splatted into the water. Ben turned to see Durant standing beside him, wiping his lips with the back of his hand.

"There's a ship down there, Gannon," he rasped. "A small freighter. Went down less than a week ago."

His lighter flared as he lit a cigarette. "There's something on it that belongs to me. I want it back."

Ben waited. Durant cleared his throat and continued. "On the main deck, dead center, there should be a single steel cargo container. You know the type I mean? Gotta be a million of 'em scattered around the ports of Southeast Asia."

"I know what they look like."

"Fuckin' A, slick. Here's the deal: I need you to go down there, locate the motherfucker, hook a crane line to it, and cut it off the deck. Then we pick it up, understand? Easy." Durant drew heavily on the cigarette, grinned, and blew smoke out between his stained teeth.

Ben regarded him with a level gaze "Nothing's ever easy underwater, Durant. Take my word for it."

The big man glanced purposefully over his shoulder at Sass, sitting on a spool of thick cable with an AK-toting gunman behind her. "I got faith in you, slick. If any man can get it done, you can. That is"— he sucked on his cigarette—"you *better.*"

Ben looked off to the horizon in frustration. "Look, Durant, you don't even know if the ship's upright. This water's over three hundred feet deep. She may have rolled over as she sank and landed upside down on the bottom. Your container may have ripped loose from the deck on the way down and planed out to God-knows-where. It may have floated off downcurrent if it came free, or been crushed like a beer can by the pressure if it stayed welded in place. There are a hundred variables you're not considering."

Durant scowled. "Okay, slick, consider this: I'm givin' you two days to locate my container and get it up here on deck. You don't get it done, I'm gonna tie your old lady across one of these crane treads and let her entertain a couple dozen of my men while you watch. Then I'll give you another two days. And so on." He gave Ben an ugly smile. "We clear?"

Ben stared at him. "Clear."

"Good." Durant stretched his tattooed arms over his head, flexing the muscles. "Think I'll take me a siesta while you get your gear ready. Take all the time you need to get set up, slick. I wouldn't want anything happenin' to you down there." He laughed hoarsely and turned to leave, then paused.

"By the way," he said, looking past Ben's shoulder, "your woman ever tell you the name of the ship you're divin' on?"

"We haven't had much chance to talk," Ben replied acidly.

Durant let out an amused snort and pointed. "He'll fill you in."

Ben turned to see Lom Lok standing behind him, aiming an AK-47 at his stomach. The pinched face split into a seamy grin.

"Loro Kidul," he cackled. *"Loro Kidul."*

Chapter Nineteen

The old man shifted his weight gingerly on the sharp lava rock and brought a pair of rusting binoculars to his eyes. The vantage point just above the tree line at the base of the island's volcanic cone offered a commanding view of both the lagoon beaches and the sea beyond. He manipulated the focus wheel, sharpening the field of vision as much as the dilapidated glasses and his own aging eyes would allow.

The ominous black ship that had been hovering in deep water just outside the lagoon's single channel had since pulled away and anchored about a mile offshore. The old man could make out movement on her deck, but that was all.

Of more immediate concern was the activity on the beach, near the mouth of the tiny freshwater river that emptied into the lagoon's southern end. He shifted the glasses down toward the thick grove of coconut palms that all but concealed the river's entrance. Beached under the overhanging trees was a small, single-engine seaplane. Several hundred yards farther up the river, tied off to the mangroves and palms crowding the bank, was a large World War II-era landing craft of American design.

The landing craft had arrived the previous afternoon, the plane early that morning. When the old man had gotten over his initial terror and emerged from hiding, he'd counted at least fifteen men down near the river mouth, all of them armed. They were still there, sitting under the shade of the palm trees around a small cooking fire. He was feeling better since it had become obvious that this advance party, at least, did not intend to scour the island.

For the hundredth time he steadied his nerves and began to count men, guns, and equipment, forcing the information into his fragmented memory.

Accurate.

It was important to be accurate.

The tiny, smokeless fire of dried and split bamboo snapped loudly in the confines of the small, black lava cave, tossing two or three hot embers out of the fire ring and interrupting the old man's report. He paused, reached down and flicked black sand over the errant coals to extinguish them, then shifted on his haunches and continued:

"Unit strength is no more than one platoon, sir," he recited. "Standard infantry armament consisting of rifles and light machine guns. No recognizable uniforms, but the landing craft is of American military design. The seaplane appears unarmed, a reconnaissance craft only. Unit strength and armament aboard the large vessel lying offshore, unknown.

"As of this moment, they do not appear to be dispatching patrols to investigate the island."

The old man slowly raised a piece of dried fish to his lips and chewed, staring into the flickering flames of the little fire.

Thank you, Lieutenant. A most excellent report. You are to be commended for your thoroughness.

"Thank you, sir," the old man said. Reflections of flame danced in his glistening, wide-open eyes. "Can I get you anything before I sleep, sir? Some water, perhaps."

No thank you, Lieutenant. I'm fine for now.

The old man settled back onto a thin mat of woven elephant grass and curled into a semifetal position. "You'll take the first watch, sir, as usual?"

As usual, Lieutenant.

The old man nestled his gray head down into the crook of one arm. "Good night, sir."

Good night, Lieutenant.

Chapter Twenty

The sun was just starting to melt into the limpid sea on the western horizon, surrounded by a fiery abstract sky of orange and purple, when Ben took his fiberglass dive helmet from Sass and raised it over his head. He paused as he saw the worry in her eyes.

"Nothing but a couple of hours at the office for me, Sasha," he said, giving her his lopsided smile. "Don't fret, okay?"

"Oh, sure. No problem." She tried to laugh.

"Really. Be back soon. Just remember to keep that decompression chamber ready, the way I showed you, okay?"

She nodded, and Ben lowered the dive helmet over his head. With practiced skill he fitted the base of it into the fiberglass-and-neoprene neck dam he wore and locked it in place. Reaching up, he adjusted the helmet's free-flow knob until a soft current of cool air blew onto his forehead from the diffusion bar mounted above the faceplate.

He breathed in and out a few times, testing the regulator, then turned to the dive shack. Ki sat in the open door, wearing a set of headphones, one hand on the air/gas manifold. Ben tapped the side of his helmet.

"Comm check, Ki. You got me okay?"

"Roger. Loud and clear."

"Okay. I'm going. Start my bottom time as soon as I hit the water."

"Sure thing."

Ben turned and walked to the side of the *Kraken,* lumbering a bit under the weight of his heavy wetsuit, boots, weighted tool belt, and large steel bailout bottle. The umbilical hose containing his breathing line, communications cable, and pneumofathometer—a small air hose used to measure water depth—he dragged carefully behind him. An Indonesian gunman recruited as a hose tender followed, paying out slack from a five-hundred-foot coil set beside the dive shack.

Sass kept a hand on his shoulder as he moved to the edge of the deck. A long section of railing had been removed. She looked down some forty feet into the gently undulating water, as black as india ink, and shivered. The deep ocean at night was an alien place.

The main crane line's large ball-and-hook was hanging level with the deck, two feet outboard from the edge. Ben put his left dive boot carefully into the belly of the hook, locked an elbow around the cable, and touched Sass under the chin with his free gloved hand. Then he motioned to the crane operator.

The huge boom lowered, taking Ben outboard some thirty feet and dropping him to within a couple of yards of the water. He made a rotating motion with his arm, the hand pointing down, and the crane operator began to unspool cable. Ben switched on his helmet light as he splashed through the surface in a whirling cloud of silvery bubbles.

He had barely reached ten feet when he felt the cable halt suddenly.

"All stop for a minute, Ben," Ki said.

Ben looked up. In the beam of his helmet light, he

could see his bubbles frothing on the surface just over his head. "What's going on now?"

"Got a visitor."

Sass watched from the rail as the dugout canoe, which had suddenly appeared out of the darkness, ghosted closer to the *Kraken,* its white crab-claw sail hanging slack from its spindly spars. In the bow was a young boy, no more than a child, dark-skinned with a thatch of flyaway black hair. He hunkered down in the timid way children have when confronted with something strange and unfamiliar. Behind him, in the stern, steering with a broad-bladed paddle, was an aged fisherman with white hair and stringy arms. He was waving one finger back and forth, shaking his head, and chattering at the top of his lungs.

Durant moved up beside Sass, his pistol in his hand. He bumped hips with her; she recoiled, and he yanked her close again with one huge arm around her shoulders. "What the hell is this bullshit?" he growled, staring across the water at the dugout

Ki was standing in the doorway of the dive shack, still wearing the headphones. Durant motioned to him with the handgun. "Come here, slant-eye."

Ki thumbed the talk button on the dive radio. "Gotta go for a minute, Ben," he said quickly. "Be right back."

"Wait, hang on—"

Stepping out of the shack, squinting against the glare of the *Kraken*'s deck floodlights, Ki hurried over to Durant and Sass. Several of the Indonesian gunmen were standing nearby, muttering in confusion among themselves. Durant spat over the side, letting go of Sass as he did so.

"What the fuck's this old fool sayin'?" he snarled

at Ki. "I can't make out a single word. He's about to piss me off."

Ki craned his neck and listened for a moment. "He's speaking a dialect from southern Kalimantan. I don't know this one specifically, but it's similar to a couple I'm familiar with." He listened again for several seconds. "Basically, he's saying the same thing over and over again. I think he's warning us not to go in the water here."

"Eh?" Durant lifted a simian eyebrow at Ki. "Why not?"

Ki hesitated. "Water demons."

"Water demons?"

Ki shrugged and nodded. "That's what he said."

The dugout glided closer. At that moment Ben, tired of waiting, began to climb the crane line, hand over hand, toward the surface.

"What the fuck," Durant fumed, and leveled his automatic at the sailing canoe.

As the prow of the dugout slid within six feet of the crane cable, Ben emerged from the black water with a great, splashing heave, his yellow fiberglass helmet with its Cyclops-eye faceplate glistening, the glare of his dive light flashing into the face of the little native boy.

His head already swimming with his grandfather's tales of water demons, the child shrieked and threw himself prostrate onto the bottom of the canoe, hands covering his face. At that moment Durant opened fire with his pistol. Chips of wood flew as bullets smacked into the dugout's bow.

The old fisherman, who'd been out searching for one last bit of salvage from the sunken wreck, gulped, abruptly ceased his rapid-fire warnings, and turned the black water

white with his paddle as he attempted to put distance between himself and the tall gunman on the floodlit ship.
The dugout slid away rapidly into the darkness, the wail-
ing of the little boy growing fainter and fainter.

"You'll hit Ben!" Sass shouted, grabbing Durant's
gun arm and driving it upward. He swept her aside
with a curse, throwing her into Ki. When he turned
back to the sea, the canoe was gone. Where Ben's
head had been, at the crane line, there was only a
roiling of bubbles on the black water.

Ki ran back to the dive shack, Sass at his heels, and
threw on the headphones, flicking on the radio's room
speaker as he did so. "Ben!" he said ungently. "Ben,
you all right?"

"Yeah, sure. Just down here blowing bubbles." Sass
hung her head and sighed with relief. "I dropped
down when someone started shooting. What's going
on up there?"

Ki looked at Durant, who'd come up behind them
and was changing the clip in his automatic. "Un, just
some curious fisherman. Durant scared him off."

"Tell him to get going," Durant ordered. His mood
was turning ugly. Sass moved over beside Ki, distanc-
ing herself.

"You ready to go down, Ben?"

"Yeah. Lower away."

Ki stepped halfway out of the dive-shack doorway
and caught the eye of the crane operator. He gave the
hand signal to spool out crane line. "Coming down,"
he said into the headset's microphone.

Durant scowled and strode off, jamming his automatic into its shoulder holster. Sass watched him go,
unable to conceal her revulsion. A hand touched her
gently on the elbow.

"Stay cool," Ki said quietly. He smiled reassuringly. She nodded, smiling back. "Trying."

Reaching up to the manifold, Ki opened a small needle valve. Far below, a little gust of bubbles erupted from the pneumofathometer hose near the umbilical shackle on Ben's dive harness. Ki shut off the valve, and the water column forced its way back into the open end of the hose, producing a reading on a large depth gauge mounted on the shack's air/gas manifold.

"One hundred ten feet, Ben," Ki said.

"Okay. Shoot me the gas, and don't stop the crane. I'll take the breathing mix on the fly."

"Gotcha. Here it comes." Ki reached down to the base of the manifold, threw open the quarter-turn valve that controlled the mixed gas, and simultaneously closed another that locked off the air supply.

There was a rattling squeal as the thin heliox breathing gas streamed through the manifold piping and into Ben's umbilical hose. Nearly a hundred seventy feet below the ship, dropping into a cold, black void, Ben tasted the metallic tang of helium as the last bit of air was displaced from his dive helmet.

"I've got the gas, Ki," he said, his voice thin and reedy from the shrinking effect of helium on the vocal cords. "Keep on coming down on the crane line."

Ki glanced at his watch, concentrating, and marked down the elapsed time on the dive sheet clipboard he balanced across his knee. With the other hand, he continued to signal to the crane operator. "Still coming down, Ben. You see anything at all yet?"

"How deep am I now? I just passed another thermocline. Getting chilly."

Ki manipulated the pneumofathometer's needle

valve, watching the depth gauge. "Just passing two hundred sixty-five feet."

"I don't see a damn thing. It's like outer space without the stars down here. Blacker than hell. No bottom, no ship—nothing." There was a gushing noise as Ben adjusted his regulator. "Keep on coming down. I'm not deep enough yet."

"Roger," Ki responded. He fell silent, continuing to rotate his hand slowly at the crane operator.

Sass looked at him. "Ki."

He glanced up and slipped one ear out of the headphones. "Yes?"

"What do you think that old fisherman meant when he said there were water demons around here?" She furrowed her brow. "I mean, I don't want to sound like an idiot, but . . ."

Ki smiled. "It's all right, I understand." He cleared his throat. "Very often, myths and legends from local folklore have some basis in fact. In this case, however, I think it's safe to assume that it's merely superstition. Many of the people in these isolated islands still hold animist beliefs. They believe that there are spirits, both good and bad, inhabiting everything—plants, animals, rocks . . . even the weather. That old guy in the canoe was probably talking about something like that. You see?"

"Sure." Sass grinned, shaking her tousled blond head. "I guess you're right. He just gave me the chills, though, screeching out of the night like that."

"Don't you worry 'bout no fuckin' water demons, darlin'," Durant said from behind her. He lit a Marlboro. "You're safe as hell up here with me."

He grinned as Sass pushed past him in disgust and stalked over to the port rail.

"How's Mike Nelson doin'?" he asked Ki.

As if in response, Ben's voice, hollow and far off, crackled out of the radio speaker.

"All stop on the crane, Ki. I just landed on the bow of the wreck."

Sass stood at the rail, hugging her arms tightly across her chest, looking down at the sinewy reflections of the *Kraken*'s floodlights as they coiled and writhed across the oil-black water. She racked her brains. They had to plan ahead, figure out some way to overpower or outmaneuver Durant before he didn't need them anymore. It was a sure bet that their lives wouldn't be worth a plugged nickel after he'd recovered the cargo he was after.

Lom Lok wandered past, leering and making a wet hissing sound with his lips. Sass gritted her teeth and stared at the water, quelling the impulse to wrench his rifle from his grasp and beat him to death with it.

Something flashed in the black depths. Not a surface reflection, a momentary bright glow from much farther down. She blinked. There it was again. Then another. The second flash lingered, then shot off sideways before disappearing.

Then there were six—no, eight—glowing spots of light, rising together near the crane line, still very deep. It was impossible to make out any distinct shapes, only an unearthly luminescence. And then, as one, they sank rapidly and disappeared from view.

Sass clutched the rail, breathing hard. Then she turned, stumbling, and ran toward the dive shack.

Chapter Twenty-one

Three hundred seven feet below the surface, Ben sat perched on the bow rail of the *Loro Kidul,* enveloped in a cold shroud of complete and utter blackness. Keeping one hand on the crane cable, he reached up and groped at his hat light, which had gone dead, for some reason, as soon as he'd touched down on the wreck's steeply sloping foredeck. To his relief, the light flickered on again, providing the little illuminated pocket of foreground that was a night-working diver's entire world. The ship's uppermost rail curved off into the gloom, a mute invitation to follow sternward.

Gripping the rail with one hand, Ben began to scramble along it, keeping his other hand on the crane line. "Ki. Tell that tender to come up on my hose a good fifty feet. He's got too much out. There's a big belly hanging off into the darkness below me. I don't want it to get hung up on something. And tell the crane operator to swing the boom twenty feet to the right. Then we'll see where we end up. Got it?"

"Roger, Ben. Coming up on your slack, and swinging twenty feet to the right," Ki replied.

Panting, tugging the heavy crane cable along with him, Ben kicked and pulled his way along the rail. He had to stop for a moment when the cable got too far out of plumb to drag anymore, but resumed progress

when the crane boom was swung topside and it hung
vertically once again, this time near the wreck's foredeck ladder. Ben followed the cutaway sheer of the
hull until he had worked his way to the foremost part
of the main deck.

He rested momentarily, trying not to pant too much
and overbreathe his hat. Build up too much carbon
dioxide, he reminded himself, and you're gonna be
gasping like a hanged man. A cloud of isopods, tiny
sea creatures no larger than a flea, moved in on him,
whirling in his hat light like summer insects around a
streetlamp. Then they were gone, leaving the black
void clear once more.

He cracked the free-flow valve on his hat briefly to
clear the condensation from the inside of his faceplate.
It was cold, and getting colder. The heliox gas conducted heat away from his body core with each exha-
lation. As he had many times in the past, he marveled
at how warm and inviting the ocean could be at its
surface, and how deathly cold and inhospitable it often
was at depth. A vigorous shiver gripped him, and
when it passed, he moved off along the rail once again.

Unlike wrecks that had been underwater for years,
the *Loro Kidul* had absolutely no sea growth, nor even
any sediment, covering her surfaces. Somehow, intact
and unsullied as she was, she looked more ghostly in
the dim glow of the hat light than if she had been
festooned with coral heads, draped with bulging curtains of running rust, and swarming with fish. It was
as if the sea had not yet claimed her; as if she was
merely a phantom intruder from the surface world of
wind, spray, and daylight.

"Swing the crane another twenty feet to the right,
Ki," Ben instructed. "That ought to put me close to

the center of the main deck. I'm on the upper rail.
She's resting on her keel with at least a sixty-degree
list to port. When I figure I'm in the right place, I'll
drop down the slope of the deck maybe twenty or
thirty feet and see if I can run into the container. If
it's even there, that is."

"You better hope that sumbitch is right where she
was welded, slick." Durant's coarse voice came crackling through Ben's hat speakers. "You don't wanna
see me in a bad mood."

"Put Ki back on, Durant," Ben said angrily. "You
want a dive operation run for you, you stay the hell
off the radio while it's being conducted."

There was a lengthy pause, and then Ki's voice returned. "He backed off, Ben. Now, you want the crane
swung twenty feet to the right?"

"Right. Correct. Go ahead."

The vertical crane cable in Ben's hand suddenly
angled off toward the stern. He let it pull him along,
kicking his feet along the top of the rail and keeping
an eye on his umbilical hose, which bellied out behind
him as he went. He drifted through another cloud of
isopods—the only living creatures he'd seen since
leaving the surface—and gradually came to a stop as
the cable went vertical again. Below him, the deck of
the *Loro Kidul* slanted down precipitously into the
black gloom. His hat light flickered again. If it was
leaking, he hoped it would hold out for the duration
of the dive.

"Okay, Ki," Ben said. "Slack both the crane line
and the diver's hose twenty feet, then stop."

"Roger. Coming down on both now."

Ben stepped off the rail and began to descend along
the slanted deck, nudging himself clear of vents and

hatch covers with the toes of his boots. As he descended, the darkness seemed to encroach even more; he reminded himself that it was psychological. He was still moving downward with the ball-and-hook when he came up against a vertical wall of square-corrugated steel, angling out at ninety degrees to the main deck.

"All stop, all stop," he said hastily. He put a gloved hand on the steel surface and swiveled his head, casting around with the glow of his hat light.

"This is it," he said. "I'm at the container."

"I'm telling you, I saw something!" Sass writhed in Durant's powerful grasp, trying to free her wrists. "Let me go, dammit! I've got to tell Ki! We've got to get Ben up!"

"How about gettin' *me* up, darlin'?" The big man pushed his groin into her hip, leering. Several Indonesian gunmen stood nearby, chortling at the scene.

Sass rolled her eyes in exasperation. "We don't have time for this, Durant! Will you fucking let go of me? There's something down there!" She renewed her efforts to break away from him.

All at once, Durant seemed to tire of toying with her. He flung her backward and turned toward the rail, digging in his vest pocket for a cigarette. "Something down there, huh? What? Fuckin' UFOs?" His lighter flared, highlighting his apelike features. He raised a hairy eyebrow at her. "Tell me it's water demons, and I swear to Christ I'll kick your pretty ass clear to Okinawa."

"It's something, I'm telling you! There were a half dozen or more of them!" Sass was hurrying toward the dive shack. "Like floating lights, down deep . . . and they were *big*."

"Aw, bullshit," Durant muttered. He blew out a cloud of smoke, looking down at the undulating night sea, then noticed Lom Lok hovering nearby. He scowled at the little man and chewed on the filter of his cigarette.

"Keep an eye on her," Durant said. "She's fixin' to run some kinda con on me."

Ben broke the lightstick that he had wired to the crane line and agitated it, mixing the luminescent chemicals until the cigar-shaped plastic tube glowed a brilliant, eerie green. Then he left the ball-and-hook lying against the slanting deck and began a rapid inspection of the cargo container. It seemed to be distorted, and as he scrambled along its side, then up toward its top, he discovered that the steel had buckled inward under the tremendous pressure exerted by over three hundred feet of seawater. The end doors, however, he found to be intact. Dropping around to the far side, hanging by one hand from the corner of the container, he saw that it too had buckled, though not badly.

He was about to ask Ki to shoot a quick pneumo on him, since he was at his greatest depth, when his eye was caught by a sudden flash of light some distance away, out in open water. He blinked and looked again. Nothing but black, empty ocean.

Ben again cleared the condensation from his faceplate with a blast from his free-flow valve, and pulled himself up to the top of the container. In a few seconds, he confirmed something that he'd noticed on his first pass: the container's four lifting slings were still attached to its upper corners, linked by a single heavy steel ring.

"Ki. Get ready to come up on the crane line." Ben pulled himself over the container's upper edge and drifted down toward the green lightstick that marked the end of the cable. Getting a gloved hand on the lifting hook, he paused for a moment. "Ki? You there?"

Once again a sudden flash of light—reddish this time—caught his eye, high in the water column, and a good distance from the *Loro Kidul*. It flashed twice before disappearing, with a flaring burst of color resembling that of a neon sign. And it seemed to be moving horizontally. Very quickly.

Shielding his faceplate with one hand from the luminous green glow of the lightstick, Ben stared out into the blackness. He frowned inside his hat's oral-nasal breathing mask. Maybe some type of phosphorescent plankton. Weird. He'd never seen anything like it.

Then Ki's voice crackled through the ear speakers. "Sorry, Ben. Sass is trying to tell me something. You say you want to come up on the crane?"

"Yeah, about ten feet. And you need to get a depth reading on me, and tell me how long I've been down here. I've got to be running short of time."

"Hang on." Ben could hear the faint rustle of paper over the comm line. "You've been down fourteen minutes, and I've got you at three hundred twelve feet." Ki coughed. "And I'm coming up ten on the crane."

"Roger. Go ahead." As the cable started to move upward, Ben did some quick calculations in his head. "Run me on that three-hundred-twenty-foot gas decompression table. Twenty minutes bottom time.

That'll give me—what—an hour's decompression in the water, and three hours on oxygen in the chamber, right?"

"Uh, right," Ki confirmed. "An hour and ten minutes doing water stops, actually, breathing fifty-fifty mix."

"Right. All stop on the crane."

The cable stopped moving upward, and Ben tugged the ball-and-hook over the top edge of the container, toward the lifting-sling ring. It was hard work, and he began to pant as he neared it. He was about the grab the ring and drop it over the hook when he froze suddenly.

Hanging out in the open water, level with and slightly above him, were one, two, three . . . ten glowing cylinders of yellowish-red light. Abruptly, the center object flashed a brilliant, angry red. Instantaneously, the other nine flashed the same rippling color, and the entire pod shot off horizontally into the darkness at uncanny speed, and vanished.

Ben remained stock still, heliox gas hissing quietly into his hat, peering out into the empty black water. Nothing. No light, no movement. Nothing.

Sass's voice filled his ears.

"Ben! You need to get out of there now." Her voice was shaking. "The sea up here is full of these big flashing lights, changing colors and shooting all over the place! We can't tell what they are; they're too deep. Please, come up now, and we'll run a medical table on you in the chamber for omitted decompression! Ben? Ben?"

Ben never heard the last half of her transmission. His dive hat's communications wires had been ripped out of their terminals by the thing that had hit him in the neck and back like a freight train, driving him off the top of the container and out into space.

Now he was falling, his light dead, kicking and twisting in a whirl of gas bubbles, fighting with the unseen thing that was smothering the upper half of his body.

Tumbling toward the very bottom of the *Loro Kidul*'s undersea grave.

Chapter Twenty-two

Something was around his throat, squeezing with incredible force. And his upper body was being wrenched this way and that, as though a giant hand had descended over his head and shoulders and was crushing him between immense fingers. Still tumbling head over heels, he clawed at the thing that enveloped his dive hat. His gloved hands slipped over a rounded surface that was smooth, slimy, and as unyielding as hard rubber.

He landed in the ooze of the sea bottom with the thing still attached. The attacker wrenched again, twisting his head sideways onto his shoulder, and bore down on his back, pressing him face first into the cold mud. He was strangling, his breathing passage locked off by the pressure around his throat. One wildly kicking foot found a purchase against the bottom, and he flailed over onto his right side, feeling the thing pulse with muscle as it came into contact with the mud.

It let go. Ben gasped for breath, settling into the ooze on his back and bailout bottle, totally blind without his hat light. He reached up frantically and shook it. It flickered on, illuminating a cloud of grayish sediment that had been kicked up in the struggle. Digging his hands into the cold muck, he clawed his way to the side about ten feet, into clear water, and stood up.

Surrounding him, and directly overhead, were nearly a dozen hovering luminescent forms, each at least eight feet long, flashing complex patterns of red and yellow. He directed the beam of his hat light at the nearest one.

Less than six feet away, floating just above the bottom, was an immense squid. Its eight shorter tentacles—a circular array of muscular, suckered appendages—drifted and flexed in unison, and two much longer tentacles probed in and out in Ben's direction, testing, seeking. A heavy tubular body at least two feet in diameter and seven feet long supported the writhing tentacles, and terminated in an undulating, delta-wing tail. Two laterally mounted eyes, white with black pupils and the size of dinner plates, stared at Ben with lidless, alien concentration.

Two other squid drifted down beside the first, freckled with rapidly blooming and shrinking color blotches of brownish-red, purple, and sickly yellow. Then, simultaneously, all three creatures lit up with a brilliant crimson flash of luminescence and shot off sideways.

Ben stumbled backward, barely able to control the rush of primal fear that coursed through his body. His hat clanked against something hard: the lower rail of the *Loro Kidul.* As another squid rushed into the glow of his hat light, he ducked under the steel lip and burrowed back in the mud under the side of the dead ship, wedging himself against the hull plates. Through sticky tendrils of sea-floor ooze, he could see the tentacled head and eye of the squid as it hovered mere feet away. His racing mind focused in on the thought: *they don't like to touch the bottom.*

Which did him no good at all. He couldn't stay where he was. But he couldn't leave, either. As the billowing muck blacked out his light, he tried to suppress his panic and think clearly. *How do I go up when I can't stay down? How do I stay down when I can't go up?*

Without warning, the problem was solved for him. His hose went taut, yanking him clear of his muddy refuge and out into open water. He was being pulled upward, dangling by his dive harness like a piece of live bait on the end of a very long line.

The flashing forms of the huge predatory squid began to move very quickly as he ascended through the black void. Circling. Orienting

Following.

"Up on the diver! *Up on the diver!*"

Ki rotated his hand angrily at the Indonesians, who were already hauling up on the umbilical hose for all they were worth. The shiny black synthetic tubing flew up over the *Kraken*'s gunwale, from hand to hand, in a spray of floodlit water droplets.

"He's coming all the way up from a three-hundred-foot gas dive with no decompression!" he yelled at Sass. "If we don't get him in the chamber in a matter of seconds when he hits the surface, he's as good as dead! I don't even know if he's conscious now! I haven't been able to talk to him for nearly five minutes!"

"I know, I know!" she shouted back. "It's ready! He'll make it!"

If he doesn't die of an embolism in the last hundred feet, Ki thought grimly. "Come on, dammit!" he shouted. "Up! Up! *Keatas!*"

Two hundred feet below the *Kraken*, Ben was fighting for his life. A huge squid, flashing crimson, jetted forward and seized his left arm with its nest of tentacles. The tooth-lined suckers tore at his neoprene wet suit, and one appendage fastened itself across the front of his dive hat, its suckers flattening on the faceplate. He punched the animal hard in one of its hideous staring eyes. It turned him loose and rocketed backward, rippling with luminescent bands of red and yellow.

Another squid fastened itself to the back of his right leg, upending him with the force of its rush. Before he could twist around to strike at it, he felt an excruciating pain in the back of his thigh—as though his hamstring had been clipped deeply by a pair of large tinsnips. He bit his lip inside the oral-nasal mask and kicked backward with his free leg, connecting with hundreds of pounds of slippery muscle. He kicked again, with all his strength, and this time the squid let go.

He grasped the back of his right thigh. It stung in the salt water as though a swarm of bees had landed on it. He could feel the shredded neoprene, and the torn flesh beneath it, through the fabric of his glove. Blood in the water. *Not good.* The scent of it was like a magnet to all undersea predators.

Keeping a hand clamped over the wound, the leg drawn up to his chest, he tipped his head back and looked up. The floodlights of the *Kraken* were very near, he could see the wavering distortion of the water's surface. Then there was a warm rush of aid into his dive hat as Ki shut off the heliox gas and switched him back to the compressors.

Two more squid jetted past, crisscrossing in front of his eyes as they circled in closer. The black ocean seemed full of glowing forms, some close, some far off.

All of them were moving with frenzied speed, leaving sparkling trails of phosphorescence in the plankton-rich shallower water. He punched at yet another animal that charged out of the darkness, tentacles fanned and gaping. It reversed direction in a split second.

Three more lunged in to take its place, their giant eyes wide and staring.

"Pull, you bastards!" Burke roared, knocking aside one of the gunmen near the *Kraken*'s rail. He'd come down from the wheelhouse at the first sign of trouble. Leaning over the side, he gazed in astonishment at the incredible light show alongside the ship. The black sea was full of luminescent forms, rocketing around at incredible speeds, leaving long, cometlike trails of phosphorescence in their wakes. And there seemed to be a particular concentration of them below the spot where Ben's hose entered the water.

All of a sudden there was a wet *whoosh* and a ten-foot-long squid erupted through the surface like a Polaris missile. It sailed through the night air in a perfect arc, higher than the *Kraken*'s rail, its pale bronze skin gleaming in the floodlights, and splashed down in an explosion of white spray and greenish phosphorescence. Everyone on deck stood paralyzed at the sight, mouths agape.

The Indonesians on the umbilical hose shuffled back farther from the unrailed section of gunwale, eyes popping. "Air jin," they muttered. "Air jin."

"Dammit!" Burke leaped forward and seized the slack hose from the first Indonesian, hauling on it with all his strength. Ki ripped off his headphones and ran out of the dive shack, moved in beside the captain, and began hauling on the hose as well. Sass knelt at the top of the long steel ladder that had been lashed to the gunwale and which extended down into the water twenty feet below.

Durant grabbed one of the gunmen who'd abandoned the hose and slammed him back into the side of the dive shack. "Who told you to drop that fuckin' hose, eh? *Siapa?* Who?"

The Indonesian's eyes were wide with fear. *"Air jin,"* he babbled. *"Air jin!"*

"Water demon, my ass!" Durant snarled, and threw the smaller man sideways into an empty oil drum. He watched as another huge squid leaped out of the water, tentacles flailing, and smacked back down onto the surface. "Oversized fish bait is all . . ."

Sass gestured frantically at Burke and Ki. "There he is! Bring him to the ladder, quick!" She could see Ben's hat light flashing this way and that in the shadowy water, illuminating the huge, pale forms that surrounded him.

The two men heaved up on the hose, and Ben's yellow fiberglass hat broke the surface at the foot of the ladder.

The squid lunged in and fastened itself to his left shoulder, driving him hard into the steel plate of the *Kraken*'s hull. He felt a sharp sting as the animal bit down through his wet-suit jacket and into his trapezius muscle. Then he heard a faint series of popping sounds, and the squid's body spasmed violently. It let go of him and jetted off into the darkness. Utterly exhausted, Ben willed himself to grab the ladder and start climbing.

He was clear of the water and halfway up the side of the *Kraken* when the first pain hit. He'd been expecting it, had felt it before, but this one was bad. It was as if someone had hammered a red-hot chisel into the joint of his right elbow. He gasped, clutching the arm to his side and nearly falling off the ladder, and kept climbing. Something grazed his leg and smacked heavily into the hull, but he barely noticed.

The only way he was going to live more than a few minutes now was to get up on deck and into the decompression chamber.

Durant emptied the rest of his automatic's clip at the frenzied squid swarming near the foot of the ladder. The one that had latched on to Gannon he was sure he'd hit at least five times. Tough critter. It had absorbed the heavy slugs and taken off in a burst of speed, leaving a gleaming trail of phosphorescence behind it.

"Stop shooting, you asshole!" Sass screamed at him. She turned back to the ladder and leaned down, trying to reach Ben as he climbed slowly upward, rung by rung.

"Hey, it made that thing turn him loose," Durant shouted, changing clips. Ungrateful bitch.

Amazingly, the squid were still trying to get to Ben as he labored up the ladder. First one, then another, jetted clear of the water in his direction, headfirst, with tentacles writhing. Both crashed into the side of the ship and splashed back down. As he came over the top of the ladder, staggering and bent nearly double, another huge animal rocketed into the air, trailing water, and arced over the *Kraken*'s gunwale. As the nearby Indonesian gunmen scattered, gibbering with fear, the slimy bronze body smacked down heavily onto the main deck, water gushing like a jet from a fleshy funnel near its head.

Ben never saw it. He was reeling toward the open hatch of the decompression chamber, unlocking his hat from its neck dam. Clawing it off, letting it fall to the deck, he yanked the quick-release clip attaching the dive hose to his harness and collapsed through the circular opening onto the steel grating of the chamber's tiny outer air lock. Blinding pain permeated every major joint of his body, and a moan of agony escaped his lips as he lay shaking in a sodden heap on the cold grating, bent double. Vaguely, he heard the hatch slam shut and the rushing sound of high-pressure air as Sass and Ki blew the chamber down.

A fiery pain jolted up his spine and into his skull. He stiffened and shook, like a condemned man in the electric chair—and then he was back underwater again, a spirit without physical form, drifting peacefully through an endless, black, midnight sea.

Chapter Twenty-three

"He's not moving!" Sass said, her voice taut with concern. "He's just lying there, Ki!" She flexed her fingers nervously on the vent valve of the outer lock as she peered through the thick Lexan porthole at Ben. "I need to get in there and try to help him!"

"You know you can't do that," Ki replied helplessly. "If he's unconscious, it's because gas bubbles came out of solution in his brain. That's bad enough, but if I bring him back to the surface now to let you in, they'll just reexpand and maybe kill him." He shook his head, chewing his lip in frustration. ' His tissues and blood are completely saturated with inert gas. The best thing we can do is pressurize him way down on that emergency medical decompression table, all the way to one hundred eighty feet, where the bubbles will go back into solution, or shrink so tiny that they won't have any physiological effect. Then maybe he'll come around and be able to crawl into the inner lock. If he does, I can bring the outer lock back up to the surface, and let you go in with a medical kit. But I can't bring *him* back to the surface."

Sass pounded her fist softly on the wall of the chamber. "I know, I know," she whispered, staring through the humidity-fogged Lexan at Ben's motionless form. "I should have blown down with him."

"There was no time, Sass."

Ki stared at the depth gauge of the outer lock, and as the creeping needle slowly moved over the number 180, he shut off the blowdown valve. The loud hissing sound of pressurized air stopped, and he moved over beside Sass to peer into the little porthole.

"There," he said. "One-eighty. With any luck, he'll regain consciousness on his own."

"We don't even know if he's breathing, Ki!"

"You're right, you're right. But we can't *do* anything about it at the moment."

Durant sauntered over, trailing a blue cloud of cigarette smoke. "So what's up with Gannon?" he demanded. "He got the bends, or what?"

Sass wheeled and struck at him with her open hands, fingers tearing at his face. The broken cigarette fell to the deck as she laid open his cheekbone with her fingernails. "You fucking son of a bitch!" she shouted, her eyes brimming with tears. "It's because of *you* that he's lying in there!" She landed a vicious kick to his knee and a left hook that snapped his head back before he smothered her in his massive arms and pinned her against the chamber. Ki leaped forward to help, but Durant ripped his automatic from its shoulder holster and jammed it into the young officer's breastbone.

"Back the fuck up, slant-eye!" he snarled, his face a study in pure viciousness.

A swarm of Durant's gunmen lunged in to seize Ki and Sass. Ki's face was pale with barely suppressed anger, and Sass was still kicking and punching in a white-hot fury. It took five Indonesians to get her under control.

"Ben," she panted, half sobbing, *"Ben."*

Durant wiped the back of his hand across his cheek and looked at the blood smearing his knuckles. His face twisted, and he reached out and grabbed Sass by the throat. "You goddamn bitch," he growled. "You need your face rearranged some." He drew back a fist like a battering ram.

"Durant! *Durant*!" Burke's voice boomed across the main deck as he strode forward. "Don't do it! Let her go!" The command in his tone made even Durant's animal concentration waver. Rather than land the blow he was aiming, he looked over his shoulder.

"Eh?" he grunted.

"You still want your container back, don't you?" Burke stopped only a matter of inches from the other man. "It's down there, Durant."

The renegade SEAL let go of Sass's throat and turned to eye Burke. "Yeah, it is. What about it?"

"Who do you think is going to go get it for you if Gannon dies because *you* had to interfere with the two people on this vessel who know how to save him?"

For a few seconds it appeared as though Durant might leap at the tall captain and try to kill him with his bare hands. Then he laughed, his face creasing into its ugly grin.

"Right." He shrugged, digging for a cigarette. "You got that right, admiral." He looked at Ki and Sass. "Everybody's just gettin' a little strung out, is all. So, we'll just all stay cool. Stay cool." He lit his Marlboro. "Take care of Gannon," he said, jerking his thumb at the chamber, and sauntered off toward the port rail.

The Indonesians released Ki and Sass and backed away, muttering in Bahasa. Burke walked over to the outer lock porthole and looked in at Ben. He glanced up as Sass came over.

"Thank you, Captain," she said. "He'd really have hurt me."

"I don't hold with the mistreatment of women, Mrs. Gannon," Burke replied, somewhat stiffly. "I'll prevent it when I can, particularly aboard my ship." His severe expression softened momentarily, then he nodded to her and moved off in the direction of the stranded squid. The loitering Indonesian gunmen parted for him like the Red Sea opening for Moses.

Ki gazed after him. "Some men just have a natural gift for authority," he said. "There goes one of them. I have to give him that."

"He stopped Durant with only his voice," Sass agreed. "I wouldn't have believed it if I hadn't seen it. He's got no real power left on board the *Kraken,* but he made that asshole hold off on beating me half to death." She turned toward the chamber, and her eyes suddenly went wide with delight. "Ben!"

Ki whirled. Ben's face was pressed up against the inside of the tiny porthole. He grinned weakly, scratching a little at the Lexan with the fingers of one hand.

Ki snapped on the chamber radio. "Ben! Come back, Ben!"

Ben's face turned from the porthole, his lips moving as he talked at the speaker in the outer lock. "Thought everybody forgot about me out there."

Sass pressed her nose to the porthole, her fingers crowding the rim. Ben looked back up at her, bedraggled and pale, and gave her his lopsided smile. He rapped a knuckle over her nose on the Lexan, then slowly made the OK sign with his thumb and forefinger.

"What a night," he said over the radio. Sass watched him push open the door of the inner lock, glance inside, and begin to shed his soaking dive gear and wet suit.

"I guess I need to go in here," he sighed wearily.

The tigress crouched in the corner of her cage farthest from the three turbaned *Two-Legs* that were lurking outside the bars. She drew back her chops in a series of snarls, warning them off, her eyes glowing like coals. One of them pushed something through the bars and flung it awkwardly in her direction, and she bolted to the other corner with a startled roar as it flopped to the cage floor. The *Two-Legs* withdrew a little, observing.

After a few minutes, she crept forward toward the object, sniffing. The *Two-Legs* began to mutter, and she glanced up at them, freezing in place. They immediately fell silent, and she resumed her slow inspection.

She bumped it with her nose. It was cold and slimy, some kind of flesh. Pale and ugly, not red and thick with rich blood, but flesh nonetheless. She was hungry, so hungry that her hollow stomach was rubbing her backbone, but this offering strained even her uncritical palate. She picked up the tentacle gently in her mouth, and carried it back to the rear corner of the cage.

Once there, she settled down, holding the heavy tendril of flesh between her paws, and bit down into it. Immediately, she loosened her jaws. It tasted awful. Worse than the rotting meat of the saltwater crocodile, the *Buaya*, which she'd been forced to sample on one lean and hungry occasion. The flesh of the great squid was redolent with ammonia.

She rose up, sniffed once more at the pale mass, then batted it across the cage with one huge paw. She continued to bat at it, like a house cat worrying a bell-toy, until it was jammed up against the bars far from her preferred corner. Then she lay back down and licked water from the oil pan on the cage floor, trying to rid her tongue of the foul taste.

"*Adalah buruk daging. Jin daging,*" one of the watching Indonesians whispered. "It's bad meat. Demon meat."

Ten hours later, Ben emerged from the chamber, clad in a pair of black jogging shorts with a large towel around his neck, blinking in the glare of the midday sun. His thigh and shoulder were heavily bandaged with multiple wraps of gauze. Sass came in close to steady him as he wobbled a bit, putting one arm around his waist and the other on his chest.

"Are you all right?" she asked.

"I'll let you know soon," Ben replied. "If I don't relapse with the bends in the next half hour, I should be good as gold." He smiled down into her concerned eyes. "But I feel fine."

He extended his hand toward Ki. "I need to thank you," he said. "You did a helluva job up here running the station and the chamber. Like you'd been doing it for years."

Ki shook his hand. "Well, you and Jake Logan brought me up to speed pretty quickly, Ben. I had good teachers." He grinned. "Welcome back to the world."

"Thanks."

Durant strolled over to the chamber, smoking. "You all in one piece, slick? We ain't done yet."

Ben rubbed the back of his aching neck with the towel. "I'm still standing."

"I see that," countered Durant. He spat a piece of filter off his lip. "Don't bother tellin' me you need a surface interval and can't dive for twenty-four hours. I know it."

"How'd you know?" Ben asked. "Sass or Ki tell you?"

"I was a Navy SEAL, slick," Durant replied. "I got mixed-gas training. I remember the drill."

"Then why don't you go hook up your container yourself?"

The big man snorted. "And have to get locked into that chamber with all you friendlies out here takin' care of my decompression? Not fuckin' likely, pal. You're gonna do it."

Ben laughed bitterly. "You stupid asshole. Didn't you see those squid in the water last night? They nearly tore me to pieces down there. What makes you think anyone is going to be able to get any work done on the *Loro Kidul* the next time?"

"Not 'anyone,'" Durant said. He pointed a finger at Ben. *"You."*

Ben sat down on a cable spool and looked wearily at the renegade SEAL. "Durant, look: it just isn't going to work. I need to be able to move around down there to cut the container free with a burning torch, and those attacking squid aren't going to let me do it. I'd like to help you out, but you're going to have to face the fact that I can't fucking get it done if I'm having chunks of meat ripped off my body every few seconds. Understand?" He raised his bandaged leg.

"They nearly got a piece the size of a softball out of me last night. Cut deep and almost all the way through. If that squid had had another half second to close its jaws—or beak, or whatever the hell it is—I'd be lying in bed crippled right now, instead of limping around wasting my time talking to you."

Durant's expression went ugly. "You know," he rasped, "I know what your problem is, Gannon. You're like some of them guys back in the old days who washed out of SEAL training in the first week because they weren't mentally prepared. They fuckin' pussied out because they lacked motivation."

Ben stared off at the horizon. If only a large-caliber handgun, or even a reasonably heavy club, would drop out of the sky and into his hands, he could wrap up this whole miserable affair right now.

"So, I'm providing you with some motivation." He gestured with a couple of fingers and two Indonesians seized Sass by the upper arm. Ben started forward, but once again the automatic appeared in Durant's hand.

"One of these days," Ben said between his teeth, "I'm going to catch you without that fucking thing."

Durant laughed. "I'm never without this fuckin' thing." He waved the pistol at Sass. "Stick her in there," he said.

Sass bucked in their grip, but the two gunmen pulled her across the deck and up to the tiger cage. A third man opened the door of the empty half, and she was shoved inside. The door shut with a clang, and was secured with its padlock.

"It's okay, Ben," she called, gripping the bars defiantly. "Don't let him make you do it. I'll be all right."

Durant settled back against one of the crane treads, keeping the automatic leveled. "That's debatable," he said. "You see, I think she distracts you from your work, so I'm sendin' my white tiger, and her, over to my business associate, Fat Anton Jaeger. Remember him? The weirdo with the faggoty voice on the radio when we first got here? He's over there, camped out on that island." He laughed hoarsely. "He'll like her, but I guarantee you, she ain't gonna feel the same way about *him*."

"Yup. Ol' Anton's a little . . . *peculiar* when it comes to women."

Ben glared at him. "You let anything happen to her, Durant . . ."

"Put it this way, slick," the big man interrupted, "the quicker you get my container up here, the quicker we move on to the next stage of this little operation. And the quicker you get your ol' lady back, and away from Fat Anton. Trust me: you don't want to wait too long. Anton takes a while to warm up, but once he gets cookin', well . . ."

Durant waved his hand in the air in mock helplessness and turned away. He nodded to the Indonesian who had been handling the big crane, then smirked at Ben.

" 'Scuze me, slick. Landin' craft's comin'. I gotta go load me up a little female tiger and a big stripey cat."

Chapter Twenty-four

Ben stood at the *Kraken*'s rail for a long time, watching the decked-over landing craft cruise toward the island, until it was lost against the greens and browns and blacks of the shoreline. The crane had off-loaded the divided cage containing Sass and the white tigress onto the floating World War II relic—a strange bastardized vessel that looked ugly and top-heavy—and Durant had immediately waved it away. Ben had kept his eyes locked on Sass's as she looked back at him through the steel bars, until the landing craft had moved too far off for him to see her anymore.

He turned and looked across the main deck. Nearly two dozen of Durant's raggedy, turban-clad gunmen loitered here and there. Durant himself was always armed, always alert. When he slept, which was almost never, he isolated himself in some location where he could not be taken by surprise. As far as Ben knew, there were no firearms stored aboard the *Kraken*. And there was little hope of escaping in a lifeboat; the Indonesians were everywhere, constantly watching him and the other remaining crew members.

He shivered despite the equatorial sun, and wrapped the towel around his shoulders like a blanket. There was nothing for it. He had to continue playing Durant's game, especially now that Sass was out of reach, and hope that an opportunity to escape or reverse their situation presented itself further down the road.

He was trying to tell himself that she'd be all right as long as Durant needed him to salvage the container when he noticed Burke approaching, Ki at his shoulder. Three or four gunmen, cradling their AKs trailed along behind like watchdogs.

"Mr. Gannon," Burke said, "may I have a word with you?"

Ben ran his fingers through his tangled hair. "Sure, Captain. Sure."

Burke cleared his throat. "It's fairly evident that Durant intends to keep trying to recover the container from the sunken ship, regardless of the risk to us—and in particular to you, of course. In light of that fact, I'd like you to accompany me to the *Kraken*'s reading room. Do you mind?" He stepped sideways and gestured formally with his arm.

Ben managed a slight smile. "All right, Captain," he sighed. "I'll take all the help I can get."

The reading room was a small cabin located one deck below the bridge. The Indonesians had gone through it quite lightly, merely dislodging a few dozen books from the bulkhead shelves and, for no apparent reason, smashing a small glass coffee table. Burke toed the shards carefully, his hands clasped in the small of his back.

"Senseless, animalistic vandalism," he fumed. "On my ship."

Ki knelt and picked up two of the hardcover books that lay splayed on the oriental carpet, their spines bent or broken. "Apparently, the reading of works

printed in English isn't high on their list of priorities,"
he commented. He flipped one of the books over.
"*Toilers of the Sea,* by Victor Hugo. An early
twentieth-century hardcover edition, printed in England." He closed the damaged book gently. "That's
a damned shame."

"My father collected books," Burke said. "He was
a voracious reader. A self-taught intellectual. He was
able to find many rare editions during his years of
voyaging aboard the *Kraken.*"

He glanced over at the open door. The two Indonesians who'd followed them up from the deck of the
ship had lost interest and were sitting on their
haunches in the passageway, smoking and jabbering
at each other.

Burke lowered his voice and directed his piercing
gaze at Ben. "However, I did not bring you up here
to look at books. It occurred to me, Mr. Gannon, that
you might be able to protect yourself underwater by
using a *speargun.* With additional shafts, perhaps you
could hold off the squid long enough to get the container burned free. I realize that this is a rather desperate suggestion, but I'm at somewhat of a loss to
come up with a better idea.'"

"The other thing that occurred to me was that if
Durant happened to be standing nearby as you were
about to enter the water, and he assumed that you
were going to use the speargun to try to ward off the
squid and get his cargo back for him, the opportunity
might present itself to discharge the speargun in *his*
direction, at close range. My experience over the years
with lower-class Indonesians, such as these gunmen,
suggests that they may very well scatter in confusion
if their leader is suddenly killed."

Ki nodded. "He could be right, Ben. Maybe all we have to do is lop off the head, and the body will die. Most of these gunmen are just dirt-poor slum people from Djakarta or Palembang. I can do some pretty fast talking if Durant goes down—technically, I *am* a law enforcement official—and maybe I can scare them with my authority long enough for us to get clear and radio for help."

Ben nodded. "It could work. Better than any ideas I've had so far. A speargun's not going to keep those squid away, but if we can convince Durant that it will, and then get him to come in close enough for a shot . . ." He turned to Burke. "You've *got* a speargun, I take it?"

"Yes," the captain replied. "My father had it made for me in French Polynesia many years ago. I used to hunt the reefs with the native spearfishermen when I was a boy. It's a long gun, made of wood and marine-grade stainless steel. The shaft is propelled by four lengths of heavy surgical tubing. I fired it once on dry land, and it sent a five-foot steel spear completely through the trunk of a palm tree."

"I don't suppose we could just lie in wait for him in one of the passageways?" Ki inquired. "Maybe have one of us draw him around a corner into an ambush?"

Ben shook his head. "Can't, Ki. What about all these gunmen hanging around? They bird-dog us everywhere we go. We prowl around with a big loaded speargun, looking for Durant, and they're going to get wise and shut us down in a hurry. No, we've got to make Durant think that I'm going to use it on the squid, and hope he comes in close enough for me to nail him."

Burke stooped beside a teak bench and loosened two brass catches under its lip. "I keep it in here," he said, lifting the heavy seat. "It's out of sight, and in the library, so I rather doubt that any of our uninvited guests—" He stopped suddenly, staring into the storage space.

Ki stepped forward, waiting. "Captain?"

Slowly, Burke lowered the seat. "It's gone," he said. Defeated, he sagged to the edge of the bench. "How could they have found it?"

Ben looked at Ki, the disappointment in the young Indonesian's eyes mirroring his own, and slowly rubbed his temple with the heel of his hand. His head was beginning to ache with tension and fatigue.

Ki pursed his lips. "Is it possible that Mr. Bullock took it? He's been lurking off by himself as often as not. Maybe he's got his own ideas about escaping."

Burke shook his head. "No. I'm the only one who knew it was here. Bullock had no idea. In the entire time he's been aboard the *Kraken,* I've never seen him in this room once."

Ben sagged into one of the upholstered reading chairs. "Well, shit."

They looked at each other in gloomy silence for several long minutes. At last, Ki sighed and headed toward the door. "Well, I'm going down to the galley. Whatever we end up trying to do, we don't have to starve to death in the meantime. Anyone coming?"

Burke got to his feet. "I believe I'll accompany you. Mr. Gannon?"

Ben looked up at him, slumped in the chair, his hand visoring his forehead. "No, thanks, Captain. I think I'll rest for a few minutes right here."

Burke nodded, and he and Ki exited. Ben was left alone in the room, rubbing his eyes.

He was going to have to go back down to the *Loro Kidul*. There was no getting around it. Back down over three hundred feet, through what had to be a feeding ground for huge predatory squid, with no underwater protection, backup divers, or reliable surface support other than Ki. He flexed his leg. The bite on the back of his thigh was stiff, crusty, and leaking through the gauze bandage Sass had put on it in the chamber. The same was true of the wound on his shoulder, though it was not as deep.

Those voracious undersea hunters were going to rip him to shreds unless he came up with some way to hold them off while he tried to burn loose Durant's container.

A cage? He could ride down in one, but he couldn't work from it. To get the burning done he had to be able to move around freely. Still, a small cage would provide protection on the way down and, hopefully, on the way back up.

But there wasn't going to be any coming back up without a means of keeping the squid at bay while he worked outside, unprotected.

He pressed his hands to his temples and stared at his feet. His head was splitting.

At his toe, crushed open on the floor, was a small book bound in tightly woven rattan. It was open to the title page. Sun Tzu: *The Art of War*. Beneath this, the brief quote: "Know thy enemy."

Ben gazed at the little phrase for a long time. Then he got to his feet, turned to the bookshelves, and began to scan the titles for anything that might contain information on large oceanic squid.

*   *   *

An hour later, Ben was out on the main deck, walking slowly around the body of the huge squid that had jetted aboard the previous night. Having lain in the sun for over twelve hours, decay was beginning to set in. An acrid stench of rotting flesh and ammonia permeated the air. Even so, with the exception of having lopped off one tentacle for experimental tiger food, the Indonesians were loath to touch it, even to shove it over the side. Ben couldn't help making a mental comparison between these ignorant men and the cool, educated Ki. Superstitious fear haunted their hollow-cheeked faces.

He stepped over one of the squid's limp, pale tentacles. The animal was immense, heavy-bodied and well over nine feet long from the front of its head to the tip of the tail. Dead, its skin had faded to a blotchy ivory color, the natural slime that coated it now almost dry, barely oozing onto the deck plates. Ben tapped the small volume he'd found in the ship's library— *Predators of the Deep Sea,* by a French marine biologist named LeToque—against his leg, and considered the creature that had nearly killed him.

By comparison with photographs in the book, it appeared to be a very large specimen, or near relative, of *Docidicus gigas,* also known as the Humboldt Squid. Quite common in the cold waters of the Humboldt Current off the coasts of Peru and Chile, they were greatly feared by local fishermen for their ferocity, which included attacks on men unfortunate enough to fall overboard while wrestling up fishing nets or longlines from deep water.

The great squid had a circular arrangement of eight relatively short, sucker-lined arms radiating from its head, with which it held its prey. It had two much longer tentacles, with suckers concentrated only on the ends, which were used to snatch food from a distance and draw it into the embrace of the more powerful short arms. The suckers themselves were lined with sharp, chitinous teeth, which, like modified claws, aided in preventing a victim's escape.

At the apex of the radiating arms, in a powerful nexus of muscle known as the buccal mass, was the animal's mouth: a sharp, parrotlike beak with which it could cut and tear chunks from its meal. Inside the beak was the radula, a long, narrow tongue covered in minute, backward-pointing spikes, which helped to rasp and grind meat from the body of the prey and conduct it down the gullet.

The squid's giant eyes were extraordinarily sensitive, their retinas—like those of a human—lined with rods and cones. The great predator could see fine detail, in color. Its eyes—like those of a cat—concentrated ambient light, enabling it to see in near-total darkness. It had extra photo-receptive organs arrayed on its head, which picked up the minutest flashes of bioluminescence from other squid or prey animals. The squid could divide the pupil of its eye in half with an ocular contraction, enabling it to see both forward and backward at the same time.

It could change colors far more dramatically than any chameleon. Its skin was covered with chromatophores; giant, elastic-walled pigment cells that the squid could expand or contract at will, in any sequence. Also present were great numbers of photophores, or light-emitting organs, with which the animal could produce a dazzling display of luminescence, in virtually all colors of the rainbow. With these capabilities, it attracted mates, warned off rivals, and confused potential predators.

The squid was jet-propelled, moving itself in any direction with ease by ejecting a powerful stream of water from the fleshy funnel under its head. In combination with its tail fins, it was capable of instantaneous changes in direction or incredible feats of acceleration, to the extent that it could lunge in on prey with blinding speed or launch itself clear of the water like a rocket, as those aboard the *Kraken* had seen the previous night.

It had a sophisticated nervous system incorporating the largest nerve axons of any animal on earth, which gave it unparalleled reflexes. It had a brain comparable to that of a lower mammal, which gave it an unknown degree of intelligence. It had blue, copper-based blood, two hearts, and an ink sac with which it could blacken the surrounding water.

It was one of the most highly evolved, deadly efficient predators in the sea.

And he was going to have to face not one, but dozens of them, again.

Ben sat back on a fuel drum and gazed at the dead creature rotting on the deck, searching his memory for something—anything—that could give him a clue as to how to deal with the huge, roving squid that haunted the *Loro Kidul.*

It seemed futile.

And yet, there was something. Something he could dimly recall.

Something about an octopus . . .

Chapter Twenty-five

Ki closed the cover of *Predators of the Deep Sea* and whistled between his teeth. "Boy," he said slowly, "and I thought tigers were dangerous. These big squid are real killing machines. Incredible." He flipped the book back open to the color plates. "You know, this picture of *Docidicus gigas* resembles the animal lying out on the main deck, but it's not quite the same. I think we're dealing with a slightly different squid—maybe a tropical subspecies—that is very similar, but grows even larger and can thrive in much warmer waters. Look, the pattern of photophores is different on *Docidicus* in this picture, and the two long tentacles are much shorter than on our animal."

Burke shifted in his seat on the edge of the galley table. His eyes flickered from Ben to Durant—leaning back in a chair with his boots crossed on the table, smoking—then back to Ki. "I've heard of the Humboldt Squid before," he said. "They're only found in deep, cold water west of South America, as far as I know. How can these things be so similar, yet survive in an area as warm and shallow as the Java Sea? They don't belong here."

"Well, it's possible that there's an uncharted canyon in this area that leads off to the edge of the continental shelf," Ki surmised. "Maybe it provides a flow of cold, deep, oxygenated water that enables the squid to move into the shallows to hunt, then descend back into a more suitable environment once they've fed. You said it was unusually cold down there, right, Ben?"

Ben nodded. "Very cold. Especially for a tropical sea this shallow."

"That would also explain why their presence isn't known, why they haven't been caught by commercial fishermen elsewhere in this part of the world. And why the locals consider them abnormal and frightening enough to be labeled *air jin,* or water demons." Ki blew out a long breath. "I think it's just a natural anomaly, a freak chance, that an animal like this happens to be here."

"Fuckin' great." Durant's boots stomped on the galley floor as he tipped his chair forward. "The one place in the entire goddamn Indonesian archipelago that my goods sink, and it has to be crawlin' with man-eating sushi."

"Calamari," Ki corrected.

"Shut up, slant-eye." Durant's head swiveled toward Ben. "Well, slick, you said you had a way to keep these bastards off you while you burned loose the container. Let's hear it."

Ben pushed several still wet, tightly closed mussels that he'd scraped off the *Kraken*'s waterline across the table. He picked up a bottle of Tabasco sauce. "Watch," he said.

Picking up one of the mussels, he held it with the shell halves in a vertical orientation and let several drops of Tabasco sauce fall onto it, very close to the rear hinge. Then he set it down and repeated the process with two more. The remaining mussel he nudged over toward Durant. "See if you can open it with your knife," he said.

Durant snorted, but picked up the shell and pulled a short stiletto from his boot. He began to probe at the tightly closed lip with the point of the blade.

"Hard to find a place to stick your knife, isn't it?" Ben said. "Especially without slipping and running it through your hand." He tapped on the table near the other mussels. "The only place you can find a slight opening in any closed shell like a clam or a mussel is right near the hinge. Even then, some of them have such a strong adductor muscle holding them shut that you can't get enough leverage to pry the halves apart."

"Yeah, so?" Durant retorted, giving up and throwing the little shell back onto the table.

"Look." Ben pointed at one of the mussels. It had cracked itself open a quarter of an inch and was opening wider. A second one did the same, then the third.

"The hot sauce you put on them trickled inside through that tiny hinge opening," Ki said. "It's irritating their tissues so much that they're opening up to try to expel it."

"Yup." Ben smiled. "An old Gulf of Mexico oilfield trick. We used to find dozens of spiny oysters deep down on the legs of the offshore rigs. They're beautiful, with long delicate spines and brilliant colors: red, purple, yellow. They're also good to eat—they're actually a scallop, not an oyster—and we collected them for the meat, and to give away as gifts. Keep the girlfriends happy, you know?"

"Get on with it," Durant snapped. "Why do we give a flyin' fuck?"

"A spiny oyster, or a clam, or a mussel, is what

scientists like Ki here call a mollusk," Ben continued.
"So are animals like the octopus and the squid."

"Cephalopods," interjected Ki. "A branch of the
mollusks that have no external shell and multiple,
sucker-lined arms. They look a lot different from a
clam, but fundamentally, their biology is the same.
Soft-bodied invertebrates."

"This isn't gettin' my container up on deck any
quicker," Durant said.

"Wait a second, will you?" Ben shot back. "Let me
finish. About an hour ago, I remembered a story I'd
heard years back, when I first started oil-field diving,
about something that happened up in the Sea of Japan
during the mid-seventies.

"Back then the Japanese were doing a lot of experimental deep-sea drilling. They had undersea wellheads
scattered all over the place in their southern waters.
At the time, they were using saturation divers to do
the underwater flange-ups and installations. These
guys would ride down seven, eight hundred feet in
small diving bells—not much more than hollow steel
cannonballs dangling on slender cables—and then exit
once they were on bottom to perform the work.

"Usually, it was two divers in a bell, doing an eight-
hour run. One guy would suit up, drop down through
the lower hatch, and walk over to the wellhead on the
end of his umbilical hose. The other man would tend.
Then, after four hours, they'd switch.

"Okay. These two guys went down. They'd just
reached bottom at seven hundred feet, and were dangling there about ten feet from the seabed, getting
ready to go to work, when all of a sudden something
tilted the bell. This bell had a couple of small viewing
ports mounted in its sides, as well as two external

lights to help the divers stay oriented when they were working out in the darkness. The lights went out, just like that." Ben snapped his fingers.

"The lower hatch was open in preparation for the first shift. While the divers were looking out the ports, trying to figure out what in hell had plastered itself across them, the tips of three *really big* tentacles wormed their way up from the open hatch.

"They freaked. They slammed the hatch shut, dogged it, and started screaming over the radio for the support vessel to pick them up. No dice. The winches on all diving bells have tension gauges on them to prevent the cables from being overloaded and parting. They hadn't budged a foot upward when topside informed them that trying to spool up the winch was exceeding the breaking strain of the bell cable. They were stuck.

"Finally, someone on the support vessel had the bright idea of sliding a vertically oriented television camera down the cable to see if they could find out what was on top of the bell. They rigged up some lights to it, shackled it to the cable, slid it all the way down, and got a great picture of a monster octopus.

"It looked like your standard Giant Pacific Octopus, like the ones found in Puget Sound, but much larger. They estimated that it had an arm span of sixty feet. It was draped on top of the bell, just hanging out, with some of its tentacles wrapped around it and the rest latched on to the wellhead. It was so strong, apparently, that they couldn't use the winch to pull it free of the bottom without snapping the bell cable."

"They're unbelievably powerful for their size," Ki said. "Even a small one, maybe two feet across, can pop open a shellfish using its arms and suckers." He looked pointedly at Durant. "You couldn't get that little mussel open with all your hand strength, even with a knife."

"Imagine the strength of one sixty feet across," Ben said. "Nobody knows how big these things get in the deep ocean. We're only just starting to explore down there." He ran a hand through his hair. "Anyway, they're in a jam. They've got to get these divers off bottom and back up to the ship, but they can't just yank them up without breaking the cable.

"They tried to convince the guys in the bell to suit up, go outside, and see if they could prod the thing off the bell with crowbars and chipping hammers. Basically, the reply that came back was the Japanese equivalent of 'Are you out of your fucking minds? We're not going anywhere!'

"So, they had to think of something else, before the scrubbers and supplemental O_2 ran down and they ended up with two dead divers.

"Here's what they did: they collected every bottle of bleach they had on board, tied them all to big, heavy shackles, punched holes in them so they'd leak slowly, and slid them down the cable all the way to the bell. The camera was still down there, too, so they could monitor what was happening. Of course, the guys in the bell couldn't see anything.

"At first, nothing happened. But as the bleach leaked out and diffused into the water, it started to irritate the octopus. It got restless."

Ki was grinning. "Octopi and squid both breathe by inhaling water into a mantle cavity and expelling it out a funnel. The same mechanism that enables them to jet around. The gills are inside the mantle. They're sensitive to irritants, just like our lungs. I mean, look what happens when a human being is subjected to fumes or smoke. His lungs don't like it, and he goes into fits of coughing."

Durant scowled at him and lit a Marlboro. "Finish the story, Gannon," he rasped.

"Ki's right," Ben said. "After about ten minutes, the octopus suddenly lifted off the bell and drifted away into the darkness." He chuckled. "I think the support vessel broke the world's record for a bell recovery after that. Anyway, the divers made it. I heard they both retired the next day."

"I can't say as I blame them," Burke declared. "You think we can do something similar with regard to our squid problem, Mr. Gannon?"

Ben nodded slowly. "I'm hoping so, Captain. In a nutshell, it comes down to this: all mollusks, including ceph—" He stumbled on the word, and looked at Ki.

"Cephalopods," the young Indonesian filled in.

"Thanks, cephalopods. They're all soft-bodied, and react defensively when exposed to irritants. I noticed ten or fifteen drums of industrial solvent and cleaning fluid stored out on the forward part of the main deck. Is that pretty strong stuff?"

Burke lifted an eyebrow. "Absolutely. Deck-wash concentrate in ten drums; the other five are toluene. Very toxic. The deck-wash concentrate is quite corrosive. The toluene, in particular, is a bad chemical to get on your skin, especially undiluted. It burns like fire."

"Good," Ben said. "What I want to do is marry another small hose into my umbilical, leaving one open end with about four extra feet of length dangling from my harness. The other end I want to have attached to a portable fuel-transfer pump—one with enough gas to pump a high volume of light fluid down three hundred feet—that draws a mixture of toluene and deck-wash concentrate from those barrels. I'm going to try to saturate the water where I'm working with a cloud of irritating chemicals. If any of the squid try to charge in, I'll just blast them with a direct stream of chemicals from close range. It ought to back 'em off long enough to get the burning done.

"I'll ride down and back up in the diving stage we've got over by the chamber. I'll weld a few sheets of expanded metal onto it to turn it into a cage. We'll lower it with the crane's secondary lifting cable." Ben looked at Durant. "Any questions?"

The big man blew a long cloud of smoke and stared back at him. "Sounds like a long shot to me," he said. "You wouldn't be jerkin' me around, would you? Stallin' for time?"

"No, Durant," Ben stated. "I'm trying to get your goddamn container back for you, that's all."

There was a long pause as the ex-SEAL drew twice more on his cigarette, glaring at the three men in front of him.

"This better work," he growled finally. "I'm gettin' sick of floatin' around out here."

"Aren't we all," Ben said, and started for the galley door.

Chapter Twenty-six

The sweet, cloying odor of hashish drifted past the old man's nostrils as he lay motionless in the elephant grass on a little rise by the mouth of the island's small river. An effective reconnaissance of the invaders' encampment had necessitated a closer inspection; he was less than two hundred yards from the single-engine float plane, pulled up on the beach under the palm trees above the high-tide mark. A large, khaki-colored canvas tent had been erected in a particularly shady spot on the riverbank. Sixteen men were sitting or lying in the clearing nearby; talking, eating, or smoking, their weapons propped up casually here and there.

They didn't *look* like Americans. But that didn't mean anything. There were partisans and enemy sympathizers scattered throughout the islands, many of them supplied by clandestine air drops. Certainly, the landing craft was of U.S. military design, and very likely the seaplane as well.

A biting insect drew blood from his neck, but he ignored it. Still as a corpse, he squinted hard in the direction of the riverbank. The landing craft, which had departed some hours earlier and motored out to sea in the direction of the faraway black ship, was returning. In the clearing, half a dozen men rose and walked to the river's sandy edge as the clumsy vessel came growling up against the current, trailing a dirty cloud of diesel smoke.

It was running with rust, and its ribs stood proud against its warped hull plates. A large, bulky deck-house had been retrofitted—definitely not a standard U.S. military configuration—and occupied all the area from amidships to the stern. The normally open forward section of the hull had been decked over with rough timber, and sitting on it was a large metal cage containing some type of animal.

He squinted again. Maybe two animals. It was hard for him to make out details even from this short distance. Lines were thrown from the landing craft to the men on the bank as it nudged up on the sandy shallows. There was a burst of shouting, and the rest of the men from the clearing got hurriedly to their feet and trotted over to the vessel. Two wide wooden planks were propped in place from the gunwales to the bank, and the men swarmed aboard to crowd around the cage.

At a shouted command, sixteen pairs of hands lifted in unison and the cage rose into the air. Cautiously, exchanging high-pitched exhortations and warnings to be careful, they maneuvered the large enclosure off the landing craft and onto the bank. Carrying it to the edge of the clearing, they set it down beneath an immense coconut palm.

As the old man watched, the flaps of the khaki tent parted and an odd-looking man emerged, short of stature with very dark skin, kinky hair, and incredibly bowed legs. He wore a faded calico shirt, no shoes, and a loincloth that resembled a giant diaper. As he walked with an awkward, rolling gait toward the cage, he kept his shoulders hunched forward, both arms

hanging loosely at his sides, in a knuckle-dragging pos-
ture. The lighter-skinned men were quick to step out
of his way, the old man noticed.

He stopped in front of the cage, waiting. Two of
the men from the clearing opened the cage door and
dragged out a tall, blond woman—the first the old
man had ever seen in the flesh. She didn't like being
manhandled, apparently. The two men on each of her
arms had their hands full controlling her as she ex-
acted a painful toll from their shins and knees with a
series of well-placed kicks.

They propelled her up to the dark, bowlegged man,
who stared at her for a moment, poked at her shirt
once or twice, then turned abruptly and started trudg-
ing back toward the tent. He flopped an arm once in
a beckoning gesture, and the woman was pushed along
behind him, still resisting. The old man admired the
way the sun caught her hair; it looked like long feath-
ers of pale gold.

The bowlegged man ducked through the tent flaps,
and in a moment the golden-haired woman was
pushed inside behind him, twisting and kicking at her
captors. The other men drifted back to the clearing,
resuming their talking, smoking, and eating. A few of
them walked to the landing craft and began to adjust
the mooring lines.

The old man watched for another twenty minutes,
but the woman did not reemerge from the tent. The
shadows were long in the elephant grass as he crept
backward on his belly, painfully stiff from lying absolutely still all afternoon, and gradually melted into the
dense, silent jungle.

Chapter Twenty-seven

"I want Captain Burke to run the crane, Durant," Ben said as he clipped the umbilical hose into his dive harness. "If you don't mind, of course, Captain."

Burke shook his head, eyeballing Durant from beneath his dark brows. "Not at all, Mr. Gannon. It's your operation. If I can help in any way, I'm glad to do it."

"Look, slick," Durant retorted, toying with his automatic, "I don't care if you get Imelda Marcos to run it, as long as you get my container back. You want the admiral to handle the crane, that's fine by me."

"It's his ship, Durant," Ben said briefly. "He knows its systems and gear inside and out—including the main deck crane. I don't want one of your holdup men winging it in the cab when I need quick responses down below. Okay?"

"Hey. Cool." The ex-SEAL shrugged and lit a cigarette.

Ben took his dive hat from Ki. "Same deal, Ki. I need another top-notch job from you up here, just like the other night." He smiled. "And I know I'll get it. You ready?"

The young Indonesian officer returned the tight smile. "Ready as I'll ever be. You just say the word when you're down there, and whatever you need, I'll get it done. Count on it."

Ben clapped him on the upper arm and raised his hat over his head. "Thanks, partner." He lowered it into place, working his mouth and nose into the oral-nasal mask, and locked down the cam of the neck dam. Ki hurried back to the dive shack as Ben gathered his hose and turned toward the edge of the main deck.

"One, two, three," he said into the headphone mike.

"One, two, three back at you," Ben replied. "Got comm. Let's try the chemical pump one more time." He picked up an open-ended section of slender hose dangling from his dive harness, and pointed it overboard.

"Right." Ki waved a hand at Bullock, who was standing about twenty feet away, next to the chemical barrels. Beside him was a Rube Goldberg contraption of piping and industrial-grade hose, with an electric fuel-transfer pump at its heart. The sullen-faced mate flipped a switch, and instantly a powerful stream of greenish-blue liquid chemical shot out of the end of the hose. Ben turned to Ki and made a cutting motion at his throat with his free hand.

"All stop, all stop. That's enough. Jesus." He let the hose fall to his side and shook the hand that had been holding it back and forth. "That's some nasty stuff. I can feel it burning me right through my glove. I'll get in the stage, and let's get me in the water pronto so I can wash it off."

He stepped into the stage, a small, one-man platform of tubular steel that he had enclosed on three sides by welding on sections of expanded metal, and motioned to Ki, still shaking his hand. Ki signaled the crane cab, and Burke hit the retrieval lever for the secondary lifting line. Ben and stage were picked up off the deck and boomed outboard over the water. When the crane boom reached the exact position that had put the main lifting cable over the container on the *Loro Kidul* the previous night, Burke lowered Ben through the surface, then followed with the ball-and-hook of the main crane line.

"Going down, Ki," Ben said as the cool water swirled around his dive hat. "Start my bottom time. How are those idiots doing with the burning lead and my umbilical hose?"

Ki looked out the dive shack door at the two pairs of Indonesian gunmen who had been recruited to pay out the diver's hose and hundreds of feet of heavy burning cable. The cable would deliver to an underwater torch head the O_2 pressure and DC electrical current Ben would need to burn through the welds securing the container to the *Loro Kidul*'s deck. The inexperienced tenders were keeping up with the descent of the stage and diver awkwardly.

"They're managing it, Ben," Ki reported, turning back to the radio. He glanced out at the purpling evening sky. "The sun's going to hit the water here, pretty soon. You see those damn things anywhere yet? Must be dark down there." He shot a pneumo on Ben that showed the diver just passing seventy-five feet.

"Getting gloomy," Ben said, his voice crackling slightly with static. "Not much light at all. What am I at? One hundred?"

"Roger that. Just coming up on it."

"Give me the gas."

"Roger."

Ben opened his free-flow valve, and heliox gas rushed into his hat. When all the warm compressor air had been flushed out, he shut it off and adjusted the balance knob of his regulator slightly. Then he reached up and switched on his hat light.

"I've got the gas," he reported, his voice once again distorted by the helium. Ki acknowledged him, and the stage continued its steady descent into the green-black emptiness.

A squid cruised past the stage, barely three feet away.

It was a ten-footer. Its muscular body was dappled with expanding and contracting reddish-brown chromatophores, and every few seconds it gave off a quick flash of yellow luminescence. The Gorgon's head of tentacles snaked and undulated in loose rhythm ahead of the great staring eye that was locked directly on Ben. The thick, torpedolike creature sailed off into the darkness and disappeared.

Ben looked down through the grating that formed the floor of the stage. Between his heavy rubber dive boots, far below, he could see a cluster of flashing lights, milling this way and that, some tracking off laterally and disappearing. He took a deep, shaky breath, and let it out very slowly.

"Ki," he said.

"Yes?"

"They're here."

The young Indonesian cleared his throat nervously over the radio. "Uh-oh. You want the chemical now, Ben?"

"Negative," Ben replied. "Stand by, though." He swiveled his head as three squid suddenly shot into view, flashing crimson, and arced downward like a tight formation of jet fighters. In a few seconds they were gone. A shiver gripped him. The black water chilled a dozen degrees more as he descended through yet another thermocline. "How deep now, Ki?" he asked.

"Two eighty-five," came the response. "I'll get Burke to slow it down a little bit. You're getting close."

Ben was watching a faintly glowing shape move through the darkness a good way off when, abruptly, the stage was jolted sideways. He lost his grip on the vertical framework, his feet skidded on the grating, and his bailout bottle clanged on the expanded metal of the side. He whirled, breathing fast, to find that a medium-sized squid—perhaps a six-footer—had plastered itself against the stage, its tentacles splayed out on the expanded metal, suckers flexing. The delta-shaped tail fins flapped vigorously and the funnel pulsated with ejected water as the animal tried to force its way past the unyielding steel.

Ben recoiled instinctively to the opposite side of the narrow stage, then groped for the dangling hose by his side. "Give me the chemical, Ki!" he shouted, pointing the open end directly at the pale, fleshy junction of the tentacles.

The hose jumped in his hand, and an emerald-green stream of deck-wash concentrate and toluene shot out from it, enveloping the business end of the attacking squid in a billowing chemical cloud. In the glare of his dive-hat light, Ben could see the rich color suddenly start to eject from the animal's funnel.

Less than two seconds later the squid convulsed, its skin chromatophores turning an angry purplish-red, and relinquished its hold on the stage. With uncanny speed, it jetted away tail-first into the darkness, tentacles trailing, giving off repetitive bluish-white flashes like a living strobe light.

"Damn!" Ben said, elated. "That one sure didn't like a faceful of this stuff. All stop on the chemical for now, Ki." He felt the pressure in the hose subside almost instantly as Bullock turned off the pump, topside.

"The chemical's secured," Ki reported. "Glad to hear it works." He laughed, some of the tension leaving his voice. "I didn't know a squid *had* a face."

"Well, you know what I mean." Ben looked down again just in time to see the upper rail, then the sloping deck of the *Loro Kidul* loom up out of the blackness. "All stop on the stage," he said quickly as the metal platform clunked against the deck plates. The stage slowed, then scraped to a halt on the steep incline, less than four feet above the shipping container.

"All right," he said. "I'm there."

He stood still for a moment, looking this way and that, listening to the sound of his own bubbling exhalations. There were no squid in sight, not even any distant flashes out in open water, either above or below. He felt a prickling at the back of his neck, beneath the neoprene lining of his neck dam, and turned quickly. Nothing but black water.

"I don't suppose it's possible," he said quietly, his eyes searching the dark void through the condensation on his faceplate, "that the squid I hit with the chemical might have warned off the others somehow? When it booked out of there, it was flashing like crazy with colors I've never seen before. Bluish, sort of. Maybe it was a danger signal or something." He craned his neck and looked around three hundred sixty degrees. "There's nothing down here now, that I can see."

"I'm sure it's possible," Ki replied. "We know they communicate with each other using color patterns and light. But I wouldn't count on it."

"Huh!" Ben snorted. "I guess not." He tucked the end of the chemical hose up into the chest webbing of his dive harness, where it would be readily available. "All right. I'm going to hop up on top of the stage and release the burning lead and torch head."

He pushed on the square panel of expanded metal that he'd wired, rather than welded, to the stage framework. The makeshift door swung open slowly, and he pulled himself out and up onto the top of his little sanctuary. The burning lead was shackled to the main lifting padeye; he released it and pulled down an extra forty feet of slack before resecuring it. Then he lowered the torch head to the side of the container, letting the extra slack coil down into a small pile.

He looked around, standing on top of the stage and holding on to the lifting cable with one hand. Nothing. Empty water.

"Slack the diver," he instructed, and stepped off into space.

As he dropped toward the container, he breaststroked hard and managed to land on its metal roof. The main crane line with its heavy ball-and-hook had returned exactly to where he'd left it on the previous dive, only inches from the container's central lifting-sling ring. This time no charging squid blindsided him as he slipped the ring securely over the crane hook.

"Container's hooked up, Ki," Ben said. "I'm going to burn it off the deck now, and then get the hell out of here." He chuckled nervously. "I think I liked it better when I could see those squid charging around and flashing like neon signs. Too quiet down here."

"Maybe you were right. Maybe they're gone."

"Hope so." He scrambled over the edge of the container's roof and dropped down to the intersection of its side and the deck, where the burning lead lay in a small pile. "I'm going to burn off the lower welds first, then come back up and do the top ones."

"Roger. Be careful. And you've been down nine minutes."

"Got it."

Ben grabbed the torch head, draped several large loops of burning lead over his arm, and maneuvered around the end of the container. Dropping down the steeply sloping deck, he passed the big cargo doors, gripped the trim of the lower corner with his free hand, and swung down to the container's underside.

His hat light illuminated the twenty or thirty huge squid that had been hovering there in a closely packed school, giving off no luminescence at all, hidden from view beneath the container. His heart froze in mid-beat. He hung there by one hand for a split second, paralyzed with shock, and then the nearest squid attacked.

It hit him in the chest, driving him backward. His grip was torn from the corner of the container, and the coils of burning lead tumbled toward the bottom. Two other squid jetted in to latch on to his legs. He felt his dive umbilical tug hard at his harness as the animals propelled him out into the empty blackness of open water.

"Hold the diver's slack!" he shouted. "Hold the diver's slack!" He wrenched an arm free from beneath the crushing tentacles and groped frantically for the end of the chemical hose. "Give me the chemical, *now*!"

A gush of glittering green fluid boiled past his face-plate, and he felt the hot sting of the chemical on a small patch of exposed skin at the neck of his wet suit. As the toxic cloud darkened in color, he felt all three squid loosen their grip on his body. He worked his hand under the rubbery tentacles engulfing his chest, located the hose, and jerked it out of his harness.

Jamming the end up under the biggest squid's soft mantle, he held it there as he worked his other arm free and punched down at the animal that was trying to twist his left leg off at the hip. It quivered, then released him and jetted backward. Abruptly, so did the big squid on his chest. Rippling with bluish-white light, its funnel spewing green chemical, it rocketed off tail-first and disappeared from view.

Dangling on the end of his taut dive umbilical, Ben directed the toxic stream from the hose at the re-maining squid. Its beak cut through the neoprene of his wet-suit leg, was just starting to carve into his thigh, when the animal suddenly turned a mottled purplish-red, splayed its tentacles, and let go. As the others had done, it retreated into the darkness, emit-ting a brilliant luminescence.

Reorienting himself, Ben saturated the surrounding water with the stinging chemical. He could feel the heat of it on the exposed patch of skin on his neck, and through the fabric of his gloves. All around him, at a distance of less than twenty feet, dozens of huge squid circled, flashing with angry crimson light.

He was dangling by his dive umbilical a mere ten feet off to the side of the container. Adrenaline pumping, he dropped the chemical hose, which was still spewing green fluid, and stroked madly for the lower corner. Grabbing it with one hand, he seized the hanging burning lead with the other and began to haul it up an arm's length at a time, draping the loops over his thigh. The squid zoomed in and out, vectoring nearer and nearer.

Recovering the end of the lead with the torch head, he hung it over his shoulder and grasped the chemical hose again, directing the fluid stream at the approaching squid for several seconds. Then, swinging by one hand like an underwater gibbon, he worked his way along the underside of the container to the farther of the two welds that held it to the deck.

Letting the chemical billow around him, he clipped a short leash attached to his dive harness to one of the small padeyes welded to the side of the container, hung there, and inserted one of the ultrathermic burning rods from the packet at his side into the torch head. Jamming the ground lead clamp up into a gap in the container's base, he took a last glimpse around at the jetting squid, placed the tip of the rod at one end of the weld, and flipped down his dive hat's burning shield. He depressed the torch's O_2 trigger, and a burst of oxygen erupted from the end of the hollow rod.

"I'm burning, Ki," he said urgently. "Make it hot!"

In the dive shack far above, Ki threw shut a large electrical knife switch, sending current surging down the burning lead to Ben's torch head. The ultrathermic rod ignited in a white-hot flash of arcing electricity and high-pressure oxygen. It took Ben less than twenty seconds to cut through the entire six-inch length of the heavy weld.

He turned to see a squid lining him up as the chemical cloud dissipated on his left side, and got the hose up just in time. The animal lunged forward into a direct burst of green toxin. Its tentacles brushed his sleeve before it reversed direction. He sprayed chemical around himself, over toward the other weld, then unclipped his leash and hand-over-handed himself back to the other end of the container.

The second weld was burned through in less time than the first, and Ben scrambled up the sloping deck along the container doors to the uppermost side, dragging the heavy lead after him. He was panting hard now, gasping in the thin heliox gas, in danger of overbreathing his hat.

He shook the stub of the depleted burning rod out of the torch head, replaced it with a fresh one, and batted a small, four-foot squid that jetted in toward his head. The chemical cloud was dissipating quickly, as if blown away by a slight current. Ben sprayed more green liquid around in a wide arc, then jammed the rod up against the third weld.

"Get ready on the main crane line!" he half shouted, hitting the O_2 trigger. "There's only one weld left holding the container on the deck once I get this one burned, and it might—"

There was an audible *crack* as the half-burned weld broke in two, followed by a second sharp report as the remaining weld split down the middle under the strain. Ben dropped the torch, scrambling frantically for a handhold as the container fell away under his feet. The huge metal box wobbled precariously as the lifting slings on its roof snapped tight, shock-loading the crane line. It swung out from the *Loro Kidul*'s deck, hung in open water for a second, then swung back in.

Ben saw the thousands of pounds of corrugated steel coming at him and kicked sideways with all the strength he had left. The container crashed into the metal deck with a resounding underwater *ka-boom,* missing his feet by inches. It didn't miss his dive umbilical, coiling behind him, or the stage, hanging alongside the deck only a few feet from the container's original position.

The stage was smashed flat, its tubular framework crushed, pieces of grating and expanded metal whirling downward into the murky darkness. And where the dive umbilical had been pinched, a swirl of heliox gas bubbles and toxic green chemical bloomed from torn hoses.

Ben immediately felt the sensation that every commercial diver dreads: that of pulling vainly with half-empty, oxygen-hungry lungs on a breathing supply that suddenly isn't there.

Throwing a leg over the *Loro Kidul*'s rail, he reached behind his waist with one hand and brought the other up to his head. A couple of quick twists opened the emergency gas valves on both his bailout bottle and dive hat. As the cold heliox surged into his regulator, he filled his aching lungs with rapid breaths, then pulled himself along the rail toward the midline of the container, now hanging level from the main crane line.

Shoving off with his legs, he launched himself from the ship's rail toward the top of the container, and landed near its center. Two squid zoomed in, tentacles flailing; he twisted onto his back and kicked one in the underside of its mantle. His boot sank into the soft, fleshy area, and the creature veered off, the other one staying with it. Several more flashing shapes loomed nearer, coming in at high speed. There was no protective chemical cloud around him; the green toxin was billowing out of the crushed dive umbilical in the darkness some fifty feet away.

Lying on his side, Ben began to reel in the umbilical frantically. "Ki!" he shouted. "Up on the main crane line! Forget the stage, it's smashed flat! I'm on the container on the *main crane line*!"

"Coming up now, Ben!" Ki's voice was distorted, crackling, but unlike the air/gas line and the chemical hose, the comm line had partially survived the impact of the container. "Up on you, too, as you get shallower! What the hell happened down there? The heliox supply is just screaming out of the cylinders, and I can hardly hear you!"

"Shut the breathing gas off," Ben said, eyeing three ten-foot squid that were hovering about fifteen feet away, orienting on him. He recovered the dive umbilical to the damaged section and looked at it. All the hoses were pinched off, the comm line badly frayed. Heliox and green chemical boiled out of the ruptured lines. "The dive umbilical got crushed. I'm on bailout right now."

"Shit!"

"Just about what I did," Ben said. "Shut the gas off, and keep coming up on the crane. We'll figure out what we're going to do next." He waved his arm in an arc, spreading the leaking chemical around himself. "Oh, and keep the chemical pump going. I need it."

"Roger. Ben—ah—how much time do you have, breathing the heliox out of that bailout bottle?"

Ben's voice was steady. "At this depth, about six minutes."

"What?" Ki exclaimed. "But you've got at least an hour of decompression in the water. You don't want to get bent twice in two days! It could kill you!" He drew a breath. "And we've got to switch you back to air. With a ruined hose, how are we going to get you anything to breathe?"

"Working on it," Ben said. "Stand by."

The squid were keeping their distance, probing and skirting the edge of the irritating green cloud billowing around the top of the container. The black water warmed gradually as the huge metal box crept up toward the surface, leaving behind a succession of thermoclines. Ben unclipped his dive knife from his harness, felt for the check valve on his hat, and with one deft slash cut the useless umbilical breathing line away from it. Then he retrieved the damaged section of umbilical and cut away the rest of the ruined breathing line, chemical line, and pneumofathometer, leaving only the comm line intact.

Slitting the duct tape that held the various lines together, he pulled the hoses apart until he had separated a four-foot section of umbilical into its individual components. Then he shoved the lines under the webbing of his dive harness, more or less securing the jury-rigged umbilical to his body. His hat's regulator began to rattle and breathe hard as he relocated the freshly cut end of the breathing hose.

"Ki," he said calmly. "I'm running out of bailout bottle gas. How close am I to my first water stop?"

"About fifteen feet to go," Ki replied, his voice unsteady, "but how are you going to take your stops when—"

"Put compressor air to the dive umbilical, just like normal," Ben instructed.

"But how can you get air to your hat if the hose is crushed?"

"I cut off the damaged section."

"Air coming now. But there's no threaded fitting on the cut end! How are you going to screw it into your hat's valve block?"

"You worry too much," Ben said. "Tell you if it works okay."

As air spurted from the end of the breathing hose, Ben reached up under his neck dam, pulled the tight neoprene collar away from his throat. and forced the narrow hose up into his hat, the end of it resting alongside his cheek. Warm compressor air filled the dive hat, displacing what remained of the cold heliox gas.

"Ahhh," Ben said. "Tastes good." He reached behind his waist and shut off the valve of the empty bailout bottle. Locating the chemical hose once again, he waved it around a few times, replenishing the squid-repelling green cloud. The stuff stung his skin, but it was better than being eaten alive.

"You're going to give me heart failure," Ki said. The crane jolted to a halt. "All stop. One hundred sixty feet, your first water stop. You're breathing okay?"

"Doing fine," Ben responded.

"What about those squid?"

"They rushed me a couple of times," Ben said, raising his voice so Ki could hear him clearly over the loud hiss of air from the open-ended hose. "I gassed them with the chemical, and now they seem to be keeping their distance."

"Thank God for that."

"I already did. Several times."

He sat down under the lifting ring, the chemical hose in one hand, the other gripping a padeye. Squid cruised in and out, gleaming with luminescent patterns, hovering nearby but unwilling to enter the toxic cloud. Maybe they *are* intelligent, Ben thought: they can learn a lesson, and none too slowly, either.

He kicked a heel against the metal roof of the container. Durant was about to get his cargo back. The container had certainly flooded, partially crushed as it was, but that possibility hadn't fazed Durant one bit. Whatever might be inside it was apparently unaffected by immersion in salt water.

In spite of everything, Ben admitted to himself, he was curious about the contents of the container.

And more than a little worried about the fate that awaited all of them, now that the renegade SEAL was on the verge of getting what he'd been after.

A little over an hour later, Ben was picked up from the top of the container as it hung a mere forty feet below the surface. The squid made several halfhearted rushes at him as he gained the foot of the ladder, but he was out of the water and climbing before they could absorb the fact that he was no longer totally surrounded by a cloud of irritating chemical. Durant took the opportunity to pump another clip of bullets from his automatic into the bodies of several large animals that lingered around the ladder.

He stood off to the side, leaning on the starboard rail and watching lazily as Ben doffed his dive hat, peeled off his wet suit, and ducked into the decompression chamber. As Ki threw the compressed air valves and blew the chamber down with Burke watching over his shoulder, the ex-SEAL stuck a cigarette between his lips and turned back toward the water. The main crane line hung motionless, some thirty feet out from the side of the *Kraken*. The glowing bodies of squid darted through the black sea like living comets, leaving behind their now-familiar trails of phosphorescence.

Durant exhaled a long cloud of smoke. Gannon had told him that the container was damaged, and that it would be wise to put some extra slings and winches on it before picking it all the way up out of the water. That way, if a lifting padeye or two ripped out of the weakened framework, the whole mess wouldn't go all the way back down to the bottom. Smart sumbitch, that diver. Knew his business.

He glanced at his watch. It was late now, nearly midnight. Once in a while, as he gazed down into the water, he thought he could see the huge, blocky shape of the container dangling on the slender crane cable. He'd get Gannon to rig some slings to it first thing in the morning, after he got out of the chamber. Slick would be able to make a couple of short, shallow dives without getting killed by a repeat episode of the bends.

A hundred feet from the *Kraken*, a squid launched itself into the air, doing a graceful corkscrew before it splashed back down into the water. Durant grinned to himself as he watched it. Yeah. Slick could do a little rigging without getting bent.

Of course, it didn't really matter much.

Not now.

Chapter Twenty-eight

It was well past nine the next morning when, once more, Ben emerged from the water alongside the *Kraken* and doggedly clambered up the long ladder to the deck. There had been no sign of the huge squid in the sunlit depths. Uncamming his big fiberglass dive hat, he pulled it off his head and rested it against his right shoulder, holding it with one hand by the valve block. As seawater dripped off him and pooled around his feet, he looked over at Durant, undisguised mistrust on his face.

"All right," he said. "I wrapped the two sixty-foot fabric slings completely around the container, one on each end. They're shackled into the cables that lead to those two winches." He pointed at the two motorized drums that had been welded to the deck near the *Kraken*'s gunwale. "Have your men take up as much slack as possible without yanking on the load or interfering with the lift of the main crane, and that's as safe as I can make it. Even if we lose a padeye or the main cable itself, the winch lines should stop your container from going all the way back down."

Durant grinned nastily. "Fuckin' beautiful, slick. You might just walk away from this yet."

"You said we would," Ben stated flatly.

"Yeah, yeah. Sure I did. No sweat." Durant strode

off toward the unrailed gunwale, yelling a mixture of English and Bahasa commands at the Indonesians operating the crane and winches.

Ben slowly stripped off his wet neoprene jacket. He looked at Ki and Burke, standing close by, then glanced at the six or seven gunmen hovering behind them with AK-47s slung low and ready.

"Why do I get the feeling that we're running out of time," he said quietly.

"Because we are," Burke replied. Ki nodded in silent agreement.

Ben took the towel Ki handed him and rubbed it around his neck and shoulders. "Any ideas?"

"Not yet." Burke's dark eyes were flashing, and his big hands clenched and unclenched in frustration at his sides. "We haven't had a single opening. There are always at least two armed men at our heels everywhere we go. Usually more."

"That's right," Ki whispered. "Durant has small teams of them assigned to us in rotation. We can move around, as you saw in the reading room, but not without being guarded. I haven't seen any opportunities to get clear or grab a weapon." He shrugged helplessly. "But most definitely, I think we're running out of time. Durant isn't going to need us anymore once that container's on deck."

"Well, he relies on you, Captain Burke, and your unsociable first mate, Bullock, to move the *Kraken* around," Ben said. "Maybe we've got more time than we think." He looked toward the island suddenly, his eyes becoming distant. "And I have to get Sass back. Somehow."

"Yes," Burke said. "*We* have to."

"Where is Bullock, anyway?" Ki asked. "He's never with us."

"He's been staying in the engine room," Burke informed him. "Crowds of Asians that he can't control make him paranoid." He lowered his eyes, shaking his head. "It was a mistake, in retrospect, to hire Bullock as first mate. He was always highly efficient on deck, and on the bridge. But the blatant racism he exhibits, just barely under the surface—it gets in the way. An outdated, inferior kind of thinking that I shouldn't have tolerated."

Ki started to say something, paused momentarily, then was cut off by the roar of the crane's diesel engine. The three of them turned as one and looked across the deck.

Durant stood beneath the crane boom near the open gunwale, his tattooed arms upraised as if preparing to conduct. His hands waved rhythmically as he signaled the winch and crane operators to come up on their respective cables. The crane diesel whined, the air motors on the winches chugged, and accompanied by a cacophonous symphony of industrial noise, the top of the container broke the surface of the water.

The winch cables danced in the sunlight as the immense metal box turned slightly on the end of the main crane line, which was taut as a guitar string. Water poured from cracks and fissures around the end doors and corner joints as fully half of it rose into the air.

"Durant!" Ben called. "I'd stop there and let it drain, if I were you. No sense in picking up all that seawater."

The big man grinned over his shoulder, a cigarette clamped between his stained teeth, and waved a closed fist at the crane cab. Instantly, the diesel idled down and the main cable stopped lifting. "Good idea, slick," he said.

For the first time, they all got a good look at the thing Durant had wanted so badly. It was nothing but a standard ship's cargo container, constructed of small-gauge I-beam and corrugated sheet steel. It was painted gray and running with rust stains. The pressure had crumpled the sides along its entire forty-foot length, but the distorted metal had not torn open. The truck-style end doors were sprung in their jambs, but still dogged and chained shut.

"What the hell is in there?" Ben muttered, to no one in particular.

The streams of leaking water slowed to a trickle, and Durant waved his hand at the crane cab once again. The diesel belched smoke as it revved back up, and the container rose completely clear of the water, the slightly taut winch cables preventing it from rotating on the crane line.

"Boom up!" Durant yelled impatiently. "Get it the fuck in here!" He turned to glare at the crane operator. *"Cepat!* Faster!"

Nervously, the gunman in the crane cab manipulated the unfamiliar levers and managed to get the container inboard in a couple of minutes. It hung suspended about fifteen feet off the deck, dripping.

"Set it down, moron!" Durant shouted, his bestial face flushed with excitement. "Down! *Ke bawah!*"

The powerful diesel revved once more and the container descended. It landed on the deck plates with a muted *clunk* and a groaning of overstressed metal. Silence fell over the main deck as the crane operator shut down the engine.

Ben, Ki, and Burke moved in closer, followed by the gunmen, until they stood in front of the container's end doors. Durant strode up, digging in the hip pocket of his fatigues, and bent over the padlock that joined the door chains. He grappled with it furiously for over a minute, trying to insert a key, then swore eloquently and stood up.

"The motherfuckin' thing's seized up!" he fumed, throwing the uncooperative key violently into the scuppers. "Gannon! Burn this rat-bastard chain off for me!" He stomped over to the crane and uncoiled the hoses and torch head from an acetylene burning unit. "Come on!"

Ben looked at Ki and Burke, then stepped forward to take the torch. He manipulated the gas knobs, then held the tip up to Durant.

"Light," he said.

The big man dug in his pockets, found his Zippo, and flicked it under the torch tip. A long tongue of blue flame licked out, wavering in the slight breeze. Ben adjusted it into a two-inch cone of concentrated heat, then looked at Durant again.

"What? *What*?" the ex-SEAL sputtered.

Slowly, Ben held out his hand. "Glasses," he said.

Durant stared at him. Then his face crumpled into an ugly mask. He plucked a set of dark sunglasses from his vest pocket, held them out to Ben, and moved in close.

"Don't be *fuckin'* with me, slick," he said. "Believe it or not, I got a side that ain't real friendly."

Ben stayed eyeball to eyeball with the big American, unblinking, as he lowered the sunglasses into place. Then he bent down and began to preheat the link of chain he was going to cut. When it was glowing red, he hit the O$_2$ lever and blew the heavy link into droplets of molten steel. The chain halves clattered apart, the padlock dangling. Unhurriedly, he stood up and shut off the torch.

"Your glasses," he said, holding them out to Durant. The renegade SEAL snatched them with a scowl, then turned to face the doors.

"Open sesame," he said, lifting his arms. Two gunmen stepped in, released the locking dogs, and heaved the ten-foot-high doors open.

Residual trapped water flowed out onto the deck as Ben, Ki, and Burke crowded nearer. Durant stepped into the container, his arms still upraised, and whirled to face them.

"All still here," he said with a grin. "I got my goods *back.*"

Ben squinted, trying to make out what was stacked like cordwood throughout the interior. It looked like . . . large, plastic-wrapped packages, irregularly shaped.

Ki stepped up beside him, a puzzled look on his face. "What the hell . . ." he muttered. He moved forward as Durant picked his way toward the rear of the container, examining some of the toppled contents as he went. The young Indonesian officer put a foot up on the door threshold, bent to peer closely at the nearest packages, then suddenly straightened up.

"Oh, my God," he said, his voice hollow.

Ben looked at him. Ki's tanned face was white, his lips trembling. "What is it?" he whispered urgently.

Ki turned unsteadily to face him. "Tigers," he answered. "The skinned carcasses of tigers."

"What?" Ben blinked hard and stared back inside the container. Durant stepped forward into the sun-

light, carrying a large, plastic-wrapped object in his arms, a huge grin on his face.

"It don't look like a single package split open or leaked," he declared. He leaned forward and let the item he was carrying slip to the deck. Through the thick transparent plastic, the orange-and-black-striped pattern of a tiger hide was clearly visible. The dense hair was matted and wet, bathed in some kind of pink-tinged fluid.

Durant wrestled out a larger package, grunting with effort, and hauled it onto the deck beside the tiger hide. Then he stepped back, wiping a trickle of sweat from his brow, and fished in his vest pocket for a cigarette.

"Goddamn beautiful sight," he exclaimed loudly, lighting up.

Ben, Ki, and Burke stared down in disbelief. The second package contained the complete, intact body of a large male tiger—minus the hide. Red, striated muscle, silvery connective tissue, and yellowish-white fat gleamed through the plastic in the bright sun. The long fangs and intricate supporting musculature of the head and jaws were revealed in detail like some ghastly anatomy lesson. A huge, clouded eye, naked in its skull socket, stared up at them sightlessly. The sexual organs were clearly visible. Like the hide, the entire carcass was bathed in a translucent, pinkish fluid.

Ki knelt and slowly measured the relative proportions of the jaws and skull using thumb-to-finger spans. When he'd finished, he looked up at Durant accusingly.

"This is a Sumatran tiger," he said. "One of the most endangered wild animals on earth. It's illegal as hell to hunt them—for any reason." He pushed a finger into the plastic near the animal's shoulder. "This is where someone put a large-caliber bullet into its chest cavity."

Durant chuckled, exuding smoke. "You're a fuckin' forensic genius, slant-eye. They coulda used you in the O.J. investigation."

Ki got to his feet and looked back into the container at the packaged carcasses and hides. "All of those can't be Sumatran tigers," he said.

"Sure are," Durant informed him. "Seventy-four full-grown males and females, and thirty-eight cubs. And one hundred twelve hides, of course, some bigger'n others." He laughed hoarsely. "Fourteen months of huntin' to get all those beauties. Worth a fortune to the rich Chinese and Taiwanese who think tiger meat is some kind of heap big medicine. Fuckin' idiots."

Ki looked shell-shocked. "You killed over a hundred Sumatran tigers in fourteen months?"

"Most of 'em with one shot," Durant boasted. "The real fun part, though, was stayin' clear of all the government wardens. It wasn't hard for a man with SEAL trainin', because they're clumsy as hell in the bush, but I usually had to drag along a couple of these useless fucks with me"—he jabbed a thumb at the Indonesian gunmen standing nearby—"to carry bait in and the tigers out. Stupid bastards would stumble all over the place, give away my position. Nearly shot one once, he pissed me off so bad."

Ben nudged the clear, flexible plastic with his toe, moving the pink fluid around. "How'd you package them?" he asked.

"Check this out," Durant said enthusiastically. "I

fitted the bodies and hides into bags made of heavy-gauge commercial plastic wrap—food grade—with heat-sealed seams. Then I used a portable vacuum pump to suck out all the air. The last step was to pump in a strong solution of saline, hot spice extracts, and food-grade preservative." He grinned unpleasantly. "Marinated tiger. No refrigeration required."

"One hundred twelve Sumatran tigers!" Ki shouted. "Do you realize what you've *done*?"

"Sure." Durant pulled on his cigarette. "I've turned a whole lot of useless badass cats into ready-made TV dinners. Available for purchase by interested parties at one hundred fifty thousand dollars each, includin' hides and internal organs. Ten percent discount if you buy more than five at once." He stared into Ki's eyes and smiled around his Marlboro. "Figurin' only seventy-five grand for the cubs, that comes out to just under fourteen million dollars—U.S.

"Not bad for fourteen months huntin', eh? A million a month for havin' fun."

"You may have single-handedly destroyed the species," Ki said. "Once the wild population drops below a certain density, the males and females are too widely separated to breed."

"Oh, who gives a flyin' fuck?" the renegade SEAL snarled with a dismissive wave of his hand. "Anyone wants to see a tiger can go to a fuckin' zoo. Me, I'll take the fourteen mil."

"You're one evil bastard, Durant." Ki's face was drawn, his jaw muscle working as he struggled to control himself.

The big American leaned in close, the coal of his cigarette less than an inch from Ki's nose.

"Yes, I am," he said in a gravelly whisper. "And don't ever forget it."

He put his knuckles into the young Indonesian's chest and pushed him back three feet. As Ben shifted aside to make room for him, Durant raised his arms again. "There's enough bone, meat, and hair in one of these tigers to keep a rich Chinese in weird little potions for five years. He don't have to wonder if he's gettin' tiger-bone wine or dog-bone wine to cure his blues. He don't have to wonder if he's gettin' tiger-dick soup or rat-dick soup to make his own tiny pecker point north. He *knows* what he's gettin', because he's got his own personal tiger, shot dead and delivered whole—courtesy of me, Malcolm Durant."

The big man lowered his arms, his face hardening. He whirled and confronted the gunmen who stood around the container.

"Unload all these packages," he ordered. "Stack 'em over on the starboard rail. *Sekarang!* Now!"

"And you three," he continued, pulling his automatic out of its shoulder holster and turning back to Ben, Ki, and Burke, "you come with me."

Chapter Twenty-nine

Sass had been handcuffed by one ankle to a large, ornately carved wooden chest for more than ten hours. Though she'd tried initially, she'd not been able to budge it; it had to weigh over five hundred pounds. Neither had she been able to pull free, or even loosen, the black iron lifting handle to which her ankle was shackled. All she could do was lie back on the carpeted, pillow-strewn floor of the tent vestibule and watch the sunlight fade on the other side of the canvas. Yelling for someone to show his face had gotten old very quickly, and had also produced zero response.

Once during the night, after sheer fatigue had allowed her to slip into a fitful doze, she'd been jolted awake by something touching her unshackled foot. Squatting down, illuminated by the light of a flickering candle, was the bizarre-looking bowlegged man who'd escorted her into the tent. He was wiggling her toes with one hand, staring at her silently with white eyes the size of golf balls popping out of his ebony face, the other hand jammed inside the front of the voluminous, diaperlike loincloth he wore.

Sass had shrieked and lashed out with her foot, and the kinky-haired apparition had hopped backward, eyes unblinking and expressionless. He continued fondling whatever he'd found down the front of his diaper for a few more seconds, then pushed a bottle of water over to her, picked up the candleholder, and left, waddling on his bowed legs through a wall flap into another chamber of the tent.

She hadn't slept much after that, but, feeling quite dehydrated, had drunk the water.

Now the sun was climbing outside again, and it was getting hot. Kicking and tugging against the steel handcuffs only hurt her ankle, so, out of sheer frustration, she began to bang the empty bottle against the chest and shout at the top of her lungs:

"Hey! *Hey!* Come on, you guys! Can't a girl even get a chance to *pee*?"

The wall flap flew aside and the bowlegged man stood there, his pop eyes fixed on Sass like a pair of lightbulbs. She jumped at his sudden appearance, her breath coming out in an involuntary gasp. There was something very, very wrong about him.

Without a word, he waddled forward, unlocked the handcuffs, and stepped back. Still staring, he motioned with a large, swinging arm movement in the direction of the wall flap. When she didn't move, he danced from one foot to the other in agitation and gestured again. This time she got slowly to her feet and moved past him—carefully—to the opening. Drawing a breath, she ducked through, the canvas falling closed behind her.

She was in some kind of dimly lit fabric corridor about six feet long. There was ornate but threadbare carpet under her feet, as there had been in the tent vestibule, and mosquito-screen air vents were sewn into the roof canvas. At the opposite end of the corridor was a quilted curtain of purple silk, embroidered with gold stitching. And there was an odd scent in the air; heavy, smoky, and sweet.

Funny sort of tent, she thought, moving cautiously up to the curtain. She cocked her head to one side and listened. The faint sound of music was coming through the thick quilting. She hesitated, then hooked two fingers around its edge and pulled it aside.

It was very dark on the other side of the curtain, and she held it open as she stepped into the shadowy space, waiting for her eyes to adjust. The quilted barrier had been almost completely soundproof; now the air was filled with the soft, clear fluttering of classical piano music. And the scent she had detected in the little corridor had thickened to a heavy, sickly sweet mustiness.

As her eyes became used to the dimness, she saw that she was in the main room of the tent, the canvas walls of which had been draped with oriental carpets and tapestries rendered in lurid colors: voluptuous purples, bruised reds, garish yellows. Lush tropical plants in large ceramic pots, rubbery leaves dangling, stood around the floor's perimeter. Several carved wooden bookshelves, packed with volumes large and small, had been placed along one wall. A large portable stereo sat on a wooden chest in the far corner, the soft blue and green lights of the amplifier glowing and fluctuating in time to the music.

In the center of the room, facing away from her, was a huge upholstered armchair with a high spreading back, topped by an intricately carved wooden headpiece. A small wooden chest served as a side table. A trickle of smoke rose toward the ceiling from the chair, swirling lazily as the small amount of ocean breeze that could get through the roof vents caught it. On one armrest, a fat white hand kept time with the music, the fingers fluttering on invisible piano keys.

Sass was debating whether to approach the chair or back out quietly when the decision was made for her.

"Come to me," purred a thick, oily voice in accented English. The fat white hand gestured softly, gracefully. "Come to me, my dear."

In the black lava cave, the old man tossed in his sleep on the elephant-grass mat, moaning, his mind consumed by visions.

A last glass of sake. A toast to the Emperor.

A squadron of flight-suited young pilots, white *hachimaki* scarves wrapped around their heads, trotting across the tarmac toward single- and twin-engine planes that are heavy with bombs and gasoline. The red ball of the Rising Sun painted on every fuselage.

Dozens of young men like him, with only three short weeks of flight training, about to take off on their first mission.

And their last.

Commander Nakajima, the hard-bitten Zero ace who'd been pulled from combat duty near the island of Iwo Jima and assigned to train this squadron: "Are you ready, Lieutenant?"

He: "Yes, Commander."

Commander Nakajima: "Are you afraid?"

He: "No, Commander. I am content. *The true Samurai must live always prepared to die.*"

Commander Nakajima: "That time comes for every warrior who lives by the code of Bushido. And my time, like yours, is now. You are my favorite among all the young pilots I have trained, Lieutenant; the most intelligent, the most dedicated."

He pats the long, ivory-handled sword he has bound to his side with a black sash. "If I had a son, this sword of my father's would be left to him. Since I have no family, it will go with me into my final battle. Will you do me the honor of allowing me to ride in the copilot's seat of your plane? Together, we will carry death to the Americans who would desecrate our beloved homeland of Japan."

He (bowing low): "The honor is mine. Commander."

Sass stood where she was for a moment, then walked cautiously around the chair to face the occupant.

Seated with his slippered feet up on an upholstered stool, filling the wide chair from arm to arm, was one of the fattest men Sass had ever seen. Not that he was so tall—he looked to be somewhat below average height—but simply broad, an immense bladder that had somehow sprouted arms and legs.

The fat man reached up to tug on a thin black cord hanging down from the ceiling, and a soft light came on overhead, illuminating the chair with a warm glow. Sass stared. The man was bald, his head pocked with brown age spots. Thin, pale eyebrows described circular arcs over a pair of watery green eyes, lending his face an owllike appearance. A narrow, curved nose with arched nostrils stood out prominently in the center of his face, and immense layers of cheek and jowl hid his neck, giving the impression that his head was stuck directly onto his bulging body. His mouth was tiny and lipless, the chin nonexistent, and his complexion, mottled with tiny purple veins, was as pasty-white as typing paper.

He was dressed in loose-fitting white pajamas and a long robe of purple silk. In his right hand, which was encrusted with heavy, elaborate rings, he held the tiny bowl of an unusual pipe: the stem was nearly two feet long, not wider than a pencil, and tapered to a small mouthpiece at its upper end. Holding the bowl in his prodigious lap, the fat man rested the mouthpiece on his shoulder. The last remnants of an ember were just burning out in the pipe, sending a final thread of smoke curling toward the ceiling.

As the piano music reached a soft flourish, the fat man began to keep the meter with a graceful back-and-forth movement of his left hand.

"Mozart," he said suddenly, his voice a high wheeze. "Pure genius. A talent of Promethean proportions. Not unlike Jaeger." The watery green eyes seemed to focus on something far away. "Yes . . . like Jaeger."

Sass stirred uncomfortably. Instantly the eyes flickered over to meet hers, and the doughy face rearranged itself into a bulging squint of a smile.

"I am Anton Jaeger," the fat man said. "Please, sit." He motioned again with his left hand, and Sass turned to find a collapsible rattan chair near the bookshelves. She drew it up and sat down, keeping more than an arm's length away.

Jaeger wiped a film of sweat off his upper lip with a stained silk handkerchief. "I heard you padding about, my dear," he said, nodding his jowly head. "Oh, yes. Yes indeed. Sasha Wojeck the Creeper. Creep, creep, creep . . ."

Sass pulled back warily, eyeing the pale troll in front of her. She was *not* comfortable having her full name rattled off by . . . whatever this thing was.

"Naturally," Jaeger continued, "you have a typical female distrust of someone who knows your name, and with whom you are unfamiliar. Quite understandable. Yes, quite. So we will trade. I will tell you about Jaeger. A personal account of the most extraordinary man I know: myself. But first, the Black Smoke . . ."

As Sass watched, Jaeger reached over to the side table and plucked the top off a small ivory box carved in the shape of a sperm whale, covered with fine scrimshaw. Delicately, his fat fingers extracted a small lump of some black, tarry substance and deftly rolled it into a ball. Then he dipped the ball into a metal canister beside the ivory box, worked it back and forth, and withdrew it covered in a thick layer of finely cut tobacco. Inserting the ball into the bowl of his pipe, he tamped it down gently with another pinch of tobacco, lit a match, and drew heavily on the mouthpiece. The whole process of filling the pipe and lighting it was performed with a hypnotic, ritual smoothness.

Jaeger blew out a thin line of dark smoke. The air became newly pungent with the acrid, heavy odor Sass had noticed upon entering the room. Again, it smelled strange, yet somehow familiar . . .

"Opium," Jaeger said. "The Black Smoke. A gift from Nature to the imagination of Man. A key to the Doors of Perception—William Blake, incidentally. You've heard of him?"

Sass shook her head. "Somewhere, maybe."

"A rather tedious and murky English poet with a few very interesting ideas. Currently an academic favorite, but long dead, of course. Genius is never recognized in its own time." He shook his head sadly. "A situation with which I am closely familiar."

He drew on the pipe, then pulled himself erect in the chair and began to speak more clearly.

"Anton Jaeger was born in Java in 1934, into a wealthy Dutch trading family. I am he. A precocious and gifted child, he soon displayed a proclivity for playing the piano, thus entering the company of other musical prodigies such as Mozart and Chopin. He received the best private tutoring available to colonial families in Java, but was prevented from ever reaching his full potential by his arrogant bitch of a mother and a tyrannical father who refused to send him back to Europe to study in the great musical institutes. Instead, he was forced to endure life in the knowledge that he would never pursue his natural ambitions, but would be relegated to learning the trade of his father—nothing more than a well-to-do peddler of exotic spices.

"The Empire of Japan intervened on young Anton's behalf in the early days of World War Two, interning his father and mother and looting the Jaeger estate. He was never to see his parents again. But he spent the balance of the war under the protective wing of a Japanese commander who had the good taste to appreciate a fair-haired, smooth-skinned young lad who could make beautiful music on the piano. In return for Anton's physical willingness and musical offerings, the Japanese officer educated him in the various delights of the East: marvelous drugs and intoxicants that delivered heavenly visions, men and women so skilled at providing sexual pleasure that among the elite who desired their services they were revered almost as gods. Anton was a willing, and hungry, pupil."

Jaeger paused to draw on the opium pipe, closing

his eyes in rapture as he did so. He held the smoke in his lungs for nearly a minute, then exhaled slowly with a long *aaaahh*.

"It was in the company of men and women such as these that young Anton discovered his other natural talent, one that rivaled his gift for music: the pursuit and refinement of the techniques of physical pleasure. I was not always the ugly creature you see before you now," Jaeger declared, making one of his curious narrative jumps from the third person to the first. "There was a time when Anton was beautiful, my dear girl, beautiful. Slim and blond and clear-eyed. Can you imagine what a novelty that was to the pleasure princes and princesses of the Far East? They loved young Anton, and saw to his complete education in their area of expertise."

"Then came the years of wandering, from the fortresses of the opium warlords of the Golden Triangle to the sex palaces of Bangkok. From the penthouses of Calcutta to the royal harems of Dahrain. And on to Europe, to Marseilles, and Cannes, and Monte Carlo. A long journey of service to some of the wealthiest and most discerning people in the world. How they loved Anton! How they appreciated the techniques he taught them! For you see, I had taken the principles of the Eastern masters to the next level—refined them, and made them my own." The sudden jump in narrative person again. Sass noted that it had the effect of keeping the listener at a distance, then drawing him or her in without warning.

"And finally, back to Java! To Indonesia! The potential, my dear! A tropical paradise, relatively untainted by Western notions of law and morality. A treasure chest containing some of the most potent

chemical and herbal stimulants on earth, documented
down through the centuries by the proponents of Traditional Chinese Medicine. And the population re-
source! The intermingling of races and bloodlines in
this area has produced some of the most exotic and
lovely examples of the human figure imaginable, both
male and female. And their relative poverty and their
lack of education—their innocence, if you will—make
them most receptive to any alternative that might ele-
vate them from their current state of deprivation. Oh,
I saw the potential for a man of my talents, my dear.
Oh, yes."

Sass realized that she was staring, and dropped
her eyes.

"Ah, but how I ramble on," Jaeger said, his little
mouth smiling in his fat face. "You'll forgive an old
man his memories, won't you?"

He suddenly cut loose with a burst of high-pitched
giggling. Sass felt the hairs prickle on the back of her
neck. She rose to her feet, glaring at the fat man in
the chair who sat leering up at her with those shining
green eyes, the mouthpiece of his pipe sliding slowly
across his wet lower lip.

"You see, my dear, I am a collector; a collector—
and broker—of beautiful men and women." More giggling. The watery green eyes snapped onto Sass's.
"With them, I provide, shall we say, personnel and
recruitment services—*hee-hee-hee*—to various long-
standing clients, such as the Chinese Triads and the
Japanese Yakuza, and assist them in maintaining the
stables of their sex operations. Not to mention my
own humble houses of pleasure in Djakarta, Bangkok,
and Palembang.

"There is a decent profit margin in white slavery,

but it is often necessary for me to perform random quality-control inspections of my stock. I'm sure you understand, my dear, *hee-hee-hee!*"

He kicked back the footstool, swung his legs down, and heaved himself out of the chair, standing unsteadily with his arms spread out for balance, the pipe dangling from his loose, wet lips. The rolls of flesh beneath his purple housecoat jellied with every step as he advanced toward Sass, his damp, sausagelike fingers reaching out.

"Oh, Mister Fung, my best Taiwanese client, will be so pleased! A supply of genuine tiger parts to ensure his own health and virility, the gift of a live white tiger as a professional courtesy, and a lovely blond American woman to add to his stables! Perhaps even his own personal stable!" A line of drool cropped from Jaeger's glistening lower lip as he touched Sass's shoulder, his green eyes staring.

Sass went over backward in the rattan chair trying to put distance between herself and the bloated ghoul who was literally salivating on her leg. Skidding away from him on the seat of her pants, she came up hard against one of the small bookshelves. It swayed, then fell forward, dumping books on top of her. As she fought her way clear, her hand settled on a heavy Burmese teak candleholder that had been standing on the bookshelf. Scrambling to her feet, she raised the heavy wooden ornament and spun to face Jaeger.

"Stay away from me, you sick freak!" she shouted, backpedaling slowly as the fat man continued to plod forward. "I'll split your head wide open!"

Jaeger lowered his pale hands, smiled, and shook his head slowly.

"I think not," he said.

Sass heard the quilted curtain behind her whip back, and then someone seized her from behind, knocking the candleholder from her hand and pinning her arms to her sides. Instinctively, she tried to stomp on her assailant's feet and twist free, but when she did so the arms encircling her tightened like bands of steel, crushing the breath out of her lungs. Struggling feebly, she felt herself going light-headed, the pressure around her torso continuing to increase.

Through pounding of blood in her ears, she heard Jaeger's shrill, wheezy voice: "Put her over here, Gilbert. On the pillows near the central pole."

She felt her feet leave the floor as she was lifted and carried across the room to one of the big wooden uprights supporting the tent. Nearly blacking out, she was flung to the floor on her back and her wrists yanked over her head. There was a snapping of metal locks as she was handcuffed to the pole. As she gasped for breath, she felt first one, then the other ankle forced out to the side and similarly manacled to some heavy object.

In a few more seconds her head cleared, and with some effort, she was able to focus her eyes. Looming over her, staring down with bulging eyes, were Jaeger and the kinky-haired, bowlegged man with the ebony skin. The fat man's wet mouth twisted itself into a loose-lipped parody of a smile.

"I believe you've already met my trusted servant and companion, Gilbert," he wheezed. "One of the more remarkable things about him, in addition to his muteness and unusual strength, is the fact that he possesses a seventeen-inch penis." He leaned down, sweat dripping from his jowly chin. "Of course, you'll require proof . . ."

Chapter Thirty

Jaeger's glassy eyes wandered over Sass in appreciation as she wrenched at the handcuffs binding her wrists to the pole. Her efforts were futile. She was trapped flat on her back like an insect stuck to flypaper.

"Tut-tut," Jaeger clucked. "You mustn't thrash around and damage yourself. If you scar up your wrists, you'll decrease your dollar value." He leaned forward. "You have to realize that, above all, I am a *businessman*. Unscarred and uninjured, in perfect working order, a magnificent specimen of blond Caucasian female such as yourself is worth tens of thousands of dollars to me. I'm not about to let that slip through my fingers. If you insist on trying to vandalize your own body, I'll be forced to have you sedated in order to protect my financial interest."

He collected his pipe from the floor, grunting with effort as he labored to bend over. Tamping the bowl with one pudgy finger, he relit it, inhaled, and blew out another long, thin stream of dark smoke, his eyes closed in pleasure. Then he shrugged the purple robe off his sloped shoulders and gazed down at Sass again. She glared back at him, willing her lower lip not to tremble.

"Are you afraid?" he whispered, slipping a hand into the front of his pajama pants.

"No," Sass said. "Pissed off." It was all she could do to keep the fear from showing.

"Ah." Fondling himself, Jaeger looked over at the bowlegged man and took a quick pull at the opium pipe. "Hurt her a little bit, Gilbert."

Gilbert grinned happily and jumped forward. Seizing Sass's leg, he dug his fingers into the nerve bundle behind her knee. She couldn't quite bite off the scream of pain. Gilbert released her and hopped backward on his haunches. Her leg continued to jump and throb for a few more seconds before the excruciating pain subsided.

"That's right, Gilbert," Jaeger cooed. "Not too much. We don't want to leave any marks, *hee-hee.*"

Sass looked wildly around the room, desperation rising within her. They were crazy, both of them. Crazy and dangerous.

Jaeger stood over her, fondling himself rhythmically. "Are you afraid?" he repeated.

Sass didn't have to pretend. "Yes."

"Of me?" the fat man whispered dreamily.

"Yes."

"Ahhh, wonderful . . ." He turned his head slightly, keeping his staring eyes on Sass. "Gilbert; her pants."

Sass cringed as the dark little man unbuckled her belt and yanked her jeans down to her ankles, leaving her clad in only her green bikini bottoms. He pawed at her crotch momentarily, then looked up pleadingly at Jaeger.

"No, Gilbert," the fat man instructed, "leave them on. I like the color, and they shouldn't present much of an impediment." His face was flushed, and his growing excitement was evident through the loose folds of his pajama trousers. "Help me, please."

He put out the hand that wasn't occupied to steady himself on Gilbert's shoulder, and got clumsily to his knees between Sass's pinioned legs. She looked up at his panting face and quivering torso, caught the damp scent of body odor and opium, and turned away with a grimace, utterly repulsed. Jaeger grinned down at her, his mouth wet and loose, another line of drool falling slowly from his lower lip.

"Ah, *now* you are afraid!" he declared, weaving slightly on his knees with his hand still moving steadily at his groin. "Now let me show you what Gilbert has for you." He nodded over his shoulder. "Gilbert!"

The dark, bowlegged man moved up beside Jaeger and dropped his diaper around his ankles. His male member hung like a thick hose to his knees. Sass averted her eyes in disgust, looking instead up at Jaeger. "This is insane," she choked.

"You'll notice the penis pins Gilbert has inserted just behind the glans of his considerable equipment," Jaeger droned, swaying with his eyes half-shut. "Those are *palangs,* a traditional male adornment of the primitive Dyaks of Borneo. The penis is drilled with a clean nail, the wound or wounds kept open and allowed to heal, and then the *palang*—a hardwood, ivory, or bone pin about an inch and a half in length— is put in place." He paused. "In Gilbert's case, it's more like three inches, *hee-hee-hee*!

"Poor Gilbert; he's been so misunderstood in the past. He is originally from the Gilbert Islands, of course, far to the east of here. He developed the unfortunate habit, as a teenager in his home village, of sexually attacking young girls with his disproportionately large member, and then smashing their heads in with a rock when they protested.

"Coupled with the fact that he has an insatiable sex drive, a large streak of innate sadism, and some degree of mental retardation, the elders in his village—wishing to remove such a person from their society—decided to pass a very old and currently illegal sentence on him: death by stoning. By chance, I happened to be in the area to hear about all this and, interested as I was, whisked him away, so to speak."

Sass stared up at him in horror, not believing what she was hearing.

"Needless to say," Jaeger slurred on, "he was very grateful, and has been my assistant, footman, and occasional playmate for many years now." He reached out and patted Gilbert's hip. "He's a good boy.

"Knowing the intriguing sexual practices of the Dyaks, I had Gilbert drilled twice and fitted with stainless-steel *palangs*. The Dyak men attach small wooden paddles and animal-hair brushes to theirs, in order to provide more pleasure for their women. Gilbert's are considerably more versatile. For example, observe: he's about to equip his with one of the other options."

Sass forced her eyes over to the freakish little man standing next to Jaeger. He was fiddling with the end of his immense erect member. She caught a glimpse of a triangular piece of steel between his fingers, about the size of a man's thumbnail.

"Those are razor blades," Jaeger murmured. "Gilbert and his male equipment become quite formidable when armed in such a way. I turn him loose on women under my control who don't exhibit the requisite obedience." His eyes suddenly snapped wide open, two liquid green orbs shining down on her. "Like you."

Sass gasped. It was unimaginable. It couldn't be happening . . .

"Yesss," Jaeger whispered, staring down at her with lidded eyes, his hand moving rapidly in his trousers, "you are afraid . . ."

All of a sudden, in a merciful flash of intellect, something clicked in Sass's brain. It's not me that excites him, she thought. It's my *fear*.

She looked up at Jaeger staring down at her, wheezing and gulping like a bloated fish, and composed her face. Then, looking right into his eyes, she yawned.

It was as if an electric shock had suddenly pulsed through the fat man's body. He trembled, his concentration broken, and reeled back on his heels.

"What—what are you doing?" he stuttered, his hand still moving at his groin.

"Trying to forget how much you're boring me," Sass replied. She let her eyes roam off to the side of the room.

"Wha—*what*?"

"You heard me, ugly. Do what you're gonna do, but get it the hell over with so I can take a shower. The only thing that frightens me in here is the way you smell."

"I'll have Gilbert carve you up from the inside out with his palang *blades!"* Jaeger shrieked, spittle flying from his lips.

"No, you won't," Sass stated calmly, every ounce of self-control employed in keeping her terror locked down. "You're a businessman. You're not going to allow anything to damage your blond Caucasian female, remember? Uninjured, I'm worth tens of thousands of dollars. You're not going to let that slip through your fingers. Unquote."

Jaeger's eyes bulged out of his head, and he withdrew his hand from his trousers, sagging back on his haunches in despair. The lump at his groin was gone. *"You've ruined it, you bitch!"* he shrieked. *"You've ruined it!"*

"So what?" Sass said bluntly. "Even if you'd managed to get that thing in your pants up and running and inside me, I doubt if I'd have noticed anything that small. Probably would have died of boredom."

"Aaaugh!" Jaeger warbled out a ragged scream and fell over on his back, gasping for air. Good, Sass thought. Die of a heart attack right now. She was starting to feel a rush of elation when Gilbert stepped in front of the obese man wallowing on the floor, grinning insanely. He was very excited.

Sass writhed, trying to close her knees as he moved up on her and gripped her pelvis. Oh, no, her mind cried out silently; no, no, no . . .

A fat white palm smacked into the side of Gilbert's kinky head, sending him sprawling. "Bad Gilbert!" Jaeger howled. "Bad Gilbert! Bad Gilbert! No, no! Bad!" He slapped at the little man furiously, his pudgy body shaking as he windmilled his arms. "She's not for you! Bad, bad Gilbert!"

Gilbert cowered away on the carpets, ducking and scrambling like a kicked puppy; Jaeger turned away and waddled breathlessly to the curtained entrance of the room. "Come!" he shouted. *"Datang!"*

In less than five seconds, two armed guards appeared from behind the quilted curtain. Their eyes widened as they noticed Sass, shackled hand and foot, clad only in a shirt and green bikini bottoms with her jeans around her ankles. Jaeger gestured wildly in her direction.

"Get her out of here!" he gasped, his voice a cross between a falsetto shriek and a tubercular wheeze. "She ruined it for me! *She ruined it!* Put her back in the cage with the white tiger!"

The two guards hurried forward and began to unlock the handcuffs holding Sass. When her hands were free, she managed to grab her jeans and pull them back up over her hips before being yanked roughly to her feet. As she was dragged toward the entranceway, she could hear Jaeger's slurred, high-pitched voice rise and fall in the smoky air:

"There, there, Gilbert. Good boy, good boy. That's my good Gilbert. Anton is sorry he had to hurt you. Anton is sorry you couldn't play with the new woman . . ." The bowlegged little man whimpered like a chastised animal.

Then Sass was through the quilted curtain and being hustled out into the daylight. The guards propelled her down the sandy path, across the clearing—to the hoots and hollers of the men lying there—and up to the tiger cage. The door swung open and she was shoved inside once more, falling to her knees. The door clanged shut and, her heart hammering in her chest, she was left alone.

Except for the white tigress, who hadn't stirred from her favorite corner, despite the commotion of Sass's return.

Chapter Thirty-one

"Come on, slant-eye, move your ass!" Durant shoved Ki hard through the hatchway of the *Kraken*'s rope locker, located deep in the bowels of the ship just forward of the engine room. The young officer stumbled over a spool of braided nylon hawser, his handsome face contorting with anger. Ben caught him and helped him regain his balance. Livid, Ki started toward Durant, his composure strained to the breaking point. There was a *clack-clack* as two AK-47s were leveled at him on either side of the ex-SEAL, the turbaned gunmen who brandished them flexing their fingers on the handgrips.

Durant waved his automatic in Ki's face. "Don't be no hero now, slant-eye." He dropped the pistol to waist level, tilting it down. "You could spend the last hour of your life screamin' like a white bitch with a bullet through your kneecap."

"He's not doing anything, Durant," Ben said, pulling the young Indonesian back gently by the shoulder. "Don't waste your ammo."

"Don't sweat it, Gannon," Durant rasped. "I got lots. But I'm on a schedule, so I'll take a pass on putting a hole in the slant. Think of it as your reward for gettin' my goods back for me." He grinned and stepped back toward the hatchway, keeping the pistol level. The gunmen backed out into the passageway behind him, AKs at the ready.

"What now?" Burke demanded, his deep voice echoing in the small room.

Durant stepped out into the passageway and pulled the hatch half-closed. "Simple," he said. "I got the landing craft from the island comin' out again. I'm off-loadin' the tiger carcasses and hides onto it from this tub. Then we're leavin'."

He stepped back suddenly from the hatch. It swung open again and Bullock was shoved through the opening, catching his shins on the raised lip and falling heavily to the steel floor. He groaned, cursing under his breath, and grabbed his bruised legs.

Durant reappeared, looking in at them over the muzzle of his pistol. "Well," he said, "it's been a slice, y'all. Have a nice trip."

Burke stared at him. "I thought you said we were leaving after you transferred your cargo."

"No," the big man corrected, "I said *we* were leavin'. That don't mean *you*, admiral. You're goin' on a trip."

"What do you mean, a trip?" the captain shouted. "Where?"

Durant's face creased into its gargoyle grin. "To the bottom. One way."

Before the stunned men could react, the hatch slammed shut and the outer dogs spun, securing it. Ben leaped forward and threw all his weight into reversing the inside wheel, but it was too late. Something had jammed the mechanism from the outside. Durant's laughing face appeared in the steel hatch's tiny, six-inch porthole.

His voice was just barely audible through the heavy glass:

"You didn't think I was gonna leave all you witnesses alive to put the *federals* on me, didja? If you were gonna make a move, you should have done it days ago, dumb-shits." He laughed again. "This whole ship's one big piece of incriminating evidence, just like the lay barge was back at the pipeline location. I'm sinkin' it, and you're going along for the ride."

He tapped the porthole glass with the barrel of his automatic.

"*Salamat tinggal,* losers!" he shouted, and disappeared from view.

No one spoke for several seconds, then Bullock, still lying on the floor, broke the silence. "What'd he say?" he asked.

Ki looked down at the first mate, then at Ben and Burke in turn, before translating:

"What he said was 'good-bye.' "

Durant emerged from the starboard hatch of the aft superstructure and strode across the main deck to the pile of tiger carcasses near the rail. The landing craft was just maneuvering alongside the *Kraken,* positioning itself under the hanging gangplank that had been deployed on the starboard side. The Indonesian gunmen crowded around the rail, some catching mooring lines, others already picking up plastic bags of tiger parts.

"Let's go!" Durant shouted. "Load it up! *Menggerakkan!* Move!" He turned to Lom Lok, who was standing nearby with three other gunmen. "C'mere, you." The little man hurried over, clutching his AK-47 to his chest. "Did you and those other zombies open the seacocks in the engine room, like I showed you?"

"*Ya,* Mistah Durant." Lom Lok nodded, grinning and showing his yellow teeth. "Water come in, you betcha!"

"And did you smash that other set of automatic bilge pumps? The ones halfway up the keel, near the galley?"

The little man's sallow face blanched. "Other pumps?" he repeated.

"Yeah, shit-for-brains! *The other pumps near the galley!*" Durant's hair-trigger temper boiled up instantaneously. "You were supposed to smash them, too! Like we did to the ones in the engine room!"

Lom Lok's twitchy eyes flickered around rapidly. "Other pumps?" he said again.

"You useless little bastard," Durant snarled. "Openin' the seacocks don't do no good if you haven't disabled the automatic pumps! They're battery-powered; even without generators runnin', one pair of 'em can pump all the water out of this tub as fast as it comes in for more than a week! What the fuck's the matter with you?"

He brought one huge, tattooed arm around in a roundhouse swing, his open hand catching Lom Lok on the ear and slapping him nearly off his feet. "*Get back down to the galley, you little prick, and disable them pumps!*"

"*Ya,* Mistah Durant, *ya!*" Lom Lok screeched, dashing off toward the starboard entry hatch of the aft superstructure.

Shaking his head and scowling, Durant dug a crumpled Marlboro out of his vest pocket, jammed it into his mouth, and lit it. "I gotta get me some better help," he muttered aloud. He turned to look at the other gunmen, who had formed a staggered line and were busily passing the plastic packages of dead tiger down the gangplank to the landing craft. "Come on, come on!" he yelled, gesturing impatiently. "Faster! *Cepat!*"

Ben and Burke both groaned with effort as they put every ounce of their combined strength into turning the dogging wheel of the rope locker's hatch. The metal creaked under the considerable strain, but refused to budge.

"Damn that bastard Durant," Burke panted. "He's got the outer wheel pinned with something; maybe a crowbar or the handle of a fire ax."

"Can we break the glass in the hatch's porthole?" Ki suggested. "We can't get through, but maybe we could reach down to whatever's jamming the dogging mechanism."

"Not a bad idea," the captain agreed. "We'll need something substantial to even chip that glass, however; it's virtually bulletproof."

"What about this?" Ben offered, holding up a heavy, two-foot-long steel needle. "Marlinspike."

"Perhaps." Burke took it and turned back to the hatch.

"Maybe I can find a bigger one," Ben said, hunting through the stacks of wire, rope, and cable. Ki joined him.

"What's a marlinspike for?" he asked.

"For splicing rope," Ben replied, lifting aside a spool of manila. "You stick it through the strands to separate them, then braid the two pieces of line together." He forced a smile. "Actually, a true marlinspike is made of wood. What I just gave Captain

Burke is more properly called a fid. It's steel. You use it like a marlinspike when you're working on wire or cable."

"Oh, who *fucking cares!*" Bullock yelled from his seat on a large spool. "We're all going to *die* in here!"

"Mr. Bullock!" Burke barked, wheeling. "I remind you that you are still the *Kraken*'s first officer, and that I expect you to conduct yourself in a professional manner! Get up and assist the others! *Now,* sir!"

The despairing mate peered up at his captain, shaking, then rose and began to paw through the nearby coils of used rope. Burke turned back to the hatch, hefted the steel spike by its narrow end, and rapped it sharply on the glass. Nothing. He drew back and hit the thick port again, harder. This time a tiny surface chip flew off and bounced on the steel floor.

"Try this, Captain," Ki said, holding out a small seaman's hatchet. "It was over in the corner."

"Thank you, Mr. Padang," Burke acknowledged, taking it. He took careful aim, then chopped hard at the port. A vertical split appeared in it, all the way through.

"Now we're getting somewhere," Burke said, and chopped again. The glass shattered into a dozen jagged pieces, some falling to the floor, others remaining in the porthole frame. Working quickly, the captain cleared the rest of the glass from the opening with the blade of the hatchet.

"You're the tallest one here, Captain," Ben said. "Can you reach down to the outer dogging wheel?"

"I'll try, Mr. Gannon." Burke turned sideways to the steel hatch and stuck his arm through the porthole. As he did so, a three-foot-high tower of stacked small-diameter wire spools toppled over, for no apparent reason.

"What did that?" Bullock asked fearfully.

Ben stood still for a moment, feeling his feet under him, then cleared his throat. "The ship," he said. "The ship's listing. She's starting to sink."

In the flooding bilges beneath the galley, Lom Lok had just finished smashing loose the power cables to the two big pumps with a fire ax when he heard the faint sound of running footsteps over his head. No one else was belowdecks besides him. Everyone was loading the tiger carcasses into the landing craft, then boarding themselves. He swung the AK-47 down from his scrawny shoulder. The captain, the diver, and two others had been imprisoned in the rope locker, to be sunk with the ship. They must have gotten free.

He stepped up to the level of the galley floor and stuck his head through the bilge-access opening. Nobody in the galley. Nervously, he glanced back down at the rising water, feeling the list of the ship increase by the second. The salt water lapped at his heels, then a few seconds later was swirling around his ankles.

He jumped up into the galley and began to trot aft through the lower passageway toward the rope locker, his rifle in front of him. If he could gun down the Americans and their Indonesian friend, he would be on Durant's good side for days. But he had to hurry. Already, the floor of the passageway was slanting so much that he could barely run, and water was beginning to trickle over the lip of the galley hatch.

There wasn't much time, but he could hear the sound of banging, and the screech of metal being dragged over metal. It was coming from the engine room, just around the corner from the rope locker. A quick plan formed in his mind. He would duck through the hatchway, kill the four men, and then escape to the main deck up the engine room's stern ladder; the tiny hatch at its top had been propped partly open the entire time he had been aboard the *Kraken.* He'd noticed several of the other gunmen running a length of chain through its dogging wheel, but they hadn't closed it tight, so he assumed it was still usable.

He grinned to himself. Durant would reward him for this, accord him some respect. He would gain some degree of standing among the other gunmen. All for pulling a trigger for a few seconds.

He splashed through the knee-deep water to the engine-room hatchway, paused to level the AK, then stepped quickly through the canted opening.

"I can't reach it!" Burke fumed, gritting his teeth as he strained to force his shoulder farther through the porthole. "The cursed thing's too low! I can just brush the top of the wheel with my fingertips, but I can't get a grip on it or feel what's jamming it!" He gave up and withdrew his arm, then slammed his fist on the steel hatch.

"Is there any other way out of here, Captain?" Ki asked, eyeing the seawater that had begun to pour through the ventilation gratings along the floor of the rope locker. The room had tilted to a thirty-degree angle, all of its contents—spools and bundles of rope, cable, and wire—sliding into a jumbled, soggy pile along the lower wall.

"Not a one."

The ship continued to list until it became impossible

to stand on the slippery floor. One by one, they dropped to the lower end of the room, wallowing waist deep in foaming salt water, stumbling on the tangle of rope and cable beneath their feet. The last one to drop was Burke, sliding away from the locked hatch with a sharp oath. He splashed into the water beside Ben, struggling for balance.

Bullock's eyes were the size of baseballs, his face haggard and drawn. "We're going to drown!" he whispered hollowly, his lips trembling. "We're going to drown like rats in here!"

"Shut up, Bullock!" Burke bellowed. "You'll drown ten minutes before the rest of us if you don't *shut up!*"

"Think, think," Ben said urgently. "Any ducts, vents, anything we can get through?"

"Nothing big enough," Burke replied, shaking his head.

"Any other tools in here?" Ki asked. He looked down at the foaming brine that was rising to his chest. "Kind of late to look for them now."

"Just splicing tools, Mr. Padang," Burke said. "I'm sorry." His face had eased into an expression of composed, disciplined acceptance. The inevitable was coming. Joshua Burke would not permit his last few minutes on earth to be marred by a loss of dignity or self-control. The *Kraken* was his command—right to the end. "Everyone get ready to swim," he said, his voice even.

As the water rose to Ben's chin, he looked at Ki. The shorter man was already swimming, breathing hard, his eyes frightened, but his mouth still set in a determined line.

"Wish we could have had a glass of *arak* together,

Ben," he panted. "It would've been free." He managed a grin. "My dad owns a distillery."

Ben nodded, smiling back, and then the overhead light went out. In the belowdecks rope locker, the darkness—blackness—was total. Ben choked on salt water as his feet left the pile of debris.

Bullock started to scream. *"Aaaagh! Aaaagh! Aaaagh! Aaaagh!"* Short, gasping shrieks of pure terror that pierced the mind and pulled panic up from the gut like a squirming, living thing. Ben spat seawater and thrashed out toward the horrible sounds. His hand fell on top of Bullock's head and he shoved him under the water, cutting off his noise. Seconds later, he released him. The mate came back to the surface, gasping and blowing, but otherwise silent.

The floor was nearly vertical. The *Kraken* was wallowing on her side, her huge sponsons taking time to flood, forcing her to lie over before she went to the bottom. The groans of stressed steel began to echo throughout the ship as her decks and bulkheads worked and flexed unnaturally.

Ben thought of Sass. Thought of her blond hair flying in the wind as she rode the bow pulpit of the *Teresa Ann*. Thought of all the days spent sharing wind and spray, sunlight and blue skies. Thought of the nights when they became one living thing, tangled in the soft darkness, warmed by the glow of a single candle.

The glow of a single candle . .

Ben tried to blink the stinging salt water out of his eyes and focus. A pinpoint of reddish-yellow light was glowing in the blackness, several feet above the level of the water.

"What's that?" Ki shouted, coughing.

Ben blinked again, squinting, and then a stream of molten sparks erupted from the glowing dot and showered down on them. He ducked under water as a droplet of slag fell on his hair and began to burn his scalp. Backpedaling into Ki, he forced them both away from the rain of white-hot liquid steel.

Ben broke through the surface again and stared. "Someone's cutting through the bulkhead with an acetylene torch!" he yelled. "What's on the other side of that wall?"

"Forward section of the engine room!" Burke shouted back.

The stream of sparks and molten slag was moving rapidly in a wavering arc, leaving a cleanly cut trail of burned steel behind it. Assuming the arc continued around to its point of origin, it would describe a circle about two and a half feet in diameter—if, Ben thought desperately, whoever was doing the cutting could beat the rising water. It was going to be close.

The brilliant spray of molten steel moved through the lowest part of its arc and began to curve upward again. Seconds later, the ragged cut hissed and threw off steam—barely visible in the torchlit darkness—as the water hit it. A deep, grinding moan of stressed metal echoed through the ship just as the flying sparks reached the original burn-through point, completing the circle. Then, abruptly, the torch went out, and the rope locker was plunged into total darkness once again.

Except for a dim red light emanating through the circular cut in the bulkhead. There was a sudden bang, and the rough disk of steel turned slightly in its burned perimeter. Another bang, and it cocked sideways four inches more, letting in the eerie crimson glow from the other side of the bulkhead.

"That light's from the emergency battle lanterns in the engine room!" Burke shouted. "They're red!" He coughed as the salt water foamed up around his mouth.

Ben was at the circular opening in two quick strokes. "The cutout disk has a couple of slag hangers jamming it up!" he yelled. "We've got to try to knock it out of the hole!"

"Here!" Ki sputtered, emerging from beneath the water beside Ben. "I just kicked this! Try it." He passed Ben a small cylindrical tank. "Fire extinguisher!"

Ben grabbed it and, treading water hard with only his legs, smashed it into the jammed disk of steel. It turned again, another two inches. The water rose to cover the lower third of the hole, pouring through into the engine room. That was good, Ben thought fleetingly; it meant that the water level in the engine room was lower than that of the rope locker. He hammered the extinguisher into the disk again.

"Almost, Mr. Gannon!" Burke shouted. "Try again!"

Before Ben could raise the extinguisher a third time, another violent blow impacted the disk from the engine-room side. With a ringing crack, the panel of steel broke free of the slag holding it and splashed into the water. The unobstructed circular opening glowed a dull red, water swirling through its lower third. A miniature sun setting into a foaming indoor sea.

Then a face appeared in the opening, partially blocking the red light.

"You come, Cap'n!" Chang called urgently. "You and other men come right now!"

Chapter Thirty-two

"Out of my way!" Bullock shrieked, thrashing past Ben to the bulkhead. He seized the upper edges of the opening with both hands. *"Yaaaaaagh!"* There was a sizzling sound as the skin and flesh of his fingers cooked instantly on the still-hot steel. The pain didn't slow him down. Kicking and squirming, he levered himself through the hole and disappeared. Seconds later, Chang came into view again, splashing water on the hot edges of the opening.

"Come, come!" he urged.

"Go, Ki!" Ben said. "No time to argue."

"Right!" The young officer stroked up and slipped through the hole with the agility of an otter. Instantly, his face reappeared beside Chang's. "Ben, Captain, there isn't much time! Hurry!"

"You're next, Mr. Gannon," Burke said. His voice was calm, commanding.

"My pleasure," Ben replied. He heaved himself into the narrow opening, catching his shoulder briefly on a claw of burned metal, and then tumbled through onto a flooded grating in the engine room. The entire room was ninety degrees out of its normal orientation; they were standing on what had been a vertical surface. The battle lanterns bathed the large compartment in a hazy red light, creating a labyrinth of shadows and shapes. Seawater had filled the engine room past the halfway point, blocking off most of the exits. On the other side of the brimming pool of red-tinged water, Ben could see Bullock floundering toward the stern ladder and hatch.

"Where Mista Bullock?" Chang said anxiously. "Where he go?"

"He's headed for the stern hatch," Ben answered.

"No! Not that way!" Chang exclaimed. His nearly sightless eyes darted back and forth over the flooded compartment. "Mistah Bullock!" he called out. "You come back! You not go that way! Too late! You come with Chang!"

"Go fuck yourself, you old gook!" came Bullock's echoing reply. "I'm getting out of here!"

"Forget it, Chang," Ben said. He put a hand on the old man's shoulder. "Tell us what to do."

"Get the Cap'n first," the old steward stated, reaching to help Burke as he squeezed his broad shoulders through the opening. The captain splashed to the steel grille, panting, then rolled to his knees. He looked up at his old crewman and gripped his arm.

"Well done, Chang," he breathed. "Well done."

"Yes, Cap'n." Chang turned, feeling his way along the bulkhead, and sloshed off along the grating. "All follow now. Hurry!"

With Ben, Ki, and Burke trailing behind, the old steward proceeded across the semi-inverted room, navigating with his fingertips and what small amount of vision he had left. Even in the maze of shadows and crazy angles, his sense of direction was uncanny. There was no hesitation as he led them over pipes, around engine blocks, and across hidden, submerged gaps.

At the entrance to the passageway leading forward, now three-quarters full of seawater. Chang paused. "Now we swim," he said, and stepped off the grating. There was a splash, and then he disappeared into the flooded corridor.

Ben leaned down to follow, then went rigid as he came face-to-face with Lom Lok. With an oath, he started backward, thrashing in the water.

The little man's eyes and mouth were wide open in death, his head lolling onto his shoulder. Just below the vee where his throat met his collarbone, dead center, a five-foot steel spear had penetrated his upper sternum, pinning him like a collected insect to the heavy teak frame of the passageway hatch. The clouded, lifeless eyes stared at Ben, as inanimate as ball bearings in the red glow of the battle lanterns.

Burke leaned over and fingered the steel shaft. "My speargun," he whispered.

"I take, Cap'n," Chang said, reappearing in the passageway opening. "In case I meet man who try to stop me from helping you escape." He glanced at Lom Lok. "He come around corner with rifle, to kill me, and maybe you. He too slow. Very fine speargun your father have made for you, Cap'n. Shoot very straight, even for old man with bad eyes. Begging your pardon for taking without telling you." He paused to breathe. "We go now, please?"

"God, yes," Burke muttered, his voice awestruck. "Mr. Gannon, Mr. Padang, shall we?"

"Yes, I think we better fucking shall," Ben agreed. He leaped into the water beside the old steward, followed by Ki and Burke. They moved off down the flooded passageway, pulling themselves along by the electrical conduits bracketed to the ceiling, their heads

barely above water. The red light of the battle lanterns
faded behind them; those mounted in the passageway
had not survived their immersion in seawater.

Chang forged ahead, hand over hand, into the darkness. Blind as bats, the others followed, putting all
their faith in the old man.

"How the hell does he know where he's going?"
Ben whispered. "Feels like we're heading deeper into
a flooded coffin, dammit."

"I don't know," Ki panted, floundering along behind him, "but at the moment, he's got my vote."

"Chang knows every inch of this ship," Burke said.
He spat seawater. "And he knows it blindfolded. He's
taking us to the quickest way out; you can depend
on it."

Ben coughed. "Not that I'm complaining, but why
didn't we just head over to the engine room's stern
hatch, like Bullock? We'd have come out on the poop
deck and been free and clear."

Not slowing his progress for a second, Chang spoke
over his shoulder: "No good, Mistah Gannon. Hatch
no good. Pirate chain it up from outside to keep Mistah Bullock in while he run engines. Look like it open,
but only open partway. Not enough for man to fit
through. Still chained." He stopped moving as he
came to a two-foot-diameter ventilation duct, covered
by a thin screen. His voice was tinged with sympathy:
"Mistah Bullock, he not get out that way."

At that moment, back in the engine room, Bullock
was clawing his way along the top rungs of the nearly
horizontal ladder to the stern hatch. The battle lanterns beneath him were starting to flicker, their red
glow fading in and out. The rising water, now occu-

pying fully three-quarters of the compartment, was beginning to affect them.

But it didn't matter. It just didn't fucking matter. He grinned through his panic as he scrambled the last few feet up and across to the hatch. In a few seconds he'd be out. He could see daylight shafting through the partially lidded opening, and catch the odd puff of fresh air breezing into the dense humidity of the engine room.

Those stupid assholes had followed the old chink steward. Even after he'd sided with Durant and his gunmen. Even after he'd helped to sink the lay barge and drown all those yellow niggers trapped below-decks. The mate spat. His cooking had sucked, too. Heavy on the ginger and lemongrass. He hated ginger and lemongrass.

Well, fuck 'em. At least that slanty-eyed Indonesian officer who kept sucking up to the diver and talking like he was some kind of American blue blood was going to bite the biscuit. And the hell with Burke, too. Serve his pompous ass right to drown trapped in his own ship. Talking to him as if he were some kind of dog he could kick.

He worked his shoulders up into the tubular frame of the hatchway and peered out through the crack. The flat-calm sea was lapping against the main deck, right at the level of his head. Off in the distance, he could make out the silhouette of the island. It was going to be a long swim, but with the aid of something to float on, he'd make it. He hoped there weren't any sharks around.

The hatch was propped open just enough to fit his head through, no more. Feeling the water rising around his waist, he put his shoulder against the heavy steel lid and pushed.

The hatch moved an inch, then stopped with a metallic *clunk.*

Bullock blinked and looked down. Water was swirling around his chest.

A second later, the battle lanterns below gave out. The red glow vanished, and the interior of the engine room went black.

In a frenzy Bullock battered his shoulder against the hatch. It moved up and down an inch every time he rammed into it: *clunk . . . clunk . . . clunk.*

The *Kraken* settled another foot, and seawater began to pour through the narrow gap onto Bullock's head. He began to whimper in panic, clawing and tearing at the edge of the hatch, his fingernails turning broken and bloody.

As the water rose to his chin, welling up from below and pouring in from above, he began to scream. Grasping the lip of the hatch, he forced his head through the gap, scraping the skin from his temples and ripping one ear halfway off. He didn't feel it. With his head completely outside, his neck wedged between the edge of the hatch and the deck seals, he stared up at the burning blue sky, his eyes bulging in stark terror.

He screamed and screamed, a disembodied head perched on the poop deck of the slowly dying *Kraken,* until—gently—she settled another two feet. The shimmering surface of the Java Sea crept up the nearly vertical deck plates . . . and covered the hatch in eighteen immaculate inches of blood-warm, crystal-clear water.

And then there was no more screaming.

*   *   *

In the flooding lower passageway, Chang locked his gnarled fingers through the screen covering the ventilation tube and shook it. "Help, please," he said to Ben.

Ben jammed his fingers through the mesh, took a deep breath, and inverted himself on his arms, planting his feet on the steeply angled ceiling. Now completely underwater, he gave one massive heave and wrenched the screen loose. Kicking it away, he popped his head back up into the fast-shrinking air gap. There was less than six inches of breathing space left.

"Come now!" Chang gasped. "Into vent!" He lunged into the slanting tubular hole and clawed his way up. "This big funnel ventilator to main deck!"

"Go, Captain!" Ben shouted. "You're closest!"

"I can't fit through here!" Burke replied, feeling the opening. "It's barely two feet wide! I'll get stuck and block the rest of you! You go! I'll try after you follow Chang!"

"Dammit to hell, my shoulders are nearly as wide as yours!" Ben shot back. "Let Ki go, then!" He groped for a handhold on the electrical conduits in the utter darkness.

"No!" Ben felt Ki brush past him. "Put one arm down by your side, Captain! The other straight up by your ear! Angle your shoulders and pull yourself along! Kick if you can, and I'll push the bottoms of your feet!" He sucked in a breath of air. "It's a caving technique for getting through small passageways! Go! Go!"

Burke didn't argue. With a tremendous splash, he heaved his upper body into the tube, Ben and Ki shoving him along. They could hear him grunting with effort as he dragged himself through the tight space.

"Try to keep your lungs as empty as possible, Captain!" Ki yelled. "It shrinks your chest diameter! Stay loose and flexible, and for God's sake *don't stop!*"

The water bubbled around the lip of the tube; the air gap in the passageway was gone. Their heads brushing together in the narrow vent, Ben and Ki looked at each other in the darkness.

"One of us has to stop breathing and get out of the way for the other to hoist himself up inside," Ben said. "You're slimmer and faster. You go. I'll push you from below, if I can." Before Ki could argue, he sucked in a deep breath and dropped out of the vent. A second later, the young officer felt his shoulders maneuver under his feet. Pushing down with his legs, he clambered swiftly up into the tube.

Beneath the surface, Ben shoved up on the back of Ki's thigh. As his lungs began to burst, the kicking legs moved upward, clearing room in the tube for his head. Ben broke through the foaming water with a ragged gasp.

"Come on, Ben!" Ki yelled, his voice muffled by his own body blocking the vent.

Ben dropped one arm to his side, extended the other up alongside his head, and angled his shoulders as much as possible. Using knees, elbows, and fingers, he pried his way into the tube, feeling like a cork jammed into a wine bottle. Burke was right: the vent was far too small for a big man to get through.

But the captain was doing it. And so was he. In between them, Ki alternately pushed Burke and extended his foot back for Ben to use as a handhold. Progress was agonizingly slow, but they were moving.

At first Ben ignored the water welling up around his feet, but when it reached his knees, then his thighs, he realized that he was about to become a victim of the law of diminishing returns: the water was rising in the tube faster than they were climbing.

"We need to hurry it up!" he shouted, forcing his aching muscles to work harder. "She's going down!"

"We're nearly there!" Ki yelled back. "Burke says Chang is at the opening of the deck funnel. But he says the damn thing has a steel grating screwed over the opening to stop crewmen from tossing trash into it! He doesn't know how Chang's going to get through it without a torch!"

"Don't tell me that!" Ben panted. "I don't want to do all this work for nothing!"

He kept moving up, inch by inch, tugging on Ki's foot when he could, expecting any second to find himself forced to stop when the men ahead of him encountered the grating. But it didn't happen. Suddenly, Ki's foot disappeared, and the slim officer scrambled ahead rapidly. "Then, as if someone had turned on a floodlight, sunshine beamed in from the broad, trumpet-shaped opening of the deck funnel.

With one last effort, Ben dragged himself out of the narrow tube and into the funnel's wide mouth. The Java Sea, blue and tranquil, stretched out before his eyes, its surface glittering in the late-afternoon sunlight as though it had been sown with diamonds. He was free.

Ki's head and shoulders appeared around the lip of the funnel. "Let's go!" he said urgently. "She's sinking fast! We've got to get clear or we'll be sucked down!"

Ben humped himself forward and stuck his head and shoulders out into the fresh air. Ki was sitting astride the shaft of the funnel, just above him. The main deck was almost completely vertical, the surface of the sea—less than ten feet below—lapping along it from bow to stern. Fully two-thirds of the deck was underwater. Most of the *Kraken*'s topside equipment, including the huge walking crane, was gone. Oil drums, wooden gratings and pallets, and assorted floating debris littered the surrounding water, bobbing gently in the slight current.

Burke and Chang were treading water next to the deck, each with a hand on a wooden pallet that floated between them. The old man looked very pale, Ben noticed, as though he was running on his last reserves of strength.

There was a scuffling sound overhead, and he twisted to look up. Ki had clambered vertically to the upper rail and was peering over the gunwale, keeping his head low. After a few seconds, he picked his way back down to the funnel, his face flushed with effort.

"The landing craft is hanging around out there between us and the island," he called softly. "She's only about three hundred yards away. They must be waiting to see the *Kraken* go down."

"And to make sure we don't pop up, by some miracle," Ben added, "if I read Durant right."

"Then we've got to keep the *Kraken* between us and them for as long as possible," Burke growled, looking up from the water. "And we can't risk trying to cut loose one of the lifeboats, as I'd hoped. That'd be a dead giveaway."

"Dead is right," Ki said. "Durant's through playing. If he catches a glimpse of us, he'll come roaring over here with machine guns blazing. What are we going to hide behind once the ship sinks? It's still two or three hours until nightfall. He'll spot us for sure."

There was a sudden tremendous groan of stressed steel, and the *Kraken* began to settle fast, going down by her stern. Geysers of white bubbles erupted along the exposed section of the aft superstructure, and displaced air whistled from the remaining vents.

"Time to leave!" Ben shouted to Ki as aerated water foamed up the tubular shaft behind him. Drawing a foot up and bracing it on the funnel's lip, he dove outward with all his strength, a blast of white foam accompanying him. A half second later, Ki launched himself off his perch above Ben in a clean swan dive. Both men hit the water at the same time, knifing through the surface and going deep, sheathed in bubbles.

Coming up, Ben stroked over to Burke and Chang. Grabbing the edge of the floating pallet, he began to whip-kick vigorously. "Let's get away from her." he panted.

Ki joined them and the four men labored to put distance between themselves and the foundering *Kraken,* shoving the pallet through a trash field of gas cans, oil drums, and plastic buckets. From behind them came the roar of surging water, accompanied by shrieks of escaping air and the grinding of buckling plates. Fifty yards later, they paused and looked back.

The *Kraken*'s black bow was pointing skyward at a steep angle, four-fifths of her hull underwater. Metallic groans and cracking sounds filled the calm air. She was rotating slowly on the axis of her keel, taking her time about dying.

They watched in silence, hanging immobile in the clear water. Ben glanced at Burke; the captain's face was ashen beneath his dark brows. "My ship," he whispered once. He said nothing more.

"Chang," Ki asked, "how did you get through the grating that was over the funnel mouth? I remember seeing it when I first came aboard the *Kraken*. It was too heavy to tear through with your hands."

"That true," Chang replied. His teeth were starting to chatter. "I take out screws holding it—two, three days ago—and replace them with little wooden pins. I do it slow, one at a time. No pirate notice. When we come up funnel vent, grating easy to kick out." He smiled serenely through his discomfort. "I make extra way out after I overhear Durant tell other pirate he plan to lock you deep in ship, then sink her."

Ki puffed his cheeks and blew out a short breath. "At the moment, I'm really happy you went to all that extra trouble."

"There she goes," Ben said.

Accompanied by one final geyser of air and foam, the *Kraken*'s bow went completely vertical. She hung there for a long second, a dark wedge against the pure blue sky, and then sank beneath the glimmering surface of the Java Sea. Bubbles boiled up into churning heaps as she disappeared, then gradually subsided.

A quarter mile beyond the *Kraken*'s grave, the landing craft lay motionless. Then, with a distant roar and a puff of black smoke, it got under way, gaining speed quickly.

Toward them.

Chapter Thirty-three

The landing craft was motoring directly toward them, its broad, flat bow pushing a wall of white water. Ben could clearly see men standing on both the foredeck and the elevated bridge, rifles close at hand..

"They're going to make a pass through the debris field!" Ben said. "Keep low, and don't do any splashing!" He twisted around, his eyes darting over the floating junk. "Dammit, we need somewhere to hide!"

"Maybe under a bucket?" Ki suggested.

"No," Ben replied. "That section of compressed-air hose! Grab it, Ki!" The young officer snatched the eight-foot piece floating nearby and passed it to him. "Thanks."

As fast as he could, Ben crimped the hose near its middle and worked it back and forth. When he felt the tough rubber begin to wear through, he took a deep breath, ducked underwater, and put one foot on the weak spot. Then, grasping the hose with both hands, he yanked hard. It parted with a dull snap.

He bobbed back to the surface and, working fast, threaded the two sections through the wooden slats of the pallet, each with one end stuck up in the air several inches and the other dangling beneath the wooden frame. He shot a quick look over in the direction of the landing craft. It was coming fast.

"Here it is," he said, talking quickly "Captain Burke and Chang on one hose, Ki and I on the other We hang underneath the pallet and take turns breathing. Keep still, don't kick, and don't drop the hose Two deep breaths, then pass it. Exhale into it first to clear the water, but don't blow like a whale or Durant'll see us. We'll be able to tell how close the landing craft is by how loud its engines are. We stay under until they get real faint. Got it? No time if you don't. Let's go."

Simultaneously, the four of them ducked under the surface and positioned themselves beneath the pallet, each man dangling by a couple of fingers near one of the hoses. It took all their concentration not to choke on seawater as they began to pass the makeshift snorkels back and forth. If only one of them lost control of his breathing and had to flounder up for air, their location would be given away.

The rhythmic thrumming of the landing craft's screws grew louder by the second.

"Over there," Durant rasped, exhaling smoke. "Near that pallet." He shifted the AK-47 he'd commandeered to the other arm and plucked the Marlboro from his lips. "Something ain't right about it."

"Ya," grunted the skull-faced Indonesian helmsman, changing course slightly. The landing craft cruised up to within thirty feet of the pallet, then coasted to a halt as the helmsman throttled down and put the engines in neutral. The five-foot-square frame of rough wooden slats bobbed and dipped in the imperceptible swell, surrounded by a number of plastic buckets. A rainbow haze of oil or diesel fuel shimmered on the water.

"Four buckets," Durant growled, "and four sum-bitches I ain't seen dead yet." He spat. There was no way they'd gotten out of the rope locker, but he hadn't seen Lom Lok since he'd sent him below to smash the forward bilge pumps. Not that he gave a rat's ass, but the old steward—the one who'd jumped ship and buddied up to his men as soon as they'd taken over the *Kraken*—was nowhere to be found, either. It felt wrong, and it pissed him off. Gannon was clever; if there was a way out, he might have found it.

He looked again at the pallet and the four buckets floating beside it, and brought the AK to his shoulder.

"Fuck it," he said, and depressed the trigger.

The percussive rattle of Durant's AK was like a signal. Instantly, the rest of the gunmen opened up on the buckets, the pallet, and everything else floating nearby. The landing craft literally shook from the combined recoil, ripples spreading outward from its waterline. Plastic bits and chunks of wood flew through fountains of spray as the buckets and pallet disintegrated.

"All right, all right! Stop firing, morons!" Durant yelled at the top of his lungs. *"Tangkap!"*

The hammering rifles fell silent as a cloud of cordite fumes drifted away from the landing craft. Durant looked out across the ruined debris that was still floating. There wasn't a piece of wood or plastic larger than a pack of cigarettes. And no sign of anything human, living or dead.

He searched for another minute or two, unwilling to ignore the gut feeling he had, then finally plucked the cigarette from his mouth and snapped it over the side.

"The hell with it," he growled. "We can't shoot up

every bucket and pallet out here. Gotta be dozens of 'em." He turned and scowled at the helmsman. "Well, what are you waitin' for? They're dead as fish bait. Take this piece of shit back to the island."

Hanging beneath the pallet, Ben was relieved to hear the throbbing of the landing craft's engines grow only so loud, then taper off. Then there came a muted popping and rattling that he recognized as gunfire. It was some distance away, though, thank Christ. He glanced around underwater. So far the other three were managing to stay in position and breathe calmly.

Even the old steward. Maybe *especially* the old steward. He moved with a control and economy that belied his years. Ben took the hose as Ki passed it to him, pressed the end firmly against his lips, and exhaled into it. They'd had the old man all wrong.

The vibrating growl of revving engines suddenly filled his ears. The landing craft was on the move again. Maybe good news, maybe not. He listened. Within a minute he was sure: the vessel was moving away from them.

He let the noise fade to a barely perceptible hum, then tapped Ki on the shoulder. In a few seconds, all four of them were on the surface again, gulping in the unlimited fresh air.

The landing craft was a black speck on the watery horizon, moving toward the island. Ben gazed at it for a moment, then cleared his throat. "Well, folks, here we float," he said. "With only one place to go."

"That's going to be a fair swim," Ki remarked. "Does anyone think we ought to try to build a bigger raft out of this floating junk?"

"In my opinion, we should stay with this pallet,"

Burke said, "and start kicking for the island as soon as possible. It'll be dark soon, and we don't want to waste energy thrashing around out here trying to collect flotsam. We're losing body heat as it is, even in this warm water. We should go now while we still have our strength, with this one flotation aid. It's relatively small and easy to push."

"Captain Burke's right," Ben agreed. "We're only going to get weaker the longer we hang around out here. And we don't know what tides or currents may be working against us. Not to mention the fact that it's not generally considered healthy to be kicking and splashing at night two miles out in a tropical sea."

Ki glanced down. "Think those squid'll be back?"

"Maybe, but I don't think they're the main worry." Ben shrugged. "I have a feeling they stay deep unless something—a rising bait or a diver—draws them up. I was thinking more about sharks."

"That's a comforting thought," Ki noted. "Well, I'm all for getting on with it, then. I'd prefer not to have my legs chewed off in the darkness by some tiger shark, if you don't mind."

"I don't mind a bit," Ben said. "Captain? Chang? You ready?"

"Absolutely." Burke nodded.

"I ready," Chang affirmed. He coughed a little, and Ben looked at him carefully.

"Chang," he said, "if you get tired, you should lie up on top of the pallet and let us push. It's going to take a good four hours to make it to the island, and that's if we're lucky with the currents. You could even get up there now. You've done enough."

The old steward shook his head adamantly. "No, Mistah Gannon. I fine. I push for island along with

Captain, you, and Mistah Padang. No problem." He
held his head a little higher out of the water and
forced a smile.

"All right." Ben rested his arms on the edge of the
pallet and began to kick. The others followed suit.

"Pace yourselves, gentlemen," Burke advised, taking up a position next to Chang. "We won't make it
if we're all exhausted after the first hour."

The first hour passed quickly, the second less so. By
the time the sun had set completely, wreathed in the
usual kaleidoscope of fiery colors, Ben's legs were on
fire from the sustained effort of kicking, and the rest
of his body was stiff, cold, and aching. The island, with
no regular inhabitants and therefore no lights, was
rapidly becoming an indistinct black blot in the gathering dusk. Now, well into the third hour of swimming, it
still seemed dishearteningly far off. As an experienced
seaman, Ben knew the illusion: if you're sailing toward
a shoreline ten miles distant, the land mass doesn't
seem to grow appreciably in size for the first nine.

The knowledge was small comfort, shivering in the
dark water as the sky turned indigo blue, then velvet
black, and gradually became carpeted with stars. The
island was distinguishable only as the very dark area,
low on the horizon, where the stars weren't. Ben drew
his legs up to his chest one at a time to stretch out
his aching back, and wondered how Chang, who was
nearly twice his age, must be holding up. The old steward had been kicking doggedly for hours without a
word of complaint.

"How's everyone doing?" Ben asked. He was surprised at the sandpapery rasp of his own voice. Sea-
salted vocal cords, he thought.

"Tired, Mr. Gannon," Burke replied, "but far from done in."

"Still here," Ki acknowledged. "You can call the cruise ship anytime now."

Ben laughed through his fatigue. "I wish. I'd settle for a rowboat." He turned slightly. "Chang?"

The old steward didn't answer. "Chang?"

"Chang!" Burke quickly threw an arm around the old man, who was lying with his gray head cradled on his crossed arms, still kicking. "Are you all right?" The captain's voice was taut with concern.

Slowly, the old steward raised his head. His expression, as always, was placid and neutral, but around his eyes the skin had drawn into tight lines of pain. He was breathing in an odd rhythm: quick, shallow puffs that terminated in a little catch. His left arm was locked in close to his body, the hand balled into a fist.

"Yes, Cap'n," Chang said softly. "You not worry about me."

Burke firmed up his grip on the old man, and looked across the pallet at Ben. "Something's wrong," he said. "We've got to get him up on the raft."

"No, no, Cap'n!" Chang shook his head. "We not stop now. Too close. We go on, please."

"But, Chang—" Burke began, and was cut off when Ki let out a sudden yelp of alarm.

"Something just bumped into my legs!" he exclaimed. "Scared the hell out of me!"

Oh, oh, Ben thought. "Everybody stay still for a moment," he called. "Keep your legs up under the pallet." He twisted his head around, searching the nearby surface. "Anyone see anything?"

"Unfortunately, *yes,*" Ki replied, pointing a finger.

A tall, triangular dorsal fin appeared about ten feet

away, rising out of the starlit sea like the tip of a
butcher's knife. It glided around them in a tight arc,
cleaving a perfect V through the oil-black water. As
it passed behind Ki, who was frozen in place, it sank
slowly beneath the surface again.

"Shit," the young officer breathed.

They clung to the pallet, dangling in the night sea,
each one expecting any moment to feel the crunching
of serrated teeth on his leg. It was a game of water-
borne Russian roulette, with the executioner circling
behind, unseen, loaded revolver ready, waiting to
make his choice. The water lapped gently on the edge
of the pallet, like seconds ticking out of a clock.

"There," Burke growled.

The fin slid up through the glassy surface again.
behind Chang this time, and continued its arc around
the little knot of men. As they followed it with their
eyes, afraid to look away, a second fin rose into view
beside the first. The twin triangles began a second lazy
circuit around the pallet, now leaving double V ripples
on the black water.

Ben frowned as the fins bypassed him again. The
nearer one was mottled white, the other jet-black.
And they moved in perfect unison, one never falling
behind the other or veering off on a new course.

Sharks don't swim paired up like that, Ben thought.
As he continued to watch, the fins changed direction
and curved away from the pallet in a tight turn. The
nearer fin became the farther fin, and in presenting its
opposite side, changed color from white to black. The
reverse was true of the second fin.

Ben began to smile. As the triangles cut closer to
him once more, he lifted himself up out of the water
on the edge of the pallet, then lunged for a spot di-

rectly between them. Plunging down blindly, arms extended, his open palms contacted a broad, flat surface that felt both slippery and sandpapery at the same time. The surface heaved, there was a sudden rush of displaced water, and then it was gone.

Ben popped back up into the night air and reached the pallet in three quick strokes

"What exactly is it you think you're doing?" Ki exclaimed, his eyes wide with shock. "When you leaped onto those fins like Tarzan, the whole ocean exploded! We thought you'd just been bitten in half! Are you crazy?"

"Maybe," Ben replied, panting, "but not suicidal. That wasn't a pair of sharks. Not even one shark."

"What were—was—it, then?"

Ben chuckled. "A manta ray."

Ki stared at him. "Really? You could see that? How?"

"But there were two dorsal fins, Mr. Gannon," Burke protested. "What kind of ray has two tall fins on its back?"

"None, that I'm aware of," Ben answered. "What you saw were the two tips of the manta's wings, curved upward and breaking the surface of the water as it came in." He began to kick, pushing on the pallet. "Let's get under way again. We don't want to be out here all night."

"But how did you know?" Ki persisted, resuming his kicking. "The rest of us couldn't make out what it was at all."

Ben coughed out a little salt water. "Fifteen years diving in the oil fields, you see a few things. In spite of breathing in weird gases for a living and drinking too many late-night roadhouse beers with the crew, you even remember a few. First time I ever saw a manta come in like that, with its wingtips raised, was offshore in the Mississippi Delta, from an oil rig we were diving on. The water was too muddy to see down into at all.

"Like you, we thought it was a pair of sharks showing their dorsal fins. But the ray breached through the surface and we saw what it was. Fooled us all. The thing is: mantas are black on top and white underneath—including their wings. When it swims by you, you're seeing the *top* of the far wingtip, and the *underside* of the near one. Okay, could be a black shark and a white shark swimming in tandem, right? Until the manta turns around, and the fins reverse positions. Now you can see that one side of each fin is white, and the other is black. Unless there are some two-toned sharks swimming around the ocean in pairs, that's always got to be a manta ray."

"And *I'm* supposed to be the wildlife expert," Ki muttered.

"That's impressive, Mr. Gannon," Burke said. He shifted his arm around Chang's shoulders, supporting him. "You're far more knowledgeable than you like to let on."

"I just try to pay attention, Captain," Ben replied with a wry smile. "Like I said: you work out on the water year after year, you get to see a few things. You know that yourself."

"True enough." Burke nodded. He frowned off into the distance. "Are we getting closer, do you suppose?"

"Hard to tell," Ben said. "I think that black shape looks bigger. Ki?"

The young Indonesian squinted. "Could be. I'd sure like to believe so."

There was the sound of suppressed coughing, and Chang raised his head, his feeble eyes turned up toward the stars. "Island very near now," he said softly.

Burke lifted the old steward a little higher out of the water. "It is, Chang?" he asked, all the strident command gone from his voice. "Can you see something we can't?"

Ben said it before he could stop himself: "Chang hasn't seen very much for quite a long time, Captain. He's nearly blind. You haven't noticed yet?"

As Burke looked over at Ben in shock, Chang spoke again, his voice a faint whisper:

"Not see, Cap'n. *Smell and hear.*" He smiled up at the stars. "Jasmine flower and night cricket."

Chapter Thirty-four

The old man moaned once more, cursed with restless sleep that would not end.

Blue sky and white clouds. Formations of Mitsubishi A6M-5 Zero fighters, Yokosuka D4Y-2 Suisei dive-bombers, and Tenzan B6N-2 torpedo-bombers cruising high above the open Pacific in orderly waves, piloted by young men who have never flown into harm's way before, proudly wearing their *hachimakis*.

His gloved hands on the vibrating controls of a Yokosuka P1Y-1 Ginga bomber, one of the few twin-engine planes designated for use by the Special Attack Group. Commander Nakajima sitting behind him in the separated bubble cockpit, reciting a haiku poem he'd written that morning.

Then, far below, the gray bullet shapes of the American fleet, wakes curving into random arcs behind them as they take evasive action. Up ahead, the first wave peeling off and beginning to dive.

Sudden terrible concussions and the sky pocked with ugly black smudges of smoke. Lines of red and green tracer shells spitting up from the ships' gun turrets, crisscrossing the high air with death. More planes diving down through the awful hail of anti-aircraft fire. Planes tumbling through the sky in burning shards;

planes exploding into high-octane infernos all around, on every side, above and below.

Final yells of "Banzai!" and screams of fear and agony coming over the radio. His friend and wingman Teruo, from flight school, flying beside him one second; the next, his Zero a ball of fire. A trio of U.S. Navy Corsairs—huge, terrifyingly fast flying tanks with immense gull-wings—knifing through his squadron, guns blazing. A lone P-38 Lightning—the twin-tailed, dual-engine fighter so feared by Japanese aviators that they have named it "the fork-tailed devil"—overtaking a diving Tenzan torpedo-bomber and machine-gunning it into a comet of flame.

His hands shaking on the controls of the shell-buffeted Ginga. Fear like a strangling claw on his throat.

Commander Nakajima: "Now, Lieutenant, now! The carrier! Dive!"

He tries to answer, but cannot force sound from his paralyzed vocal cords. Instead, he throws the controls forward, sending the Ginga into an abrupt nosedive. Vaguely, he sees his target: the gray, rectangular deck of the American aircraft carrier. Violent explosions: ear-shattering noise and bone-jarring concussions. The rising scream of the slipstream outside the cockpit canopy.

Commander Nakajima: "Arm the bombs, Lieutenant! You have forgotten to arm the bombs!"

He gropes for the handle of the cable that, when pulled, will allow the arming propellers to spin off the noses of the four five-hundred-pound bombs mounted beneath the Ginga's fuselage. His fingers will not close around it.

Commander Nakajima: "Pull it! *Pull it!*" His hand

claws forward, but he cannot reach into the front cockpit from the rear seat.

A fountain of green and red tracers smashes into the plane, spraying toward his eyes. The Ginga shudders as though coming apart at the seams. Explosions on every side. An upward rain of merciless antiaircraft fire, targeting him. The American gunners have a lock on the snow-white *hachimaki* scarf around his forehead. The carrier deck grows huge through the splintered cockpit windscreen.

His hand trembles on the arming cable. Commander Nakajima screams obscenities at him, clawing at his shoulder. A terrible bang just behind him, and another type of scream from the commander. The planes of his comrades falling in flames all around him, smashing into the sea, not one in twenty successfully completing a kamikaze dive into an American ship.

And suddenly, he knows with absolute certainty that he *does not want to die.*

The strangling fear that has all but paralyzed him now turns him into a virtuoso pilot. His mind a blur, he drops the arming cable and pulls the crippled Ginga out of its suicide dive in the nick of time. The twin-engine bomber careens past the bridge superstructure of the American carrier, so close that he can look into the staring eyes of the life-jacketed, helmeted captain and his officers.

Commander Nakajima (coughing wetly): "What— what have you done, Lieutenant? *What have you done?*"

He cannot answer. He puts the early-afternoon sun just behind his right shoulder and flies south, barely thirty feet off the water. The Ginga—a medium-range light bomber—has fairly large fuel tanks, and they are full. They have been topped up so that his kamikaze dive might end in an even larger and more damaging explosion on the deck of an American ship. He cannot release the bombs mounted beneath the fuselage, but they are not armed. And he can still deploy the undercarriage.

And with the Ginga's large fuel tanks, he can fly for hours. Many hours.

He knows he cannot go home. Not now. Not ever.

But he can fly. Away from fire and death. Away from his awful fear.

Away from his shame.

Sass hugged her knees to her chest and gazed across the cage at the white tigress lying sprawled on the other side of the dividing bars, her rib cage expanding and contracting as she huffed in little breaths of cooling air. The night was filled with the sounds of insects: the buzzing of flies, the humming of mosquitoes, and the chirping of crickets. Through the brush she could see the flicker of the cooking fire in the clearing, and in the opposite direction, up the little sandy path, the light from Jaeger's tent was visible, glowing between the palm trunks.

The landing craft had departed early in the afternoon, and returned near dusk. Though she hadn't been able to see much, there had been a great deal of raucous carrying-on, as if there was some cause for celebration. The ghoulish Anton Jaeger, followed by his loping little gargoyle of a servant, had made his way down the sandy path toward the riverbank, waddling past the cage like some silk-draped bipedal walrus—without giving her the slightest glance.

She'd heard Durant's guttural voice quite clearly

over the high-pitched chattering of the Indonesians.
Perhaps Ben had recovered his cargo for him. She'd
listened, but hadn't been able to tell if he was in the
company of the men in the clearing. More likely he
was still aboard the *Kraken.*

She shivered. "Kraken," she knew, was an archaic
word for the giant squid, which had supposedly risen
from the depths in centuries past to haul many a
square-rigged ship to its doom—if you believed the
period woodcuts and etchings, anyway. Now Ben was
diving from a vessel named the *Kraken,* through an
aggressive swarm of real-life krakens; smaller, but no
less dangerous. It was one of those weird coincidences
that works on the mind, creating the illusion that some
kind of malevolent conspiracy of the fates is targeting
you or someone you love. Sass refused to let the superstitious paranoia snowball in her thoughts, but
prayed that he was still safe.

Searching for something to distract her from un-
pleasant musings, she began to examine the lock on
the cage door. It was a standard heavy-duty padlock,
key-operated. She patted her disheveled hair for a moment, then gave up with a sigh—when you really
needed a hairpin, damned if you could find one.

She yanked on the padlock once and let it drop
from her hand with a bang. No way to open it.
Slumping down again with her back against the bars,
her eyes fell on the door of the tigress's side of the
cage. The heavy steel hasp had no lock on it, but was
held shut with a simple metal hitch-pin. Makes sense,
she thought; tigers can't pull pins. Why bother pad-
locking a door if you don't need to? The hitch-pin
wouldn't come out unless a human hand pulled it, and
nobody in their right mind was about to do that.

She stared off into the black jungle, wishing that Ben would step out of the foliage and take her far, far away from the likes of Anton Jaeger and Malcolm Durant. Before they got around to making her the center of attention again.

It was less than an hour until dawn, but the dream— the nightmare—that had haunted the old man's sleep for over fifty years still would not relinquish its pitiless grip. The little cave reverberated with his unconscious cries as he writhed on the elephant-grass mat.

Flying through squalls of gray rain and around glowering thunderheads. Ocean below, then small islands, then a huge land mass with jungled, mountainous terrain. More ocean, tiny islands, and coral atolls. Not a sign of human presence.

Only the occasional moan from Commander Nakajima.

The fuel-gauge needles bouncing on empty. The starboard engine beginning to miss. Below, a small island with a black volcanic cone, a shallow lagoon on one side, and a long strip of white beach.

He prays that the landing gear will deploy properly. With four five-hundred-pound bombs bolted to the underside of the wings and fuselage, there will be no walking away from a belly landing. He feels the wheels unfold and lock into place, their air resistance slowing the Ginga and causing an uncomfortable vibration.

He lines up on the near end of the beach and begins his rapid descent and approach. The palm trees wave their lush fronds at him—hail the conquering hero— and the lagoon flashes past on the seaward side of the cockpit, an impossibly beautiful watercolor wash of translucent green and blue. He feels the awful claw of fear tighten on his throat again. Even unarmed, the bombs could easily detonate during an emergency landing.

The wheels touch the firm sand and he throttles back the engines, fighting the controls. The Ginga shudders violently, barely maintaining a straight course—and then the starboard wheel hits a soft depression in the beach. Like a breaking twig, the support strut snaps away from its mounts in the underside of the engine nacelle, and the wing drops into the sand.

He screams in terror as the careening plane spins and the world explodes into a chaos of shattering glass, tearing metal, and billowing, blinding sand. The bombs must go off, the bombs must go off . . .

But they do not.

Later, in the small black lava cave he's found, he props his severely wounded commander up against a soft heap of dry grass.

He: "Don't worry, sir. I'm going to take care of you. We'll be safe in here."

Commander Nakajima (blood leaking from his lips): "You—you have dishonored yourself, Lieutenant. And me. There is only one—*aaaagh*—one remedy. Give me your pistol. I—I'm too badly injured to commit proper seppuku, even if I had my short sword."

He (busily propping the commander's feet up on some dry grass): "I'm going to take care of you, sir. You don't need my pistol."

Commander Nakajima: "Curse you, Lieutenant. Then let me die. I re—refuse to live in shame with the likes of you. You have not even the—the courage to redeem yourself."

He (his mind reeling): "I'm going to take care of you, sir."

Commander Nakajima: "Damn you. Damn . . . you . . ."

Chapter Thirty-five

It was well past midnight when Ben felt his foot touch the hard coral of the island's barrier reef. A minute later, all four of them were wading carefully across the sharp, irregular bottom in three to five feet of water, still pushing the pallet. They would need it when they stepped off the edge of the reef into the inner lagoon.

Burke was virtually carrying Chang, who labored on with his left arm crooked tightly across his chest. He had consistently refused to lie on top of the pallet and allow himself to be pushed along by the others. "Raft too small," he'd said. "I sink it low in water, and slow everyone down too much."

There had been no unwelcome marine visitors rising out of the black depths since the departure of the manta ray. The odd splash here and there—serving to remind them of their vulnerability and keep their nerves thoroughly jagged—but no contact with any of the great predators that routinely haunted the midnight sea. If they stayed lucky for another quarter mile or so, Ben thought, and the lagoon held no bad-tempered inhabitants, they were going to make it.

Across the glassy-calm expanse of starlit water, at the far end of the island, Ben could see a light flickering through the trees. Campfire, most likely. That would be Durant and company. And that other player—the high-pitched voice on the radio—what was his name? Something European-sounding . . . Jaeger.

They stepped off the edge of the reef into deep water again, and began to swim the pallet across the lagoon. Trees and rock formations gradually materialized out of the darkness, underlined by a narrow strip of sandy beach that gleamed palely in the starlight. The rhythmic sound of tiny swells washing at the lagoon's edge reached their ears.

Ki was looking over at the shimmying dot of firelight at the far end of the island. "I suggest we head for those rocks," he said quietly. "There's soft sand to land on between them, and we'll be concealed from view."

"I agree, Mr. Padang," Burke growled. "Even if it's unlikely that we'd be spotted, we don't want to take any chances."

Ben spat a little salt water. "Sounds good to me, too. We're going to need to hole up for a few hours, anyway—rest a bit and figure out what we're going to do next. We've got to get Sass back, and"—he glanced at the old steward—"Chang needs medical attention. We've got to get him out of here. And us, too, preferably."

Burke hefted the old man's gray head on his shoulder. "When I was at the *Kraken*'s helm on the day we first arrived at this island, I noticed what looked like a seaplane at the far end of the lagoon. It must belong to this Jaeger person. Perhaps we could force the pilot to fly us out."

"No need." Ki smiled. "I've been flying small planes since I was twelve years old." Ben and Burke looked at him. "I told you—I'm a rich kid. Rich kids get to play with expensive toys."

"Thank Christ the world isn't fair," Ben remarked. "You're a godsend, Ki. You can really pilot that seaplane, even if it's a design you haven't flown before?"

"Sure. Small planes are small planes; they all work fundamentally the same way. I'm not saying I can throw it around the sky like the factory test pilot, or recognize every bell and whistle on the dash, but I can get it airborne and fly it in a straight line the hell out of here."

Burke smiled grimly across the pallet. "Outstanding, Mr. Padang. If we plan carefully, and use the element of surprise to our advantage, I'd say we stand a reasonable chance of escaping. Mr. Gannon?"

Ben nodded. "Right, Captain. Remember, it's not just that Durant and Jaeger don't know where we are: they think we're *dead*. There's no reason at all, on this deserted island, for them to be expecting any kind of trouble. I'd imagine their guard would be down pretty low." He paused momentarily. "The only thing is, with millions of dollars worth of contraband tiger parts on their hands, I doubt if they'll be hanging around for very long. Whatever we're going to do, we probably need to do it at first light. If they take off on us, we're stuck here."

"Agreed," Burke said. He teetered slightly in the water. "My foot just hit bottom."

"Mine, too," Ki echoed.

Ben felt the firm sand under his feet and began to wade. A small opening in the black lava rocks could be seen just off to the right, revealing a fifteen-foot strip of pale beach. "Over there," he said. "Looks like we made it."

Their collective sense of relief was quickly shattered when Chang emitted a choking moan and slipped from Burke's grasp, his head disappearing beneath the surface.

They pulled the old steward onto the pallet and dragged it up onto the beach. Lifting him off the wooden slats, they carried him over to the base of the black lava rock formation and laid him gently down on the soft sand. Burke cradled the old man's head and shoulders in his lap, trying to make him comfortable.

Chang's eyes fluttered open. "Hear cricket?" He smiled. "Cricket sing."

Ben and Ki bent near, touching the old steward's hand and sleeve. His left arm trembled as it hugged his chest, the fingers locked into a fist. He grimaced as a knifelike pain cut through him.

"Chang," Burke whispered.

The old man's face relaxed. "I here, Cap'n," he said, breathing hard.

Burke's brows knitted, and his voice shook slightly. "Now, you must relax, Chang. You've overstrained yourself. I won't tolerate any more of your heroics, do you understand?" His commanding tone trailed off into a choking sound, and he bent his head low.

"Ahhh." Chang smiled up at the night sky. "I understand, Cap'n."

Burke's head came up, his eyes stricken. "Why did you do it, Chang? Why did you come back for us? For me? After the way I treated you. You were free and clear. You could easily have stayed with Durant's men, then slipped away once they'd returned to the mainland."

The old steward fixed his eyes on Burke's, smiling
paternally as though addressing a favored, wayward
child. "Old Cap'n Isaac, he ask me to watch out for
Joshua. He say Joshua too young, too quick to make
judgment. He say Joshua too proud. Pride blind a man
to mistakes. His own mistakes." He paused to draw a
rattling breath. "I make Cap'n Isaac a promise. Promise to help Cap'n Joshua grow older . . . and learn
to see."

Chang blinked once, slowly. His face was serene,
happy. "I keep my promise."

Burke couldn't speak for a moment. When he did,
his voice was barely audible:

"Chang. I must ask you . . . those men in the
barge . . ." He shook his head. "You were closing all
the air vents, shutting them in. You helped Durant's
gunmen sink that barge, Chang . . . Helped them murder all those men."

The old steward smiled again. "Men not dead," he
said. "Barge not sink."

The captain glanced up at Ben and Ki in confusion.
"What do you mean?"

"Look." Chang reached out with one hand and held
it over a little pool of seawater that was caught in a
depression in the lava rock. "Barge flood from bottom
up only." He cupped his hand, spreading his fingers
apart slightly. "Water push out air, then barge sink."
He lowered his hand into the pool, and the seawater
flowed up through his fingers, covering it.

"But keep air inside, close all vents in top deck,
and barge not sink." He withdrew his hand, cupped it
again with the fingers pressed firmly together, and lowered it back into the water, trapping a pocket of air
in his palm. His hand stayed on the surface. He looked

up at Burke. "I close all vents to keep barge from sinking," he reiterated.

Ki looked at Ben. "Is that possible?" he asked.

Ben nodded. "Absolutely. Durant's men were trying to sink the barge by opening the seacocks in its bottom. Chang knew that the barge was airtight except for the upper vents. When he shut them, he trapped a huge pocket of air inside the hull, and the water could only rise so far. The barge sank enough initially to make Durant think it was going down, but after we left, the water and air pressure equalized, and it stopped." He gazed down at the old man. "Pretty damn clever."

"Of course," Burke said slowly. "I should have recognized what he was doing at the time. But all I could see was that black headband he'd put on . . ." His voice trailed off.

"But wouldn't the men inside have run out of oxygen eventually?" Ki inquired. "How long could they have stayed alive in there? They were still trapped."

Ben smiled. "Chang even found a way to do something about that," he said. He touched the old steward's sleeve. "Chang. When I saw you reach into the life jacket storage shed on the deck of the barge, after you'd closed all the vents—you were tripping an EPIRB unit attached to one of the life rings, weren't you? Inverting it so that a constant emergency signal would be sent out to the marine rescue authorities?"

Chang smiled. "I manage to trip three."

Ben shook his head in wonder. "With three emergency beacons broadcasting at once, I'd say there's an excellent chance that rescue vessels arrived at the barge in less than six hours. The pipeline location wasn't all that far from land. The only lousy part is, none of the men in the barge would have been able to tell the authorities where the *Kraken* went. They'd certainly have reported the fact that she'd been hijacked, though."

"No wonder Durant wanted her sunk," Ki said. "Everyone from the Indonesian military to the American navy is probably out looking for her."

"She was a unique vessel, hard to miss," Ben agreed.

Burke looked off into the distance, his brow furrowed.

"All I saw was what I wanted to see," he said quietly. "All I heard was the sound of my own voice."

Chang's face suddenly contorted in pain. He waited until the spasm subsided, then reached out and touched Burke's collar with one trembling hand. His eyes shone as he gazed up at the burly captain.

"I keep my promise, Cap'n Isaac," he whispered.

Then his hand dropped away, his head sagged, and his eyes closed.

The old debt was paid.

They worked frantically on the old steward for over an hour, administering CPR, taking turns at artificial respiration and chest compression, but it was no use. Finally, Ben and Ki sat off to the side against the black rock, watching as Burke continued to try to revive Chang, driving himself to the brink of exhaustion.

At long last, he sat back on his haunches, his head bowed and his broad shoulders heaving, and put his face in his hands. Then he slid across the sand to the wall of rock and stared up at the stars.

Ben and Ki said nothing, giving him time.

Finally, Burke turned and looked at them. "We'll put him up in that cleft of rock," he said, "above the tide line where the crabs won't get at him easily. I'll wrap him in our extra clothing as best I can."

"Of course, Captain." Ki nodded.

Burke's deep voice had regained its commanding tone. There was not a trace of hesitancy or doubt as he spoke.

"Then, gentlemen, I suggest we make our way toward the camp, collect your good lady, Mr. Gannon, and commandeer that seaplane.

"It's high time we left."

Chapter Thirty-six

Cautiously, with one finger, Ben parted the cluster of leafy vines obscuring his view of the camp. Behind him, concealed in the jungle, Ki and Burke waited. Over the past hour they'd managed to work their way through the dense undergrowth to within a hundred yards of the clearing. Around the smoking remains of the cooking fire, nearly thirty Indonesian gunmen lay sleeping, most of them beneath individual mosquito nets propped up by small sticks. Their rifles lay close at hand beside them.

Ben examined the layout of the camp for several minutes before letting the vines ease back together and rejoining Ki and Burke. They squatted together in the predawn jungle, their heads close.

"I don't see a single guard," Ben whispered. "No lookouts, no perimeter of any kind. I guess they feel pretty safe."

"This is the middle of nowhere," Ki breathed. "Not likely that thirty armed bandits are going to be assaulted by the odd wandering fisherman."

"Right." Ben crushed a mosquito that had chosen to eat its last meal on his right temple. "What about that seaplane, Ki? Think you can get it started up and turned around for takeoff? Maybe those pontoons won't even slide over the sand."

The young officer pursed his lips. "It shouldn't be a problem to get it running," he said softly. "There's probably an engine ignition key, but I'm sure it'd be in the cockpit. If not, I can jump the ignition lock. Three wires—easy. And if the tie-downs holding the plane are cut away, I should be able to goose her across the sand and into the water. We get that far and we're home free—there'd be nothing they could do to stop us from accelerating down the lagoon and taking off."

"Except shoot at us," Burke growled.

"Well, yeah . . . There's that."

"Occupational hazard at this point, I think," Ben whispered.

"But there *is* a problem," Ki went on. "They must have used their manpower to drag the plane nose first up into the trees like it is. It's facing the wrong way, into the jungle. I can't turn it around with the engine; it has to be done manually. Once it's been turned toward the lagoon, I can just hit the throttle and skid across the beach and out into the water."

"Maybe we can sneak over there and haul it into position before everyone wakes up," Ben said. He glanced up at the lightening sky. "We've still got about forty minutes before sunrise, and I didn't see anyone walking around."

"I think we could do it." Ki nodded. "It's a small plane. Shouldn't weigh much."

"Sass is in that split cage with the tiger," Ben whispered. "I saw her lying inside. It's over by the river, near a little pathway that leads up to a big, fancy-looking tent. I figure Durant and this Jaeger guy must be in there."

"All the hired help gets to sleep out with the mosquitoes," Ki muttered.

"I guess," Ben said. "Anyway, I've got to get her out of there. I can't even think about climbing into that plane without her."

"Neither can we, Mr. Gannon," Burke said. "Be assured of that."

"Thanks, Captain." Ben rubbed his eyes. "Damn, I'm tired. Look, how about this: I'll work my way down to the river, just upstream from the camp, and swim along the bank until I'm opposite the cage. Then I'll try to get over to Sass and free her.

"You two move around the clearing to the seaplane and check it out. Make sure you're going to be able to get it started, Ki." He paused. "Think there's any way you and the captain can pull it around by yourselves without attracting attention?"

"Maybe," Ki replied. "If we just dig in hard and try to turn it from the rear of the pontoons, we might be able to. Some heavy limbs for levers might help. The trees block the view from the clearing, so if we don't make too much noise, and nobody comes walking in our direction, no one should see the plane moving."

"Okay. If I get Sass out of there, we'll work our way around the clearing and back to you at the seaplane." Ben glanced at Burke. "Anything to add, Captain?"

"Just a couple of comments," Burke said. "If you can't get the cage open, come back to us and we'll plan a more forceful course of action: perhaps seize some weapons and try to take Durant and Jaeger hostage. And the other thing is, it might be better if we move around separately. That way, if someone gets caught, one or two of us will still be free to hide in the jungle and try to help later. As best we can, anyway.''

"Good point," Ben concurred. He blew out a long breath of air. "Okay, that's it, then. Are we ready, gentlemen?" Ki and Burke nodded. "Good luck to us all."

He shook Ki's and the captain's hands in turn, then stood and moved off silently into the thick tropical undergrowth.

The mosquitoes attacked with unrelenting ferocity as he picked his way over the mangrove roots toward the edge of the narrow river. Though he was completely enveloped in a dense swarm of the stinging insects, he paused momentarily to eye the turbid, lazily flowing water. These islands were home to the estuarine crocodile; a mankiller that routinely snatched careless humans who bathed or fished along little coastal rivers just like the one he was about to enter. Not a nice way to go.

Ben could see no sign of crocodiles, but knew that didn't mean anything. In the murky water, a sixteen-footer could be lying on the bottom right beneath his feet, and there wasn't a hope in hell that he'd see it. He'd have to trust his luck. Which—except for Chang—hadn't been all that good lately.

He took a deep breath and slipped off the mangrove roots into the water. The current began to carry him along, his legs occasionally brushing against sunken tree limbs and other underwater snags.

He was just putting the thought of crocodiles out of his mind when the mangroves turned into a flat mud bank and he came within arm's length of a gigantic knobbly head lying along the water's edge. It was attached to an equally gigantic knobbly body that seemed to go on and on as he drifted past, with only the top half of his head exposed.

Above the long, ragged-toothed smile of a mouth, a yellow saurian eye blinked open lazily. It regarded him for a moment as the current carried him downstream, then slowly closed again. Ben didn't breathe as he passed the massive, scale-plated tail, two feet thick at its base, and continued on down the river. The huge reptile never moved.

As he rounded a slight bend, the bow of the landing craft came into view, the vessel lying up alongside the six-foot-high undercut riverbank. There was a lone Indonesian on deck, sitting on a mooring bitt, smoking. Quietly, Ben stroked sideways twice, then ducked underwater.

After counting to thirty, he came up beside the landing craft's steel hull, out of sight of the gunman on the bow. He stayed low as he was carried past the stern, the muddy water gurgling around the rudder post. There was no one else to be seen.

Breaststroking hard for the bank, he felt his elbows, then his knees, touch down on the mud-and-sand bottom. His heart pounding, he crawled out of the water and glanced back at the landing craft. Then he climbed swiftly up the steep riverbank and slide beneath the broad leaves of a low-growing scrub palm.

To his right, thirty yards away, he could see the yellowish sides of the large tent that probably housed Durant and Jaeger. The narrow path to the clearing was just ahead of him, and beside it, on a small rise less than fifteen yards to his left, sat the tiger cage.

A shaft of sunlight appeared on his forearm, illuminating the old commercial diving tattoo. He glanced out toward the lagoon. The sun's upper limb had just poked over the eastern horizon, throwing an orange glow into the clear morning air.

Soon, Ben thought, the whole camp would be awake.

Get moving.

Sass rolled up onto one elbow as the early-morning light fell across her face. Realizing that she was still in the cage, she ran a hand through her tangled blond hair and tried to steel herself against the surge of despair that welled up in her chest. Crying wasn't her style, but Jesus, she sure felt like it.

She rolled over the other way, trying to unstiffen her back, and looked straight into Ben's face.

"Ben!" Sass nearly came through the bars trying to get to him.

"Shhhh!" Ben pressed his forehead to hers and hugged her tightly around the shoulders, barely feeling the steel that separated them. "Quiet, sweetheart, quiet." She smothered his lips with hers, running her hands over his face.

"Mmmpf—okay, Sass, listen," he whispered urgently. "We're going to steal these people's seaplane. Ki can fly it. He and Burke are over there right now getting it ready to go." He lifted the big padlock. "You know where the key to this damn thing is?"

She shrugged helplessly. "Every time I've been put in this cage or taken out, a different guy's done it. Seems like at least half a dozen people have keys. But they carry them all the time, I think."

"Shit!" Ben pulled on the lock, then exhaled air between his teeth. "No tools, like bolt cutters or a hacksaw. Maybe on the landing craft." He glanced over toward the river. "I'm going to have to try to get onboard and prowl around. I can't just walk into that clearing over there and start shaking guys down for the key. 'Excuse me, boys, but would you mind not shooting me while I search everyone?' That just won't cut it."

"Ben," Sass said, her eyes wide on his. "You should just go. Go while you have the chance." She pressed her lips together for a moment to keep them from trembling. "If you waste time trying to get me out of here, they'll catch all of you. If you fly out now, you can get help and come back."

"No way."

"Ben—"

"No way." He gripped her chin through the bars. "I'm not leaving you here with that murdering son of a bitch. By the time I got back, they'd be gone, and so would you. I don't even want to think about where or how. So just forget it." He got to his feet. "I'm going over to the landing craft. There must be tools aboard it, somewhere."

"No, Ben; *don't . . .*"

Suddenly, there was the sound of running footsteps on firm sand. Ben whirled, raising his fists, and Ki slid to a halt beside the cage. "Hi, Sass," he said breathlessly.

Ben crouched beside him. "What are you doing here?"

"I worked my way past the tent, then ran over here," the young officer panted. "There was a block and tackle lying beside the seaplane. They must have used it to make it easier to haul the thing up the beach. Anyway, it makes turning the plane a snap. We rigged it from the end of one pontoon to a palm tree and had the plane spun a third of the way around in one pull. Burke can finish it off himself; he told me to go and help you."

"Any tools aboard that seaplane?"

Ki thought for a second. "Small tool kit under the pilot's seat. Pliers and screwdrivers, I think. Why?"

"Because," Ben said in exasperation, "I can't get this fucking padlock open. No key."

"Really?" The young Indonesian lifted the lock and examined it. "Well, you've got *this* Ki." He smiled at Sass, looking out anxiously between the bars, and dug into his pants pocket. Producing a small Swiss army knife, he fingernailed open the diabolical array of blades, files, and awls, and selected a pick with a right-angled bend at its end. He inserted it into the keyhole, and after three or four quick twists, the lock fell open. Ben and Sass stared at him.

"You're damned handy to have around," Ben said.

Ki swiftly removed the lock from the hasp and dropped it on the ground. "You don't want to know why I know how to do that," he said with a grin. "Dad doesn't own a lock factory."

"Tell me later, over that glass of *arak*," Ben returned. He swung open the cage door, taking Sass's hand as she stepped out. "Let's get back to the plane, and the hell out of here."

They crept silently onto the narrow path, keeping low, just in time to meet one of the Indonesian gunmen shuffling out of the undergrowth, his AK-47 slung across his shoulders, zipping up the fly of his raggedy trousers.

"*Yi-yi-yi-yi-yi!*" The gunman let out a shrill yell of alarm as he fumbled for his weapon. By the time he brought it to bear, Ben, Sass, and Ki were a good thirty yards away, heading inland through the dense foliage along the upper edge of the riverbank—at a full sprint.

The early-morning silence was shattered by the staccato roar of the AK as the gunman got off a long burst. His aim was poor. Tree bark flew and leaves shredded well behind the three fast-disappearing fugitives. In the cage, the white tigress jumped up with a startled roar of her own. She dashed back and forth within the small enclosure, her chops pulled back, fangs fully exposed.

The gunman stumbled down the path, tugging at the bolt of his jammed weapon.

"Awas!" he screamed in Bahasa. "Look out! They're free!"

Chapter Thirty-seven

The faint rattle of small-arms fire brought the old man awake with a start. He glanced around the interior of the black lava cave in confusion, then got his bearings. Another burst of gunfire. It could only be coming from the camp at the river's mouth.

He rolled painfully to his knees, every joint creaking, and groped for his pistol belt. Sliding the old revolver out of its rotting, age-stained leather holster, he broke it open and spun the cylinder. The five empty chambers gleamed in the dim light.

"I remember what you said, Commander," the old man muttered. " 'If you won't commit suicide, Lieutenant, then I expect you to justify your miserable existence by holding our position on this island against the Americans and their allies until you are relieved by the forces of His Imperial Majesty.' " He drew out a cloth-wrapped package from beneath his sleeping mat. "That is a direct quote, I believe, sir."

Yes, Lieutenant. I recall saying that to you, some time ago now.

The old man began to unwrap the package. "I want you to know, Commander, that I intend to atone for my failure during the kamikaze attack. This island is held by the military forces of the Empire of Japan, in

service to His Imperial Majesty, Emperor Hirohito."
He paused. "This position will be defended."

*I would expect no less from you, Lieutenant. Duty
must be served.*

The old man finished unwrapping the dirty cloth
and held up one of the five heavy-caliber pistol shells
it contained. Even after more than fifty years' expo-
sure to the intensely humid tropical climate, there was
not a speck of oxidation on any of the brass casings.
Like the old revolver, they had been rubbed clean and
recoated each week with a thin layer of moisture-
proof turtle oil. For over half a century.

The old man's gnarled fingers shook as he inserted
the shells into the cylinder of the pistol. "I know what
I did was inexcusable, sir. By my act of cowardice, I
put a blot of shame on my entire family. My beloved
mother, my honorable father . . . even my little sisters." His eyes filled with tears as he fumbled with the
last shell. "And my ancestors."

*But all men are afraid sometimes, Lieutenant. How
could they not forgive you your moment of weakness?*

"I could not go to an honorable death with my comrades. Not even with my friend Teruo; not even after
I saw his Zero burned to a cinder on my starboard
wing."

*Teruo understands, Lieutenant. Your friend loved
you like a brother.*

"I betrayed my Emperor."

*His Imperial Majesty forgives you, Lieutenant. He
knows you will do your duty now.*

The old man snapped the pistol shut and looked
across the cave with his tear-stained eyes. "Yes, Commander," he said. "I will." He paused. "Commander
Nakajima?"

Yes, Lieutenant.
"Can you forgive me?"
Yes, Lieutenant. I forgive you.

Ben, Sass, and Ki dashed by the landing craft at full tilt, disappearing into the undergrowth before the cigarette-smoking crewman on the bow could react. Vines and sharp-edged leaves whipped across their faces as they scrambled along the top of the riverbank in desperate haste. A chorus of shouts rose from the clearing, followed by the sporadic popping of gunfire.

Ki, in the lead, sprinted past a surprised-looking gunman who was squatting in the bushes with his pants around his ankles. As Ben and Sass came by, he leaped to his feet and grabbed her, his pants still down. She shrieked involuntarily as he yanked her sideways, breaking Ben's grip on her hand. Sass and the gunman spun through the foliage in a whirling parody of a dance.

She saw the tree trunk coming out of the corner of her eye and sidestepped. The gunman didn't, and whirled himself headfirst into it with a loud smack. He sagged, but managed to keep his grip on Sass's arm. She wrenched away, then stepped in and landed a field-goal kick to his groin. As his eyes rolled up white in his head, Ben charged through the foliage and hit him with a shoulder in the midriff, driving him back. The gunman's breath came out in a whoosh. Ben fell to his stomach at the top of the embankment, and the lighter man went backward into space, falling toward the river.

He landed on top of the giant saltwater crocodile that had been basking on the mud bank when Ben drifted by. As Ben and Sass watched, transfixed in horror, the massive reptile spun around with blinding speed and snapped its jaws shut on the dazed Indonesian's upper torso. He managed one bewildered scream as the crocodile yanked him sideways like a rag doll, thrashing its tail like a huge, scaly bullwhip, and submerged with its victim into the muddy turbidity of the river.

"Come on, come on!" Ki called softly, appearing out of the undergrowth. "We've got to get farther up into the jungle before they get organized! *Come on!*"

Breathing hard, Ben scrambled to his feet, grabbed Sass's hand, and plunged into the green tangle of leaves and vines once more, hot on Ki's heels.

Durant came down the sandy path from the tent at a fast trot, buckling his shoulder holster over his olive-drab vest. He snatched a quick look at the cage, empty except for the pacing tigress, and sprinted into the clearing. The sleep-addled gunmen were wandering around in confusion, chattering to each other in rapid-fire Bahasa. Durant grabbed the nearest man by the collar and lifted him up on his toes.

"What the fuck happened?" he demanded. "Where's the girl?"

"She go, boss!" the little man squawked. "Diver man take her into jungle!"

"What?!"

"True, Mistah Durant! Diver man, he come back!"

Fuck. His gut instinct hadn't been wrong. Either it was his goddamned ghost, or Gannon had gotten clear of the sinking ship. It was fucking impossible, but he'd done it. And that probably meant that some or all of the others who'd been with him were running around loose, too.

Jaeger came waddling up, his purple robe hanging untidily around his pallid, obese body. "What has happened, Malcolm?" he inquired moistly.

Durant looked at him in disgust. "That fuckin' Gannon. Man here says he sprung the bitch and took off into the jungle."

"No."

"Yeah, that's right. Can you fuckin' *believe* it? That sumbitch has some *cojones* on him, and no mistake." He snatched an AK-47 from a nearby gunman and began pointing his finger. "*Anda. Anda. Anda.* And you, and you." Five of the more capable-looking Indonesians hustled over to him, fully armed, their eyes hard and quick in their lean faces.

"Goodness gracious, Malcolm," Jaeger said, yawning. "Whatever are you going to *do* about this?" He rubbed a finger under his nose and sniffed in a gesture of effete boredom.

Durant hefted the AK easily, broke out the banana clip, glanced at it, and slapped it back home. "Well, fat man," he said with his ugly grin, "I'm gonna do what I do best: I'm going huntin'." He beckoned to the Indonesians with a crooked finger, then turned to go. "Only this time, it ain't for no fuckin' tigers."

"This way!" Ki called, waving a hand. "Maybe we can hide our trail in the elephant grass!"

Ben and Sass toiled up the vegetation-choked incline. "Where are we?" Ben panted. "Feels like we're heading up toward the base of the volcano."

"That's right," Ki said, pointing. "See it through the trees, there?"

A gap in the leafy canopy revealed the steep black lava cone, no more than a quarter mile away. Just ahead, the jungle opened out onto a flat plateau of eight-foot-high elephant grass.

"You think they found Burke?" Ki asked.

"He was over by the seaplane, right?" Ben helped Sass over a boulder with an arm around her waist. "I don't see why they would have. The whole damned camp was focused on us. He should have been able to slip away. I hope."

They climbed the last few yards to the top of the rise, leaving the jungle behind. The slight ocean breeze stirred the elephant grass and cooled the sweat on their brows. They had a commanding view of the entire eastern side of the island, including the lagoon and the half-concealed river mouth. The seaplane was just barely visible underneath the palm trees. In the clearing, men scurried back and forth like ants.

Ben shaded his eyes and squinted. "Damn," he muttered. "I believe the plane is facing out toward the lagoon now. Burke must have gotten her turned around."

"Anybody nearby?" Sass asked.

Ben shook his head. "Not yet. Everyone seems to be running around in the clearing . . . and over to the river, where the landing craft is."

"Probably getting loaded up to leave," Ki said.

"Looks like it."

Sass looked at them both. "You don't think they'd just go away and leave us alive on this island, do you?"

"In a word, sweetie," Ben said, scanning the jungle, "no."

"Durant doesn't like loose ends," Ki added. "Like, for instance, witnesses."

A sudden burst of machine-gun fire tore into the

ground at their feet, throwing up dirt, dry grass, and rock splinters.

"Run!" Ben yelled, shoving Sass after Ki. The three of them sprinted into the elephant grass, disappearing immediately among the tall, waving stalks.

A minute later, Durant reached the edge of the plateau, his five Indonesian gunmen spreading out on either side of him. Without a word, he leveled his AK-47 at hip height and began firing into the tall grass. The others opened up as well, sweeping the little plateau with a waist-high barrage of automatic weapons fire. The elephant grass disintegrated as the hail of bullets chopped through it.

Durant kept firing until the banana clip of his AK was empty. Flinging it away, he banged home a fresh one and held up a hand. "Cease fire, assholes!"

As the final echoes of gunfire died away, he stepped forward into the ruined vegetation, the barrel of his rifle tracking back and forth like a single deadly antenna.

Sass lifted her head, spitting bits of dead grass. Beside her, Ben and Ki were sprawled facedown in the dry humus. By good fortune, most of the bullets had gone overhead, puncturing the air with their characteristic *whizz-snap!* The three of them rose carefully to their feet.

"Anyone hurt?" Ben whispered. "No? Good. Let's get going." He took a step forward and winced. "*AAggh!*"

Sass dropped to one knee beside him. There was a ragged hole in the left calf of his jeans—no, *two* holes; less than an inch apart. Blood was already soaking

through the faded denim, the crimson stain blossoming
like some kind of obscene flower.

"You've been shot, Ben!"

"Thanks for letting me know, sweetheart." Ben grimaced. He put an arm around Ki's shoulder. "We
can't stop here. Let's go. If I can't run, at least I can
still hobble fast."

Sass cocked her head sideways as she got under
Ben's other arm. "I can hear them coming through
the grass!" she whispered urgently.

"Come on!" Ki hissed.

They moved through the dense brown stalks as quietly as possible, Ben cursing under his breath with
each painful step. From behind them came loud rus-
tling sounds as Durant and his men probed forward.
Now and then they could hear one gunman calling to
another in Bahasa.

They emerged from the far side of the stand of elephant grass onto a rocky, open slope that led up
toward the northern base of the island's volcanic cone.
There was little cover, but nowhere else to go. They
began to traverse the incline at a run, Ben limping
along in the rear.

"Hurts less when I run than when I walk," he
gasped. He waved a hand as Sass and Ki slowed for
him. "Go on, go on! I'm coming."

They scrambled up into a deep cleft in the black
rock and ducked under an overhanging ledge. Ben
flopped to the ground beside Sass and gingerly inspected his injured calf.

"Hurts like a bastard, but it's not that bad," he said,
gritting his teeth. He probed the edge of one hole with
his forefinger. "See that? Punched right through the

meat of my calf. In one side and out the other—without hitting any bone or arteries, thank Christ."

Sass slipped her arm out of her shirt, gathered the sleeve in both hands, and ripped it free. Working quickly, she bound it tightly around Ben's bleeding leg. " There, she said, trying to smile through her fear. "Gave you the shirt off my back."

"Gannon! Hey, *Gannon!*"

Durant's coarse bellow reverberated off the rocks of their hiding place. They froze where they lay, keeping absolutely silent.

"You know, you ain't got nowhere to hide on this fuckin' island!" the ex-SEAL shouted. "It's too small! There ain't no place to run to! You hear me, Gannon?"

Ki stirred, shifting a leg, and Ben put a finger to his lips. The young officer nodded grimly.

"Who you got with you, Gannon? That slant-eyed college boy who talks like he's some kind of *real* American? How about the admiral? Burke there, too?" There was an ugly chuckling sound. "I gotta hand it to you, man: I wouldn't have bet a plugged peso that you'd get out of that ship."

Durant's voice was getting louder. Ben leaned over toward Sass and Ki. "He's walking up the slope as he talks," he whispered, barely mouthing the words. "Looking for us." He picked up a coconut-sized chunk of lava rock "Ki. You and Sass head out the other end of this cleft we're in. Get over the rise and around the base of the volcano to the far side. Put some distance between yourselves and Durant."

"What about you?" Ki said.

"I'm slower, but I'll be right on your tail."

Sass stared into his eyes with alarm, clearly not believing him. "I'm staying with you," she said.

"No." Ben squeezed her shoulder. "I don't want to argue. Go. Right now."

"But—"

At that moment there was a cracking sound and a rain of loose rock spilled off the overhang above their heads. Someone uttered a high-pitched oath in Bahasa, and a pair of legs, clad in ragged trousers, slid into view. The dangling sandal-shod feet kicked frantically as they sought a toehold.

"Grab him!" Ben shouted. He and Ki threw themselves at the legs and dragged the gunman off the ledge. He came down in a tangle of calico cloth and ammunition belts, losing his turban as he thudded into the hard ground. His AK-47 slid off the overhang with him, hitting Sass in the thigh as it fell.

She scooped it up, leveled it at the entrance to the rock cleft, and pulled the trigger just as Durant stepped into view, sighting down the barrel of his weapon.

The AK jumped in her hands with a stuttering roar as the rock walls were pulverized into a cloud of black dust and lava chips. As she let up on the trigger, she could hear the ex-SEAL cursing in pain and rage at the top of his lungs, out of sight around the corner.

Ben cracked the lava rock into the struggling gunman's temple, then batted Sass on the shoulder. "Let's get out of here!" he shouted. She whirled, stepping over the limp body on the ground, and sprinted past Ben, handing off the AK to him as she went. Ki followed, and the three of them made for the far end of the rock cleft, Ben covering their rear.

Sunlight glinted off the crystallized lava rock as they approached the far opening. As Sass and Ki clambered up and out, Ben whirled, dropped to one knee, and fired a long burst back the way they'd come. Someone screamed, and he was sure he saw a body topple amid the flying rock chips and dust. Another turban-clad gunman appeared in the narrow cleft, and he unleashed a second burst.

The gun jammed. He jerked the trigger several times, then dropped the useless weapon to the ground and began to scramble madly over the rocks that lined the opening, the pain of his wounded calf burning all the way up into his groin. A blast of AK fire fractured the boulders behind him as he rolled out into the open and up against Sass. She gripped his arm with both hands.

"Ben," she whispered, her eyes despairing. Beside her, Ki crouched, his body quivering with adrenaline, a look of desperate uncertainty on his face.

Following the cleft had led them to the edge of a black lava cliff—and a sheer drop of nearly two hundred feet down to a maze of foaming water, rocks, and coral.

Shouting voices echoed from the cleft opening behind them. Ben looked around in desperation. Along the steep side of the volcanic cone there was a short pathway, leading up to what appeared to be another opening in the rock.

"Up there!" he gasped. Heaving himself to his feet, his wind nearly gone, he stumbled up the slope, leaning hard on Ki. Sass kept a hand on his waist, steadying them both. Behind them, there came the sound of more gunfire.

Ben glanced back. Rock dust was flying around the opening of the cleft. "Those idiots are still shooting down that passageway," he panted. "Durant must be having trouble making them go on through " He grinned weakly. "Guess I must have hit someone."

"Not as much fun to shoot at people when they can shoot back," Ki said bitterly. "Bastards."

"Wi—wish we could *still* shoot back," Sass wheezed.

"Maybe we can get—get through this—opening up here," Ben gasped, his chest heaving. "We—"

Ki stopped suddenly, staring up the slope. His mouth dropped open.

"Holy shit," he murmured.

Ben and Sass followed his gaze. Standing in the gap in the rocks up ahead was a squat, aged man with wispy gray hair and oriental features. His head was bound with a ragged scarf that had once been white, possibly, and he was wearing what appeared to be the remains of a military tunic. The lower part of his body was wrapped in a loincloth, and his spindly legs were bare but for the woven grass sandals that protected his feet. He held a pistol in one hand, and an ivory-handled sword in the other.

Ki continued to stare, his eyes flickering over the old man.

"What's going on, Ki?" Sass whispered. "Who is that?"

The young officer didn't answer for a moment, realization dawning on his face. "I don't believe it," he muttered. "It can't be. The last of these men came out of hiding thirty, forty years ago "

All of a sudden, he grabbed Ben's and Sass's arms and lunged forward, dragging them with him.

"*Ki o tsukete!*" he yelled. "*America-jin! Tasukete, Samurai!*"

Chapter Thirty-eight

The old man squinted hard as the three people on the slope resumed their climb toward him. "Watch out!" shouted the slender man in the lead, in perfect Japanese. "Americans! Help us, Samurai!" The old man could just make out his Asiatic features and straight black hair as he pulled the other two along behind him, one of them limping badly.

He stepped back inside the cave entrance, shaking the ivory-handled samurai sword free of its sheath, and took up a position behind a buttress of lava rock. "Three friendlies coming in, Commander Nakajima," he called over his shoulder. "The Americans are chasing them."

Prepare to defend this position, Lieutenant.

"Yes, sir."

Gasping for air, Ki stumbled into the cave, half carrying Ben, with Sass two steps behind. They collapsed onto the black sand floor, totally spent. Ki turned his head to stare at the old man who crouched behind the rock bulwark, muttering to himself in run-on Japanese.

He hadn't been wrong. The ragged military tunic hanging from his stooped shoulders dated from the Second World War, as did the heavy, short-barreled pistol he brandished. The stained white scarf that he wore around his head, binding back his wispy, shoulder-length gray hair, was undoubtedly a *hachi-maki*—the traditional adornment of a Japanese samurai warrior going into life-or-death battle. And the wizened, bent little man was the right age: well over seventy, at the very least. Lines of time, weathering, and some terrible, unknown pain were etched deeply into his face, as though they had been carved there with a knife.

The old man continued to mumble to himself, staring out of the cave entrance. In spite of his own exhaustion and fear, Ki felt a surge of pity well up inside him. Clearly, the old soldier was not entirely sane

"Samurai," he said softly.

The gray-haired old man turned to look at him with eyes that were at once both wild and knowing, bright with tears.

"Samurai," Ki whispered again.

The old man held his gaze for a long moment, then slowly turned his face back to the cave entrance. Wordlessly, he set his pistol on top of the rock buttress and pointed a gnarled, unsteady finger behind him, toward the dim recesses at the rear of the cave.

Ki lay there on the black sand for a few more seconds, unable to tear his eyes away, a strange sinking comprehension filling his chest with a dull ache. Then he rolled toward Ben and Sass, who were still panting for breath beside him.

"Let's go," he said. "I think there's a back door to this cave."

"What—what about the old man?" Ben wheezed, getting to one knee. "He's all alone in here."

Ki didn't look over at the old soldier again. "He's

been all alone in here for a long time, Ben," he said softly. "And he.wants us to go."

The old man's body stiffened as he saw three gunmen emerge from the rock cleft at the bottom of the slope. They paused to look over the edge of the cliff, then fanned out and began stalking their way up the incline in skirmish formation.

Behind them, a fourth figure appeared; a huge man whose height and build dwarfed the first three. He wore heavy black boots, camouflage pants, and an olive-drab vest—classic U.S. military garb—and carried a heavy rifle effortlessly in one hand. And although the old pilot had never actually *seen* any Americans, this man walked as he had always imagined they would: erect, with long strides, loose-limbed like a panther. Americans, he had been told, walked the earth like they owned it.

"American patrol approaching, Commander Nakajima," the old man blurted over his shoulder. He crouched back behind the rock buttress, fingering the trigger of his revolver. The old familiar claw of fear began to tighten on his throat. He swallowed, and to his surprise, it lightened its grip.

Stand fast, Lieutenant. I will cover the rear.

"Yes, sir."

He peered out at the big American striding up the incline toward the cave. The man was grotesque, apelike. Looking at him, it was easy to believe the wartime propaganda about American soldiers. They were lovers of red meat, and ate the luckless Japanese they took prisoner. Their bodies were covered in hair, like animals, and like any predator they smelled of blood, rot, and death. They were semihuman and without morality. Such creatures, who threatened the very heart of Japan itself, were well worth killing.

But such a foe. The old man swallowed again to keep the knot of fear in his throat from choking him. He pressed himself back against the rock wall.

"Very close now, sir," he called hoarsely.

Courage, Lieutenant. We will hold them, you and I.

As Ben, Sass, and Ki moved deeper into the cave, groping their way along the wall, the old man's rambling voice followed them. Most of the time, not even Ki could understand the staccato, stream-of-consciousness Japanese. To Ben and Sass, it was incoherent gibberish.

"What's he *saying?*" Sass whispered, her eyes slowly adjusting to the dimness.

Ki stepped over a rock, his feet crunching in the coarse sand of the cave floor. "It sounds to me like he's talking to someone."

"Talking to someone?" Sass shook her head incredulously. "Who?"

"Maybe him," Ben said, stopping in his tracks. He pointed toward the far wall.

Sass leaned forward, peering into the darkness, then recoiled against Ben's arm. *"Oh!"*

On a bed of dry grass, propped up against the black lava rock, was a human skeleton. It was draped in the moldering remains of a military uniform, and here and there a few withered strips of flesh still clung to the yellow-gray bones. The baleful skull was tipped forward so that its grinning jaw rested on the clavicle. Nearby lay a small fire ring of lava stones and a woven-grass sleeping mat.

The old man's muttering voice reverberated faintly

within the confines of the cave as Ben stepped over the fire ring and knelt beside the skeleton, grunting as his injured leg flexed. He looked over the remains for a moment, then ran his index finger along the top crest of the pelvis.

"Metal fragments," he said softly. "Embedded in his hip. And shattered bone." He peered down into the center of the pelvis. "More sharp junk in there. And fragments stuck through the lower spine." He looked at Ki as the young Indonesian knelt beside him. "This man died in a lot of pain."

Ki nodded slowly. "And a lot of years ago." He pointed at a tarnished insignia on the skeleton's disintegrating uniform collar. "Second World War-era Japanese military dress. He was a flier."

Ben's eyes widened. "The old man back there?"

"The same, I think. Similar uniform. Not khaki, like a ground soldier. Blue—the color of a pilot."

"*Guys,*" Sass interrupted, "I hate to break up the history lesson, but now isn't the time for this!"

Ki glanced back toward the cave entrance, then got to his feet. Ben did likewise, leaning on him for support.

"Right," he said. "Let's go."

The old man flattened himself against the rock wall as the first gunman crept into the entrance to the cave, rifle leveled, his sharp eyes flickering beneath his black turban. Obviously an American sympathizer; a guerrilla. The old pistol that had not been fired in more than fifty years came up and barked once. The bullet slammed into the side of the gunman's head, knocking him into an untidy heap on the cave floor.

A second gunman leaped over the body of the first

and ducked for cover behind a large boulder, squinting into the darkness in an attempt to pinpoint the origin of the shot. The old man covered the distance between them in three quick strides and brought the ivory-handled samurai sword around in a flashing arc. The lethal blade sliced through the back of the gunman's unprotected neck like butter, nearly severing his head from his body.

The old man paused, looking down at his dead opponent. The most incredible thing was happening instead of paralyzing him, strangling him, all his fear was turning to pure energy. He felt flushed with power, invincible. The high blood of the warrior was literally *singing* through his veins.

Behind you, Lieutenant!

At the sound of Commander Nakajima's voice the old man spun to the side with the agility of a twenty-year-old. He *was* twenty years old again. It was a miracle, wrought by the gods of war, just for him. The burst of point-blank machine-gun fire shattered the boulder just behind him.

Stamping his rear foot, his elbows high, he lunged forward with the samurai sword, letting loose an attack yell. The third gunman's eyes bugged as the razor-sharp blade slid through his solar plexus, emerging from his back a full two feet. The old pilot ripped the sword free as the skewered man sank to his knees. A quick step back, and the blade flashed down again, splitting the gunman's skull from crown to jaw.

The old man turned and leaped farther into the cave's interior as a tall shadow blocked the light at the entrance. Machine-gun fire hammered at his heels as he disappeared around a corner, rock splintering into shards and dust behind him.

Durant ground his teeth and charged after him with a bellow. The little finger of his left hand had been blown off when Sass had cut loose with the AK in the rock cleft. Now, pain and frustration were driving him into a berserk rage.

In his maddened state, he got careless. As he pounded around the corner, he didn't see the old man hiding in a narrow crevice just to his left. The samurai sword sliced across his left hip, laying him open to the bone. With a howl, he spun away, bringing up the AK with his right hand.

The old pilot dodged out of the crevice as Durant sent a barrage of bullets jackhammering into it. The ex-SEAL turned to follow him, clutching his side, and tripped backward over a rock. As he hit the cave floor, he half lost his grip on the AK.

The old man whipped up the pistol, took a graceful millisecond to balance himself, and lined up the sights on Durant's forehead.

"*Yaaaagh!*" the big man shrieked in helpless fury, his eyes huge, seeing it coming.

The old man squeezed the trigger.

There was a dull *snap* as the fifty-year-old cartridge misfired.

Then the cave shook with the chugging roar of Durant's AK.

The old man felt no pain as the bullets hammered into his chest. He was aware of being lifted backward, gently, and of floating through the darkness as if in a slow-motion dream. There was a slight crunching sensation beneath him, and then he was staring up at the rock ceiling of the inner cave; the same ceiling at which he'd stared, night after endless night, for over fifty years.

He shifted his eyes slightly, and there was Commander Nakajima's face, smiling down at him.

"Have I done well, Commander?" he asked.

Yes, Lieutenant. You have performed admirably. A true son of the Rising Sun.

"Thank you, sir."

Suddenly, there was Teruo, his friend and wingman from flight school, smiling over Commander Nakajima's shoulder.

"Teruo," the old man said, delighted.

And then there was a sea of young faces, young men with jet-black hair and laughing eyes, handsome and invincible in their flight uniforms. Behind them sat a silver armada of gleaming warplanes, adorned with the red ball of the Rising Sun, underneath an endless sky of immaculate blue.

"Yorushi!" the laughed in chorus. "Where have you been all this time? We've been waiting for you!"

And as Flight Lieutenant Yorushi Kurosawa closed his eyes and went, at last, to join his comrades, his final earthly thoughts were of how he had restored the honor of his family.

And of how his bones would one day be carried back to Japan and given to his little sisters, grown now, who would remember him in their prayers as they knelt beside the thousand-year-old Shinto shrine in his hometown of Hiroshima.

Chapter Thirty-nine

Durant leaned against the rock wall of the cave, grimacing in pain as blood from the deep slash in his left hip leaked out between his fingers. He stared down at the body of the old man with the flashing sword, little more than a heap of dirty rags now, lying across the partially scattered bones of a human skeleton. The tilted skull grinned up at him mockingly.

Crazy. It was fucking crazy. Lunatic old motherfucker had come out of nowhere, taken out three of his best men—two with a fucking *sword,* for chrissakes. Nearly taken *him* out, too. It was just sheer dumb-ass luck that the pistol had misfired; he'd been looking right down the barrel at the slug with his name on it.

Well, the old bastard was worm food now. Durant spat in the direction of the body and lurched off toward the rear of the cave, letting the blood from his hip wound leak down his leg. He flexed the four remaining fingers of his left hand around the AK-47's barrel.

Not quite fucking Miller Time yet.

The cave had continued to narrow as Ben, Sass, and Ki worked their way deeper into it, finally becoming little more than a horizontal tubular shaft some four feet in diameter. Just when it seemed as though they must be crawling blindly toward a dead end, the shaft tilted upward, then rose like a chimney. Hand- and footholds were numerous, and they hadn't climbed more than fifteen feet before Ki, in the lead, called down that he could see blue sky through an opening about thirty feet above him. They redoubled their efforts, and in five minutes Ben and Ki were helping Sass out of the chimney's mouth and into the sunshine.

They were on a rocky hillock about fifty feet above and a hundred yards away from the front entrance to the cave. A continuous line of black lava cliffs followed the western edge of the island, dropping vertically more than two hundred feet to translucent green shallows and jagged gardens of yellow coral.

"I don't see Durant or any of his men," Ben said. "They must still be in the cave."

Sass glanced anxiously back down the chimney. "They've got to be coming up this way, then." She picked up a chunk of lava. "How about if we drop a few rocks on their heads?"

"Not a bad idea," Ben replied, "but we don't know if there might be two or three coming up this way, and the rest heading back out the main entrance to cut us off. We don't want to stay here." He glanced at Ki. "I think we need to split up again. Make our way back to the seaplane. Hopefully, we'll run into Burke somewhere."

"If these guys waste time trying to decide who to chase, so much the better for us." Ki nodded. "I'll take off around the far side of the volcanic cone, okay?"

"Sure. Sass and I will work our way up into those rocks, then back around the edge of the plateau where the stand of elephant grass was." Ben looked at his watch. "Let's try to meet about two hundred yards down the beach from the plane. Say about . . . two hours from now."

"I've got a better idea," Durant growled, peering at them through the sights of his automatic rifle. He shifted his elbows slightly on the rock that had concealed the secondary chimney from which he'd risen, unseen. "You all stay *exactly* where the fuck you're at, or the blond bitch will be the first one to get turned into hamburger."

The hike back down to the camp was brutal. Durant had tossed them two sets of handcuffs and made it clear that he didn't give a shit one way or the other if he marched down two captives manacled together, or three. When he'd put the muzzle of the AK against Sass's forehead, Ben and Ki had each rapidly locked one of their arms to one of hers, and started walking.

Climbing through the rocks was a slow, painful undertaking, handcuffed into a trio with Sass in the middle. By the time they reached the upper banks of the river, their wrists were raw and bleeding from the constant friction of the steel manacles. And Durant had been in a simmering rage the whole time, alternately spewing dire threats and cursing at the pain of his wounds.

Sass faltered as they passed the high bank where the unfortunate Indonesian gunman had met his end courtesy of the giant saltwater crocodile, and Durant kicked her viciously in the back of the upper thigh.

"Move it, bitch," he snarled, "or I'll blow your arms off at the fuckin' shoulders and let these two assholes drag the pieces around for a while!"

Sass staggered on, leaning on Ben and Ki, until they came to the edge of the camp clearing. The gunmen, who had been loitering in the shade of the palms, stopped talking among themselves and began to hover closer, inspecting the captives—two of whom had recently returned from the dead, apparently. They'd all known that the diver and three others had been locked into the belly of the sinking *Kraken.*

Ben leaned over, catching his breath. As he did so, he noticed that the cage containing the white tigress had been moved to the edge of the clearing, next to a short footpath that led over to the riverbank where the landing craft was moored. The animal was pacing in a tight circle, agitated, emitting small throaty snarls as she repeatedly pulled back her chops. You don't much care for these people either, do you, girl? Ben thought.

Durant walked stiffly around in front of them as Jaeger and his grotesque tagalong Gilbert arrived in the clearing from the direction of the tent. Vaguely, Sass wondered if the fat man ever changed his robes; the purple and white silk garments had the crusty, yellowed look of month-old bedsheets.

"Ahhh, Malcolm!" Jaeger beamed, waddling up to the ex-SEAL. "A successful hunt, I see." He glanced around slowly, a look of false distress on his bloated face. "Didn't you take five of your men with you?"

"Expendable assets that got fuckin' *expended!*" Durant snapped. He winced as the pain in his hip lanced through his abdomen, and gestured at one of his remaining gunmen. "Go get me a bottle of bourbon, you."

The Indonesian glanced at Jaeger, who gave a quick nod, and trotted off toward the tent. The fat man smiled over at Sass. "Hello, my dear," he cooed. She looked him up and down, then averted her eyes.

"You haven't damaged her too badly, have you, Malcolm?" Jaeger scolded, looking at her raw wrists. "She's worth money, as you are well aware."

"She might be worth a whole lot more to me if I just started cuttin' little pieces off her," Durant growled. He held up his blood-blackened left hand, minus the little finger. "Look at this shit. Damn bitch hosed me down with an AK. Took my fuckin' pinky clean off."

"Goodness *gracious!*" Jaeger exclaimed. "We'll have to get that bandaged up right away. And that other problem, too." He fluttered a hand in the general direction of Durant's hip. "I've never seen you this beaten up before, Malcolm. You can't hunt down three unarmed people, one of them a woman, without losing *five* gunmen and getting half killed yourself?" He shook his head. "You may be losing your touch, I'm afraid."

The Indonesian who'd gone for the bourbon returned, and Durant snatched the bottle from him. "What the fuck's that supposed to mean, fat boy?" he shot back. He bit the seal off the bottle, unscrewed the cap with one hand, and tipped it up. Jaeger's eyes narrowed as he watched the big man chug down the golden-brown liquid.

"Well, Malcolm," Jaeger said, "it means that some of *my* men have been having a chat with some of *your* men, and it seems that, all in all, you're a rather difficult person to work for."

Two Indonesians moved up on either side of Durant, unrolling strips of gauze bandage. He passed the

bourbon to his free hand and held out the injured one,
letting the AK-47 drop to the sand.

"Well, ain't that a shame," he said. "These little
monkeys are fuckin' lucky I pay them at all, the way
they keep screwin' up."

"But poor management of one's personnel can
come back to haunt one," lectured Jaeger. He smiled
thinly. "You should remember that."

"I'll keep it in mind."

"You do that," Jaeger said, "because *now*"—he
raised the index fingers of both hands—"your men are
my men."

"What?" Durant grunted, and Jaeger lowered his
fingers.

As one, the two Indonesians on either side of him
dropped their bandages and whipped out short wavy-
bladed *kris* knives. In mirror-image choreography,
they both turned and drove their blades up into Durant's belly.

The ex-SEAL's face blanched in shock, his eyes
staring at Jaeger. Then, from behind, two more Indonesians stepped up and plunged their serpentine-
bladed knives deep into his back, just below the level
of the kidneys. Durant blew out a spray of bourbon
and sagged to his knees.

"You . . ." he gurgled, shaking, and fell over onto
one shoulder, clawing at the sand.

"You know," Jaeger said conversationally, walking
around him, "when you first approached me about
organizing transport and acting as broker for your
most interesting cargo of illegal tiger carcasses, I
thought, well, charging a fee for the use of my ship
and taking a percentage as middleman would be
nice . . . But wouldn't it be even *nicer* if I just took

the whole cargo and sold it myself?" He chuckled. "I mean, I had the ship, the manpower, the contacts with the purchasers—what earthly reason was there to split the profits with the likes of you? I'd prefer to have *all* of fourteen million dollars rather than just *part* of it, wouldn't you?"

He stepped carefully over the legs of the dying man, lifting his fetid skirts as he did so. "So I had my own ship, the *Loro Kidul*, hijacked in the Sunda Strait! Isn't that just *too* delicious for words, Malcolm?" His face fell somewhat. "And it would have worked beautifully, too, if it hadn't been for one of your more overzealous employees—the odious Captain Jakob De Voort, I suspect—managing, apparently, to kill all my people who'd gotten aboard. Which in turn caused the *Loro Kidul* to wander up here on her own and crash into a reef." He tut-tutted. "Such trouble."

"*Gaaaggh . . .*" Durant gurgled.

"I'm glad you see it my way," Jaeger continued. "You and De Voort have really made things much more complicated for me than I would have preferred, now, haven't you?" He paused to sniff. "Well, in the process of interfering with my seizure of the *Loro Kidul*, De Voort seems to have gotten himself conveniently killed. At least he did one thing right. And now, if you'd be so kind as to hurry up"—Jaeger gathered his skirts and bent low over Durant's head, his voice rising to a shriek—"and *die . . .* I've got other business to attend to before loading up that exquisite female tiger and vacating this wretched little island!"

Durant made one last attempt to rise, arching his back and clenching his teeth as his arms strained to push his body up from the sand. Then he shook violently and collapsed onto his face. his breath coming out in a long, wet rattle.

"Ahhh," Jaeger sighed, smiling skyward with his eyes closed. "For once in our short, stormy relationship, Malcolm, you oblige me without an argument. Thank you, my darling man, thank you." He toed Durant's lifeless body as Gilbert capered beside him, emitting a strange hooting noise.

"The keys to those handcuffs will be on the earthly remains of our dear departed friend," Jaeger announced. He yawned and fluttered his fingers at the nearby gunmen. "Unlock the woman."

Sass shrank back against Ben as four Indonesians grabbed her and a fifth rifled Durant's pockets. Coming up with the handcuff keys, he stepped forward as several more gunmen restrained Ben and Ki, prying them away from Sass.

"Wait, Jaeger!" Ben shouted, fighting hard against the four pairs of arms holding him. "You're a businessman, right? We can talk, make a deal . . ."

Jaeger looked absently off into the jungle. "What on earth for?" he asked. "You have nothing I want. As a matter of fact, you've been such an inconvenience that I'm thinking of staking out both you and your official-looking friend"—he looked Ki up and down—"and having your feet roasted off to stumps over a slow fire." He licked his wet lips and stared the young Indonesian in the eye. "My God, how I hate government-bureaucracy types. No imagination whatsoever, and always meddling, meddling, meddling in my affairs."

He turned away and crooked a finger in Sass's direction. "Bring her to me."

"*Jaeger!*" Ben yelled, and then a forearm clamped

across his throat, cutting off most of his air. He went to the sand with four gunmen on top of him, fighting like a madman. Next to him, Ki bucked and heaved in the grip of his captors, to little avail.

Sass gasped in pain as her arm was yanked up behind her back and she was thrust toward Jaeger. She kicked and twisted, trying to keep distance between them, forcing the men holding her to shuffle across the sandy clearing, off balance. Jaeger waddled in pursuit, the hideous Gilbert at his heels.

"Unfortunately for you, my dear," he puffed, "I've decided that your humiliating treatment of me in the tent the other morning cannot pass unpunished. My ego simply won't permit it, I'm afraid. A character weakness on which I'm continually working, I assure you." He smiled, his lips glistening, and fumbled with the crotch of his soiled white under-robe.

"I've decided that in light of the tremendous profit I'm going to realize once I sell off the contraband tiger parts to my wealthiest clients, I can afford to absorb the financial loss of one blond Caucasian female, damaged beyond repair." His hand moved rhythmically beneath his robes as he began to caress himself. "Watching Gilbert carve you up from the inside out—once I'm finished with you—will have a therapeutic value for me that you can't begin to imagine, my dear."

He smiled down at the deformed little man beside him, who was licking his lips and fingering several of his small triangular *palang* razor blades, his free hand digging into his diaper. The gunmen standing around the clearing began to grin and shuffle closer in anticipation of the coming show, snickering among themselves.

Jaeger's watery green eyes went round and lidless as he stared at Sass, as if slowly entering a trance. He waddled forward, his mouth hanging open, the pale lips slick with saliva. "Put her on the ground," he ordered, his voice slurring. "Hold her down."

He blinked at her once, owllike, his eyes gleaming in his bloated face.

"Tell me, my dear Sasha," he wheezed softly. "Are you *afraid*?"

Chapter Forty

Ten yards away, Ben wrenched his right arm free and broke the jaw of the gunman directly above him with one vicious punch. The Indonesian reeled back with a howl, but the combined weight of the other six men piled on top of him kept him pinned into the sand.

As Jaeger advanced on her, Sass felt the gunmen holding her try to force her over onto her back, giggling lasciviously as they did so. They were enjoying themselves. She wasn't sure who enraged her more: the depraved ghoul about to force himself on her, or his little team of snickering sycophants.

She twisted sideways and sank her teeth into the finger of the gunman holding her left shoulder, feeling the bone crunch. He screamed and turned her loose, trying to yank his hand away. Her left arm unrestrained, she whirled and drove her stiffened fingers into the eyes of the man on her right. More screaming erupted as she kicked, clawed, and punched her way free.

Stumbling across the clearing, sobbing for breath, she lost her balance and fell against the door of the tiger cage. Immediately behind her, the white tigress snarled and leaped to the rear of the enclosure, her fangs bared.

Sass backed up against the bars, her legs kicking in

the sand, and watched helplessly as the angry gunmen approached, with Jaeger close behind. He was smiling at her; a sick, demented aberration of a smile.

Her head banged against the hasp of the cage door. The nearest Indonesian reached for her, giggling, his skull-like face split into a thousand delighted wrinkles.

She reached up without looking, gritted her teeth, and pulled out the pin that secured the door. It swung open on its own.

She froze in place, holding her breath.

The expressions on the faces of Jaeger and his men turned instantly from leering anticipation to mute shock.

The white tigress poked her great head out the door and sniffed at Sass's temple. Sass closed her eyes and didn't move. She could feel the huge animal's hot breath tickling her ear, the coarse whiskers scratching her neck.

The tigress pushed her wet nose directly against Sass's hair and breathed in and out. The scent of the female who had slept beside her. Then she turned her head toward the clearing.

The white tigress launched herself from the cage in a furious headlong charge, the pent-up energy of weeks of captivity exploding in her muscles. The Indonesians stumbled backward. Shrieks of raw terror erupted around the clearing as men scrambled desperately to get away from the white-and-black-striped blur of savagery that was hurtling toward them.

Jaeger stood directly in her path, his green eyes the size of saucers. He had no time to even attempt to heave his bulging body out of harm's way before she was on him, hitting him in the groin like a freight train, her teeth and claws slashing. He went over onto his back with a wild, high-pitched scream.

She worried away at him, hunched between his frantically kicking legs, while he shrieked and floundered in his torn, bloodied robes. The sound coming from his throat was inhuman.

She left him lying on his back, still screaming, with blood soaking through his shredded clothing from his stomach to his knees. He pawed at himself feebly as the tigress lunged over his head and continued her dash around the perimeter of the clearing, swatting down two gunmen in the first fifteen feet.

Her predator's blood was up. She'd grown to hate the turbaned *Two-Legs* that had poked, prodded, and tormented her during her captivity. She would kill every one of them that came within reach.

The gunmen fled into the surrounding jungle in disarray, dropping their weapons behind them in a blind panic. There was no time to aim and fire, no time to think. The charging tigress was too fast, too powerful. The fear that gripped them was that ancient, primal type—the fear of being hunted down and eaten—that makes the mind stop working and the legs take over.

Sass watched transfixed as the tigress leaped onto the knot of men holding Ben. Wild shrieks, and they scattered, leaving two of their number dead. The tigress pounced on a third as he clawed to get away, breaking his neck with one swipe of her paw. Sass saw Ben roll clear, then scramble to all fours.

A shadow loomed over her, blocking out the sun. Gilbert grabbed her hair, cackling insanely, his bulging diaper dropping free around his scrawny hips. Sass threw a punch at him, and he seized the oncoming hand with lightning speed, hooting at her. Forcing her back with his body weight, he kneed her legs apart, maddened with excitement.

As Sass fought him with all her strength, she heard a blast of gunfire. The deranged little man's body shook violently as he was hammered off her and thrown up against the bars of the cage. He fell forward onto his face, stone dead, his diaper around his knees and his dark-skinned buttocks jutting up into the air.

Sass rolled onto one shoulder and looked up to see Burke standing twenty feet away at the edge of the clearing, a smoking AK-47 still in firing position at his shoulder. The burly captain lowered the weapon and leaped toward her, moving with surprising speed for a man of his size.

"Come on!" he shouted, grabbing her hand. "The seaplane!" He turned and looked across the clearing at Ben and Ki, who were running toward them at a sprint. "Mr. Gannon! Mr. Padang! Hurry!"

Behind them, the white tigress tore the arm off a screaming Indonesian who'd paused to take aim at her. The undergrowth surrounding the clearing was full of fleeing gunmen, most without their weapons.

Ki stared back at the writhing man who'd just lost his arm to the enraged tigress. "Talk about disarming someone," he panted.

"Jesus, Ki!" Ben shouted. "Not now with the jokes! Let's go, let's go!" He pushed the young Indonesian along in front of him, and grabbed Sass's free hand.

Ki needed no prodding. He dashed into the lead as they ran along the little sand pathway that led past the tent to the edge of the beach. The seaplane sat as Burke had left it, facing the lagoon, all its tethers and tie-downs cut away.

Ki yanked the cockpit door open and clawed his

way inside, sliding into the pilot's seat. As he turned the key and pumped the fuel primer, two Indonesians emerged from the jungle about a dozen yards down the beach and began to fire at the plane.

Burke threw up the AK and loosed off a long burst at them. Sand kicked up as they dove for cover. One of them rolled over as he hit the ground, howling and clutching his shin. Another gunman appeared in the trees near the first two.

Ben half lifted, half threw Sass into the rear seat of the cockpit and jammed a shoulder against one of the wing struts as the engine caught. The propeller whirled into a silver disk as Ki gunned the throttle.

"Push, Captain!" Ben yelled. The two strong men shoved for all they were worth as the seaplane's pontoons began to move on the sand, the engine screaming at maximum rpm. They stumbled across the beach with the sliding plane, Burke firing two more bursts one-handed from the hip as he pushed. Random bullets began to smack into the fuselage as the pontoons hit the water.

"Get on, Captain, get on!" Ben hollered over the roar of the engine. He leaped up out of the knee-deep water onto the top of the pontoon as the plane gathered speed, spray nearly blinding him.

On the other side, Burke dropped the AK into the water and threw a leg over the second pontoon, holding on for dear life. The seaplane bucked over small waves as Ki took it farther out into the lagoon. A barrage of slugs tore into the tail, shredding its leading edge.

"Get in!" Ki shouted at Ben through the open door. He threw open the door on his side of the cockpit for Burke.

"Come on, Ben!" Sass screamed, reaching out her hand. Blinking through the sheets of spray, he grabbed it and heaved himself into the copilot's seat. The glass of the rear-seat window opposite him disintegrated as a burst of gunfire hit it, showering Sass with broken shards.

Burke's spray-soaked face appeared next to Ki's shoulder in the open door. The young Indonesian leaned forward, making room, and the captain lunged behind him into the rear seat, his long legs kicking. The two cockpit doors banged shut as Ki turned the fast-moving plane to the north, heading up the lagoon.

The engine roared, the plane shuddered, spray whipped through the broken rear window—and then they were airborne, the glassy green shallows flashing by only scant feet below. Ki kept the angle of climb low and controlled as they shot over the yellowish-brown coral of the barrier reef, then out over the deep blue water of the open sea. The plane gained altitude steadily.

At five hundred feet, Ki began a slow bank around to the south, wiggling the ailerons cautiously. "Seems like they're okay," he muttered. "Got a vibration through the controls, though."

"The tail took a burst," Ben said, wiping the spray from his face. "I saw it. Tore up the surface some."

"That's probably it." Ki nodded. "If it doesn't get any worse, we should be okay." He tapped a gauge. "Plenty of fuel, anyway, thank God."

The seaplane began to pass over the island again as it headed south, the black volcanic cone rising well above them on the right. Sass blinked as she stared at the jumble of lava rock at its base. "That old man's still in the cave," she said softly. "He must be. How else could Durant have gotten past him?"

No one said anything. Ben reached back and squeezed her hand.

They were passing over the clearing. Below, they could plainly see the bodies of Durant, Jaeger, Gilbert, and at least half a dozen others sprawled crookedly on the light sand. The entire lower half of Jaeger's white-robed body was bright red. As they watched, his arm flopped across his chest, then back out to the side.

"He's still alive," Ben said.

Ki glanced down. "Maybe not for long."

A few Indonesian gunmen were wandering around the perimeter of the camp, moving as if in a daze. Several more stood near the landing craft. None of them made any attempt to fire up at the seaplane.

Burke was looking back toward the north end of the lagoon.

"Chang," he whispered, pressing his fingers against the glass. Then he fell silent.

"We'll head for the island of Belitung," Ki said. "It's well within range, only a few hours, and the authorities have a large presence there." He grinned ruefully over his shoulder. "We have a long story to tell. All of us."

"Tell me about it," Ben remarked. He rubbed his eyes.

"Look!" Sass cried suddenly.

They stared down at the jungle on the right side of the plane. Far below, flashing between the trees, was the sleek, running form of the white tigress. She was more than a quarter mile from the clearing and moving fast, heading into the high, inaccessible country on the southwestern shoulder of the volcanic cone. From the way she bounded through the jungle, with long, effortless strides, it was clear that she was not injured.

As the seaplane passed over the southern tip of the island and headed out across the shimmering blue water in the direction of Belitung, Sass pressed her forehead against the glass and gazed down at the fast-disappearing white shape loping through the trees.

"Run, sweetheart," she murmured. "You're free. Run until you can't run anymore."

Epilogue

Ben finished coiling the jib halyard and hung it neatly from its cleat on the *Teresa Ann*'s mainmast. He paused for a moment, looking across the boat-cluttered harbor at the glass-and-steel skyline of Singapore, then limped across the roof of the main cabin to the steering cockpit. Sass smiled up at him over her coffee, a blanket tucked around her legs.

"How's the leg this morning?" she inquired.

Ben flexed his calf, wincing a little. "Better. Feels less shot today."

"No leaking?"

"Nope."

"Good." Sass put her head back against the cockpit's teak coaming, the cool breeze ruffling her blond hair.

It had been a month since they'd made good their escape from the unnamed little island north of the Karimata Strait. Ki's piloting had been flawless: they'd hit Belitung dead on after only a few hours in the air. Following a week of debriefing by the Indonesian authorities and representatives from the American consulate, they'd been permitted to go about their business.

They'd elected to splash the *Teresa Ann* and sail up to Malaysia, mostly to put Indonesia behind them and reassure themselves that life had regained some semblance of normalcy. The harbor at Singapore, they'd discovered, was comfortingly noisy, crowded, and heavily policed. The city itself was modern, safe, and clean, with several first-class hospitals. A good place to let wounds heal and minds clear.

The *Teresa Ann*'s anchorage was a bit bumpy, crisscrossed as it was by wakes from the continuous parade of passing vessels, but well sheltered from the weather and close to the city docks. Ben steadied himself with a hand on the wheel as his boat rocked gently over yet another set of the ship-generated swells.

"Someone's coming our way," he said, squinting at a fast-approaching Boston Whaler. Then his face split into a smile of recognition. "It's Ki!"

"Really?" Sass twisted in her seat on the cockpit bench. "Great, but what's he doing here?"

The Whaler swung in a tight arc and coasted up beside the *Teresa Ann,* its small outboard motor sputtering. At the wheel, Ki grinned and waved a clear bottle. "Hey! Catch my lines!"

Ben secured the dingy's painter and gave the young Indonesian officer a hand up over the rail. "Welcome aboard, stranger," he said with a smile, clapping him on the shoulder.

"Hiya, Ben, Sass!" He wobbled the bottle by the neck. "I'm bearing gifts, and I'm not Greek, so it's okay!" Returning Sass's friendly kiss on his cheek, he flopped down on the cockpit bench. "How about that glass of *arak?*" he said. "This is the primo stuff, straight from Dad's distillery."

"I'll get glasses." Sass grinned, heading for the companionway. Ben stepped aside for her, then sat down on the bench opposite Ki.

"Good to see you again," he said. "We hardly had a chance to say good-bye back in Bandar Lampung, what with all the official running around you were doing. Us too," he added.

"Well, we need to catch up," Ki responded. "So I flew up here from Djakarta early this morning. Thanks for staying in touch, by the way, so I'd know where you were."

Ben waved his hand. "No sweat. Glad to do it. We were hoping we'd see you again. How was the flight? Comfortable? No delays?" He laughed.

"Considering I was in Dad's Learjet," Ki said, grinning, "it wasn't half bad."

"I should have known." Ben chuckled, rolling his eyes.

Sass returned with three tumblers. "Here," she said, passing them out, "they're glass, not plastic, so maybe that rocket fuel you're about to pour won't eat right through them."

Ki laughed and popped the cap off the bottle. "I should bring you up to speed on the latest developments regarding our little misadventure." He poured three generous shots and sat back, sipping from his glass. "Ahh. Burns like molten honey, doesn't it?"

"Yup," Sass croaked, her eyes watering. "Good, though."

Ki crossed his legs. "First of all: Burke. The *Kraken* was fully insured, but Lloyd's of London was moving a little too slowly over the phone to suit him. So he went roaring off to England on a midnight flight and— I guess—pounded on some desks at the home office. It must have worked, because he was back in less than five days, with a very satisfied look on his face—*and*, he told me, a very large certified check from Lloyd's."

"Hell," Ben said. "If I was a claims manager and Joshua Burke came at *me* in fifth gear, I'd give him all the money he wanted." He grinned over at Sass.

"Likewise," Ki agreed. "The first thing he did when he got back was take care of Chang's body. Wouldn't do anything else until he did." He sipped his *arak.* "There's a strong streak of human decency running through that man, underneath his Captain Bligh exterior."

"I think we all saw that," Ben said. Sass nodded.

"Anyway, he's looking for a new ship, he says. He sends his regards."

"And ours to him." Ben drained his glass and set it down. "What about Jaeger and his men? And all those contraband tiger parts?"

"Well, as you recall," Ki said, "two helicopter gunships full of Indonesian commandos were dispatched immediately to the island. They rounded up the surviving gunmen and confiscated the tiger parts. Apparently, Jaeger's men were so disorganized that they hadn't even tried to get away aboard the landing craft. A lot of them were injured, too. They'd either been shot, or mauled by the tigress."

"Ugly," Sass commented. "By the way, we never heard: did the men in the lay barge survive?"

Ki nodded. "Just like Chang said. The barge stopped sinking because he'd closed the vents, and the emergency beacons brought a coastal rescue vessel out in less than four hours. They released the men, then towed the barge in. No casualties, no damage."

"What an incredible old man," Sass murmured. "And then there was that old soldier in the cave . . . the one who literally saved us. Were you able to figure out who he was and what he was doing there?"

"When I went back with investigators after Jaeger's gunmen had been arrested, I recovered both Chang's body and the body of the old man in the cave," Ki said. "He'd killed three of the gunmen chasing us, but it seems that Durant then shot him, unfortunately. I was able to find an old bracelet that identified him as Flight Lieutenant Yorushi Kurosawa, a World War Two pilot. I contacted the Japanese government's war-history office in Tokyo; they're sending a team of investigators down to take charge of his body and the skeleton in the cave, along with the artifacts."

"Fifty-plus years is a long time to fight one war," Ben said softly. "Poor old guy."

"I think he may have gotten what he wanted, in the end," Ki said. "I don't know why I think that, but I do."

"What happens to all those tiger parts?" Sass asked. "And what about the white tigress?"

"Well, the tiger parts will be earmarked for scientific research," Ki said. "Lots to learn on a cellular and genetic level. The government has left the tigress to me as a pet project—excuse the pun. Since she's a rare white variant of pure Sumatran tiger—a species which is even more endangered now, courtesy of Malcolm Durant—we want her well cared for. For now, I'm leaving her on the island! It's safe, uninhabited, and easy to monitor.

"Because there are no large game animals on the island, we're transporting a herd of goats onto it to give her something to hunt. There's always the possibility that she could swim off to another island—tigers can swim twenty miles with no problem—but I don't think she will. With plenty of easy meat around, she'll stay where she is."

"What about Jaeger?" Ben growled. He picked up the second glass of *arak* that Ki had poured for him. "He still with us?"

"Yes, he's alive," the young Indonesian sighed.

"Too damn bad," Ben commented acidly.

"I can't say as I feel any different than you do," Ki said. "He's a known career criminal; a white slaver, smuggler, pirate, murderer, and all-around degenerate. But he's in custody now—or was, the last I heard—and is going to have to face some tough justice if he ever recovers from his injuries."

"The tigress tore him up pretty bad, I guess?" Sass remarked.

"You don't know the half of it," Ki said. He took a swallow of *arak*. "He's not ever going to be the same man he was before. Not that that was so appealing," he added.

He blew out a long breath before continuing.

"She didn't just maul him. She *emasculated* him. Chewed his genitals right off." He and Ben unconsciously crossed their legs at the same time. "He nearly bled to death, but all that loose clothing he wore wadded up around his groin and saved him." He shuddered a bit. "Right now I imagine he's wishing he *was* dead."

"Even remembering what he put me through," Sass said, "I can't say that I would have wished it on him. It's too horrible. Talk about the punishment fitting the criminal."

Ki smiled over at Ben. "That's not all. Do you remember the day we talked about Traditional Chinese Medicine in the dive shack aboard the *Kraken?* When I told you all about how it's believed that tiger-penis soup stimulates virility, fertility, et cetera?"

"Sure," Ben said. "Folk beliefs, without much scientific basis."

"Well, maybe not," Ki continued. "Maybe it works in reverse, too."

"What do you mean?" Ben and Sass glanced at each other, puzzled.

Ki began to smile. "Just this: the tigress made a quick meal of Jaeger's genitals, apparently. And now . . ." His voice trailed off into a half-embarrassed chuckle.

"What?" Ben prodded, starting to grin.

"What, Ki?" Sass urged.

Ki looked at them. "She's pregnant," he said. "She's already located a den. That's the other reason I know she's not going to swim off that island."

The little cub came into the world blind and confused, missing the comforting warmth of his mother's womb. He was soon followed by two brothers and a sister, the white tigress grunting gently with the effort of the birth. She licked them clean, nudging them up against her belly, and inspected them. All were healthy. The tiny cubs squirmed and twisted, helpless, until each was guided by its mother to a teat.

When all four had latched on by their milk teeth, the white tigress settled back against the lava rock of the little den and gazed out with her peridot-green eyes at the moonlight shimmering on the black surface of the Java Sea. The night was absolutely still.

Absolutely devoid of the noises of man.

The white tigress lowered her great head and nosed gently through her contented litter.

Until they, and finally she, drifted off to sleep.